I0773454

Emerald Skies

Primordial Gods Book Two

P.S. Nail

Primordial Tree Publishing

Copyright © 2022 P.S. Nail

All rights reserved. No parts of this publication may be reproduced, distributed, or transmitted in any form or by any means, including photocopying, recording, or other electronics or mechanical methods, without the prior written permission from the author, except by a reviewer who may quote brief passages in a review.

This is a work of fiction. Names, characters, places, and incidents either are the products of the author's imagination or are used fictitiously. Any resemblance to actual persons, living or dead, events, or locales is entirely coincidental.

Written by P.S. Nail

Illustrations by Diletta De Santis

Editing by KDL Editing and Heather Shields

ISBN: 979-8-218-01996-9 (paperback)

ASIN: B09NLD9PQV (e-book)

First Edition: July 2022

Dedication

To my grandmother, Cora Nance.

I couldn't think of a better way to immortalize you than adding a recipe of yours to each book in this series. I hope I have made you proud. I miss you daily.

And

To the readers

As a fellow fantasy romance reader, I hope this book continues to bring you the escapism your fantasy-loving heart desires.

ALSO....

Aunt Vicky! Because every book *has* to be dedicated to her. Her words, not mine. *wink*

Contents

Note from the author

I hope everyone enjoys the world I have built and I apologize in advance for any tears you may shed while reading—but not really. *wink*

I want ALL the emotions to come out in you!

You may fall in love, laugh, cry, or get horny, and if so then I did my job right. ENJOY! *–P.S. Nail*

P.S. There is a chocolate chip cookie recipe in the back!

Information

Content warning: This book contains explicit adult sexual content, profanity, blood, death or dying, and graphic violence. There are also mentions of anxiety and depression, and it touches very briefly on infertility.

For information on this book, please visit the author's website https://psnail.org/

To see a full colored version of the Primordial Realm world map, please visit https://inkarnate.com/p/RpLqpr--ps-nail/

To purchase officially licensed merchandise, please visit https://www.primordialtree.com/

Glossary

Caster: A person born with the ability to cast either fire, wind, or water. magic.

Changeling: A being who lives on the Demon land and can make themselves look and smell like someone else. They look like small, pale, deformed children in their true form.

Chimera: A fire breathing animal made up of three different animals. A lion, a goat, and a serpent.

Debaser: A person who abducts people and trades their souls for money or power.

Dusted: You will have to read to find out the definition. *wink*

Emergence: When a female species becomes fertile after being concealed.

Flapped: When an Angel's or Fae's wings fling open unexpectedly due to an overly emotional response—stressed, scared, excited, lustful, etc. Most common in young children.

Gale: To use one's mind to move across a single land mass in an instant.

Guardian Mark: A tattoo in the middle of one's chest that appears at birth that marks them as a King's Guard. Also known as a mark of a guardian, or King's Guard tattoo.

Hertis Rote: My Heart's Root. An ancient term of endearment for a person you love.

Ignitus: The magic in a person that can be used to light their skin on fire. Usually only applicable to a Demi-God.

Introspector: A Demon that has the ability to get into people's heads, read their thoughts, know their past, and turn them into a living puppet at their whim.

King's Guard: A person sworn to protect the kingdom and usually born with a guardian mark.

Messenger Imp: An Imp whose duties are to relay letters from one place to another in an instant. They cannot enter a private room without permission.

Portal: A doorway, gate, or other entrance that one can use to transport themselves or items from one land mass to another within seconds. Portals can only be used with a day pass, or if you have a guardian mark. *See also, Guardian Mark.*

Shield: A way of blocking your mind from others who can read thoughts.

Hallowshade
Direbreak
Portal
Portal
Castleva
Ashbern Crater
Berry Beach
Amethyst Falls
Ashbern
Elderfall
Ethereal Pastures
Portal
Dazeth
Portal
Gailshire
Arnlean
Magecrest
Fairy Beach
Tessalone
Anahita
Cerulean
Portal

Angelcrest
Arcross Mountains
Portal
Valmeyer
Windcrest
Portal
Vanhall City
Portal
Blackveil Castle
Spellchild Castle
Arna Mountains
Pyreland
Portal
Winter's Peak
Mayhem
Mayhem Harbor
Wistar Isle
Mazuria
Nebulous Forest
Closed Portal
Nebulous
Dungeon
Mistlaven

Primordial Gods

Voltarean: The God of Night, the maker of the Vampires, reigning from the country of Mayhem.

Toberon: The God of Day, the maker of the Fae, reigning from the country of Tessalone.

Reign: The God of the Sun, the Maker of the Angels, reigning from the country of Valmeyer.

Lykaon: The God of the Moon, the maker of Lycans, reigning from the country of Direbreak.

Ailwin: The God of the Forrest, the maker of the Elven, reigning from the country of Dazeth.

Apothee: The God of the Earthen, the maker of Plants and Animals, reigning from the country of Ashbern.

Volcanis: The God of Fire, the maker of Fire Casters, reigning from the country of Mazuria.

Abzule: The God of Water, the maker of Water Casters, reigning from the country of Cerulean.

Zephyr: The God of Air, the maker of Air Casters, reigning from the country of Windcrest.

Tartarus: The God of Sulfur, the maker of Demons and other malicious creatures, reigning from the country of Mistlaven.

UNTIL DEATH, DISMISSAL, OR DISHONOR.

Cinder

I t was three days after I had come to live at Castleva manor. I was in the kitchen making some cinnamon rolls for Cash. I had told him that I could cook, and he bet me I couldn't. If the cinnamon rolls came out good, I would win. Since the win was winner's choice, I had a really good idea of what I was going to pick.

After icing the tops of two cinnamon rolls, I put them on a plate. With a prideful smile, I quickly made my way to the dining room where Cash was patiently waiting for me.

"They are done!" I said cheerfully.

"They smell really good, but let's see how they taste."

He rubbed his hands together in excitement. I slid the plate in front of him and his eyes widened.

"They look good, too!"

"Thanks. Try one." I pulled out the chair next to him and took a seat.

He picked up a roll and looked at it with hungry eyes. Opening his mouth, he took a huge bite. I watched as his tongue slid out and licked a shimmer of icing off his lip. I have never wanted to be icing more in my life!

"Well?" I asked before he even swallowed completely.

"These are delicious, Cinder!"

"So, I win?" I asked with excitement.

"You win, but I kind of won, too, because these are amazing!" He took another bite.

"Yes!" I clasped my hands together in front of me.

"So, what are you choosing?" he asked with a full mouth. "I have already run naked around the garden twice now."

"Oh!" My eyes widened at his words. I wish I would have been there for that. "How about a kiss?" I asked sweetly. His eyebrows raised as I held my breath.

Cash was a lover of food. I hadn't been around long, but I could tell his life revolved around what he was going to eat next. So, when he threw the cinnamon roll down and leaned into me, I really felt like a winner.

"You want a kiss for your win?" he asked.

"Yes, if that's okay?"

A wide grin came upon his face

"That's another win for me."

He raised his hand and laid it on my cheek and his thumb rubbed up and down. My heart raced as he leaned in slowly. My lips parted slightly in anticipation, and then it happened—my first kiss!

His lips pressed gently against mine. They were warm, and tender—the feeling far more amazing than I had hoped for—than I had dreamed for!

He pulled back and I could feel my cheeks flushed as he stared into my eyes. I licked my lips lightly and could taste a small amount of icing on them and it made me smile.

"You taste like cinnamon," he said, and I giggled.

"That wasn't me, Cash. You had cinnamon roll on your lip."

"Cinnamon was my favorite thing in the realm, until you came."

My heart raced as I stared into those beautiful Angel blue eyes of his.

"You're my favorite thing," I confessed with a smile.

"Thanks, Cinnamon," He winked at me.

"Cinnamon?"

"That's my new name for you."

"Why?" I giggled.

"Well, your name is Cinder and Cinnamon has some of the same letters, plus you taste like it."

"That was the roll!" I laughed hard as he leaned in and placed one more single kiss on my lips.

That moment had been the best moment in my twenty-one years. Little did I know how much my happiness was about to change....

Chapter 1

Cinder

His beautiful blue eyes sparkled as he searched in the garden, looking for the most perfect flower to give me. This was a daily routine the Angel did, and I would never get tired of it. Plucking one from its stalk, he stood up and met my eyes.

"Here you go, my lady." Slowly lowering his head, he bowed to me. He was always playfully formal with me, and I loved it.

"Thank you, dear sir. I am forever grateful for your kindness." I curtsied, returning the same playfulness.

"There is no flower perfect enough for my lovely Cinnamon, but this one will do." He stuck the flower behind my ear as I smiled.

"Thank you." I blushed.

"I have something else for you."

"Oh. What is it?"

Cashmere held up a gold necklace. Dangling from it was a pair of angel wings. My heart thundered in my chest as I admired its beauty.

"I picked it up at a jewelry shop. I hope you like it."

"I love it. It's perfect, Cash."

"May I put it on you?"

"Yes, please." I turned away from him.

He brushed my hair away from my neck and it sent shivers down my back. Sliding the necklace on me, he latched it.

"Let me see," he said.

I turned around and faced him.

"How does it look?"

"It's almost as beautiful as you, Cinnamon."

"Thank you."

"You're welcome, my lady." He grabbed my hand as we continued through the gardens.

"What are your plans today, Cash?"

"I'm getting an early workout in with Asher for the next hour. I'll be done just in time to change my clothes before breakfast. Then we can take our walk before my next class on Valmeyer."

"We already took our daily walk."

"Only because you wanted to watch the sunrise. We can still take our walk like we usually do after breakfast." He smiled as he pulled my hand up and kissed it.

"I would like to visit Valmeyer someday."

"I would love to show you the Angel land. How about this weekend?" he asked.

"That would be wonderful." Excitement filled me as I thought about visiting another land. I was born in the country of Mazuria and had never been to any of the other lands except for the land I now lived on, which was Ashbern.

"You can meet my parents," he said.

"So soon?"

My heart raced as I thought about being taken home to meet his parents. Most men didn't do that until they were ready for a formal mating. Cash was the first man I had ever been interested in, so having a relationship was completely new to me. I wished for him to ask me someday, but I wasn't ready for a mating yet. I was only twenty-two.

"Absolutely. I have told my mother so much about you, and she is dying to meet the woman who has captured my heart."

Cash and I had been spending time together every day. He was taking things slow and gentle for my benefit, and I followed his lead. All we had done so far was hold hands, hug, and share light kisses on the lips. I had been feeling so close to him lately, I just wanted a little more. I was ready for a real kiss.

"Cash."

"Yes, Cinnamon."

"Can we kiss?"

"We have already kissed, Cinder. But if you want to kiss again...." He smiled big.

"I mean. Can we kiss deeper, like with tongue?"

Cash stopped walking and turned toward me. He placed his hand gently on my cheek and said, "I will do anything you want when you're ready."

Looking into his beautiful blue eyes, I was mesmerized. He was sweet, understanding, and kind. He was also hot, and I enjoyed looking at him. Cali said that the men chop wood shirtless sometimes. I had yet to see it, but I was patiently waiting for the day.

"I'm ready now," I said.

"Are you sure?" He ran his thumb over my cheek.

I nodded as my lips curled up into a smile.

Leaning in slowly, he tilted his head. I closed my eyes as soft lips pressed against my own. Placing my hands on his back, I parted my lips as the kiss deepened. I slid my tongue into his mouth, and he did the same. After a few seconds, Cash pulled away.

"Wow, Cinnamon."

"Thank you." I smiled at his words. The kiss felt amazing, and I was going to think about it all day.

"I have to go meet Asher now." He pulled his long blonde hair up into a bun as I watched. I couldn't help but blush at his beauty.

"I will see you at breakfast, then."

"Yes, you will." He kissed my cheek and walked away. I watched the muscles in his back through his shirt as he headed toward the training building.

Walking toward the front of the manor, I thought about how different my life had been since moving. It had been weeks since I arrived with my suitcases at Castleva Manor. Imprisoned by the Demon King Erebus, I was saved by my sister, Ember, and the rest of the King's Guard. It was not safe for me to go home, and Ember insisted I stay here under the watchful eye of her and her crew.

Other than the little time I got to spend with Cash, boredom and lack of being needed were all I had experienced since my arrival. Since I wasn't a guard, I had no job duties or missions.

An hour later, I was in the kitchen helping the servants make breakfast.

"You are doing an excellent job there, my lady, but it is unnecessary for you to help." The female servant smiled politely.

"Thank you, but since I have nothing to do around here, I would like to help in the kitchen. I love to cook, and I think helping you will alleviate my boredom."

Noreen was an Elven and a new resident at Castleva, too. She was hired because one of the elder servants retired a couple of weeks ago. She was a little shorter than me and had long, brown, curly hair and dark-brown eyes.

"You are more than welcome to stay, my lady." She gave me a strained smile because she didn't want me in the kitchen. I sighed.

"Noreen, I have told you before to call me Cinder. We're friends now." Not letting her uneasiness stop me, I stuck the biscuits I had rolled out into the oven. I had nothing else to do, so I was not leaving this kitchen.

Hearing people walk in, I looked over my shoulder and saw Cash and Zayn. I quickly tried to dust the flour off the front of me before they saw.

"Good morning, Zayn." I smiled.

"Good morning, Cinder, Noreen." Zayn ran his hand through his dark, shaggy hair as he smiled.

"Good morning, my lords." Noreen was always proper since she used to be a servant at the duke's castle. The other servants weren't.

"Smells good in here, Cinnamon. Are you cooking?" Cash always had a permanent grin on his face, and I loved it.

"Yes, I am." I blushed and wiped my hands off on a towel.

"Wow, you're an amazing woman." His statement made me gleam with pride. Getting nervous, I immediately turned around and checked the biscuits. They weren't even close to done.

"We will see you in the dining room, Cinder," Zayn said. "Come on, buddy." Cash grinned and watched me as he followed Zayn out of the kitchen.

"To the Gods." I looked at Noreen with my eyes wide, and she giggled at my reaction. Since she was only six years older than me, it was easy for us to become close.

"I think you may be smitten."

"I'm very smitten. We had our first real kiss in the garden this morning and I haven't been able to stop thinking about it since. I put my tongue in his mouth." I giggled and blushed.

"That is wonderful. Is it too bold to ask how it was?" she asked.

"Not at all. It was amazing, Noreen. I just want to do it all day, every day now." We both giggled like school-aged girls. "He also gave me this necklace."

Placing my fingers on the angel wings, I lifted it up to show her, and she leaned in to inspect it.

"That is beautiful."

The door opened and brought my attention away from Noreen.

"Cash told us you were cooking," Calista said as she and Zila walked into the kitchen.

"Yes, I'm helping Noreen with breakfast."

"Why?" Cali had a mortified look on her face.

"Because I'm not a King's Guard, and I have no life or job duties."

"Oh, we are going out this weekend. You should come." Zila nudged her with her elbow. "What, Zila?"

"That's not a place for a proper lady," Zila said.

"I'm not a lady." I sighed loudly, hoping everyone would get the hint.

"Cash calls you 'my lady,' why can't we?"

"He does it jokingly, Cali. It's our thing."

"But you are unmated and a lady of this house, so you are a lady in the eyes of the kingdom," Zila said.

"I'm just Cinder." I sighed again.

"Yeah, that is exactly why you shouldn't go. You are Cinder, not a girl who hangs in saloons." Zila smiled sweetly at me.

"Well, I am of age and unmated, so it's ultimately my decision." I gave them a regal smile. Afraid that they would call me a lady again, I slowly eased my smile and body.

"Then it's settled. You will come with us to Direbreak." Cali clapped her hands excitedly. Zila shook her head in disagreement as a frown settled on her face.

"Direbreak? The land of the Lycan?" I asked.

"Yes." Cali winked at me.

"What are we going to do there?"

"We are celebrating my brother's birthday. I'm throwing him a party." Zila smiled proudly.

"Yes! We will drink alcohol, dance, eat, kiss men, kiss women, whatever we choose." Cali clapped her hands.

"Cali!" Zila's voice sounded like one of a mother correcting her child.

"It's fine, Zila. I have nothing to do around here. Only so much food needs to be made."

Cali let out a squeak as the two females strolled off to the dining room and I continued helping Noreen.

Halfway through our breakfast, my sister and my new brother by mating walked in. They were both smiling. Val pulled her chair out and she took a seat. He took one next to her.

"Good morning, Cinder," my sister said.

"You two are late again." I frowned at them. Ember completely ignored my comment, and Valarian quickly averted his eyes.

"Why are you covered in flour, Cin?" Ember looked at the mess I had on the front of my beautiful dress. I should have worn an apron.

"I just wanted to help the servants, so I cooked breakfast with Noreen." No one understood how boring it was without job duties.

"Oh." Ember's face filled with surprise. "You cooked?"

"I made the biscuits." I shrugged.

"And they are delicious." Cash smashed another biscuit into his mouth.

"They truly are delicious," Zila said as she grabbed another one.

Ember's face looked like she didn't believe them. She grabbed a biscuit and sniffed it, and her actions offended me. She took a bite of it, and her eyes widened at me.

"These are delicious," she mumbled with a mouth full of biscuit.

"Let me taste." Valarian leaned over to her. She put the biscuit up to his mouth, and he took a bite. The simple and sweet gesture had me longing to touch Cash. I placed my hand on his leg and met his eyes as he grinned at me.

"Whoa, those are delicious. Excellent job, Cinder." Val said with a full mouth. I looked back and smiled proudly at them both.

"I told you that she's a good cook." Cash leaned in and nudged his shoulder against mine.

Staring at Cash's beautiful face, he had a full, thick beard and gorgeous blue eyes. He also had a perfect body. He grabbed another biscuit and grinned before shoving half of it into his mouth.

How can he eat so much and stay as fit as he is with those hard muscles and —

"Cinder, shield." I glanced over at Val. He gave me an empathetic smile.

Looking at Ember, her face looked the same. I blushed and looked down at my hands as I put my shield up.

I had practiced shielding my thoughts with Valarian, but only a few times so far. I had been getting good at remembering to put my shield up to block my thoughts, but anytime Cash was around, I just lost all ability to focus.

"I'm truly sorry, Valarian." Only Vampires could hear thoughts. Thank the Gods Valarian was the only Vampire that lived here.

"No need. Keep practicing, and you'll get it." He smiled at me as my sister kissed him on the cheek.

"You're the best, most amazing man ever," Ember said to him. He kissed her neck in return, and she giggled. I realized I had never seen her truly happy before, and it was heart-warming seeing her like this.

"That's funny, Red. You told me the same thing yesterday," Zayn gave her a disappointed look.

"You're the best man ever, too, Softy." Ember winked, and the Angel smiled at her.

"Hey, what about me?" Cash asked. My eyes shot to him. I wanted to tell him he was an amazing man, but I stayed quiet.

"You're just Cash," Asher said. Cash threw a piece of a biscuit at him, but Asher used his wind magic making it fly back and hit Cash.

"You all are amazing men when you're not being children." Ember shook her head.

"Thanks, Ember." Cash winked. "You can stay home this weekend, Ass. I mean Ash."

"Oh no. I need to get the hell out of here for a while." Asher cracked his knuckles. "I'm getting uneasy sitting around."

"Indeed, with the lack of missions this last week, I'm bored." Cali sighed.

They're bored? How do they think I feel? I looked up at Valarian and immediately put my shield up. He nodded and smiled.

"I haven't been bored," Ember said with a sly smile.

"Of course not. You two have probably been doing it everywhere." Cali dramatically waved her hand around. Ember shrugged her shoulders and smiled proudly. I blushed at the thought of my sister having sex everywhere. Glancing over at Cash, I hoped he didn't notice.

"Are you guys going to the Howling Moon this weekend?" Zayn asked, looking at my sister and Valarian.

They locked eyes with each other. I believed they were engaging in a silent conversation. Valarian said he would teach me how to converse privately with our thoughts once I was good at shielding, and it excited me to learn.

"We'll stay here this time, since we are still on our honeymoon," Ember said. Valarian pulled her towards him and kissed the side of her head.

"Come on, it has been weeks." Cali crossed her arms and pouted. "It will be fun. Even Cinder is going." The entire room got quiet, and everyone looked at me.

"You most certainly are not," Ember said as her eyebrows furrowed together.

"Yes, I am." I straightened my shoulders and held my head up high. I knew this was about to be a standoff.

My sister was only a year older than I was, but since our mom was taken, she'd always wanted to protect me, which sometimes meant treating me as a child. I noticed everyone's eyes were directed at us. Embarrassment filled my body and my face.

"You aren't going to a place like that." The tone of Ember's voice was daring me to argue with her. Challenge accepted.

"Why? I am of age, am I not?"

"Yes, but it isn't a place for a girl like you."

I was sick of people assuming what kind of girl I was.

"Oh, but it *is* a place for a girl like you?"

"It's different, Cinder."

"How?" I tilted my head at her, waiting for the answer.

"Because I'm stronger than you."

"Well, it must be nice being so perfect." I stood up and forcefully shoved my chair in. "And strong."

"Cinder, come back," she said as I stomped out of the dining room, ignoring her.

As I lifted my dress and jogged up the stairwell, my heart was racing. I continued to my room, slammed the door, and immediately locked it. I knew Ember would be right behind me.

Plopping down on my bed, my blood boiled as I tried to catch my breath. She was not my parent, and she had embarrassed me in front of everyone. Not to mention she called me weak, which I didn't need to be reminded of. I heard the door handle shake, then a knock.

"Cin, come on. Let me in."

"Go away, Ember!"

"Cin, please." Her voice sounded sad. I let out a long breath as I walked over to the door and opened it.

"What do you want?" She pushed past me, barging through my door.

"Don't be angry with me," she said.

"You hurt my feelings, not to mention the fact that you made me look like a child, Ember!"

"I'm sorry. I didn't mean to hurt your feelings."

"But you did, without a care. You're so much better than me, and I know that. You don't have to throw it in my face any chance you get."

"That's not what I meant."

"But that's what you said, and it hurt."

"I did it out of love, Cin. I don't want you going there."

"Why not?" I asked.

"It's not a place for a young girl like you."

"Stop saying that. You don't know what kind of girl I am. Plus, you aren't much older than me."

"But I'm a trained King's Guard."

"Well, it's not your choice." I crossed my arms and glared at her.

"Yes, it is." She crossed her arms, matching my stance and facial expression.

Hearing the door squeak, we both looked over to where Valarian had peeked his head in. "Cinder, I don't want to intrude, but I may be the voice of reason."

"Come on in," I said. I really didn't need two people to humiliate me, but Val was always nice to me.

"Cinder is here of her own will, love," Valarian said.

"And?" Ember asked.

"And she can make her own decisions."

"You're no help, Val." Ember gave him a look of disapproval.

"Let him speak. Go ahead, Valarian." I liked where this conversation was going. We both stared at him as he glanced back and forth between us. He took a deep breath.

"I think Cinder should go celebrate with the others if she wants to."

"That's ridiculous, Val."

"Why is it ridiculous?" I asked.

"I won't be there to protect you." Ember shook her head.

"She will be with the King's Guard. She will be protected." Valarian wasn't going to back down from Ember and I was grateful to him.

"What if the Demons attack again and our friends are busy defending all the citizens? Who will defend her?" Ember asked.

"I'm trained to defend myself," I said.

"Well, you—"

"Not formally," Ember said, cutting Val off. "That mercenary barely trained us. He charged me way too much for too little training. I learned so much more after coming here."

"I'm still trained, Ember!"

Val tried to speak again. "You aren't trained well enough to defend yourself against—"

"Exactly!" Ember nodded her head in agreement. Val gave her a look of disapproval and took a deep breath.

"Ladies!" Valarian's voice stopped both Ember and I from our bickering. "Like I was saying..." He looked back at Ember, daring her to cut in again. She curled her lips up at him and gave him a sultry smile. He shook his head and looked back at me. "You aren't trained formally. We never know where a Demon could be. Even with the group, I would be more comfortable if *we* trained you on offense and defense."

"Valarian Carter Grey, don't you dare." Val ignored Ember.

"So, I talked to Zayn. We're going to get permission from the king to train you like a King's Guard."

"What?" Ember's face filled with confusion.

"If you would like?" Val was completely ignoring Ember now. I loved it.

"I would!" I clasped my hands together with joy.

"Good. So, until then, if you decide to join in the... festivities, you need to make sure that one of us guards is there to protect you. No going alone, ever." A smile slowly radiated across my face as I looked at my sister. Her face had gone pale, and her mouth was hanging open.

"Thank you, Valarian!" I hugged my new brother, and he lightly patted my back.

"You're welcome, Cinder." He pulled back and looked into my eyes. "I know you are mature enough to handle yourself and will make the right decisions when the time comes."

"I won't let you down." I hadn't been this happy since I got here.

"What?" Ember said again.

"Come on." Valarian grabbed her hand and pulled her out of my room. Her eyes were locked on mine the whole time, her face still in shock.

As soon as they were gone, I shut the door. I was so excited and happy I did a little dance, then I froze as a realization hit me.

Honestly, I didn't want to go out to a saloon. I had only agreed out of boredom. After that, I got angry when Ember told me no, and I just wanted to fight for the right to make my own decisions.

Deciding that I should be happy about this win, and it would probably be fun, I took a seat in my chair and did a little knitting while I patiently waited for Cash to take me on our walk.

About ten minutes past our normal walk time, I sighed and left my room. He was probably busy, so I decided I would walk through the gardens, hoping he would catch up.

Chapter 2

Ember

While being dragged down the hall by Val, who I was going to murder as soon as we got to our room, we ran into Cash.

"Where are you going?" I asked, knowing he was going to Cinder's room. I was heated and was ready to yell at everyone.

"It's time for Cinder and I to take our walk, plus I just wanted to make sure she was okay. You were a little harsh on her." Cash's eyebrows furrowed at me.

"She is fine."

"Well, I still want to check on her." He walked away.

"Cash, wait." He turned to look at me. "I know you like my sister, but please don't do anything to take her honor away."

"I would never do that." His face was confused.

"I know you're no saint, Cash."

"What's that supposed to mean?" he asked.

"You have been with plenty of women. She is a virgin and... ahh." Val yanked me up, threw me over his shoulder, and carried me away.

"You're out of control," he said as he carried me to our room. I looked over his shoulder and saw Cash turn back around, away from Cinder's room.

Good.

Val set me down in our room and shut the door. I crossed my arms as I glared at him.

"You shouldn't have told Cash that." He shook his head at me.

"Why not? I think he should know that she is a virgin, so he knows to take his time with her."

"It's not your business to tell. You were being mean, love."

"Don't call me *love.* I'm still mad at you."

He crept up to me, and I put my hand out, stopping him. I knew he was going to kiss me and make me smile.

"Don't, Val."

"Ember." His violet eyes locked onto mine.

"Don't say my name like that, either."

"Like what? Ember." He practically purred my name. It sent shivers through me and a smile crept across his face.

"You shouldn't have done that. That is my sister, Val."

"That's where you are wrong, love."

"What do you mean by that?" I asked.

"We are mated in the eyes of the kingdom, so she is my sister now, too."

"But—"

"There's no *but*, Ember. If I am to protect her and love her like a sister, I get a say."

"She's too young, Val." A hard breath escaped me. I was glad that he wanted to protect her, but I felt like it was my job.

"She's only one year younger than you, and you're mated." His lips slowly curled up in that sexy way of his.

"But I don't want to go out, and I need to be there to protect her if she goes." He curled his arms around my body, pulling me close. I looked at the ground, avoiding his face. It was hard to be mad at him when he was so beautiful.

"Look at me." He gently forced my chin upward with his hand.

"What?" I pouted.

"She's a girl who just left the only lands she has ever known. She spends all her time walking in the garden or hanging out with Noreen while we are busy."

"Yeah, but—"

"I wasn't finished, Ember."

"Continue." I rolled my eyes at him because I knew what he was about to say was going to be the truth. What I did was wrong.

"And she's lonely because the only person she truly knows is you, and you're too busy enjoying our new life together."

His words hit me hard. It didn't even occur to me that Cinder would be lonely. She was always such a cheerful person. "Now I feel bad."

"Don't feel bad. It would help if you were more understanding about her feelings. She is a grown woman, and she needs the room to make her own decisions. She also needs to feel like this place can be her life because she doesn't now."

"Is that what her thoughts have been saying?" I asked, knowing he wasn't going to tell me.

"You already know that I'm not going to tell you. It's already intrusive enough that I know."

"Is she thinking about Cash?" I made eye contact with him and held his gaze. I knew he couldn't lie to me. He crossed his arms and went stone faced. "That face tells me yes." I pointed at him.

"Would it be so bad if she was? Cash is a good man. A very honorable man."

"I know he is. I was just mad."

"You should apologize to him and talk to your sister about things."

"Why isn't she talking to me like she used to?"

"You are always with me, love."

I hadn't been hanging out with my sister because I enjoyed my newfound love and mated life. But I had an idea, and I was hoping it helped.

"I think I know something that might help. I know the perfect place to take her!"

"Where, love?"

"Magecrest market." I smiled like I had all the answers.

"I miss the days when I could hear your thoughts."

"Why is that?" I asked.

"It would be easier than wondering what goes through that crazy mind of yours."

"Oh, you love me."

"I truly do." He kissed my neck.

Standing up on my tippy toes, I licked my lips, priming them for good kissing.

"Not going to happen."

"And why not?" I asked in my most sensual voice.

"Because it will lead back to that bed, and I have to go talk to the king. You need to find Cash and Cinder and apologize to them both."

"Fine." I walked away and threw myself back on the bed flat as Val laughed at me. He walked over and kissed my forehead.

"Zayn's here. I'll be back." I heard a knock on the door as soon as Val said the words. "He said we better not be naked again." I laughed as he opened the door to my best friend.

"Hey, Softy." I smiled at the Angel.

"Hey, Demon Spawn. We will be back."

"Have fun." I sighed as the two most important men in my life left the room.

After laying there for a while in full contemplation, I realized what I had to do. I walked down to my sister's room and knocked.

"Cinder?" I stood there for a minute and there was no answer.

I wonder where she went.

As I continued walking down the hall, I figured I would ask Noreen if she had seen her. Apparently, they were good friends now. I made it to the kitchen and found Noreen washing the breakfast dishes.

"Hey, Noreen, have you seen Cinder?" She looked over at the clock.

"This is about the time she takes a walk through the gardens with Cash."

"Oh, okay. Thank you."

"You're welcome, my lady."

As I left the kitchen, I stopped and stared at a painting of flowers that hung in the hall.

How did everyone else know what my sister was doing, but I did not?

My mate knew, and I didn't. Even the servant knew where she was at this time of day. I hadn't been a good sister these last few weeks, and I had some making up to do to her.

The door flung open, pulling me from my thoughts. I glanced into the foyer and saw Cinder.

"Hey, can we talk?" I asked.

"Sure." She had a sad smile on her face, and it hurt my heart to think of her as anything but happy.

"Want to walk with me? I have to check on Arna."

"I just walked through the gardens, but I suppose I could walk again."

She followed me as we left the manor. Once we were on the side of the estate, I realized that I would have to speak first.

"I'm sorry, Cin. I was not trying to treat you like a child. I'm just so used to taking care of you by myself."

"I thought about it, and I understand. I know you only did it because of what happened to mom, so I forgive you," she said.

"And I'm sorry for saying I'm stronger than you. You're strong in your own way."

"Don't apologize for that. It is true. Hopefully, the king will agree to my training, and I will get stronger."

"I also want to apologize for not being as good a sister as I could have been these last few weeks."

"You just got mated. I understand you guys need time for yourself. It's just lonely here sometimes."

"I know, Val told me."

"What? He tells you about my thoughts?" She whipped her head toward me and stopped walking. She looked upset.

"No, he doesn't. I have asked, but he refuses to. He just explained that this is all new to you and I need to be around more."

"Well, that's refreshing." Her body eased as we started strolling again.

"Since he won't tell me your thoughts, you're going to have to. We both need to communicate better."

"I can do that," she said with a smile.

"Is there anything you want to talk about?" I asked.

"No. Not really."

"How are you and Cash doing?"

"We're wonderful. We walk in the garden every day and he is so kind and polite. Don't get mad, but we had our first kiss today."

Looking over at her face, she blushed, and I smiled.

"How was it?" I asked, swallowing down the anxiety of my sister courting someone. I was grateful, knowing a kiss was all she had done so far. Cash just moved higher on my list of respect.

"It was wonderful. I can't wait to do it again. He treats me so well, Ember. I'm so happy with him." Listening to her gush about Cash made me feel bad for what I had said to him. I was going to apologize when I saw him.

"That's good. I'm happy for you, Cin."

"Thanks. Is there anything you want to say?" she asked.

"Well, the first thing I want to say is that I want to go on an all-girls trip to a special place that I like to visit."

"That would be wonderful." She clasped her hands together in excitement. "Where to?"

"It's a surprise."

"When can we go?" she asked.

"I figured we would see if Cali and Zila want to go with us, and then we will head out immediately." We passed the outdoor training arena and headed toward the new barn that was being built by the Elven.

"Oh, I am so excited, Ember."

"Good, I'm happy that you are happy." We both smiled at each other and laughed.

I heard a squawk and looked up. Lowering itself in front of us was a giant red bird with a solid black head. It was my Familiar, and we were bonded.

"Arna!"

Hello! She landed in front of us.

"Have the Elven finished your barn?" I asked.

I just flew over. It looks like it's almost done. I'm so excited, Ember.

"That's wonderful. I'm happy for you."

Indeed. I'm off to find something to eat. I was going to catch some fish, but racoon sounds good.

My stomach turned at the thought.

"Okay. I will be back later to check on you. I have some things to do."

Okay. Bye. Tell Cinder, I said bye.

"Arna said bye." Unfortunately, since I was her bond mate, I was the only one who could hear her. Well, Val could, too. He could talk to her through thoughts, but only because he was a Vampire.

"Bye, Arna!" Cinder waved as Arna flapped her wings and took off.

"I never would have guessed, in a million years, that I would be in love with a bird." I shook my head as I watched Arna disappear into the sky.

"Me neither." We both giggled as we continued walking toward the barn.

As we approached, we saw Cali and Zila walking away from the Elven.

"What are you two doing?" Cali asked.

"I was about to ask you the same thing," I said with raised eyebrows. "We were just checking to see if the barn was close to being done."

"We were just checking, too." Cali smiled.

"Cali wanted to look at the shirtless Elven," Zila said bluntly.

"Well, that was just a bonus." Cali winked one of her pretty blue eyes at me. I shook my head and smiled.

"You didn't even ask about the barn." Zila shook her head.

"It slipped my mind." Cali shrugged her shoulders, and I laughed.

"Well, now that I have you two together, I have something to ask you. I want to take Cinder on a shopping trip. Do you both want to go?"

"Yes!" Cali clapped her hands excitedly. "Can you stay away from Val for that long?"

"Hush your mouth. Of course, I can."

"I would love to go." Zila smiled sweetly.

"Yay. This will be fun," Cinder said. Her huge smile made me happy.

"We'll meet you in the study in roughly twenty minutes," I said.

"Perfect. We'll be there," Zila said as she and Cali strolled off.

On our journey to the barn, we were met by a handsome chocolate-brown eyed Elven named Oren Navarro. He was a tan male, with long dark hair, and a full beard. I had met him a few weeks ago when the Elven first came to build the barn. He told me he was a guard for the Duke of Dazeth, and I wondered why he wasn't here with us since he was only twenty-four years old, but I never asked.

He was shirtless and sweaty, so I had a full view of the gold King's Guard Tattoo in the middle of his chest. It was a log of wood with an axe stuck in it.

Elven were born from the bloodline of Ailwin, the God of the Forest.

Glancing over at Cinder, her eyes were wide as she gawked at him.

"Good afternoon, ladies," Oren said.

"Hey, Oren. How is it going?" I asked.

"The barn is coming along great. It will be done in the next few days."

"That's amazing. It looks great already."

"Thank you, Ember. We Elven are *known* for our building skills."

"I can see why. Arna will be happy."

"Once the barn is finished, I would appreciate it if you relayed a conversation between us. I would like to know how she likes it."

"I can do that," I said.

"It must be amazing being able to talk to her." He had a curious smile on his face.

"It truly is."

"I wish I could do that. It sounds wonderful."

"You may regret those words, Oren. She is a bit sarcastic."

"I can tell. She lands sometimes and stares at us and squawks. I feel it's her telling us to hurry."

"If you knew Arna, you would know how true your words are." I smiled at him. "Thank you for doing this."

"It's our job, and the king pays well, but you are welcome."

"Well, we must get going."

"Can I ask you a question first, Ember?" Oren shifted uncomfortably.

"Sure."

"Umm. I was wondering if you, if all of you, wanted to come to Dazeth in two weekends? It's burlesque night. It only happens every few months."

"That would be fun," Cinder said.

Immediately picking up on his discomfort, I wanted to make sure he knew I was mated.

"I will have to ask my mate, but maybe."

"Okay. You can bring the rest of the King's Guard, too."

"I will let them know we have an invitation," I politely smiled. "We will see you tomorrow."

"I have one more question, Ember."

"Okay. Go ahead."

"Is Calista mated or betrothed to anyone?"

Oh, he has a crush on Cali. I immediately relaxed.

"Cali is currently unattached. She is more of a free spirit."

"She is free-spirited, and that's what I love, um, like, about her."

"I will invite her and everyone else, of course."

"Thank you, Ember."

"Any more questions?" I asked with a giggle.

"No, that was all." He laughed nervously. "Have a good day, ladies." He turned and went back to work.

"Oh, maybe they will get mated," Cinder said as we strolled away.

"I don't think Cali is the mating type, but you never know." I shrugged my shoulders.

We made our way back to the manor. Once we were inside, Cinder went to talk to Noreen, and I headed to the study to find Cali and Zila so we could get our plans rolling.

Chapter 3

Cinder

Parting with my sister in the foyer, I practically danced my way to the kitchen to find my friend.

"Noreen, guess what?"

"What, my lady... Uh, Cinder." She smiled at me.

"I get to go on a trip today with all the girls." I clasped my hands together at the excitement of the day.

"That is fantastic. I am so happy for you."

"Thank you! I'm excited, too. Oh, I wonder what I will wear? Do you think I should wear a blue dress, or a yellow dress? I think the yellow would go best with my new necklace. This is going to be so much fun."

"I am sure you will look beautiful in anything you wear."

"Thank you, Noreen. You're too kind. I'm going to head off and pick out a dress."

"Have fun, Cinder."

"Thank you. I'll be back later." I smiled as I left the kitchen.

Heading up to my room, excitement was bubbling up inside of me. I wanted to dance with all the newfound energy I had.

Once I was in my room, I pulled out every dress I had, trying to find something nice but not too fancy to wear. Settling on a yellow sundress with white flowers, I quickly changed. Since it was close to autumn, I grabbed a white shawl and threw it on in case it got chilly.

Excitement filled my body as I left my room and headed toward the stairs. I saw Cash walking toward me and my excitement rose even higher.

"Hi, Cash." I smiled widely as I looked into his beautiful blue eyes.

"Hey, Cinder." He gave me a light smile. It wasn't his usual big, cheerful smile. It was very unlike Cash.

"I missed you during our walk."

"I was busy." He shrugged his shoulders.

"I figured. Do you like my dress?" I asked as I fluffed out the bottom.

"Yes, it's nice." Noticing he was being reticent and distant, I needed to know why.

"Everything okay?"

"Yes, I have things to do. I will talk to you later, Cinder." He continued walking.

Did I do something wrong? I wondered as I continued toward the stairs, not understanding why he seemed so gloomy. I had never seen Cash anything but happy and he never called me Cinder. As I descended the stairs, I saw the three girls waiting for me.

"We were just coming up to get you," Ember said.

"Oh! You look so pretty, Cinder."

"Thank you, Calista."

"Okay, let's get going." Ember went out the manor's front door, and we followed.

"Have you ever been to any other lands?" Zila asked. Like all Lycans, Zila had beautiful silver eyes.

"I haven't. Only Mazuria and here."

"You will love Tessalone," Cali said as she clapped her hands.

"The land of the Fae?" I asked.

"Yes!" Cali squealed.

"Cali, it was supposed to be a surprise," Zila said.

"It's fine," Ember said. "She would find out in about five minutes, anyway."

Zayn and Valarian were standing outside, talking. Both men wore completely black royal clothing.

"Why are you wearing royal raiment?" Cali asked.

"We have a meeting with the king today," Valarian said.

"Oh, I forgot." Cali shrugged.

"You both look very handsome."

"Thanks, Cinder." Zayn winked at me. "Where are you ladies going?"

"They are taking me to Tessalone!" I couldn't contain my excitement.

"Nice. Have fun, ladies. Come on, buddy." Zayn walked off.

"I'll see you when you get back, my love." Val grabbed my sister, leaned her back, and passionately kissed her. We watched longingly, hoping we would find love like that one day.

"I love you," she whispered.

"I love you, too, Ember. You girls have fun." Val smiled at us and walked away.

"How does it feel to be mated?" I asked.

"It has its advantages, that's for sure. He tends to smother me in bed. He has to cuddle me at all times."

"Aww. That sounds amazing!" Cali clapped her hands.

"It is, most of the time." Ember giggled. "Alright, let's go." They stepped on the portal, and I followed.

"The portal is rough, but it gets easier with time. I finally got used to it," Ember said, and I nodded.

"I can hold your hand." Zila reached her hand out to mine, and I took it.

"Thank you." As soon as I said the words, we flew through the world.

I felt a gust of cold air hit me mixed with wisps of the warm atmosphere. It was like a storm was about to happen. I felt the rush, and it was scary, yet somehow fun. Like I was going fast, but nothing I couldn't handle. My heart raced with excitement at the feeling. Then we landed.

"Are you okay?" Zila asked. My heart still thundered, and I felt slightly off balance, but not that bad.

"I'm fine."

"You did way better than Ember." Cali nodded.

"Well, that was like my sixth or seventh time."

"Wow. I was still getting sick on my dozenth time," Ember said. "I'm glad you aren't as bad as I was."

"Okay, ladies, let's have some fun." Cali strolled off the portal, and we followed.

We walked on a sandy beach and crossed a big bridge overlooking the sea.

"This place is beautiful," I said.

"You haven't seen the best part yet, Cin. Just wait." Ember smiled big.

We walked a little while and eventually came across a vast area of farmland. I saw tons of vegetables and fruits being grown.

"The Fae are the growers, correct? That's where a lot of food on the ships comes from."

"That's correct," Ember said. I looked over and saw a grape vineyard.

"Do they make wine, too?"

"They do." Zila smiled.

"This is where the wine we have with dinner comes from," Cali said.

We entered a large field of beautiful sunflowers. They were enormous.

"What do they do with these?" I asked. All three of the girls looked at each other.

"I honestly don't know. Maybe for sunflower seeds?" Cali looked puzzled.

"I can ask Natsu if we see him," Zila said.

"Who is Natsu?"

"Zila's crush," Ember and Cali said in unison. I looked over at the beautiful Lycan.

"Fine, fine. Whatever. I have a crush," she admitted.

"To the Gods! I can't believe you admitted it." Cali squealed and clapped her hands.

"Shut up, Cali." Zila walked ahead of us.

"What's wrong with her?" Cali asked.

"I don't know, but everyone seems cranky," I said.

"I haven't seen her mad in a while," Cali said. "She is so sweet and goes with the flow. Like Cash."

"Cash seemed upset today, too. I saw him in the hall on the way down. He didn't go with me on our walk, either."

"I wonder why?" Cali asked. "Is there a full moon?"

"Can we gale now?" Ember asked, completely changing the subject.

"Of course," Cali said.

"Zila, we're going to gale," Ember hollered. Zila quit walking and waited for us.

"I'm sorry, Zila." Cali gave her an empathetic face as she walked up. She reached out and gave her a hug.

"It's okay." Zila smiled and turned toward me. "Let's show Cinder some fun."

Ember wrapped her arms around me, and we galed away.

We all landed just outside of a vast town. As we walked closer, I noticed it was an enormous market. I saw multiple stands with a variety of items.

"This is amazing."

"I knew you would like it, Cin." Ember smiled proudly.

"The king said since you are living with us, he will provide you with anything you need. So, get whatever you want," Cali said.

"No way." I clasped my hands together as more excitement filled me.

"Even if she isn't a King's Guard?" Ember asked.

"The king insists. He pays for anything the servants want, too. He's an incredibly kind man," Cali said.

"Yeah. That's just how he is. It's weird at first, but you'll get used to it," Zila added.

"I'm going to go look for some sexy new undergarments. I will catch up with you ladies soon." Cali walked off.

"I want to go look at boots. Do you mind, Cinder?"

"No, go ahead, Zila." I smiled.

"Thanks." She strolled off, leaving me standing there with Ember.

"I'm sorry I haven't been a good sister."

"I already told you it's okay, Ember. So, where is the first place we are going?"

"I wanted to show you the spice stand first. It's over here."

Ember strolled toward the stand as I followed her. There were hundreds of herbs and spices. Anything you could think of was here. I picked out ten different herbs and a dozen spices in total.

"You have a lot of good things here. May I ask, what are you making?" the lady running the stand asked as she put them in a cloth bag for me.

"I'm a baker, or at least I want to be. I enjoy making desserts, mostly."

"You should open a stand here. You could sell your desserts."

"Oh." I stood there wondering what that would be like. I would love to open a stand. I didn't know how to go about it, but I wanted it badly. Maybe it would keep me from being as bored.

I wonder what I would name it. Maybe I could call it Cinder's stand. No, that's dumb. Cinder's Baked Goods? No. Baker's Stand. Ugh. Maybe...

"Are you okay, miss?" the woman asked.

"She's fine." Ember grabbed my arm and pulled me away from the stand. "What's wrong, Cinder?"

"I want to open a stand and sell baked goods."

"Okay. What else?"

"Nothing. I think that would solve a lot of my boredom."

"Why did you look so shocked?" she asked.

"I'm not shocked. I was trying to come up with a name for my stand."

"Oh, geez." Ember laughed as she shook her head. "Let's go find out how to get one."

We grabbed my bag of goodies and wandered around for a while until we ran into Zila.

"Hey, Zila. Cinder wants to open a stand and sell baked goods. Do you know how to find out some more info on it?"

"I don't, but I know someone who will know." Zila smiled.

"Of course. Natsu!" Ember said.

"Let's go find him." Zila smiled big as we headed toward the back of the market.

We walked until we found a man that appeared to be a Fae. He was over six feet tall with tan skin, deep brown hair, and sparkling amber eyes. He was smiling hugely as we approached.

"Zila, it is lovely to see you again," he said as he bowed.

"Nice to see you again, Natsu." Zila's smile was the purest and sweetest I had seen from her. I realized Natsu was the one they were talking about—the one that she had a crush on.

"Hello, Ember."

"Hey, Natsu. I would like you to meet my sister, Cinder."

"It's nice to meet you, Cinder." Natsu grabbed my hand and kissed it.

"The pleasure is all mine." I pulled up my dress and curtsied in return.

"We have some questions, Natsu. If you have time?"

"Of course, Zila. I always have time for you." He smiled at her, and she smiled back. My heart filled with pure joy as I watched the two of them. I knew that they would definitely be mated someday.

"Perfect. We were wondering how to get a seller's stand for the market?"

"What are you selling, Ember?" Natsu Asked.

"It's for my sister."

"Oh, do you have a business, Cinder?"

"I don't yet, but I would like to."

"What will you be selling?" he asked.

"I want to sell baked goods."

"That's magnificent. I can take you to the woman that handles the market. Follow me." He held out his arm, and Zila took it. Ember and I followed behind.

We strolled up to a small booth that sold homemade soaps and oils. The Fae woman was slender and had blonde hair.

"Emilia, this is my friend Cinder. She is interested in opening a booth at the market."

"Oh, wonderful. We could probably get you one by springtime."

"Oh. Okay." I sighed.

"Is there not any way to get her one earlier?" Zila asked.

"Not unless one opens up."

"I thought Miles was closing his stand before the fall?" Natsu asked.

"He mentioned that, but has yet to turn in his paperwork."

"That is unfortunate for Cinder." Natsu gave me a sad look.

"It's fine." I smiled politely.

"You can fill out this form and get on the list." Emilia handed me a piece of paper, a quill, and ink.

"Thank you." I filled out the form and gave it back to her.

"Perfect. If one opens, I will send a messenger Imp."

"Thank you so much, Emilia."

"You're welcome, miss."

We left the stand, and my heart was heavy once more. I was hoping this idea would change my life. I absolutely adored Cash, but I was ready to do something other than walking in the garden every day.

"I'm sorry you couldn't get a stand just yet. But I will talk to Miles and ask what his plans are."

"That's okay. Thank you for your troubles, Natsu."

"The pleasure is all mine. You ladies have a great day. I must get back to my crew." Natsu bowed to us, gave a bright smile to Zila, and walked off.

"Zila, he is just the sweetest," I said. She blushed at my words.

"Let's find Cali and get back home." Ember took my arm with a somber face.

I knew she wanted this for me, just as bad as I wanted it.

We found Cali and went back to Castleva Manor. I dropped my spices off in the kitchen and headed up to my room. I hadn't been back for long when a knock sounded upon my door. Opening it, I saw Val and Zayn.

"Oh, hello. Come in." They walked into my room. "Where is Ember?"

"We didn't tell her we were coming here. She would get cranky again." Zayn smiled.

"We talked to the king, and he said that we can train you like a King's Guard," Val smiled as my mouth dropped open in shock. "I will spar with you, teach you self-defense, and some fighting skills. You will—"

"Thank you, Valarian!" I slammed into him and hugged him.

"You will also have training with different weapons until you decide which is the one you would like to use," he finished. "I put Cash down to train you on Axes."

"We're all going to help. I'm going to teach you and Ember and how to use swords. She mentioned she wanted to learn," Zayn said. "Cali said she can show you the katana if you're interested."

"How wonderful! Thank you, Zayn." I pulled him in for a hug.

"You're welcome," he said into my hair as I squeezed him.

"Ember is going to be...." I let go of the hug, scared to finish my sentence.

"Don't worry. She'll get over it," Val said.

"Indeed, she will." Zayn laughed.

"When do we start?" I asked.

"Tomorrow morning at sunrise. Wear pants," Val reminded me.

I looked down at my dress and sighed.

"Do you have pants?" Zayn asked.

"Just pajama pants."

"We will send a tailor up after dinner to take your measurements. Order as many things as you want. The king will take care of it." Zayn winked.

"Get some fighting leathers, too. I will send Cali up when the tailor gets here, and she can help you figure out what you need to order. You can probably borrow some pants from her in the meantime," Val said.

"Thank you both."

"You're welcome." Val turned toward the door. "We will see you at dinner."

"Bye, Cinder," Zayn said as he shut the door.

Excitement and nervousness filled my body. I had done some lessons with Ember and her expensive mercenary trainer. I could protect myself against citizens, but I wouldn't be able to against Demons or anyone trained. Ember had proved that to me a few times. She always won when we sparred. I just hoped that this training made me good enough to make her proud of me.

Chapter 4

Ember

Sitting on the library floor reading, I waited for Val to come find me and tell me how the meeting with the dukes went. I had just gotten to a spicy scene when he walked in with Zayn.

"Ugh." I slammed my book shut.

"What's wrong, love?"

"I just got to a good part, Val."

"Oh, chapter fourteen?" Zayn asked.

"Yes!" I smiled excitedly.

"You're so weird." Val gave Zayn a suspicious look.

"I read romance, so I know what the ladies want." Zayn smiled. "You should try it, buddy." He clasped Val on the shoulder.

"I don't need a book to tell me how to please my woman. Right, love?" Val winked at me.

"Ahh. Too much. My best friend is right here." I pointed to Zayn. Val crossed his arms in that lazy stance of his and smiled at my discomfort.

"I'm just saying, if you read romance—"

"Shut up, Zayn. Subject change, please." I looked at the two grinning men and shook my head. "How was the meeting?"

"It was good. The dukes all expressed their concern and the king listened." Val walked over and took a seat on the floor next to me.

"Did you see my uncle?" I asked.

"I did, love. He said to tell you hi."

"What else happened?"

"Not much else." Val shrugged his shoulders.

"So, we have no plans for when the Demons attack again?"

"Not as of now." Zayn took a seat in the chair close by.

"Has there been any attacks that I don't know about?"

"Nope." Zayn shook his head.

"Erebus is planning something, I just know it. He isn't going to let this go." I shook my head. "He isn't going to let me go."

"Are you still having nightmares?" Zayn asked.

"Not every night, but yes. Did the king say if he found out any information on how Erebus is invading my dreams?"

"He's got some scholars on it, but no luck so far." Val put his hand on mine to soothe me.

"I hate Erebus. I wish I could kill him so I could move on with my life."

"If you're so sure he won't stop, he may come for you. Then you would get the chance to kill him." Zayn ran a hand through his shaggy hair.

"That's why I'm doing the extra training."

"Speaking of extra training, are you still wanting to learn how to use a sword?" Zayn asked.

"Yes. Why?" I knew exactly where this conversation was going when Zayn shifted in his seat.

"Well, the king agreed to training Cinder, so I was going to train you both at the same time."

"Don't get mad, love," Val said.

"I'm not mad." I sighed. "But I have a request."

"Okay." Zayn had a suspicious look on his face.

"I don't want my sister knowing anything about the Demons. If any attacks happen, I want it kept secret. King's Guard only. She doesn't need to know about the meetings either."

"Why?" Zayn asked.

"Because I'm going to do everything in my power to make her happy, and it would be easier if she didn't have to worry about being attacked or abducted every time she turns around."

"So, you want us to let her live in blissful ignorance?" Zayn ran a hand through his hair.

"I mean, yeah. Kind of."

"I disagree with this," Val removed his hand from mine. "We shouldn't keep things from each other, which includes Cinder."

"Please, Val."

"It's a bad idea. It will backfire, love."

"If it does, I will deal with it. I just want her to be happy."

"I have to change my clothes." Zayn stood up and headed for the door.

"Softy." He looked over his shoulder at me. "Please?"

"She's your sister, so I'll do whatever you like, but I'm with Val. I also think it's a bad idea." He left the library.

"Zayn's mad at me now."

"He'll be fine. He just doesn't enjoy lying."

"We aren't lying, Val. We're just withholding information."

"Withholding information is a fancy way of saying we are lying."

"I disagree."

Val sighed and shook his head. "How was the market?"

"It was fun."

"I'm glad you made up with Cinder. Did you apologize to Cash?"

I looked shamefully into his eyes and swallowed. "I didn't have time."

"Ember."

"Cash is fine."

"You know what happens when you don't clear the air? It gets stagnant. Find Cash and apologize."

"Fine. I will after I'm done reading."

Val stood up and held out his hand. "Come on."

"I was going to stay here for a while."

"That sounds fun, but you have a class with Katzia. She just wielded to me asking why you're late."

"Shit. I forgot I had training today." I took his hand, and he helped me up.

"She said to meet her outside by the big oak tree."

"Are you coming with me?" I asked.

"Not today. I want to change into something more comfortable before dinner."

"Okay." I could feel the tension between us. Val was mad at me for making him lie. "Can you take my book upstairs?"

"Yes." Val kissed my cheek. "Try not to burn the tree down," he said as he walked away.

Wondering if I should feel bad, I made my way out of the manor. I found Katzia standing by the big oak tree just outside the wards.

"You're late."

"I know. I forgot I had class today."

"If you're not going to respect my time, I will not respect yours either."

"I'm sorry, Kat."

"You will make it up by staying late."

"But that will cut into dinner..."

"You can eat after. Let's get started. Take a seat."

With a tremendous sigh, I took a seat on the blanket she laid out and crossed my legs.

"What are we doing today?" I asked.

"Since you still cannot control your ignitus, I figured we would proceed from a new angle. This is going to require you to focus."

"Isn't that what we've been doing?" I asked.

"This is going to be different. After some research and some thinking back, I believe we have been approaching it wrong. We have been focusing on trying to get you to light your ignitus. But I fear that you haven't bonded to it, and that's why you can't control it. We need to focus on getting you to bond with it first."

"Is that why it only happens when I'm angry?"

"I assume so, yes."

"How long did it take you to bond with yours?" I asked.

"I bonded with mine the first week."

"I have had mine for two months."

"You have."

"How did you know when you were bonded?"

"I felt it connect. When I first got my ignitus, it was yellow. Once I bonded, it turned colors." Without even batting an eye, she turned her ignitus on. A low rolling fire slid across her skin. "It's now the bright red with flecks of blue that you see today."

"Mine is orange now, so what color will mine be?" I asked.

"I'm not sure. We will know once you're bonded. Let's start by having you lay down." I laid back on the blanket and shifted until I was comfortable. "I want you to close your eyes and relax your body, Ember."

"Okay." Closing my eyes, I took a deep breath and blew it out slowly.

"I want you to think about everything in the world and describe it to me. I need three descriptions from each of your senses. First, what do you feel?"

"I feel relaxed."

"No. What do you feel with your body?"

"I feel the softness of the blanket."

"What else?"

"I also feel the firmness of the ground."

"And?"

"I can feel wind blowing lightly on my skin."

"What do you smell?"

"I smell the outdoors."

"That's too vague."

"I smell grass, mostly."

"What else do you smell?"

I took a deep breath. "I can smell the flowers from the garden."

"Last one."

"I smell a fire burning."

"Yes. The Elven were burning some wood earlier. Now, what do you hear?"

"I heard the Elven building in the barn, but they stopped."

"What else do you hear?"

"I can hear thunder rolling in the distance."

"Get up."

"Why?" my eyes popped open, and I looked at her with confusion.

"Get up," she said again and I hopped off the ground.

"What's wrong, Kat?"

"It's about to storm. Class will have to be canceled." She grabbed the blanket off the ground. "I must get to the portal. I will see you next week." She galed away.

Standing there for a few seconds in shock, I decided I should probably go inside, too. The manor was inside the wards, so I wouldn't be able to gale. As I walked, the fresh smell of the rain hit me right before it poured down. I took off jogging as the rain beat against my skin.

Rain-soaked and cranky, I slammed the door as I entered the manor.

"What's your problem?" Asher looked at me and his eyes widened. "Oh, got wet, huh?"

"You think." I slid my wet shoes off.

"Why are you wet?" Cash asked as he strolled in.

"There is magic water falling from the clouds in the sky."

"Whatever, Ember." Cash shook his head and walked away.

"What's his problem?" Asher asked.

"Shit. I pissed him off. Cash wait." I followed him into the study. "Hey, I said wait!" He turned to look at me.

"What, Ember?"

"Can we talk?" I asked.

"We have nothing to talk about." He strolled up to the minibar and poured himself a drink. "Do you want one?" he asked. I shook my head no.

"I'm sorry for what I said to you earlier, Cash."

"No. You were right, Ember. Your sister needs someone more like her. A better man than I can be." He turned away.

"Cash, stop." I grabbed his arm. "I was mad at Val. It had nothing to do with you."

"You sure made it about me."

"I'm sorry. Please don't be mad at me, Cash."

"It's fine. Really. We're good." He smiled lightly. It wasn't a Cash smile and I knew he wasn't fine.

"She really likes you, Cash."

"I know she does."

"So, you will continue to see her?" I asked.

"No." He shook his head.

"Why not?"

"Because even though you didn't mean what you said, it made me think."

"Cash...."

"Cinder is too good for me. She needs someone better. Someone more honorable."

"You're good enough for her."

"I'm not sure I am, Ember."

"Why would you think that?"

"She's a virgin."

"I shouldn't have told you that." I shamefully shook my head.

"I already knew."

"She told you?" Surprise filled me.

"She is very open and honest." His words made me cringe, since I wasn't being open or honest with her.

"Then what's the problem? She isn't worth waiting for?"

"She one thousand percent is. I just don't think I'm worthy enough to be the one who gets to wait."

"Why not?"

"Because I have bedded plenty of women, Ember. Like you said, I'm no saint."

"I didn't mean it like that, Cash. Even if it was true, Cinder is very understanding and wouldn't hold it against you."

"No. But I will hold it against myself." He walked away, leaving me standing in the middle of the study. This time, I let him go.

The day started off shitty and was ending even shittier. I hurt multiple people I love today, and I may have completely ruined my sister's chance of true happiness. My relationship with her was getting better, but it wouldn't be once she found out what I said to Cash. Every male, except for Asher, was mad at me. I hoped I could fix everything before it was too late.

Making my way upstairs, I went to my room. When I opened the door, Val was sitting at the table, reading.

"What happened, love?" he asked.

"Are you reading?" Val set the book down and prowled up to me.

"I just figured I would see what my woman likes." He kissed me.

"I like what you do to me." I smiled.

"Is that why you're so wet?" he said before going into the bathroom and grabbing a towel.

"It started raining during my class. Kat took off, and I got soaked." I pulled my shirt off.

"Do you want to be more soaked?" He handed me the towel.

We got mated in the eyes of the kingdom a couple weeks ago. Neither of us could get enough of each other, and we had been having sex everywhere.

"I thought you were mad at me." I pulled off my pants and dried my skin.

He stepped closer to me and slid his hands into my wet hair. "Not when you're naked." He slammed a kiss on my mouth.

Dropping the towel, I slid my hands behind his back and pulled him into me. Kissing away from my mouth, his lips traveled down to my throat. Tilting my head back, I was ready for a bite. Val stopped, and I righted my head.

"What's wrong?" I asked.

"I love you," he whispered. "Even if you make me do things I don't want to do."

I slid my arms around his neck and looked up at him. "I love you, too, Val. I'm sorry that—"

"We will talk about that later, love."

He picked me up, and I wrapped my legs around his waist. Walking us over to the bed, he laid me down on it. He removed his shirt and pants as I watched. I crawled over to the edge of the bed and grabbed his shorts.

"I got these."

As I pulled them down, his cock sprang out. Cradling it in my hand, I lowered my head and kissed it. Running my tongue around the tip, he jerked. I opened my mouth wide and took all of him inside of it, and he let out a deep growl. I rolled my tongue around and sucked on him until he was breathless.

"To the Gods."

I looked up at him from under my long lashes as he growled again. Unable to resist touching me, he shoved me back onto the bed.

"I wasn't done," I said with a laugh.

"I don't care." He crawled onto the bed and stayed on his knees. He lifted my leg and started kissing the inside of my ankle. "Have we tried here yet?"

"No," I moaned.

In a flash, Val struck out and bit my ankle, making me moan loudly, as the venom from his bite flooded my veins. The warmth spread up my body and settled in my core, making my clit twitch. After taking in some of my blood, he released the bite and continued kissing up my leg.

"Hurry," I moaned. I wanted to orgasm before the bite wore off.

"So impatient," he said as he dropped my leg.

"Val, come on."

Settling between my legs, he laughed. Kissing my lower lips, I felt his breath caress my skin, sending shivers through me. Spreading my lips apart, he sucked my clit into his mouth, and I moaned. Pulling back slightly, he rolled his tongue around. My body was tense as I felt the orgasm building. Grabbing his hair, I pulled hard as he growled, and I felt the vibrations rumble against me.

"Don't stop," I whispered.

His tongue darted inside of me and pulled the wetness up to my clit. My muscles clenched, and I exploded. My fingers tightened in his hair as the blissful feeling took over and I came into his mouth.

Val crawled on top of me, my wetness glistening off his smile. His warm cock pressed against me as I spread my legs.

"You taste delicious," he said.

"Stop talking and fuck me."

"You're being a dirty girl today, love." He tilted his head and smiled. His now-elongated, blood-coated fangs made me shiver.

"I thought we were having hate sex." I smiled playfully.

Spreading my legs further, he slowly slid inside of me, and I dug my nails into his ass as I moaned. Lowering his head, he sucked on my nipple as he rolled his hips. My body was in full bliss mode. The entire day faded away in the blissfulness my mate was giving me.

Having an urge to come again, I pushed up on his chest.

"My turn," I whispered.

In an instant, Val rolled and took me with him. Landing on top of him, with him still inside of me, I immediately started rolling my hips as I dug my nails into his chest. He squeezed my hips as I grinded on him.

"Slow down," he said.

"I can't." My fingers dug into his chest as my insides clenched around his cock. "I'm going to come." My orgasm took over as my body moved on its own.

"Fuck." Val's body tightened as warm wetness filled me. I fell against his chest as I tried to catch my breath.

"Sorry. I didn't mean to make you go so soon," I said. The stress of the day had taken its toll on me, and I needed the release.

"It's fine. We can do it again later, love." He kissed the top of my head. "We need to clean up before dinner, anyway."

Looking at the clock, he was right.

"Shit, there isn't enough time for both of us to shower." I sat up and looked into his eyes. I was about to bolt and get in the shower first.

"I guess you will have to stay a dirty girl, then." He tickled me and I fell to my side, laughing. He hopped off the bed in one fluid motion and ran into the bathroom.

"Don't you dare," I screamed as I jumped up and ran after him.

Chapter 5

Cinder

After spending some time knitting, I went down to the kitchen and helped Noreen with dinner. We made chicken alfredo and bread and had just finished setting the table when Cash walked in.

"Oh, hey, Cash." Grabbing a bottle of wine, I screwed in a bottle opener.

"Hey, Cinder. Where is everyone?" He glanced around nervously.

"I'm sure they will be here in a minute." I smiled at him as I pulled on the top. But it wasn't coming out. "How was your day?" I asked as I fiddled with the bottle.

"I forgot something in my room." Cash turned and left.

An overwhelming sadness filled my body. I didn't know what I did to make Cash distant, but I hoped it wasn't my lack of knowledge of courting, or possibly that I was a terrible kisser. Looking down at the stupid wine bottle, I was about to throw it against the wall when Zayn walked in.

"Hey, Cinder." He smiled kindly at me.

"Hey, Zayn." I yanked as hard as I could, and nothing was happening.

"Let me help you." Zayn took the bottle from me, and I heard the pop as he opened it like a pro.

"Thank you. I was about ready to throw it."

"No need when you have powerful men around." He looked down at the table filled with food. "Did you help with cooking again?"

"I did." I took my seat at the table.

"Everything looks delicious." Zayn took a seat next to me.

"Thank you."

"It smells great in here." Cali came strolling in, Zila behind her. They both took a seat.

Cash walked in. Not making eye contact with me, he took a seat on the opposite side of the table and my chest felt heavy since he usually sat next to me.

"I'm starving." Asher walked in and grabbed a piece of bread.

"Wait for the others," Cali said, and Asher dropped the bread. "Well, take it now. You already touched it." Asher grabbed the bread again.

"You're in my seat, Cash."

Cash looked up at Asher. "Sit somewhere else."

Asher stuck the bread in his mouth and shrugged, then took a seat next to me. The room got quiet as tension spread through it. We waited for Val and Ember for ten minutes. Cash didn't look toward me one time.

Zayn finally spoke. "They're late again. Let's eat."

Everyone started making their plates. I made a small salad and sat it in front of me.

"Do you want some wine?" Zayn asked.

"That would be great, thank you." I looked over at Cash. He was watching Zayn while he poured my wine.

He glanced at me for a split second, then went back to eating. Looking down at my plate, I had completely lost my appetite. Pain filled my chest. I grabbed my wine and took a swig.

"Cinder helped make dinner again," Zayn said.

"It's delicious, Cinder." Asher grabbed more bread.

"It's very good." Zila smiled kindly at me.

"Thank you, all."

The door opened and Val and Ember entered. I didn't have the energy to scold Ember for being late tonight, so I stayed quiet. They both took seats and made their plates.

Our meals were usually accompanied by talking, laughing, and having fun. Tonight, everyone was quiet. After ten minutes of silence and the two bites of salad I had, Valarian cleared his throat.

"So, we will all be sparring in the morning. Be out there at sunrise."

"Can we go swimming one last time before the summer ends?" Asher asked.

"Yes! That would be fun." Cali poured herself some more wine.

"That would be fun. I would love to show you more of the lands, Cin."

"I don't have a suit." I looked at Ember and shifted uncomfortably.

"You can borrow one of mine."

"Thank you, Cali."

"Maybe Sunday, since we have my brother's birthday party on Saturday." Zila took a bite of her food.

"Crap. I didn't realize that's why you guys were going to Direbreak." Ember looked at Val.

"We can go, love." He smiled at her.

"So, I guess we are going," Ember said.

"Yay!" Cali clapped her hands.

"Look out, Direbreak, the King's Guard is coming." Asher looked at me, wondering if I was going after the morning's argument with my sister.

"And me as well." I smiled proudly.

"Oh, I will get you a sexy dress to wear." Cali squealed with excitement. Ember shifted uncomfortably, but didn't say anything.

"I would love that, Cali. Thank you." Glancing at Cash, we locked eyes for a second before he put his fork down, stood up, and walked toward the door.

"Where are you going, buddy?" Zayn asked.

Cash said nothing as he left the room.

"Cash has been in a bad mood all day." Asher picked up his glass. "An unhappy Cash gives me no hope for a happy life," he said before taking a swig.

"So, what kind of dress are you going to let Cinder borrow?" Ember looked over at Cali, completely avoiding talking about Cash.

"Oh, I have a couple different black ones that…"

The sound of them talking faded away as my mind raced. I jabbed a piece of salad with my fork, then set it down and let out a sigh.

"Are you okay?" Zayn whispered.

"I think so."

"Do you want to talk about it after dinner?" he asked.

"I may need to talk."

"What do you think, Cinder?" Cali asked.

Looking up at her, I had no idea what she was talking about.

"Okay." I also didn't know what I was agreeing to and didn't care right now.

"Perfect! Come to my room tomorrow and you can try it on." Cali smiled at me. I gave her a light smile back.

"Excuse me." I stood up and pushed my chair in.

"Are you done, Cin?" Ember looked at me with a concerned face.

"Yes. Since we are training tomorrow, I'm going to retire early tonight. Goodnight, everyone."

My heart ached as I made my way upstairs and turned into the hall. I should have known better than to think a man like Cash would have anything to do with someone like me. I wasn't a King's Guard, and I was a virgin. I felt like a fool.

Chapter 6

Cinder

Waking up at the crack of dawn was not ideal, but Valarian told me to be downstairs early because today was my first day of training. I didn't have anything other than dresses, so I borrowed a pair of leggings and a shirt from Cali. She also gave me a tank top. She said to wear it in case I got hot and needed to take my shirt off. That wasn't going to happen, but I wore it under my shirt, anyway. I had put my hair in a braid, like Ember told me to. One last look in the mirror and I headed out my bedroom door.

Making my way down the stairs, I saw Val and Ember waiting for me at the bottom.

"Are you ready?" Val asked.

"Yes," I said nervously.

"Okay, we're waiting for the others."

Hearing feet and talking, I looked up and saw Cali, Zila, Zayn, and Asher coming down. My heart thundered in my chest when Cash came down right after.

"We're here!" Cali said.

"Alright, let's head out." Val opened the door, and we all followed him out of the manor.

Ember was holding hands with Val. Cali and Zila were walking together. Asher was walking off to the side alone, spinning his staff. Cash was way ahead of everyone and Zayn fell in step next to me.

"It's weird seeing you in anything other than a dress," Zayn said. Looking down at my clothes, I agreed.

"You saw me in pants at the Elevation of the Duke of Mazuria."

"I didn't know you as well. Now I'm just used to seeing you in dresses." Zayn laughed.

"Do I look bad?"

"No, not at all. Just weird, but in a good way."

"It feels weird, too. But it's not that bad. I suppose I could get used to it."

"You look beautiful either way. Don't fret." He smiled, and I blushed.

"Thank you."

"Are you ready for this training?" he asked.

"I guess. Am I going to get hurt?"

"No, we won't hurt you. Well, Ember might. She kicks my ass every time we spar. I still win, but she gives me hell."

"Oh." More nervousness now filled me.

"I'm kidding. She won't hurt you. The part about her kicking my ass is true, but so is me winning." I laughed nervously as we walked up to the big outdoor arena.

The training area was immense. There was a big circle in the middle and benches around it. Valarian walked out into the middle of the circle and Cash followed. Everyone else took a seat on the benches, so I followed suit.

"Alright. So, I asked everyone here today so we could do some expedited training with Cinder. We are going to do what we usually do and pair up. One-on-one. Cash and I will be the coaches. Now that there are an even number of women, my mate can stop beating up the men." Val looked over at Ember and she smiled proudly.

"Told you," Zayn whispered, and I giggled.

"Same rules apply as before. I will repeat them, so Cinder knows. No biting or eye gouging, and no magic. This is a sparring class, not a magic class. Right, Asher?" Val's eyes shot toward Asher, and he smiled.

"You throw one rock and suddenly you're singled out," Asher said, and I giggled.

"Also, the new rule we had to add, thanks to someone." Val looked at Ember and she shrugged her shoulders while she grinned.

"Which is no dick punching," Cash said, as he adjusted the front of his pants. "I'm not sure I have fully recovered since then."

"Told you she is mean." Zayn nudged my arm.

I threw my hand over my mouth to keep from laughing.

"First up are Asher and Zayn."

Zayn and Asher both stood up and removed their shirts. My eyes went wide as I looked at their King's Guard tattoos. I hadn't seen them before.

They made their way to the center of the big ring in the middle. Zayn went up to Val as Asher went up to Cash. They both talked to their coaches and then entered the ring.

Val stood along one side and crossed his arms. Cash stood on the other side and gave Asher pointers the whole time. I watched closely as punches, blocks, and kicks were thrown. After about ten minutes, they were both covered in sweat as Val called the match. Zayn won.

"Next up, Zila and Cali."

The two women immediately went to their coaches. They both were wearing tank tops and leggings. I had seen Cali's tattoo plenty of times because she wore low cut shirts, but I had never seen Zila's wolf tattoo.

Zila went to Cash, and Cali went to Val for a coach. After their words of encouragement, they entered the floor. I watched in surprise as sweet, shy Zila gave Cali a run for her money. Halfway through the fight, I realized I was going to be paired with Ember, and started getting nervous. Finally, the fight was over. Val said that Zila won, and both women took a seat.

"Cash, it's you and me, buddy."

Valarian took his shirt off and entered the ring. He did a few stretches and my eyes wandered to Cash. He had his long blonde hair in a low bun today. I watched as he slid his shirt off, and I nervously bit my lip. My heart seemed to have a mind of its own because it sped up like it was in a race. His chest was hard, and I could see his golden King's Guard tattoo. It was a sword with angel wings on the side, just like Zayn's and Cali's. His stomach was nothing but abs, and his arms were huge. It suddenly became hot outside and sweat beaded up on my body. I could feel my cheeks flush.

Cash glanced over like he could feel the lust coming off me, and we locked eyes. He smiled a true Cash smile and turned away. My mouth fell open and my breathing grew heavy at the sight of his back as I watched him stroll into the circle. To my surprise, his entire back was tattooed—a giant pair of black angel wings. A slow smile radiated across my face as I thought about running my nails down his back. I quickly tried to put the thought out of my head.

Cash's muscles moved with every punch and kick that he threw. I locked my eyes onto him, unable to look away from the glorious sight. I watched as his muscles tightened and loosed. It was like a wave rippling across his body with each precise move. It sent shivers through me, all the way to the area between my legs, and I started panting.

I was so busy staring at Cash's body that I didn't pay attention to any of the actual moves they were doing. That wasn't good because the match was over, and Val was calling my name as I watched Cash take a swig of water.

"Cinder?"

"Yeah?" My head whipped over to Val.

"I said it's your turn."

"Oh." I hopped off the bench.

To my surprise, Ember took her shirt off and strolled over to Val, wearing a tank top and leggings.

Not wanting to be the prude one who stays covered up, I pulled my shirt off and looked over at Cash. His eyes widened slightly, and I tried hard to ignore it. Looking away, I walked around the circle and headed toward my coach.

"Hi," I said as I strolled up to Cash.

"Hi." He smiled. "Are you ready to kick her ass?"

"I doubt that will happen."

"I have been watching her fight for months. There are three things to know about her that are the most important. She always throws a right punch before kicking out with her left leg. When she kicks with her right leg, she always steps forward slightly first, so you must pay close attention."

"What's the last thing?"

"She loves to run her mouth. She likes to get into people's heads, especially if her opponent is bigger than her. When we spar, she gives me a hard time. Try not to talk back, it just encourages her to talk more crap."

"Okay." I swallowed hard as I stared into his eyes. I wanted to ask him if we were okay, but I didn't.

"Come on. I will show you some stances."

Cash strolled into the circle and I followed. The ground inside the ring wasn't hard. It was squishy under my feet, like they had covered it in some type of mat.

"Spread your feet shoulder width apart." I did what he said. "I'm going to touch you, okay?"

"Yes, please." Cash smiled, and I realized just a yes would have been sufficient.

Cash moved my body around, tilting my head and arms in different directions. I could smell his skin when he was near—bergamot and sandalwood

"When she goes to punch, you're going to block like this." He moved my arm, showing me what to do. After about ten minutes of my one-on-one training with Cash, he stopped and looked me in the eye.

"Are you ready?" he asked.

"I think so." My breathing was heavy from his closeness, and I didn't hear half the words he said because I was too busy staring at his body.

He laid his hands on my cheeks. "You got this, Cinnamon. Just try to remember everything I said."

"I will try." Cash smiled and left the ring and I watched as Ember walked up.

"Are you both ready?" Val asked.

"Ready," Ember said.

I took the stance Cash taught me. "Ready."

Ember stood back and waited for me to start. I approached her slowly, hoping I remembered the techniques Cash taught me.

"You got this," she said.

"I know, do you?" I swung a fist at her and she dodged it.

"Nice," she said.

"Shut up," I said through gritted teeth and she laughed at me, so I threw another punch.

"Your punches are slow. I can see which arm you're going to use before *you* even know."

Trying hard to ignore her and focus, I tried one of her own moves against her. I threw out a right punch, and as she dodged, I kicked out my left leg and got her in the thigh.

"Nice!" I heard Cash from over my shoulder.

"That was nice. It won't happen again." Ember gave me a sly grin.

I saw her step forward slightly and knew she was going to kick her right leg out, so I took two steps sideways. She stumbled when her leg didn't land on me and I threw out a punch, getting her in the face.

"Holy shit. Yes!" Cash was clapping loudly and pride filled me.

"I see Cash was busy telling you all my secrets. Unfortunately for you, I can change them." She stepped forward again. Expecting a kick, I stepped to the right and ran right into her left fist. She had never hit me in the face before. It was the worst pain I had ever felt.

"You're good, Cinder. Shake it off." Cash was an excellent coach, I'd give him props for that. He inspired me, that's for sure.

I kicked out my leg, and Ember caught it. She twisted it up and I fell flat on my back.

"Get up, quickly!" Cash yelled. I rolled onto my stomach and crawled away before I jumped to my feet.

"If I was a Demon, you wouldn't have gotten off the ground that easily. Remember that." Understanding that she gave me an advantage, I nodded.

I threw out a punch, and she dodged it. Throwing another one, she dodged it again. She threw out one and got me in the shoulder.

This went on until I was panting and sweating. I threw out a punch, and she grabbed my arm. She twisted me around to where she was holding me from behind.

"If this happens, you have three options. You can headbutt them in the face, which hurts your head. You can also elbow them, or you can stomp their foot."

"I'm out of energy," I said breathlessly, hoping to catch her off guard.

"Are you done?" Ember asked.

"Yes." She let go of me and I instantly stomped her foot.

Not moving away quick enough, she shoved me and I fell face first onto the mat.

"Get up quick!" I heard Cash yell.

As I crawled away, Ember hopped on my back. She put her hand to my throat.

"If I was an enemy, this would be a knife and you would be dead."

"Match," Val said as he strolled into the ring. "You did a good job for your first time, Cinder."

Ember hopped off me and I sat up. "Thanks, Val."

Cash came up to me and lowered his hand. I took it and he helped me off the ground. "You did an excellent job."

"Thanks, coach." I smiled and looked down at his chest. Glancing back up into his beautiful blue eyes, I couldn't look away.

As he stared at me, I noticed his face filled with as much lust as mine. Then I saw the shift in his features. He was struggling with something, and I didn't know what it was.

"You're welcome," he said and then quickly walked away.

Chapter 7

Cinder

Yesterday's morning sparring was exhausting. After breakfast, I relaxed in my room for a bit and changed clothes. I skipped lunch because I was sore and didn't feel like walking down. Val said I shouldn't be healed because my soreness was from building muscle, not an injury. I disagreed, but I sucked it up and never asked Cali to heal me.

We had a normal quiet dinner and nothing exciting happened. I went to bed early again that night after I spent an hour knitting and thinking of Cash. He was attentive during training, but I feel it was only because he was my coach. Once the match was over, he went back to being distant.

Looking at the clock, it was around three o'clock in the afternoon. Deciding I needed something to do to pass the time until dinner and get my mind off Cash, I left my room and headed downstairs.

Heading into the kitchen, I looked around. Noreen wasn't here. I opened the cupboards and poked around inside. Finding the spice cabinet, I took a mental note of the different spices that I had bought, along with the ones the servants had. Continuing to look inside each one, I hit the jackpot when I opened the last cabinet. It was filled with cookbooks.

Digging through them until I found some good dessert ones, I made a pile next to me on the floor to take. I found six dessert cookbooks. The one handwritten by Cora Nance seemed the most promising.

Picking up my pile, I thumbed through them and came across a recipe for a caramel cake. Wanting to make this now, I pulled out the dry ingredients and utensils I would need. Deciding I should preheat the stove first, I got down on my knees and looked inside. I had never lit one before.

"What are you doing, Cinder?" I jumped in surprise.

"Oh, you scared me, Zayn." He had changed from his sparring clothes and was now in his normal pants and tight black t-shirt.

"I'm sorry," he said with a smile.

"It's okay." I smiled back at him.

"What are you doing on the floor?" He tilted his head.

"I was trying to figure out how to light the stove. I have never done it before."

"Oh, here. I'll get it," Zayn reached his hand out to me, and he helped me off the floor. "You are too pretty to be crawling around down there." I blushed at his words as he turned away.

Zayn added wood to the stove, took a match, and lit it.

"There you go. Just make sure you open this chimney vent before you light it."

"Thank you, Zayn."

"You're welcome. So, what are you making?"

"A dessert for after dinner. It's just for practice, but I may get a booth at the market, so I want to be prepared."

"Oh, that's outstanding."

"I hope it helps to pass the time. I get lonely here sometimes since I don't have missions like everyone else." I shrugged my shoulders and tried to keep my face from saddening.

"I'm sorry, Cinder."

"It's okay. Let's pray to the Gods that I get this stand soon."

"Do you know where Ember is?" he asked.

"No. I haven't seen her."

Zayn let out a long breath. "Do you want some help?" His smile was flat as he looked at me.

"Umm, do you know how to cook?"

"I do. My mother was a baker, and she taught me."

"Okay. Then yes." I smiled big. I was happy to have a cooking partner.

He walked over to the hook on the wall, grabbed an apron, and slid it on. He grabbed another apron and came back over to me. Reaching out his hands, he slid the apron over my neck and then placed his hand on my cheek.

"This will keep you from getting dirty this time."

"Ow, it caught my hair."

Zayn went behind my back and eased my hair out of the loop of the apron. His thumb brushed my neck, and it sent shivers down me.

"There you go."

"Umm, thank you, Zayn." I blushed slightly, confused by the attention.

"No problem. So, which recipe are we making?"

"I wanted to make this caramel cake." I pointed to the recipe in the cookbook.

"Perfect. I see you have the dry ingredients. I'll grab the wet ones."

As Zayn grabbed what we needed, I used the sifter and added flour into the bowl. Once he came back with the ingredients, I continued measuring out things for the cake as he worked on making the icing. About thirty minutes later, I was sliding the cake into the oven.

"It's hot in here now." Zayn grabbed the collar of his shirt and pulled it out like he was letting some cool air in.

"It truly is," I said as I wiped the sweat off my forehead with the back of my hand. I met Zayn's eyes, and he laughed. "Whatever is so funny?"

"You have flour on your forehead now."

"Oh," I laughed. "Oops."

"Here, let me."

Zayn grabbed a towel, raised it to my face, and slowly wiped the flour off me.

"Thank you."

"No problem." He smiled at me as I stared into his beautiful blue eyes. They were the same color as Cash's. Warm and inviting.

"What are you two doing?" Cash asked, and I jumped as his voice yanked me back to reality.

Feeling extremely uncomfortable, I grabbed the towel out of Zayn's hand and immediately started wiping my hands with it.

"We are making a cake, buddy. Want to help?"

"I'm good." Cash gave me a flat smile and left the room.

"What's his problem?" Zayn asked with furrowed eyebrows.

"I think I did something wrong. He's mad at me or something." I shook my head, as more confusion settled in me.

"I highly doubt that. He wouldn't get mad at you, Cinder."

"He's been distant for two days. We didn't even go for our walk in the gardens two mornings in a row."

"That's odd. You guys walk every day."

"I guess I will walk alone if he doesn't want to go."

"I'll go with you if you want. Just let me know if you ever need a walking partner."

"Thank you." I smiled at his kindness.

"Let's clean up while the cake bakes," he said.

Wiping all the flour on the counter into a pile, I accidentally knocked a wooden spoon onto the floor. I crouched down to pick it up at the same time as Zayn and we bumped heads.

"Ow."

"Oh, I'm sorry, Cinder. Are you okay?" he asked with a laugh.

"I'll be fine." Zayn and I both stood back up.

"Let me see." He grabbed my face in his hands and looked me over. "I think you will be okay, except for that."

"What is it?" I asked.

Zayn ran his fingers through the flour on the counter and rubbed it across my cheek.

"That flour right there," he said with a smile.

My mouth dropped open in shock and then I laughed. Grabbing a handful of flour, I smiled wickedly at him.

"Don't you dare, Cinder!"

"You mean this flour?" I chucked it at him.

We both started laughing hysterically as we threw flour at each other. The kitchen door opened and Noreen walked in, and we both immediately froze. She looked around at the mess we made and her face paled.

"We need the kitchen to start preparing dinner."

"We are cleaning it up, Noreen. My apologies," Zayn said as I tried to stifle a giggle.

"Thank you, my lord."

"Can you come back in, say, fifteen minutes?" Zayn gave her a sweet smile.

"That would be fine." Noreen left the room, and we both laughed.

"Okay, Cinder. Let's clean for real this time."

"We better be quick, or Noreen might freak out."

We finished cleaning the kitchen just as the timer for the cake went off. I removed it from the oven and set it on the cooling rack.

"It looks perfect," Zayn said.

"We make a great team."

"We do." He held up his hand, and I gave him a high-five.

"I want to make this lemon cake in a few days, but I need some lemons. I also noticed that we don't have nutmeg."

"You can pick some up at the market."

"Yes, hopefully I'll remember."

"Well, it was fun cooking with you," Zayn said as he removed his apron and hung it back on the hook. "I'm going to change before dinner."

"I should change, too." I looked down at my dress. The apron helped, but I was still messy. I removed my apron and hung it up, too.

"I'll walk you up. Come on." Zayn walked with me, and we parted ways at the top of the stairs as I headed to the east wing.

Having just enough time to bathe and get dressed, I laid out a beautiful blue dress for dinner and turned the water on in the bathroom.

After I was bathed and dressed, I headed out of my room. Walking toward the stairs, I saw Zayn coming out of his room. His was the first door in the west wing.

"Hey, Cinder. Headed down for dinner?"

"Hi, Zayn. Yes, I am."

"Perfect, I'll escort you." Zayn held out his arm and I took it. We descended the stairs and turned toward the dining hall. Upon entering, we both took our normal seats. Zila and Cali were already seated and both smiled at us.

"Hello ladies, and Zayn." Asher walked in and took his normal seat.

For once, Ember and Val were on time. They walked in and sat down.

"Holy shit. The stars have aligned." Asher smiled at them. "You guys stopped having sex long enough to eat?"

"Shut up, Asher." Ember stuck her middle finger up at Asher and he laughed.

"Let's eat." Cali picked up the tray of roasted chicken and put some on her plate.

"We have to wait for Cash," Zayn said.

"Oh. He isn't coming. He said he wasn't hungry." Cali passed the plate of food to Zila.

"Cash isn't hungry?" Asher asked.

"I know. I was shocked." Zila sighed. "I hope he is okay."

I watched as Val locked eyes with Zayn and Zayn nodded. Val stood up and kissed Ember on the forehead. Zayn stood up and left the dining room, and Val followed him out.

"What's going on?" I asked.

"Val said they're going to check on him." Ember shrugged her shoulders.

Most of the rest of the dinner was quiet. I think everyone was concerned about Cash. Val and Zayn didn't come back until the end of the meal.

"Ember." Val nodded his head toward the door. His face was serious. Ember sighed as she stood up.

Zayn walked over and took a seat next to me.

"Everything okay?" I asked.

"Yep." He didn't make eye contact with me as he made his plate. "I'm starving."

"I'm retiring to my room. I have some reading I want to do." Zila stood up and left the dining room.

"Does anyone want to play cards?" Asher asked.

"Sure!" Cali stood up. "I love cards."

"I'm good, buddy. I'm going to go to my room after I eat." Zayn poured him some wine and sighed.

"Cinder?"

"Thanks, Asher. Maybe next time." I smiled as they left the room. "Are you sure everything is okay, Zayn?"

"Everything is fine, Cinder. Val and I are handling it." He looked over at me and smiled.

"Okay. I'm going to head up. Have a good night."

"You, too."

I felt bad leaving Zayn to eat alone, but I wanted to be alone for once.

Chapter 8

Ember

When Val ushered me out of the dining room, I knew I was in trouble. Trailing behind him all the way upstairs in silence was nerve-racking. He opened the door to our room, and I entered. Closing the door behind us, he turned to look at me.

"Shit." A hard breath escaped me.

"Do you know what your meddling did?" Val crossed his arms as he glared.

"Val."

"For once in your life, be quiet, Ember." My heart raced at the tone of his voice. He wasn't yelling yet, but his voice was deeper than normal. "You dropped a venomous seed in Cash's head, and it has now sprouted into a shit show."

"I didn't mean for any of this to happen."

"I know you didn't. You could have stopped it immediately, but you're too stubborn to do so."

"What could I have done better? Apologize sooner?"

"You could have just not said it at all, love. You questioned Cash's honor. He's probably the most honorable man I know. His head is fucked up, and it's your fault. This entire thing is going to blow up even more when

Cinder finds out, not to mention the fact that you have put this entire house in jeopardy."

"How so?"

"We are King's Guards and can get called on missions at any time. There could be a Demon attack tomorrow for all we know. You want us on the battlefield mad at each other? That causes instability in our system and our fighting. You don't think I haven't noticed the uncomfortableness you've caused in the house this week, too."

I threw my hands out beside me. "What do you want me to do then, Val?" I yelled.

"Fix it!" Val slammed the door as he left the room.

Plopping on the bed, I put my face into my hands. I had unintentionally messed up so many things... Cash was a mess, Val was mad at me, and since Zayn went with him to talk to Cash, I'm assuming he'll be mad at me, too. Once again, I pissed off most of the men in the house. I needed to talk to Cinder first thing in the morning. If she hears it from someone other than me, she will never forgive me.

Exhausted from the day's events, I changed into pajamas and grabbed my book. I laid there reading for hours before Val came back.

"I was hoping you were still up," he said as he came into the room.

Shutting my book, I rolled away from him. I heard two clunks as his boots hit the floor and a hard breath escaped him. The bed shifted as he crawled into it. He scooted up behind me and nuzzled his face into my neck.

"I'm sorry for yelling, my *hertis rote*." he whispered.

"I yelled first, and I deserved it."

"No, you didn't, love."

Rolling toward him, I looked at him with tear-filled eyes.

"I absolutely deserved it, Val. My sister just wanted to have fun, and I caused a bunch of drama. I couldn't just keep my mouth shut and let her. I'm overprotective, and it's a huge flaw of mine."

"That's not a flaw, love. Being so protective of the ones you love is one of your many outstanding qualities." He wiped a tear from my cheek. "You were doing what you thought was right. But maybe next time consult me or Zayn first." He smiled and I let out a sad laugh.

"I'm sorry. I'll fix everything. I promise."

"No need to apologize to me, love. Just do what you need to do to fix the relationships with the people you love."

"So, I shouldn't say sorry for being so stubborn?"

"Absolutely not. That is also one of your great qualities."

Curling his arms around me, he pulled me closer to him as his lips slowly pressed against mine.

"Get some sleep. Tomorrow is going to be a long day."

Cuddling up as close as I could to him, I laid my head against his chest. My thoughts were loud, so I closed my eyes and focused on the sound of his heartbeat until sleep took over.

When the sun rose, anxiety came with it. Today was going to be a long day. Finding Cinder and letting her know what happened was first on my list. Then I had to find Cash and fix things with him.

Sitting in the chair, I reached down and tied my boots. I let out a hard breath before I stood.

"It'll be okay, love." Val came strolling out of the bathroom.

"I hope so."

"Stick to the plan you have. Treat it like a mission, but with more feeling." He smiled. "Are you ready?"

"Yes," I indeed was not ready.

After one last kiss, Val opened the bedroom door, and we headed downstairs. I planned on telling Cinder as soon as breakfast was over.

We walked into the foyer, and I saw Cinder standing there holding a letter in her hand.

"The messenger Imp just dropped off some letters. The king has requested you both." Zayn handed Val a letter.

I looked into Cinder's tear-filled eyes.

"I got my stand." She held her letter up to me.

"That's amazing, Cinder. I'm so happy for you." My entire insides clenched as nausea hit me. There was no way I could tell her right now and ruin this happy moment.

I looked over at Val with a panicked face.

You should wait until we get back from seeing the king, Val wielded to me.

"Zayn is going to escort me to Tessalone. The letter said I could come and look at my booth. I could have it open in as little as a few weeks. Isn't that wonderful?" Cinder smiled brightly, and I smiled back.

"It's fantastic. Be safe."

"She will be safe with me." Zayn smiled. "Are you ready to go, Cinder?"

"Can I grab a shawl really quick, Zayn?"

"Of course. I will meet you by the front door."

Cinder left the dining room, and I locked eyes with Zayn. "I will guard her with my life. Don't worry, Ember."

"Since when do you call me Ember? Are you mad at me, Softy?"

"I just wished you would have talked to me instead of letting things get this far."

"I've been busy, Zayn."

"You're no busier than anyone else. We all have duties and things to deal with, yet we make time. I spent yesterday baking a cake with your sister because she mentioned she was lonely. Where were you?"

"I took a ride with Arna to Mazuria, like I do every week."

"Cinder could have gone with you."

"I didn't think about it, Zayn!" My voice got higher as I went on the defense.

"I know that didn't take all day. What else did you do?" he asked.

"I went hunting with Val."

"Once again, Cinder could have gone with you, but I'm pretty sure Val can catch food on his own." Zayn looked at Val.

"I told her that." My head shot in Val's direction.

"Be quiet, Val." I looked back at Zayn. "Thank you for spending time with her."

"Don't thank me. It's what you're supposed to do with friends." Zayn turned away but stopped at the door. "Cinder isn't the only one that misses you, you know."

After Zayn left the dining room, I turned to Val.

"I can't handle this, Val." I threw my hands over my face.

"Calm down, love."

"What the hell am I supposed to do? I broke Cash's heart and Zayn is mad. Cinder is going to be mad once I tell her what I did, and I can't tell her now and ruin her happiness."

"It's just terrible timing." Val pulled me in close to him. "We can talk about it later. The king has requested our presence."

I nodded.

Val held my hand as we left Castleva Manor and strolled outside the wards. We galed as close to Castle Elderfall as possible, but the king's wards were the biggest in the lands, and it was a far walk.

He knew I needed to think, so we walked silently most of the time. Once I saw the red maple trees in the distance, I let out a tremendous sigh of relief. I was ready to get this over with so I could fix everything.

"I don't know what I'm going to do, Val."

"You will do what's right, love. That's all you can do."

"I just wished the letter would have come one day later, or I would have said something one day earlier."

"You can't quickly change the direction of wheels already in motion. All you can do is move out of the way of the buggy or hop on."

"Since when do you make up metaphors?"

"Zayn told me that once when I told him I was scared."

"What were you scared of?" i asked. In my mind, Val feared nothing.

"Of falling in love with you." My eyes shot up to him.

"You were scared of falling in love with me?"

"Yes." He smiled. "But I got over it."

"When did this happen?"

"Do you remember the evening that you came to my room and gifted me the bear and couldn't keep your thoughts to yourself?" He smiled big as I nodded. "I knew I loved you that day, but I kept denying it. Then the next day you kissed me in the cave, and I knew immediately that I would do anything to please you for the rest of my life."

"And that scared you?"

"Not at all. I feared you not being able to love me back. Your father taught you to hate Vampires, so it scared me that your attraction to me was possibly just lust, and you would never feel deeply for me. Zayn pushed me to ignore those thoughts and told me to go with the flow. He said something about taking risks and finding something magical or some shit."

"He literally said the same thing to me!"

"He was making sure we got together. I will forever be grateful to him."

"Did you know I feared you wouldn't love me?" I asked.

"I didn't. But how can I not, Ember? You're an amazing person."

"I have flaws. Like, when I don't keep my mouth shut."

"That's not a flaw either, love. That's your powerful will. It's one of the many reasons I fell in love with you. That and the dirty thoughts that run through your head."

"I can't believe there was a time where I couldn't shield."

"I miss it sometimes." His eyes met mine as he smiled.

"I will remember to wield you some random dirty thoughts." I laid my head against his arm as we walked.

"You can, but I have a lot of fun making up what I think you're thinking."

"You can tell me some of those thoughts later." I looked up at him with lust filled eyes.

"Of course. After we fix things with our friends first." He gave me a light smile.

"Yes, that' s first on my list."

My mind immediately went to Zayn. It hurts my heart to think of my best friend and what he has done for us. He had to have been listening to us both complain and worry about the other. He must have had our secrets buried deep inside of him, yet he kept his composure and steered us both kindly in the right direction. That's what I should have done the moment I upset Cash. I should have fixed what I broke, but I didn't. Like Val said, I can't stop the wheels, so I guessed I would have to hop on that buggy and see what kind of ride it takes me on.

"Are you okay, love?"

"Yes? Why?"

"Tears are rolling down your face."

"Oh." I wiped the tears away. "I was just thinking about Zayn, and everything he has done for us. I was also thinking about all the things I have broken."

"So, what are you going to do?"

"I'm going to hop on the buggy."

"That's my girl." Val kissed my cheek as we strolled up to the castle.

The gray brick castle was just as gorgeous as I remembered. Strong and tall and surrounded by beautiful red maple trees. As we walked up the stairs, the doors opened on their own. We stepped inside and Meyers, the king's royal servant, greeted us.

"Welcome. Your Majesty and his guest are waiting in the throne room. Follow me."

Guest? I wonder who it is, Val.

I guess we will find out, my love.

We followed Meyers through the halls of the castle. We passed the marble statues, and for once, I got a good look at them. One of them looked just like King Reign.

"Are these statues made to look like the Gods?" I asked.

"Yes." Meyers stopped walking. "They are the exact resemblance of all ten of the Primordial Gods."

"Whoa."

"You have never seen them, my lady?"

"I have passed them but have never had time to look at them."

"This one here is your maker, Volcanis." He pointed to the statue, and I stepped closer to it as I looked it up and down.

"Is this really what he looks like?"

"It is." My eyes wandered toward Val. "I met him the night he brought you back, love. The resemblance is remarkable."

Glancing back at the statue, my heart filled with the love I had for my God. I bowed my head to the statue.

"Thank you for bringing me back, and for Arna." Deep down, I was hoping Volcanis heard my gratitude.

Turning away, I walked up to the one that looked like the current king.

"Wow, you're right about the resemblance, Val. This looks exactly like King Reign." I tilted my head as I admired it.

"They're the same height as the Gods, too," Meyers said.

"Which one is Tartarus?" I knew I was going to regret asking this question, but I had to know.

"It's this one right here, my lady." I strolled over to the statue Meyers pointed at and looked up at it. "All the Gods are over seven feet tall, but Tartarus is the tallest of them all."

Uneasiness filled my body, and I slowly backed away from the statue. Seeing my reaction, Val grabbed my hand.

"The king is waiting. Let's move on," Val said.

"Of course, my lord." Meyers continued walking, and we followed him.

Are you okay, love?

I'm okay.

Tartarus won't hurt you. He won't have a chance. We won't let Erebus raise him.

I know, Val.

Once again, I was lying. Fear ran through my veins as the face of Tartarus flashed through my mind over and over. He was bigger and stronger than Erebus could ever dream of being, and that frightened me.

After our long walk with my thoughts, we finally made it to the throne room. The doors opened wide, and we stepped onto the crimson runner that led toward the throne. Looking up, I saw the mystery guest that was waiting for us, and I smiled.

Chapter 9

Cinder

My life was finally getting better. I had received a letter stating that my stand was ready and I was going to go look at it. Grabbing my shawl, I quickly headed down to meet Zayn.

"Are you ready?" he asked.

"Yes. I'm so excited, Zayn. It will be nice to have a job again and not be lonely or bored."

"I'm happy for you, Cinder." He opened the door to the manor and smiled.

"I have so much to do to prepare. I'm going to have to make a bunch of desserts to practice. I want to make tons of different types of cakes, pies, and maybe some other kind of pastries. Variety is the key to good business, or so I think. I don't know. I've never owned a business before, so I'm just guessing."

"I think you're right. The more variety you have, the more people you can accommodate."

"Indeed." We stepped into the portal.

"What are you going to name it?" Zayn asked.

My mind raced with ideas, but I had not settled on a name yet.

"I don't know, Zayn." I shrugged my shoulders.

"We can go over some names on the walk."

Zayn wielded the portal to go, and the blissful rush came quick. The excitement of now owning a business mixed with the feeling of the portal was marvelous. Once we landed in Tessalone, I smiled at the portal guards as we stepped off.

As we walked across the sandy beach, my mind wandered. The excitement was so much to bear that I couldn't contain it—I was dying inside to tell Cash. A small part of me knew that what I had with him was over, but an enormous part of me refused to believe it. I was on top of the world in the best mood I had ever been in my life, and nothing could ruin that today. Not even thinking about Cash. So, I would continue holding onto that hope for now.

"So, have you had any ideas on what to name it yet?" Zayn asked, as we crossed the bridge and entered the Fae lands.

"Not any good ones. I'm hoping something comes to me."

"It will. We can gale from here unless you want to walk through the farmlands first."

"I'm too excited. I just want to get there as quickly as possible and see my booth."

"Okay. I'll have to gale you since you don't know the lands yet."

"I know." We stopped walking, and Zayn put his hands out.

"May I?"

"Of course," I said. Zayn smiled and slid his arms around me. My heart raced with pure excitement for my future as we galed away.

We landed just outside the wards of town and I immediately started walking.

"Do you know where we are going, Cinder?"

"Well, there is a woman named Emilia who runs the paperwork for the stands, so I assume we go to her."

We quickly made our way through the market until we found Emilia's stand.

"Cinder, how lovely to see you. I'm assuming you got my letter."

"I did. I'm so excited. Thank you, Emilia."

"No need to thank me, it was Natsu's doing."

"Oh." Surprise filled me. I would have to thank him when I saw him.

"Follow me and I will show you where your stand is."

We followed the blonde-haired Fae back to the front of the market.

"Most of the food stands are at the front because they get the most traffic. The number of shoppers we get on the weekends is overwhelming sometimes. The days are long, and you will want a bathroom break, so I suggest bringing some workers until you see how much traffic you're going to get. This is your stand here. It's a very suitable spot."

We stopped in front of a stand that wasn't far from the entrance.

"It's perfect!"

"The previous owner thought so, too. He retired, and that's why he sold it."

"Oh. I thought this was for rent?" I had some money saved up from working at the bakery, but not enough to buy a booth.

"Some booths are, but that's very few. Most people buy them because it's much cheaper in the long run."

"How much do I owe?" My heart sped up in fear that it was too much.

"You owe nothing." She smiled kindly at me.

"Why not?"

"The king has already purchased it for you, my dear. He came here himself and signed the paperwork and paid yesterday. You are now the owner until you decide otherwise."

"The king came here for me?" I asked.

"Yes. You should have seen it. He was smiling the whole time, and the crowd was going crazy. He even bought a sandwich before he left." She smiled and held out her hand.

Overwhelming joy hit me as I took the deed. I looked at it through tear-filled eyes, wondering how I could repay the king's kindness. A hand reached out and rubbed my back. I glanced up at Zayn.

"Congratulations, Cinder." He kissed my cheek.

"Thank you." My voice cracked as my eyes went back to the paper.

"You two enjoy your day. I must get back to my booth. Welcome to the family, Cinder." Emilia strolled off as I continued to stare at the paper.

"I'm an owner, Zayn," I whispered.

"You are. I have never been so happy to see you smile this big." I looked up, and he was smiling brightly at me, as I smiled back.

Confusion hit me as I stared into his beautiful blue eyes, and I wondered if he would make a suitable mate. But when the word *mate* popped in my head, all I pictured was Cash's eyes, warm and inviting. He was always grinning while they sparkled. I quickly recovered and pushed the thoughts out of my mind.

"Do you want to look at your new booth?" Zayn asked.

I nodded my head.

Strolling behind the booth, I looked around. The previous owner did an amazing job of keeping it in good condition—it was immaculate.

"It's perfect, Zayn."

"Close. I think it could use some sanding and a fresh coat of paint." He ran his hand down the wood of the stand.

"I don't know how to do that," I confessed.

"Don't worry, I can do it for you. We can get some paint on Cerulean."

"The land of water magic?"

"Yes. There is a town called Anahita that has a huge market. The woman at a shop there makes the best paint in all the lands. She has a variety of colors, too. We can even get paints to make a sign once you come up with a name."

"That would be amazing. Thank you, Zayn."

I threw my arms around him and hugged him. He rubbed his hands up and down my back as I laid my head on his chest.

"You're welcome. I hope this makes your life happier."

"I'm sure it will."

Not sure if it was the loneliness or the fact that I was missing Cash, but I felt safe and content in his arms. I was happy being hugged for much longer than I should have been. Listening to the sound of Zayn's heart thundering in his chest soothed me so I closed my eyes.

"Are you okay?" he asked.

"Yes. Why?"

"You've been hugging me for a while now."

"To the Gods, I'm so sorry." I let go of the hug and Zayn laughed.

"It's okay. You're just a little overwhelmed with excitement."

"Yes. That must be it." I knew for a fact that wasn't it. I was lonely and I missed Cash dearly.

"Since we didn't get breakfast, would you like to grab a bite to eat with me?" He smiled kindly at me.

"That would be lovely."

"Great. There is a stand down here that sells the best sandwiches."

Zayn walked off and I followed. We made our way down to the stand and got in line. After five minutes, it was our turn.

"Hey Zayn. The usual?" the worker asked.

"You got it, Adyn."

"Who is your lady friend?" Adyn asked.

"This is Cinder."

"Nice to meet you, Cinder. What would you like?"

"Nice to meet you. I will have the same."

"Coming right up!" Adyn turned to make our food.

"You just ordered the same thing as I did, but you have no idea what I ordered." Zayn laughed and shook his head.

"Well, first you said they have amazing sandwiches. Then I noticed the worker knew your order, so I assumed you were a regular and you had tried them all. Which means you have narrowed it down to the best sandwich they have, and always get that one when you come here. Since I want to try the best one, too, I figured it would save me time if I just went straight to the one you get."

"You surprise me sometimes, Cinder."

"Why?" I asked with a laugh.

"You just do." We locked eyes, and he smiled big.

"Here you guys go." The worker broke our eye contact.

"Thanks, Adyn."

"You're welcome. It was nice to meet you, Cinder. I hope Zayn brings you around more often."

"Oh, believe me. I will." Zayn carried our tray of food through the market as I followed him.

A thousand thoughts ran through my head. Did I like Zayn? Or did I just like the attention he was giving me? Did the loneliness from missing Cash fuel these newfound thoughts I have?

"This is my favorite spot," Zayn said as he set the tray on a picnic table under an enormous maple tree.

"This tree is gorgeous."

"Just wait until this fall when it turns colors."

"I bet it's beautiful." I looked up into the middle of the tree. There were two squirrels chasing each other and I giggled at the sight.

"Here is your food." Zayn set a sandwich, a small wooden bowl, and a glass in front of me.

"Thank you."

"It's a turkey special sandwich, fruit cup, and an iced tea, by the way."

"You were dying to tell me, weren't you?"

"Kind of, yeah." We both laughed. "So, I know you haven't picked out a name, but have you decided on a color scheme yet?"

"No. I guess I can decide once I see the paint options." I took a bite of my sandwich. My eyes went wide, and I looked at Zayn.

"I told you they were delicious." I nodded as he took a bite of his food.

We ate in mostly silence. The food was delicious and I had a feeling I would get this sandwich often for lunch, since I would be at my stand a lot. Once lunch was over, Zayn took the tray and dishes back to the booth while I waited on the bench. Tilting my head, I watched as a rabbit ate clovers.

"Well, hello." I jumped, and the rabbit took off running, when I heard someone speak.

"Oh. You scared the rabbit away." Looking up, I saw a male Fae with brown hair smiling at me.

"I'm sorry, darling. I just wanted to say hi to a beautiful lady."

Usually flattery made me smile, but his words made me cringe. I gave the male Fae a flat smile, trying to cover up my discomfort.

"What is your name, my lady?"

"Cinder." I leaned to the right and looked past the Fae, hoping Zayn was close by.

"My name is Morgan. It's nice to meet you, Cinder. Are you here with anyone today?"

"Yes. I'm with the King's Guard." I immediately noticed that he stiffened at my words.

I didn't say how many Kings' Guard I was with. I just wanted him to know they protected me because he gave me the creeps.

"Is Valarian with you?"

"He is not."

"Good. I can't stand that Vampire."

"Excuse me?" My eyebrows furrowed together.

"He's a worthless ass." His words pissed me off. If I would have had a rock, I would have thrown it at him for talking about my brother.

"You don't know what you're talking about. Please excuse me." I stood up.

"Wait." He grabbed my arm and my heart raced. "Stay for a bit."

"I have prior engagements." I ripped my arm out of his grip and gave him a dirty look.

"Cinder, are you okay?" I had never been more grateful to hear Zayn's voice.

"Oh, the honorable Zaynith Storm appears." The Fae moved closer to Zayn. "She's fine. We were just chatting."

"I wasn't talking to you, Morgan. Come on, Cin." Zayn took my hand and I gripped it tightly.

"Hey, I was talking to her." Morgan stepped in front of Zayn and stood nose to nose with him.

"I suggest you move," Zayn said through gritted teeth.

"Is this your lady, Zayn? Because if not, then I request a chance to get to know her."

"She *is* my lady." Zayn let go of my hand and pulled me into a side hug. Confusion filled me, but I stayed quiet. "We are betrothed, which means she is taken, in case you are too stupid to know what that word means. So, don't ever speak to her again. She is off limits, especially to you."

"My apologies." Morgan put his hands up and backed away with a smirk on his face. "I wouldn't want to dishonor a King's Guard's woman."

"I highly doubt you care about anyone's honor, Morgan." Grabbing my hand, Zayn turned to stroll away, pulling me with him.

"See you around, Cinder," Morgan said in a low voice. Zayn stopped walking and dropped my hand. Whipping back around, he stepped up as close as he could to the Fae.

"If you ever speak to her again, the amount of blood that Ember caused you to lose will be *nothing* compared to what I do." Zayn's words were low and powerful, sending chills down me. "Do you fucking understand me?"

Zayn stood tall and proud—Morgan was only a few inches shorter than him. My heart raced as the men stared each other down for what felt like an eternity. Morgan finally gave in first, turning away and leaving.

Zayn let out a hard breath as he turned toward me. "Are you okay?" he asked.

Placing his hand on my lower back, he escorted me back toward town.

"I'm fine, Zayn."

"Did he hurt you?"

"No." I shook my head as I tried to control my racing heart. "Why did you tell him we were betrothed?"

"I'm sorry. I was hoping it would make him leave you alone. He has a thing about asking if women are taken. It's like he sees them as property instead of people, or some shit."

"Don't be sorry, I didn't mind. I was glad you came back when you did. He creeped me out from the moment he started talking."

"What did he say to you?"

"He was asking if Val was here. I said no and then he went on to say that Val was a worthless ass and it pissed me off."

"Watch out everyone! Cinder said a curse word." We walked past a crowd of people and a couple glanced over at Zayn with confused faces.

"Shut up." I blushed. "People are looking."

We both laughed as we continued walking past town.

"Ember will kill him if she finds out he talked to you."

"What did you mean when you said Ember made him lose blood?" I asked.

"We were at Zila's brother's bar, the one we are going to this weekend. Morgan was there and grabbed Ember's arm and tried to make her slow dance with him. Val yanked him away from her."

"What happened next?" I imagined Val ripping his head off, but since he was still alive, I guess that didn't happen.

"Ember punched him in the face, then put her dagger to his throat, or so I've been told. I missed it, unfortunately."

"That sounds like my sister." I smiled as I thought of her braveness. She is an amazing person and I looked up to her.

"Are you ready to head back?" he asked.

I nodded. We left town and stepped outside the wards.

"We can gale from here." I stopped walking as Zayn stepped up to me. He slid his arms around me and stared into my eyes. "It was nice seeing you happy. Well, before Morgan showed up." He smiled, and we galed away.

Once we landed, he let go and started walking. As we headed over the covered bridge and back to the portal, my mind wandered off into treacherous waters. Zayn was a sweet man and completely took care of me today. He also protected me against Morgan.

We stepped on the portal while I was still in deep thought. The rush hit me, and I realized the exhilarating feeling the portal gave me was the same feeling Cash gave me. He was also a sweet man who would've protected me if he would have been there, but he was completely avoiding me. What that meant, I didn't know yet, but I had plenty of time to figure it out.

Once we landed, we stepped off the portal and strolled toward the manor.

"I had fun today."

"Me too. Thank you for escorting me, Zayn."

"It was my pleasure. Do you want to go get paints tomorrow?"

Hearing an axe hitting wood brought my attention away from Zayn. Looking toward the sound, I saw Cash on the side of the house and my body stopped walking in reflex.

Running my fingers across my lips as I thought about our kiss. He was shirtless and had his hair in a bun, I couldn't look away. Cash raised his axe high in the air and, in one swift motion, split the wood in half. My breath caught at the sight.

"We will talk later, Cinder." Hearing my name brought me back to reality. I looked back at Zayn, and he was smiling big. "Bye," Zayn said before he walked away.

"Bye." My eyes immediately looked back towards Cash.

Deciding to be brave, I made my way to him. As I strolled over, I had no clue what I was going to say. As I watched him, I wanted to say that I missed him dearly and couldn't live without him. I also wanted to tell him how gorgeous and strong he was.

"Hi," was the only word that would come out of my mouth instead. It wasn't my best moment, but it was an opening.

"Hey." He continued grabbing wood and splitting it and I realized I would have to lead this conversation.

Figuring I should just keep the conversation light and friendly, I started with my news.

"So, I got my bakery stand."

"I heard. Congratulations." He said the words, but the tone wasn't the one he usually used. It was like he was going through the motions and saying what he had to say.

He turned his away and grabbed more wood. I stared at the sweat glistening off his back. The giant pair of tattooed angel wings seem to come to life as his muscles moved underneath it. I swallowed hard as my breathing labored.

Turning around and meeting my eyes, he stopped. "Do you need anything else?"

I shook my head and turned away. Tears threatened to come out, but I told them I was in control and there was no way I was letting him see me cry.

"Hey, Cinder."

"Yeah." I looked over my shoulder at him and swallowed.

"I'm really happy for you. You make me proud." He grinned a real Cash grin and then went back to chopping wood.

As soon as I righted my head, I smiled big, but I wasn't going to let him see that either.

Chapter 10

Ember

After seeing who was waiting for us, I couldn't help but smile as we strolled up to the throne. Meyers walked ahead of us and took his normal stance, crossing his hands in front of him—ready to make his introduction.

Val and I stopped and bowed slightly.

"We will drop formalities today, Meyers. Thank you." The king's voice was firm but loving.

"There's my beautiful niece." My uncle Hendrick grabbed me in a big hug. "Nice to see you again, Ember. I missed you dearly." He kissed the top of my head.

"I missed you, too." I smiled brightly as he turned toward Val.

"Valarian Grey." He held his hand out to Val. "I know I saw you yesterday, but we didn't get to talk on a personal level. Are you taking care of my niece?"

"Always, sir." Val shook his hand and smiled.

"I'm your uncle now. Call me uncle or Hendrick." He patted Val on the arm.

"So, we brought you here today because we need to see your dagger, Ember. May I see it, please?" the king asked as he held out his large hand. Confusion played on my face as I stepped forward, removed my dagger, and handed it to him.

As King Reign placed both hands on my dagger, it glowed. It had only done that once before - when Zayn held it the night that I stabbed Val.

"Oh, wow. They bonded it with some powerful magic." Hendrick tilted his head as he watched the king look at my dagger.

"I think we can replicate the spell." The king held the dagger out to my uncle. "What do you think, Hendrick?"

"Let me see this thing." As soon as the dagger left the king's hand, it stopped glowing. Hendrick turned it around, inspecting it from every angle.

"Why does it only glow in certain people's hands?" I asked.

"It only glows in Angel's hands and only when we will it to." The king sighed.

"Can you tell me why?" I asked hesitantly.

"Because Angels have light magic, and it is the complete opposite of the sulfur magic the Demons use." The king leaned forward and rested his chin on his hand. "Would you like to hear a story?"

"Of course." I smiled.

"I love this story. I will get the chairs, Your Majesty." Meyers started dragging a chair over to me. Val and Hendrick helped by grabbing their own chair.

We all took a seat as Meyers stared at the king with a huge smile on his face.

"You can get a chair too, Meyers."

"Thank you, Your Majesty."

The king's servant grabbed a chair and as he dragged it across the marble floor, it made a screeching sound. The king ran his hand across his forehead as he sighed. It took all my strength to keep from laughing. Meyers quickly took his seat as the king cleared his throat.

"12,000 years ago, there were ten land masses that were completely empty. One lonely tree sprouted right here in Ashbern. It was a baobab tree which is now known as the tree of life. The tree grew to enormous height and bore golden fruits. One day, ten perfect buds formed on this tree. Months later, during a blood moon, the buds opened. That was the night that the ten Primordial Gods were born. We were born babies like anyone else, but there was no one around to take care of us. After hours of crying alone under the tree, a maiden, borne from the moon, flew down from the skies. Her name was Hekata. She was a Moon Goddess in her own realm. Her primary goal was to raise us until we were ready to birth the world with our fruits. And that is what she did."

"Whoa," I whispered.

"He is not done." My eyebrows raised as Meyers shushed me.

"Hekata's first task was to get us shelter from the elements. She used her magic to create a hole in the giant tree, which was where we would live for the next twenty-two years. After feeding us all upon her breast and examining us, she quickly learned that we each had a unique tattoo and distinct eye color. What that meant, she didn't know. As we got older, she realized we were not brothers by blood, but were all different species. Once we learned to use our powers, she slowly figured out what each symbol meant.

"My brother Lykaon was the first to show his powers. He turned into a black wolf one day. All of us boys ran around screaming in fear because we had never seen an animal before. He turned back into his normal form and laughed. We were only six when he became the first Lycan." The king had a reminiscing look on his face.

"I was bathing in the creek a few weeks later when I suddenly sprouted gray feathered wings out of nowhere. Along with that came the power to heal emotions and physical wounds. I became the first Angel."

Gray wings? I thought, and the king smiled when he heard, but didn't answer me.

"The same day, Toberon sprouted shiny wings that had a rainbow of holographic colors in them, making him the first Fae."

The king's face saddened as he took a deep breath and let it out.

"That night, during a treacherous thunderstorm, Tartarus sprouted wings. His batlike wings were veiny and thin with skin like leather, making him the first Demon. He was mad that he didn't have feathers on his wings, so he would always try to pull my feathers off. That was the first time I realized my brother hated me." The king shifted in his seat and sighed.

"You'll love this part, Valarian." Meyers smiled brightly at Val.

"My brother Voltarean sprouted fangs and became the first Vampire. He walked around daily, smiling. He loved showing everyone his fangs. He could eventually tell us what we were all thinking. It quickly got annoying." I looked at Val and he laughed.

"My three brothers, Zephyr, Volcanis, and Abzule, developed magic caster skills, which came in handy. Wind, fire, and water. Zephyr would use his wind to knock twigs from the tree. Volcanis would gather them from the ground and make campfires at night for us to stay warm. Abzule would bring water to the camp through midair." The king smiled at the memory.

"Ailwin got pointy ears. He eventually fell in love with trying to build things out of wood. He built small forts and then, eventually, a boat. That is why the Elven are known for their building skills. Ailwin couldn't sail the boats he built, so he left that up to Toberon. Without those two, we would have never ventured away from our tree home." The king put his elbows on his knee and leaned forward.

"That was nine brothers, all with their own weird attributes. Apothee was the only one without. One night we were sitting around a campfire and Apothee was telling us stories. He would think of weird creatures and describe them to us. He held two sticks on his head and said the animal looked similar to what his shadow looked like in the campfire's light. I spotted the first deer the next day. Each night, he would tell us different stories about animals. Some of them were covered in fur, and others had wings like ours. Every time he would describe a creature to us, they would start appearing on the lands. Rabbits, horses, wolves, birds. Everything living today came from Apothee's mind. It was a good thing that he made animals because, once Voltarean turned thirteen, as you know Val, he required blood. Apothee also described trees, plants, insects, and crops, which also quickly appeared. We eventually had lots of different food to eat other than the golden fruit that the tree of life sprouted. Once we saw that some animals would eat others, we tried the same. That was how we figured out what meat was. Ailwin built traps to catch the animals in. Some traps worked, some did not. So Ailwin built your favorite thing, Ember. Bow and arrows. He learned how to hunt and taught the rest of us. He was also the one that wrote the book I gave you."

My mouth fell open at the revelation when I remembered the signature on the book was only the letter A—for Ailwin. The king smiled brightly before he continued.

"Hekata raised us until we were in our mid-twenties. Being with the same people all day, every day, we got restless. We all started fighting constantly—to the point that we were destroying the surrounding lands. So, our mother did a ritual and called to the moon for us to have mates. The moon Gods were listening because they sent ten full grown maidens down for us. But we weren't just gifted those maidens, we had to earn them. We Gods weren't in control, the women were."

I'm already fond of these maidens. Reign smiled at me, and I smiled back, knowing he had heard my thoughts.

"Tell them what happened next, Your Majesty." Meyers scooted to the edge of his chair like an excited child.

"Our mother taught us how to treat women, and we did what she said. We romanced them any chance we got, hoping we would be the one that they chose, but the maidens didn't hesitate to tell us no. They made us work for their love and affection. There was one maiden I was the most attracted to. Her name was Estarza. Unfortunately, I wasn't the only one attracted to her. My brother Tartarus was too." I sucked in a huge breath. The king's eyes seemed to sadden before he continued.

"After months of courting these women, some of them finally made a choice. My brother, Apothee, was the first to get mated. He was the only one that didn't leave Ashbern. He and his mate could bear no children. Every year during her emergence they tried, and she never got pregnant. She was extremely sad because of it, so he would pass the time with his mate by describing unique flowers and gorgeous trees to her. It was the only thing that made her smile. I think of his love for her every time I see a flower or a blooming tree."

My eyes filled with tears as I realized he had made the beautiful wisteria trees that I loved for her.

"Volcanis got mated next. He moved to Mazuria and eventually figured out a way to make weapons using fire. A short sword like yours, Valarian, was his favorite kind to carry." Val smiled proudly.

"After a few more of my brothers were mated, some mates got pregnant that spring. Estarza was ready to take the next step and finally made her choice."

"Who did she choose?" The words popped out before I had a chance to stop them. My hand flew over my hand in embarrassment.

"She chose me, Ember." The king smiled.

"I knew it," I whispered. I looked over at Val, and he was smiling at me.

"We were quickly mated and moved to the land that Estarza named Valmeyer. Toberon took us by boat to our land and Ailwin helped me to build our first house. Estarza got pregnant during her first emergence after mating. She bore two perfect children during that pregnancy. This time, the children were born with their wings already intact. But neither had gray wings like mine. One had black wings, and one had white. We figured out quickly that the two healing powers I had, separated into two separate powers in the babies. That's why we have Ornamental and Blessed Angels now. We had over a hundred children together over the next four hundred years. I can still name them all." Reign smiled proudly.

"I wasn't the only God whose powers split. Toberon could make plants grow high and fast, and he could also change the weather. His first-born children were also twins and his powers separated into Wielders, who could control the weather, and the Nourishers. They make plants grow super-tall, and super-fast. That is why the Fae are known for their growing skills."

The king's smile faded away. We all sat there quietly for a moment before Meyers spoke. "The portals, Your Majesty."

"Thank you, Meyers." Reign cleared his throat. "Our children needed mates of their own. So, in search of mates, the female children all eventually left home on ships to find mates on other lands and have children of their own. We quickly learned that there was a one hundred percent chance of birthing a species that was the same as the father.

Since the women were the ones to leave their homes, one species completely took over each land mass.

"Everyone had their own lands, and we all loved our lives. The lands started filling quickly, and we realized rules needed to be put in place. Ailwin and his sons built castles for each God to live in. That was how the kingdom was born.

"The kingdom was perfect with the systems we put into place, but we were going years without seeing our children, or our grandchildren. So, after years of trying, Zephyr built a portal with wind magic so we could visit each other more quickly. Any child born after he built the first portal, were born with the power to gale across whatever land mass they were on. We still had to use the portals to go across the seas, so he built a portal on every land." The king sighed and leaned back in his chair.

"I knew building a portal on the Demon lands was a bad idea. What I didn't know was that for many, many years Tartarus still wanted Estarza, and he had only settled on the maiden he had for lack of options. Not being in love with his mate, when they produced children, they looked different. Their first pregnancy also produced twins. One was born with wings, the other without. The one born with wings had the same sulfur magic as Tartarus, but both kinds had dark grayish skin and seemed to be born with evil in them. They were all fierce and mean to each other. Tartarus accepted it as their lifestyle and thrived off the evil. Unbeknownst to us brothers, Tartarus learned how to put sulfur magic into weapons. Once he did, he came for me."

I swallowed hard and shifted uncomfortably in my chair.

"One day, four hundred years after our mating, Tartarus came to visit. We had just finished dinner when he confronted me about taking his mate. One thing led to another, and he tried to stab me. Estarza got in the way trying to protect me, and he stabbed her accidentally." He swallowed hard and his eyes filled with tears.

"I fell to my knees as I tried to heal her. My light magic burned brighter than it ever had, but nothing happened. That's when we learned that Tartarus's magic was deadly to all creatures... even Goddesses. Not even Angel magic could heal a person dying from a sulfur-spelled weapon. I wanted to kill my brother for taking the only woman I ever loved, but the pain hurt so bad, I couldn't move. 'This is your fault,' he said as I held Estarza in my arms until she died. Over twelve thousand years later, I still miss her and think about her daily."

A single tear rolled down the king's cheek and my heart hurt for him. The king lowered his head. I knew the pain he was feeling. That same pain had radiated through me and consumed me the day a Demon forced me to stab my mate. Tears rolled silently down my face. Val let go of my hand and ran it along my cheek, wiping away my tears. I looked over at him.

I love you, Ember.

I love you, too.

Looking back up, the king smiled at our love.

"Where was I? Oh, yes. Killing her wasn't good enough for him. Since he blamed me, he challenged me to a fight to the death. I had just lost my mate, and I was okay with dying, so I met him outside. Unfortunately for him, our mother was waiting. She was distraught by the person he had become, so she used her moon magic to put him to sleep. Zephyr destroyed the Demon's portal, and we restored peace for a while. The Demons didn't leave their lands for hundreds of years.

"I spent the next seven hundred years enjoying my children, and their children, and so on. Once we were close to a thousand years old, my brothers' mates started growing old quickly. One by one, they died. We realized that the maiden's life span wasn't the same as ours. Eventually the lands were filled with broken-hearted Gods. Our mother thought it was best that one king ruled all the lands, and the rest would sleep. We would take turns every five hundred years. So, each king appointed their oldest son as the duke of their land. Since Apothee never had children, we would use his castle for the one reigning king, and he went first. This is my third time as the king of all the lands." The king took a deep breath and sighed.

"Then a Demon, stronger and more powerful than the others, was born. He has the strongest attributes of Tartarus and was the first born with a tattoo on their chest. His name is Erebus."

I sucked in a huge breath as fear ran through me upon hearing his name. Val grabbed my hand.

"Not long after Erebus was born, other children across the lands were born with the tattoo. They weren't like normal children. These children were curious, fierce, and wanted to protect the lands. They all had this fire in them that couldn't be stopped. Hekata had a vision about these children, so she woke the slumbering Gods for a meeting. She explained to us that her vision told her these children were the protectors of the realm and they needed to be utilized. Soon, we came up with a training system and used the lands up north to start it all. We built Castleva to replicate this castle. Everything went great, but we noticed the more the Demons attacked, the more guards were born. We originally chose the guards to protect the king, but we eventually moved the older guards on the dukes and the portals, since it was a less demanding job. That is how the King's Guard became an important part of history and it is the reason you are sitting here today." An enormous smile radiated across the king's face.

"I love that story so much." Meyers wiped a tear from his eye.

"How many times have you heard it?" I asked as I scrubbed my face free of the wetness.

"Let me see. The king tells the story about five or six times while he is reigning, and he's been awakened three times. So, over a dozen times or more."

My eyes went wide as I tried to figure out how old Meyers was since he had been with the king during all his years on and off the throne.

"He is almost as old as I am, Ember." I looked at the king as he smiled.

"How?" I confusedly shook my head.

"We are bonded. We were the first bonded pair on the lands. He was my servant when I was the king of Ashbern. I pulled him out of the water after he drowned. When I attempted to save him from dying, I didn't know he was dead and I was bringing him back to this plane, but I don't regret it."

"Me either, Your Majesty." Meyers smiled proudly.

"Meyers has devoted his life to me ever since. He sleeps when I sleep and awakens from the ground when it is time for me to reign again. He will live as long as I'm still alive."

"May I speak freely, Your Majesty?"

"For the record, Meyers has the liberties to always speak freely all day, every day, but refuses to do so."

"Is that a yes, Your Majesty?"

"Yes, you may, Meyers." The king sighed.

"I just wanted to say it has been a hell of a ride, Your Majesty." Meyers smiled and stood up from his chair. He pulled his chair back to where it came from, and I bit my lip as my uncle laughed.

"You can laugh, Ember. I laugh at him daily," the king said with a smile.

"That you do, Your Majesty." Meyers smiled proudly.

"So, I told you that long story to tell you this. There is a breed of offspring of Tartarus that can make the weapons. They're the Demons that have the same batlike wings that Tartarus does."

"I saw one of them on Mazuria the night of the attack." I glanced at Val to see if he remembered.

"I saw them too, love."

"So, we would need one of those types of Demons to make more weapons?" I asked.

"Yes, we would." Reign stood up.

"How would we get one?" I shook my head. I was willing to go onto the Demon's land and trap one, but I sure the hell didn't want to.

"We already have one." My eyes widened as I looked at my uncle. "Two Demons attacked my portal guards on Mazuria last night."

"What?" I gasped and Val squeezed my hand. "Did they kill anyone?"

"They weren't trying to get to the people, Ember. They were trying to get to the portal."

"What do you mean?"

"We killed one Demon and held the other for questioning. Once we had him in a cell, he confessed and said that they were trying to get on the portal." My uncle sighed.

"Can they use the portals?" My body filled with fear.

"Yes, they can," the king said, and I think my heart stopped beating

Chapter 11

Ember

Looking over at Val, he shifted uncomfortably and crossed his arms.

"What? All of them?" I asked. My eyes widened as I looked back at my uncle and the king. My brain felt fried as I tried to take in this new information.

"No, the regular Demons can't use the portals without a pass, just like other citizens."

"But the ones with wings can?" I asked.

"No, they can't either," Hendrick said.

"I'm not following." I glanced up at the king as he walked toward me.

"Who can use the portals?" he asked me.

"King's Guard and citizens with a day pass."

"And why can the King's Guards use them?"

"Because the magic in their tattoo allows them to use it, so anyone born with a tattoo can..." My heart sped up and I lost track of my words as the realization hit me. There were signs, but I didn't see them.

I'm a fool.

"You're not a fool, Ember." The king laid his hand on my shoulder and squeezed it lightly. "Like I just mentioned in my story, Erebus was born with the mark of a King's Guard."

Panic radiated through me, and my body went into shock as I thought about the person who was either going to mate me or kill me—I wasn't sure which. I knew Erebus had the mark because I saw it the day that we rescued Cinder. I don't know why it never occurred to me he could use the portals. All I could think about was every time that Erebus could have stepped off the portal in Ashbern and walked right up to the manor if he wanted. I swallowed hard as an important question came to my mind.

"Is Erebus a King's Guard?"

"He was the first that was born with the tattoo and the strongest Guard ever born, but he isn't considered a King's Guard. We call them Demon Guards, since they were never fit to serve the true king." Reign sighed.

They? Erebus isn't the only one? The question popped into my head, and I was afraid to say it aloud because I didn't want the answer.

"Unfortunately, yes, Ember. Erebus isn't the only Demon Guard."

"How many are there?"

"Thirteen," the king said.

"What? How will we ever take down that many?" My voice was now panicked, coming out in a squeak.

"That's why we are trying to make Demon blades," Hendrick said. "Hopefully, we get enough for each one of you to have one."

"I would also like to equip the portal and the duke guards with them, too." The king seemed stressed as he rubbed his hand across his forehead.

"Why didn't we know about this before now?" I asked. Everyone looked back and forth at each other, and a realization hit me when I saw the look on Val's face.

"You knew? You knew and didn't tell me?" Val reached his hand out to me, and I yanked mine away from him.

I'm sorry, love.

"Don't say anything to me, Valarian. Not in my head either." Looking at him with tear-filled eyes, I felt betrayed.

"Ember, you can't be mad at him because he did it on my orders." My eyes shot up to the king.

"Why would you do that?" I asked as I shook my head.

"Because I knew your anxiety wouldn't allow you to sleep, bathe, eat, or even take a breath if you knew Erebus could use the portals."

Anger filled me, along with embarrassment, so I quickly placed my hands over my face as I began to cry in front of everyone.

"We all know this is hard on you, but I need to calm your emotions for a bit because we have work to do," the king said. I didn't respond. After a few seconds, he laid a hand on me, and my body relaxed as I felt the warmth of magic hit me.

I wiped the tears away and sat up straight.

"So, how do we kill these fuckers?" I asked.

The king smiled widely.

"You two are going to go question this Demon and get as much info as possible. Ember, you will report back to me.

Val, I want you to fill Zayn in on everything. He already knows what is going on with the sulfur magic, so just fill him in on whatever else you find out from the Demon."

"Will do, sir," Val said and I nodded.

I stood up and started walking toward the door.

"Ember, wait." My uncle came running up to me.

"What?" I asked.

"Don't be mad. We did it for your own protection."

"I feel betrayed by all of you."

He put his hands on both my shoulders and looked me in the eye.

"We did it because we love you, Ember."

I shook my head and swallowed hard.

"You can be mad at me and Reign, but don't be hard on Val. He was doing what he was told."

I nodded before he pulled me in close and hugged me.

"You know you and your sister are like the daughters I never had. I love you both very much and just want to protect you."

"I know. I love you, too." He let go of the hug as Val walked up.

"You two be careful. I will see you when you get back." With a pat on Val's shoulder, my uncle walked away.

Locking eyes with Val for a second, my heart hurt slightly, knowing he'd lied. I turned and walked away. Staying about ten feet ahead of him, I quickly made my way out of the castle. Once I started walking toward the outside of the wards, he tried talking to me.

"Ember, wait."

As I stomped through the brush, I could hear him run up to me.

"No, Valarian."

"Oh, I'm Valarian again?"

"Yep," I mumbled.

"The last time you stomped away from me was in the woods when you tried to cut my throat." He laughed lightly.

"In case you haven't noticed, we aren't speaking."

"Come on, love." I ignored him as I continued walking. Once I felt the magic tingle as I crossed the wards, he stepped in front of me.

"Move."

"No," he said, and my eyes widened.

"No? Fine. I will go around you." I side-stepped him and he grabbed my waist.

He instantly galed us away and once we landed, I saw the familiar wisteria trees. We were in Amethyst Falls.

"Seriously?" I sighed.

"Come on." Val took my hand and pulled me over to my favorite tree. He lifted the branches and stepped inside the canopy.

"Why are we here, Valarian?"

He smiled big at me. I rolled my eyes and went to turn away. Grabbing me by my waist, he pulled me close to him. The scent of fresh snow mixed with the woods calmed me.

"I'm sorry, love." He nuzzled his face in my neck and I could feel his hot breath bouncing off my skin before he kissed it.

I knew he was trying to make me forgive him and I admit it, he was good—it almost worked.

"I'm not ready to forgive you, Val."

"Oh, I'm Val again?" Another kiss. "You must be less mad." Another kiss and with it came an ass squeeze.

"I'm still mad." His grip on my butt tightened as I tried to pull away.

"I really am sorry, my *hertis rote*. I didn't have a choice."

A hard breath escaped me because I knew deep down that he was right.

"It doesn't make it any better. I hate being lied to."

"We did it for you, for your safety."

"I shouldn't have been kept in the dark about this. I should have known. Did you guys think I wouldn't be mad?"

"And what do you think Cinder is going to think when she realizes you are doing the same thing to her?" My eyebrows furrowed as I looked up at him.

"That's different, Val." I pushed away from him, and this time he let me.

"Tell me how, because I would like to know." He crossed his arms in that lazy stance of his.

"She is my sister."

"And you are my mate." He gave me a fanged smile.

"She isn't trained!" My voice got a little higher than I meant.

"No, but she is emotionally strong enough to handle the truth."

"And I'm not?" My eyes narrowed at him while I waited for a response.

"Come here, love." Val stepped forward, and I stepped back.

"Answer me, Val."

He sighed and cracked his neck. I could tell that I was stressing him out.

"You are two different people. She can handle stress and you can murder people."

"That was a nice way of saying I'm crazy."

"You're not crazy, love." He stepped forward and pulled me in close to him. "You're an emotional person who wears her heart on her sleeve and there is nothing wrong with that." He kissed my neck again.

"I hate all of this," I whispered.

"I know you do." Another kiss, but this time I felt a fang graze my skin, and tingles ran through me as I ran my hands down the muscles on his back.

"Shit." Val pulled away from me. "You can't get horny. We're on a mission."

"Sorry." I smiled seductively because I wasn't really sorry.

"So, I guess you're definitely less mad now." He tilted his head at me.

"Yeah," I whispered.

Pulling me in close, his soft lips pressed against mine as I melted into his arms. Parting my lips, I slid my tongue into his mouth as I devoured him. We were both breathless when he finally pulled away.

"Okay, okay. That's enough."

"We can be quick, Val." I looked up at him with sultry eyes.

"We're on a mission, love." He adjusted the front of his pants with a pained face.

"We can be really quick," I whispered as I squeezed his butt.

"And if something happens, and the king asks for one of our hands, are you going to be the one to explain what happened when he sees our visions and sees us fucking under a tree?"

"Point taken." I released his butt, and he laughed.

"Let's go, my love." One more quick kiss and we were walking out from under the trees.

Val galed us back to the portal and stepped on.

"Do you want to wield the portal?" he asked.

"I've never done that. I don't know how."

"It's like galing. Just envision what land you want to go to." Val pulled me in close to him. "Try it."

I thought about my homeland of Mazuria and willed the portal to go. As we were speeding through life itself, Val did what he always did in the portals and placed a kiss on me. The portals were completely bearable to me now since I didn't get nauseous anymore. A few seconds later, we landed.

"You did it," he said as he stared into my eyes.

"It was surprisingly easy." He smiled and took my hand as we stepped off the portal.

"Hey guys," I said to the two portal guards.

"Hey, Ember, Val," one of them said. The other one nodded.

We walked on the outer edge of town, staying on the outside of the wards. Then we galed to Spellchild Castle. The last time I was here was when we saved Cinder. The memory made my heart speed up as we neared. We had also saved Silvaria, a Lycan that had been locked up in the prison for the previous duke. Memories of Asher's arrow going into the duke's head came back to me, and I smiled. Maybe I am crazy.

Trying to push the memories aside and focus on the mission, I looked up at the ivy-covered castle. It was just as beautiful as I remembered, with white brick and light red, pointy towers. I really hoped that Hendrick had changed the inside colors, as I had no desire to see the light blue color of the previous duke.

Val opened the door, and we entered the castle. My body eased immediately when I saw the inside was now covered in the new duke's colors. Hunter green flags, curtains, and rugs now adorned the castle.

"Welcome to Spellchild Castle. You must be Ember." The short, light-haired man reached out his hand to me and I shook it. He did the same to Val. "And you must be Valarian. The Duke of Mazuria speaks so kindly of you both, and it's nice to finally put faces to his stories." His emerald-green eyes and smile both seemed kind. My body eased even more.

"It's nice to meet you, too," I said.

"My name is Horatio, and I am the duke's new personal butler. I will escort you down to speak with the Demon, since His Grace will not be returning until tomorrow. If you would, please follow me."

Val held my hand as we walked down to the prison and went down the stairs. We entered the room, and my mind immediately went to Silvaria. I wondered how she had been since the rescue. We all needed to take a trip to Direbreak to visit her if we ever got time.

"He's in the third cell down. I will wait in the hall." Horatio left the room. I nodded to the guard standing duty as we made our way down to the cell.

"Ember Lavaris and Valarian Grey. You two have become quite the gossip on Mistlaven," the Demon said.

Is he an Introspector, Val?

No, he can't get in your mind, love. You're safe.

"It's Ember Grey now." I gave the red-eyed Demon a flat smile.

"We have questions to ask you," Val said as he crossed his arms.

"I'm stuck in here with no food and you immediately start demanding answers from me. How very vulgar of you."

Val growled, and I nudged his arm. He kept his eyes on the ashy gray-skinned Demon.

"We can make sure they feed you if you answer some questions." I smiled kindly at him, trying to build a camaraderie between us so I could get the answers we needed.

"Oh, I like her. She is a lot nicer than you, Vampire."

He tilted his head at Val and smiled. Val's eyes narrowed as he stared back. Deciding that this Demon might work better with kindness than threats, I obliged him.

"What is it you would like to eat?" I asked. "I will let Horatio know."

"I prefer deer."

"Okay, I will tell him after you answer some questions."

"Raw," The Demon licked his lips.

"Excuse me?"

"I want raw deer," he said, and my stomach turned at the thought of eating raw meat.

"Okay. I'm sure we can arrange it." I smiled again, pushing back the nausea.

"I'm going to trust you, Ember." The Demon shifted and crossed his legs. "So, what is it you would like to know?"

Thinking that he was very opinionated and wouldn't tell us how to make Demon blades, I took a different route to interrogate him.

"I have a few questions, but I'm not sure you're going to know the answers to those because they're very secretive, so we'll skip them."

"Like what?" His almost non-existent eyebrows furrowed together.

"It's not important." I shrugged.

"I'm a high-ranking Demon Guard." He smiled proudly as he pulled open the top of the brown tunic he was wearing and showed me his tattoo. "I know things most don't."

"Yeah, but you probably don't know this. It's about sulfur-spelled weapons."

"Ask me the question, Ember." His face went blank as we waited to prove me wrong.

Pulling my Demon blade out of the holster strapped to my leg, I showed it to him.

"I'm trying to figure out how these are made, but I'm assuming Erebus don't just let everyone know those secrets."

The Demon smiled arrogantly. "Oh, how wrong you are."

"What do you mean?" I tilted my head like I was dumb. He bought it.

"I have seen sulfur blades made plenty of times."

"Oh, but you can't make them. That's what I figured."

"I absolutely could!" His batlike wings popped out of nowhere. "Do you see these wings? Only a Demon with these wings has the Sulfur magic required to make those weapons."

"So, you have the magic, but haven't made them?"

"I'm a Demon Guard, Ember. My services aren't needed for such small, tedious tasks. Erebus has two Demons that he uses for that, but I could if I wanted to." His arrogant smile widened as he stared at me.

"I don't think you can." I was the one now smiling arrogantly.

"Excuse me?" His eyebrows furrowed again as he stared me down.

"Prove it, then." I locked eyes with him as his face had a look of contemplation.

"Give me your sword, Vampire."

"Fuck no." Val uncrossed his arms and growled.

"Give him your sword, Val."

"Are you crazy, Ember? He could throw it and kill you."

"Why would I do that? She has been kind to me. Unlike you."

Trust me, Val.

Val yanked his sword out of its holster and made eye contact with me.

"Fine, but you get behind me first." I did as he said and stepped behind him.

The Demon uncrossed his legs and stood up, strolling to the bars.

"You try anything, and I will rip your heart out of your chest. Understood?"

"Understood." Val held out his sword and the Demon took it from him.

Peeking out from behind Val's back, I watched as the Demon clamped the blade between his two hands, and it started glowing green. The light got brighter and brighter and then faded away.

"It's done." The Demon held the sword back out to Val and he took it.

"It doesn't feel any different," Val said as he turned it over in his hands and examined it.

"Believe me, it is." The Demon's arrogant smile was back.

"Thank you." I stepped out from behind Val. "I will make sure you get that deer."

"Thank you, Ember." His smile was kind, and I wondered if I was being tricked again or if this Demon was actually nice.

I nodded.

Val grabbed by hand as we walked away from the cell.

"Hold on, Val," I said. "I turned back toward the Demon. "What's your name?"

"Volcan Azar."

My breath caught at the name.

"That's a Fire Caster name."

"My mother was a Fire Caster and a King's Guard. Erebus took her many years ago. After they turned her into a Demon, my father mated her and had me. They say you lose your soul when you're turned into a Demon, but my mother was never like the others. The fact that she still gave me a strong Fire Caster name after she was a Demon proves that."

"Where are they now?" I asked.

"They're both long gone." His face turned somber.

"I'm sorry."

"Thank you, Ember." I nodded as I looked at his sad face and confusion filled me. "If you need any more weapons, just let me know."

"Thank you, Volcan." I smiled lightly.

"Come on, love." Val pulled on my hand, and we left the prison.

Horatio was waiting patiently for us in the hallway.

"How did it go?" he asked.

"We got the information we needed," Val said.

"That is excellent. His Grace will be pleased." Horatio smiled.

"I have a weird request," I said.

"Anything you need."

"Our Demon friend, um... prisoner wants some raw deer to eat."

"Unfortunately, I cannot do that. It will displease Duke Hendrick. We have strict orders not to feed him or open his cell until His Grace returns tomorrow."

"I will tell my uncle it was my doing." I smiled kindly. It didn't work.

"I am sorry, miss, but I cannot budge on this matter."

"Well, either you can feed him, or I will go hunt a deer and drag it in here myself–and leave blood-soaked floors in the hall–so I can feed him."

"If that pleases you." His smile was flat as he called my bluff.

"What?"

"If it pleases you to hunt a deer and drag it in here yourself, then you are more than welcome. No one in this castle is going to go against His Grace's orders and help you."

"Fine. I will!"

"You may want to get someone with a mop," Val said as I stomped past the servant.

Pulling my bow off my back, I headed straight for the woods.

"Ember, wait." Val was right on my tail.

"Don't even, Val. I'm doing this." I pulled an arrow out of my quiver.

"I know, love. I was just going to say to slow down. Hunting isn't a rushed event." He grabbed my wrist, and I stopped walking.

"Oh. You aren't mad at me?" I asked as I looked up into his violet eyes. A slow smile radiated across his face.

"No. I knew the minute he said no the first time that we would head to the woods."

I laughed as he pulled me in.

"Thank you, Val."

"Anytime, my love." His lips pressed against mine. When he pulled away, he was smiling big.

"Why are you so happy?" I asked.

"I'm going to feed off this deer before we give it to the Demon."

"His name is Vulcan," I corrected.

"Why are you using his name?"

"Because I have a weird feeling that I should trust him." I shrugged.

Val ran a hand over the back of his neck. "The last time you trusted a Demon, I got stabbed."

"Shut up. It's not like that." I laughed lightly.

"Go with your instincts, but just be careful, love."

"Always."

He kissed me gently before we continued our journey into the woods.

Chapter 12

Ember

Hours later, we were hungry, tired, and I was a little turned on as I watched Val sink his teeth into the deer I shot. Pulling away from the deer, I panted as he wiped the blood from his mouth.

"Stop watching me. I don't enjoy getting hard while I'm feeding," he said.

"Really? Because you don't mind when you feed from me." I smiled while batting my lashes at him.

"I don't want it happening when I feed from a deer." He scrunched up his nose.

"It's not me, it's the mirror-bond. I don't know why you feel my powerful emotions, Val."

"Me either, but I don't mind, love." He smiled. "Just not while I'm feeding."

Laughing lightly, I looked down at the deer.

"Are you going to carry that for me?" I asked.

"Nope. You said you were going to kill it and drag it through the halls, leaving blood everywhere. So, go for it." He crossed his arms in that lazy stance of his, and I sighed.

"Seriously, Val?"

"Seriously, love."

"Fine." I grabbed the deer by its antlers and pulled as hard as I could, it barely moved. I instantly regretted killing a huge one.

After a few minutes, I had only moved it about five feet. I was panting as I sank to my knees in defeat next to it. Trying to catch my breath, I looked up at Val with pleading eyes and stuck out my lip. He shook his head and laughed.

"I'll get it. I just wanted to see you struggle for a few minutes and regret your decisions."

"Well, it worked," I said as he lowered his hand to me and helped me off the ground.

Val reached down and picked up the deer like it weighed only a pound and slung it over his shoulders.

"Do you want to gale?" He asked.

"That's fine." I galed away and landed just outside the castle wards. A second later, Val landed next to me.

"The sun is going down, Val."

"Yep. It's probably past dinnertime."

"I may not be able to talk to Cinder tonight."

"I know, love. Hopefully, all is good when we get back."

We made our way into the castle as worry set in. I just hoped no one said anything to Cinder before I did.

"Do you think Vulcan will be happy?" I asked, as we walked the halls. Blood was dripping off the deer and leaving a trail. A mischievous smile played on my face at the sight.

"Probably. I heard his thoughts. He hadn't eaten for days before they captured him."

"That's horrible." I thought about Cinder and Silvaria being starved and felt bad for him.

We were almost at the prison area when we ran into Horatio.

"Ah, I see you have slaughtered a deer for the Demon. I am sure he will be pleased." He smiled at me.

"I'm sure he will, too," I said, sounding a little snottier than I intended to.

"Well, it is past dinner time. If you guys do not need me, I must retire."

"You're good. Thanks," Val said. I gave him a small nod, and he left.

"We have been gone all day, Val."

"We will be home soon," he said as he adjusted the deer on his shoulders.

Opening the door to the prison for Val, he stepped inside, and we went down the stairs.

"I had lost all hope that I would actually get fresh deer," Vulcan said as we entered the prison.

"I always stand by my word," I said as I strolled up to the Demon's cage.

"I see that. Thank you, Ember. A leg would have been sufficient, but I'm extremely grateful." He smiled kindly at me.

"Open the cell," Val said to the guard.

"I have been told not to open the cell."

"Then give her the keys." Val nodded his head toward me. The guard appeared stunned for a minute. "Uh, now."

The guard looked at me and I held out my hand.

"I take no responsibility for anything that happens," he said as he placed the keys in it.

"Yeah, we know." I turned toward the cell and stuck the key in. My eyes met Vulcan's before I turned it. "Can we trust you?"

"I give you my word that I will harm none of you." He stood up.

"Sit back down and don't move," Val said. "And you stay out here, love." Val glared at me, and I nodded.

"No need to be rude." Vulcan took a seat and crossed his legs.

"I'm going to trust that you will now stand by your word," I said as I turned the key, hoping that I didn't regret it.

Opening the cell door, Val entered it and set the deer on the floor. He came back out of the cell and closed the door behind him. Locking the cell door back, we both stared at Vulcan, waiting to see what he was going to do.

"Why aren't you eating it?" I asked.

"The Vampire told me not to move."

"Oh. You can eat now," I said with a smile.

Vulcan eyes traveled over to Val.

"May I?" he asked. I was a little offended that he was asking Val's permission after I already gave mine.

"Umm, sure," Val said.

Watching with curious eyes, Vulcan stood up and dropped to his knees in front of the deer. Raising his hand over it, he curled all his fingers up into a ball except for his index finger. Curiosity deepened as I watched him run his sharp claw down the stomach of the deer slicing it.

Blood poured out of the wound and dripped to the floor as he reached both hands inside, spreading the wound open. He dipped one hand in and pulled out some intestines, and my face scrunched up.

Vulcan took his claw and cut the intestines in half. Nausea rose in me as a strong smell of blood and whatever the deer ate last hit me. I pinched my nose as I continued watching him. He dropped one side of the intestines and brought the other end to his mouth, taking a bite out of it like it was a hotdog. My stomach turned as he moaned at the taste. He chewed his food and swallowed.

"I haven't had deer intestines in so long."

"I'm glad you're enjoying it." I swallowed the bile that wanted to creep up my throat back down.

"Do you want some?" He asked as he held the end toward me. "They are delicious."

I shook my head as my stomach turned. He held it toward Val

"Do you, Vampire?"

"Gross, no," Val said.

"You drink their blood. What is the difference?" he asked.

"Um. It's not intestines." Val shrugged.

"Very well." Vulcan continued eating as I struggled with the nausea.

Once he started ripping into the stomach, the smell in the room got worse, so I turned away. Twenty minutes later, a loud, satisfying sound came from his mouth.

"I'm done."

Turning back around, I watched as he stood up and took a seat on the bench that was in his cell. Looking down at the gutted deer, I knew we had to get it cleaned up.

"We can't leave that there to rot," I said as I looked at Val.

"It's too dangerous for someone to clean it up."

"We could move him to a different cell, then someone could clean it up."

"You've got to be kidding me, love."

"He can't sit in there with a rotting deer, Val."

Val let out a long sigh.

"Fuck. Unlock the cell and go stand over there." Val pointed to the guard that was on duty. I gave Val an apologetic look before I opened the cell. I quickly went and stood by the guard. His face was pale. I guess he didn't like dear entrails either.

"Walk toward me," Val said to Vulcan. He stood up and slowly made his way toward the cell door. "I'm going to move you to the next cell over. Don't try anything stupid."

Vulcan nodded, and Val grabbed his arm. He led him into the next cell over and shut the door.

"Thank you for not being rough," Vulcan said.

"Uh, no problem," Val said. He turned toward the guard. "Go get someone to come clean up this mess."

The guard nodded and left the room. Val held out his hands and I tossed the keys to him. He locked the cell door and turned toward me.

"Thank you," I said.

He nodded. "Of course, my love."

"I want to say thank you to both of you. We don't get to eat a lot on Mistlaven. Erebus has made too many Demons and food is getting scarcer with the more he makes."

My empathy for Vulcan grew. I had an opportunity to bond more, and I took it. Walking over to his new cell, I put my hands on the bars, and set my face in between them.

"I'm sorry you are treated the way you are by your... um, king. You would think he would want his men strong since he started a war." I swallowed hard as I waited for him to spill some useful information.

"Ember, if you want information out of me, all you must do is ask. I have no loyalties to the asshole who gutted my mother in front of me."

"Then why were you trying to get on the portal?" I asked.

"King's orders. I'm sure you both know how that is. I do what Erebus says, or I'm the next one gutted."

"We know about king's orders, but our king would never mistreat his soldiers or his citizens. Reign is an honorable king."

"You're lucky to have food and the ability to make your own decisions."

"We need to go, love," Val said.

"I'm sorry about your parents. That wasn't a ruse. I know how it feels to lose one, or both, in my case."

"Thank you," he said. "I'm sorry about yours, too."

"We have to go, but I appreciate your help today."

"You're very welcome." He smiled kindly as Val took my hand. We were almost out the door when he spoke again.

"Hey, Ember. The offer for more Demon blades from me still stands."

I nodded and we left the prison.

Chapter 13

Cinder

I t was time for dinner, and I hadn't seen anyone since I got back from Tessalone with Zayn.

"Hey, Cinder," Zayn said as I entered the dining room.

"Hi, guys. Are Ember and Val back?" I asked.

"Not yet," Zila said.

"Are they okay?" Worry filled me since it was getting dark.

"They're fine. They just had business with the king." Cali shifted in her seat and poured herself some wine.

"What happened? Was there a Demon attack?" I asked.

"No. Just normal guard duties. Nothing to worry about." Zayn smiled as he poured me some wine. He looked up at Cali and she cleared her throat.

"Yes. Just guard stuff. Are you excited about tomorrow?" she asked.

"I am," I said.

Cash brought my attention away as he entered the room. He took a seat and started making a plate. Everyone got quiet.

Most of dinner went by with a light conversation between Cali, Zila, and Asher. Neither Zayn, Cash, nor I said much. Once dinner was over, I got up and went to the kitchen. I grabbed the cake Zayn and I had made and took it into the dining room. Setting it in the middle of the table, everyone's eyes widened.

"What is that?" Asher asked.

"Cake, obviously," Zayn snickered.

"I know, smartass. What kind?"

"Carmel," I said as I cut everyone a piece.

Everyone started grabbing a plate with cake on it. Asher was the first to take a bite.

"This is delicious," he said.

Looking up at Cash, he watched Asher with curious and excited eyes, but didn't grab a plate. So, I picked up a plate and took it around to Cash. I set it down in front of him and his eyes met mine.

"I made it," I whispered.

He nodded slightly and looked down at the cake. Walking back to my side of the table, I took my seat between Zayn and Asher. I watched curiously as Cash picked up his fork and cut off a bite of cake. He stuck it in his mouth and his eyes widened.

"You made this, Cinnamon?" he asked while still chewing.

My heart raced at his voice and the use of my nickname.

"I did," I said sweetly, with a smile. I completely left out the part where Zayn helped me. But I was sure he already knew since he saw us.

"It's delicious." He continued eating his cake as I watched proudly.

"Can I have another piece?" My eyes wandered to Asher.

"Of course. Help yourself, Asher." I smiled as he cut himself more.

"Does anyone want to play pool after dinner?" Asher asked.

"I'll play with you, buddy." Cash grinned and my heart raced. He seemed a little happier and was eating. I took that as a good sign.

"Me too," Zayn said before he took a bite of his cake.

"Ladies?" Asher looked at Cali.

"That sounds like fun, but Zila is going to help me pick out an outfit for tomorrow. Cinder, do you want to come up and help? We need to find yours, too." Cali clapped her hands while she stared at me with an excited face, waiting for my answer.

Contemplation filled me. My feelings were torn between wanting to hang out with Cash and wanting to pick out my dress with the girls, so I didn't hurt their feelings. I hoped the plan I came up with would get me near Cash without looking like I was blowing off my other friends.

"I must take an inventory of ingredients I have after dinner and figure out what I still need. I may come up after that." Lies fell out of my mouth. I left the part out where I was going to stumble into where the men were playing pool and flirt with Cash.

"Okay. Come up when you're done. We will probably still be up." Cali smiled sweetly.

I nodded.

After dinner, everyone left the dining room. Going into the kitchen, I stood around for a few minutes and peeked in all the cabinets, trying to look busy. Hearing the men laughing, I knew they had started their game, so I wandered out of the kitchen. I went past the front door and walked into the study. There was a pool table toward the back of the large room, and that's where the men were.

Zayn was pouring drinks at the bar, Asher was racking the balls, and Cash was watching. He was running the chalk over the end of his pool stick as I walked up to him—I had never wanted to be a pool stick before, but as I watched the way he held it—the way he caressed it—that changed.

"Do you know where I can find a quill and ink?" I asked. Cash looked up at me.

"Oh, there is some on the desk right there." Asher pointed at the desk.

"Thanks, Asher." I smiled kindly, even though I wasn't talking to him.

Grabbing a quill and ink, I headed out of the room. I set them on the table in the hallway while I thought of another plan. Paper—I needed paper, too. Heading back toward the men, I walked up to Cash. Making sure I said his name this time, so Asher knew who I was speaking to.

"Cash, do you know—"

"If you need paper, it's in the desk drawer, Cinder."

"Oh. Thanks, Asher." Turning away quickly before Asher saw the scowl on my face, I opened the desk drawer and yanked out the paper.

Heading back into the hallway, I grabbed the stuff I had left and went back to the kitchen. Deciding I should *actually* take inventory, I grabbed a few things out of the cabinet and wrote some stuff down that I needed.

"What are you doing?" Zayn asked. Looking up from my paper, my eyes met his as he smiled.

"Inventory. Why are you so happy?"

"No reason." He shook his head and his smile widened. "I was just coming to remind you to add nutmeg to your list, oh and lemons."

"Yes. I almost forgot. Thank you, Zayn."

"You're welcome." He ran his hand through his hair as I stared at him, waiting to see what else he had to say. "Do you want to play pool with us?"

"Um. I do, but I didn't want to impose."

"Come on." He smiled as he reached for the quill in my hand and set it down. "This stuff can wait. Having fun should always be top priority." He took my hand and pulled me out of the kitchen.

As we walked toward the study, I couldn't help but smile. A tiny bit of me really liked Zayn—possibly as more than friends—even if Cash still had my heart.

"I found a fourth player, now we can do teams," Zayn said as we entered the study. Cash's eyes went down to Zayn's hand holding mine, and I wiggled mine out of his.

"Perfect. Have you ever played before, Cinder?" Asher asked.

"No, I haven't." I gripped my hands together in front of my body as nervousness filled me.

"I get Cash then." Asher patted Cash on the shoulder and Cash smiled lightly.

"I will take Cinder." Zayn handed me a stick, and I took it. "Do you want a drink?" he asked.

"Sure."

Zayn headed toward the bar and Cash stepped up to it first.

"I'll make it, buddy. I know what she likes." Cash grabbed a glass and started pouring things into it.

"Okay." Zayn shrugged and came back over by me. "I'm going to show you how to hold your stick once it's your turn."

I nodded at Zayn's words, but my attention was on Cash as I watched him carefully make my drink. My heart thundered as he strolled up to me.

"You'll like this." Cash grinned as he held the drink out.

Leaning my pool stick against the wall, I took the drink from him and took a sip.

"This is delicious. What is it?"

"I call it Angel Delight." He grinned as I took another sip.

"Well, I like it." My cheeks blushed as I started into his eyes.

A large crack of the pool balls filled the room and broke my eye contact with Cash.

"Cinder, come on. Asher broke, so you will go next."

"Okay." I smiled as I walked toward Zayn. He took my drink from me and set it on a nearby table. "What did he break?" I asked.

Zayn laughed. "He started the game. We are solid, so try to only get the solid colored balls into the pockets."

"What's a pocket?" I asked.

"The holes there," Zayn pointed to the holes in the table, "those are called pockets.

"Watch, Cinder. This one here is going to go into that pocket." Asher pointed his stick at a pocket. I watched as he took another shot. He sunk a ball that had a stripe on it.

"Oh, that black one is right by a pocket now," I whispered to Zayn. "I can probably hit that one."

"No, you can't sink the black ball until the end. Whoever gets all their balls in and then the eight-ball in first wins. Also, try not to hit the white one into the pockets either."

"Why not?" I asked. "It's a solid color."

"Because that's a scratch," Asher said, as he missed his shot.

"What's that?"

"This is going to be a long game." Asher sighed and went to pour himself a drink. "Your turn, Cinder."

Stepping up to the table, I had no clue what I was doing as I stared at all the balls.

"You need a stick." Cash smiled as my eyes met his.

"Oh." I turned around and Zayn handed me the one I'd leaned against the wall.

"Hold it like this." Zayn held his stick the proper way and I tried to copy it. "You're going to hit the white ball into another ball. If it were me, I would try to get the six in that pocket right there."

"Okay." I leaned down and tried to aim. I hit the white ball with my stick, and it went the wrong way.

Cash grabbed the white ball before it stopped rolling and set it back where it was.

"Try again," he said with a small smile.

I leaned down again and positioned my stick.

"Hold on. I'll help you." Zayn scooted in next to me and his body pressed into mine. He put his arm around me, showing me how to hold my stick. Glancing up at Cash, he had his eyes narrowed on Zayn.

"Now pull back and try to hit it." I did what Zayn said and I hit the ball.

To my surprise, the six ball went into a pocket.

"Yes! Good job, Cinder" Zayn held up his hand and I high-fived it.

"Thanks. Who's turn is it now?" I asked.

"It's yours again." Cash's face was blank as he bit his lip.

Leaning down, I looked around at the table. There was one ball that I might be able to hit, but I would have to go around to where Asher and Cash were standing—so I did.

Once I was on their side, Asher stepped out of the way, but Cash stayed put.

Leaning down over the table, I raised my stick.

"You're holding it wrong," Asher said. "And you won't make that shot."

"I'll help you. Let me set my drink down," Zayn said as he turned toward the side table.

"I got it this time." Cash's words shocked me, and before I could even recognize them, I smelled the manly scents of bergamot and sandalwood surrounding me. I hadn't realized how much I had missed it.

Pressing his entire body across my back, he wrapped his big arms around me and placed his hands on top of mine.

Leaning his mouth close to my neck, he whispered, "They need to be here."

Gripping my hands, he slowly slid them to where they should be on the stick. Chills ran down me as my heart thundered in my chest.

"See that white dot over there?" he asked.

"Uh huh," I moaned.

"And the one next to it?" His mouth was so close, his breath bounced off my skin, and it made the hairs on the back of my neck stand up.

"Yeah," I said breathlessly.

"Hit the ball so it goes right between them. Can you do that, Cinnamon?"

Turning my face toward him, my mouth was only mere inches from his and I swallowed hard.

"Yes," I said with a heavy breath. I felt like at any moment, he was going to kiss me as he glanced back and forth between my mouth and my eyes. Lust completely took over his face.

"No way is she going to make a bank shot," Asher said loudly, breaking our moment.

"Shut up, Asher," Zayn said in a low voice.

"Yes, she can." The manly tone in Cash's voice rumbled through my body. "Can't you?"

Cash's blue eyes stared into mine as he smiled, so I nodded. Turning my head back toward the table, I looked at the center between the two dots.

Cash turned his mouth back toward my ear, and his nose grazed my cheek before he spoke.

"Now do what I say." Cash's voice was back to a whisper. "You're going to hit the ball with medium strength, not too hard, and not too soft."

Narrowing my eyes on the ball, I took a breath.

"Now shoot."

Mine and Cash's hands moved in unison as we hit the ball with the stick. The white ball hit the number two ball, which bounced off the side of the pool table—right between the two white dots—and rolled into the side pocket opposite of it.

"Yes!" Zayn was excited as Cash stood up, removing his warm body from mine. I stood up too and tried to catch my breath.

"No fair, Cash. She isn't even on our team." Asher shook his head.

"They can be teammates now. You're with me, Asher," Zayn said.

"Sweet." Asher walked over by Zayn as my eyes returned to Cash.

"I guess we're teammates now." My smile was worried. I felt like I was going to shrink into myself as I looked at Cash's blank face.

"I guess so." A slow smile crept across his face. "Good job, by the way."

"Thanks." I smiled proudly, even though Cash technically made the shot for me.

"It's still your turn, Cinder," Asher said.

"Oh." I turned back toward the table and looked around. "I want to try this one by myself," I said over my shoulder at Cash. He nodded.

Putting my stick up on the table, I lined up my shot and took it. The four-ball hit the corner of the pocket and bounced off.

"So close," Asher said.

"My turn." Zayn took his stick and walked around the table, looking for a perfect shot.

"Do you want another drink?" Cash asked.

"Sure." I strolled over to the side table and picked up my glass. It was still mostly full, so I downed it before I handed it to Cash. He took it from me and went over to the bar.

I watched as Zayn got one of the striped balls into a pocket. A minute later, Cash handed me back a full glass.

"Here, you go."

"Thanks."

"So, this is your first time playing?" he asked.

"Yep." I nodded.

"I think you could be a natural. We will have to see," he said, grinning widely.

"Shit," Zayn said. "I missed it. Your turn Cash."

Cash made his way around the table. He lowered himself down, aimed, and took the shot. He sank the five, then the seven, and the three, before he finally missed.

"Now I remember why we don't play with you," Asher said, and I giggled.

"Do you want another drink?" Cash asked.

"I'm good right now, thank you." I smiled as Cash went over to the bar and poured himself a drink.

Asher took his shot and missed. "Your turn, Cinder." He walked away from the table with a sigh.

I stepped up to the table and took a shot. I got the one ball in and felt proud of myself for about a minute.

"Shoot," I said, and Asher laughed as I missed my next ball. My eyes met his. "I don't know why you're laughing. By my count, I have more balls than you, right now."

Zayn snickered as Cash busted out a laugh.

"You don't have more balls than me, you sank more balls than me." Asher shook his head and grinned at me.

"Same thing." I shrugged as Zayn stepped up to take his shot. He sunk another stripped ball and then missed on his second shot.

"Time to end this," Cash said as he strolled up to the table.

He leaned over it, his back muscles tightening as he took his shot. Like a pro, the four ball went in.

He stood up and looked over the table. Only the eight ball was left.

"No way you're going to make that shot," Asher said.

"Wanna bet?" Cash asked.

"Absolutely. What are we betting this time?" Asher asked.

"Let me think of a good one." Cash ran his hand through his beard.

"I got one." Asher grinned mischievously.

"Let's hear it, Ass."

"If you miss, you shave your beard, and cut your hair." Cash's face paled, along with mine.

"And if I win?" Cash asked.

"I will shave my head."

"You're already half bald. No deal." Cash shook his head. "You need to come up with something better."

"I think it's Asher's turn to run naked through the gardens," Zayn said.

"No. Come on."

"Naked or nothing," Cash said.

"Deal." Asher put his hand out.

Cash looked at me for a few seconds and I shook my head. He looked down at Asher's hand.

"Deal!" Cash shook his hand. My eyes widened and I looked over at Zayn, his mouth was agape in shock—just like mine.

"Holy shit, Cash. If you miss this shot and lose, I'm going to miss your hair." Asher grinned nervously as Cash took the shot and landed it in the pocket.

He smiled proudly as he looked at me.

"Yes!" I clapped my hands together and ran up to him. "We won." I held up my hand and he gave me a high-five.

"We did." He winked at me.

"And you get to keep your hair." I smiled big.

"I'll rack them again." Zayn started pulling balls out of a hole in the table's side, and I was confused by how they got there.

"Better hurry before he has to run through the gardens naked," Cash said.

"Who lost this time?" Cali asked. My eyes went toward the study door, as she and Zila entered.

"Asher," Cash and Zayn said in unison.

"Well, well. I hope it isn't chilly tonight." She smiled big.

"I'm not doing it in front of the ladies." Asher shook his head.

"You don't make the rules, Asher. Zayn did it in front of the whole house, including the king. Not me though, I closed my eyes." Cali made a gross face and I laughed.

"King's Guard meeting," Val said, and all our heads whipped in his direction. I gasped when I saw he was soaked in blood.

"Where is Ember?" I asked in a panic.

"She is fine, it's deer blood. We just got back from a mission, and she stayed at the castle to visit with your uncle for a while."

"Should we go to the library for the meeting?" Zayn asked.

"Here is fine," Val strolled up to us. The look on his face was serious.

Everyone got quiet and as I looked around, I realized they were waiting for me to leave because I wasn't a King's Guard.

"Well, I'm going to go to bed. Have a goodnight."

Everyone said their goodnights to me, and I shut the double doors on the way out. A smile was on my face as I headed up to my room. I couldn't stop thinking about Cash.

Chapter 14

Cinder

After having to leave the study during the King's Guard meeting, I went to my room, knitted for a bit while I thought about Cash, then went to bed.

At breakfast, they informed me that Ember had left on another mission, along with Cali and Asher. After everyone ate and took off, I figured I would make as many pies as possible for everyone to try before my stand opened. I also figured that, since Cash was being super sweet last night, I would surprise him.

Hot and sweaty from baking for a couple of hours, I saw an Angel enter the room. I wondered immediately where Cash was. He was usually not far behind Zayn.

"Hey, Cinder," Zayn said to me. He eyeballed the table filled with desserts. "It smells so good in the house."

"Hello, Zayn." I smiled politely at the sweet Angel before I saw Cash come strolling through the door, and my heart raced.

"Oh, I smelled this in my room." His eyes immediately went to the table as he scanned all the baked goods I had made today before he looked at me. "Ha-ha, don't you look adorable with flour on your cheek?" My hand immediately wiped my cheek as he smiled at me.

Cash was always such an upbeat person, and he always made me smile. My blood boiled at the way he looked at me. Well, that and I was nervous about what I was about to do.

"Hello, Cash." I blushed, looking down and wiping flour off the front of my apron. "I'm glad you're here. I have something for you."

I nervously grabbed the pie I had made for Cash and handed it to him. He looked at it with a confused face. I immediately felt silly for gifting him a dumb pie.

"You made this for me?" He met my eyes, and I looked nervously to the ground.

"Yes, I thought you would like it. Ember said that apple was your favorite."

Why had I done this? And in front of Zayn. My nerves were killing me.

"Wow, this is amazing." Glancing up, Cash had a huge smile on his face. I immediately blushed and swallowed hard. "Thank you, Cinder. It truly is an honor to get to eat your pie." I heard Zayn snicker, and my eyes shot to him.

He looked shamefully away. I didn't understand what was funny. Was he jealous? I turned my attention back to Cash. I stared into those gorgeous blue eyes of his and had to turn my head away.

"You're welcome and please excuse me, I must finish this cake." I continued mixing up cake batter when I felt a presence stand close to me.

"It truly is an honor to have you cook for me. Thank you, Cinder." Cash bowed to me. Then he kissed me on my cheek, causing me to blush. I saw him grab a fork and leave the room. I looked up at a frowning Zayn.

"He just took the whole pie. He wasn't even going to offer me one piece."

I giggled at Zayn's reaction.

"I made one for you, too. Ember said cherry was your favorite." I smiled brightly at him.

"Wow. Thank you, Cinder." He smiled as he walked over to me. He laid a sweet kiss on my cheek, and then he left the room. I shook my head at the two crazy Angels.

My new life at Castleva was going well so far, except for the fact that I had a crush on two men.

Unfortunately, it didn't matter what I did, Cash wasn't paying the same attention to me that he once had. I didn't know what I did wrong.

Maybe Zayn was a more proper fit for me. He was sweet and friendly and always gave me attention. I put the cake in the oven as I sighed before I quickly washed my hands and went to find Noreen.

Making my way upstairs, a thousand thoughts went through my head.

Zayn was always kind, attentive, caring, and his mood was always the same with me. Cash was two different people. The constantly grinning, life-loving Cash that my heart ached for, and the stone-face Cash that was afraid to be near me.

Confusion swirled through me as I knocked on Noreen's door.

"Yes?"

"It's Cinder." The door opened, and she appeared shocked.

"Is everything okay?" She had her robe on. I must have caught her at bath time. I walked into the room.

"Yes, everything is fine. I—oh, I'm sorry." There was a handsome man putting his shirt on. He had brown hair and dark brown eyes—he was Elven. I was grateful his pants were on.

"It's okay, I was just leaving, my lady." He walked up to us. "I will, uh, see you tonight, Noreen." He gave her a kiss and left.

"What's wrong, Cinder?"

"Who was that?" I asked with a smile.

"My friend." She blushed.

"Why haven't you told me about him?"

"I was going to. You have just had a lot on your mind with Cash and your stand. I did not want to be bothersome."

"Noreen, am I your friend?" I asked.

"Yes, of course."

"Well, a friendship is about give and take. You don't have to take all the time. Sometimes I can take, too. I would love to hear about your life."

"Okay." She gave me a happy smile.

I walked over and took a seat on her bed. "Sit with me and tell me."

"On the bed?" she asked. Her face looked appalled.

"Yes. That's what girls do when they want to talk about boys. Now tell me about his hot Elven man."

I patted the bed and she crawled onto it next to me.

"His name is Avan. I met him a few months ago and have only been seeing him on my weekends off, which isn't very often."

"That's exciting."

"He is here helping build the barn, so I got to see him a little more these past few weeks."

"That is amazing, Noreen. Start at the beginning. How did you meet?"

"Well..."

Noreen told me everything about their relationship. Forty-five minutes into our conversation, I had to go downstairs and remove my cake from the oven. I came back up and we talked for over an hour, and the smile she had the whole time made me happy.

"Well, I am thrilled for you, Noreen. He's very handsome."

"Thank you, Cinder." Her smile faded. "So, it's your turn. What happened?"

"I'm so confused. I like Cash a lot, but I think I'm also starting to like Zayn."

"As more than just a friend?"

"Maybe. I think so. I'm not sure."

"Did you like him at all before Cash got weird?"

"No. I mean, I liked him as a person. He's very nice and handsome."

"Are you sure that you are not just missing Cash, and that is why?"

"Maybe. I don't know. I'm confused."

"Is Cash still being weird?" she asked.

"Well, last night during the pool game, I could tell he still had feelings for me. Then today I made him a pie and when I gave it to him, he was acting like the old Cash."

"Maybe he is feeling better now."

"Maybe. I guess I will find out when I see him tonight at the party." I glanced over at the clock. "Oh no, it's almost dinnertime. Are you going to get in trouble?"

"No. We aren't making dinner tonight because everyone is going to the party. The servants are going to have sandwiches and play cards. Then I will be heading home for the weekend."

"Oh, that sounds like fun." I smiled big. "I'll leave you to get dressed." I hopped off the bed and headed toward the door. I stopped and turned toward her. "Thanks for listening to me, Noreen."

"Thanks for listening to me, Cinder." She smiled big, and I left the room.

Chapter 15

Cinder

After my long day of baking and talking, I came upstairs and took a small nap. I woke not long before it was time to leave. After showering, I quickly ran around my room as I finished getting ready for the birthday party.

Cali said I should dress more flirtatiously tonight since we were going to a saloon, so I borrowed a dress from her. It was black and hugged my body. Since it was low cut in the front, my cleavage was on display. I wasn't used to wearing such revealing clothes since our mother raised both me and my sister to be modest, but tonight, I didn't care. The dress looked good on me, and I was comfortable in it. I just hoped it did what I wanted it to do—get Cash's attention.

Looking in the mirror, I slid the necklace that Cash gave me around my neck. Staring at my reflection as the pair of angel wings dangled from my neck, my chest felt heavy. During my shower, hope had filled me that Cash had changed and might have worked through whatever issue he'd been having. Not wanting to be misled anymore, I decided that if he ignores me tonight, I will move on with my life. Holding my head high, I left my room and headed downstairs.

"Wow, Cin. You look beautiful," Zayn said as I came down the stairs. He was wearing black slacks and a dark blue button-up shirt. The top of his shirt was unbuttoned, and he was wearing a tie, but it was hanging loose. He looked very handsome, and a little sexy. I quickly averted my eyes. Asher was standing next to him—he was dressed similarly, but his shirt was white. He was handsome, too.

"Thank you." I smiled proudly as Zayn held out his hand and helped me down the last stair.

"You look too sexy in that dress." My eyes shot to Asher in shock. "I'm just saying that because Ember's going to kill you."

"She isn't my boss." My proud smile turned mischievous.

"Yeah, she's still going to kill you, though." He shrugged his shoulders and Zayn laughed.

"Is everyone ready?" Cali was wearing a super-sexy red dress with thin straps—she wore it like it was made for her. I admired her confidence as she cascaded down the stairs.

Zila was wearing a longer black dress that wasn't as revealing. She looked modestly beautiful. Her wavy hair bounced as she followed Cali down. She had a nervous smile plastered on her face.

"Damn, Cinder!" Cali clapped her hands and squealed.

"Thank you." The abundance of compliments was making me blush. "You both look beautiful."

"Where is everyone else?" Zila's silver eyes seemed worried. "It's almost time to go."

Asher cracked his knuckles. "Val and Ember just went upstairs. She got back later than us. They said they would meet us there. I don't know about Cash."

"He will be down in a second. I just finished his hair." Cali smiled big at me.

Hearing pounding feet, I gazed up as Cash came thundering down the stairs. He was dressed like the other men, but he was wearing all black. His shirt was completely unbuttoned and gaped open. I couldn't take my eyes off his chest and stomach as he frantically tried to button it.

"Sorry guys, I..." Glancing down at my dress—and my breasts—Cash's mouth dropped open as he stepped into the foyer. A gust of wind flew through the room as his wings popped out of nowhere. Shards of glass scattered as a vase exploded against the floor.

Sucking in a breath, I winced as a chunk of glass hit me. "Ouch."

"Are you okay, Cinnamon? I didn't mean..." Placing his hands on my cheeks in a panic, Cash's blue eyes looked me over.

"I'm okay," I whispered. My heart raced as I realized this was my Cash—the Cash before whatever happened made him pull away from me. Joy filled at the thought of him being back.

Dropping his hands, he took two steps back and looked down at the mess he made. Everyone was quiet, all eyes glancing at the broken vase. Cali giggled and then Zila sighed.

"Can't we just have a normal family outing without broken vases and late people?"

"Why are you so impatient tonight, Zila?" Asher asked.

"It's my brother's birthday. I just wanted everything to be perfect." Cali snickered and Zila furrowed her eyebrows at her. "Hush, Cali. Everyone outside, we are going to be late!"

Zila opened the door in a panic, and everyone piled out, except for Cash. My breathing was labored as my eyes found his again.

"To the Gods. You're bleeding." Cash grabbed my wrist and stepped closer to me.

Glancing down, I watched as the blood from my wound dripped onto the marble floor.

"I'm so sorry," Cash's voice cracked as he spoke. His thumb glided across my skin as he inspected my arm. My adrenaline was pumping high from his touch, so I could barely feel the cut.

"I'm fine, Cash." His eyes met mine again and I bit my lip as I gazed back at him.

The door opened and Cali peeked in. "Sweet Zila is about to turn into a mean wolf if we don't get on that portal."

"She's injured." Cash let out a long breath, a look of sorrow on his face.

"Oh." Cali stepped into the manor and grabbed my arm. Her skin radiated a golden light and warmth flowed across my skin as my wound completely closed. "There. Let's go."

"I have to clean the blood off me first." I looked down to see if any got on my dress.

"You guys can go. We'll catch up." Cash and Cali locked eyes, and she nodded.

"Okay. Come when you're done." Cali smiled and shut the door.

Glancing up, I met Cash's eyes as he raked a hand through his beard. His wings folded in and disappeared.

"Let's clean you up." He turned toward the hall and I watched him from behind. My body automatically started gravitating in the direction he was going. I was pretty sure it yearned for him just as much as my heart did.

He opened the door to the hallway bathroom and pulled me inside. He closed the lid to the toilet and pointed at it.

"Sit."

Cash frantically grabbed a hand towel and wet it, as I took a seat. He lowered himself to his knees in front of me, and my heart sped up once more. Picking up my arm, he gently ran a cloth across my skin and wiped the blood away.

"I'm sorry."

"It's okay, Cash. It's healed now."

"It's not okay. My wings shouldn't have..." He glanced up from my arm. "Anyway, I'm sorry."

I smiled and nodded. "I forgive you."

Looking back down, I watched as he finished cleaning up the blood. He ran his thumb across my arm where the wound had been, and my skin puckered from his touch.

"Good as new." Leaning his head down, he kissed the spot that was healed and then his eyes met mine. He dropped my arm and then cleared his throat. "Um... did you get any on your dress?" he asked.

"I don't think so."

"Good. We better get going, Cinna... um, Cinder." Cash stood up and, just like that, he put his stone face mask back on. My heart hurt once more.

"Okay," I said as I stood up, I headed toward the front door and went outside.

Cash followed behind me as I stalked off toward the portal. Watching him go from one Cash to another was frustrating. It was giving me whiplash. I was ready to confront him, but I didn't want to ruin anyone's evening, so I decided tomorrow would be better. I walked fast until I reached the portal and stepped on. Seconds later, Cash did the same.

He wielded the portal, and I felt the amazing rush. The cool breeze hit me, and excitement filled my body. Then we landed in Direbreak.

We stepped off the portal and lots of plush pine trees surrounded us.

"Wow. These trees are so tall and beautiful," I said as we started walking. "I bet this place is amazing during the day."

"Yep." He nodded.

"Where is this saloon?" I asked.

"We'll have to gale there." He let out a large and, might I add, very loud sigh.

My eyes darted up to his as my heart sped up. My heart didn't speed up from his beautiful blue eyes, his sexy body, or his gentle touch. This time, it sped up in anger.

I would take the weirdness.

I would take the sadness.

I would take the random happy moments that seem to come and go.

There was no way I was going to take him acting like it would be so hard to gale me—something friends do all the time. Something Zayn had no problem doing.

I had reached my limit.

"Sorry to be such a burden to you, sir. I will walk." I picked up the edge of my dress and held my head high as I strolled off in the direction that I really hoped the saloon was in.

"Cinder, wait. I'll gale you."

"After that sigh, you let out, it's pretty obvious that you don't want to. I'm perfectly capable of escorting *myself* to the saloon. Thank you very much!"

"Please stop."

I stopped and turned toward him.

"I wasn't going to say anything tonight, but it's also obvious that you don't want anything to do with me anymore, either!"

"It's not what you think."

"Then what is it, Cash?" I put my hands on my hips as I glared at him.

He ran his hand through his beard. "Things have just been difficult lately."

"So, instead of talking to me about your problems, you avoid me?"

"I can't talk to you about this. I'm sorry."

"Why can't you?"

"I can't tell you why, either."

"I don't understand, Cash."

"I'm sorry. I'm trying not to hurt you, but..." He hung his head low. He looked defeated and my heart hurt for him.

Slowly walking up to him, I placed my hand on his cheeks. His thick beard was soft against my skin and I missed it dearly.

"It's okay. Whatever it is, we can fix it. We can work through it together. Me and you." His bright blue eyes peered down at me, filled with regret.

"Cinder, I..." He swallowed hard as he shook his head.

"Oh." I let my hands fall away from him as a realization hit me. "There is no me and you. Is there?"

"Cinder, I don't know what to say."

"You don't have to say anything. I'm smart enough to know what's going on here."

"You don't know, though. You have no idea what's going on, Cinder."

"Then tell me."

"I can't."

"Then we are done here." I crossed my arms.

"Cinder..."

"Stop calling me that!"

Hearing the swoosh of the portal, I glanced over and saw Ember and Valarian step off, hand-in-hand.

"Hey, guys. What are you doing?" My sister's face looked worried as they walked up to us. She peered down at my dress and sighed, but she didn't say anything.

"I was just about to gale Cinder into town." Cash stroked a hand nervously through his beard.

Ember's eyes glanced back and forth between us like she could feel the tension in the air.

"Where are the others?" Val asked.

"They went ahead. I had blood on my arm—"

"What?" Ember dropped Val's hand and stepped up to me. "Are you okay? What happened, Cin?"

"I'm fine. Cash's wings knocked over a vase and I got cut by flying glass. Cali healed me and everyone else left while Cash cleaned me up."

"Oh." Ember's eyes went wide, and she looked toward Cash. He looked shamefully at the ground.

"We should get to the party, love." Val wrapped his arms around her from behind.

As soon as Ember opened her mouth to speak, they disappeared. I had a feeling Val was trying to give us alone time.

I took a deep breath and turned toward Cash.

"I'm sorry," he said as he met my eyes.

After seeing a glimpse of the real Cash, I knew he was still in there. I was going to put my emotions aside for the evening and be friendly, hoping he would come to his senses.

"We have a party to go to, Cash. I would prefer to enjoy the rest of my evening. So, for now, can we pretend like we are, I don't know, friends?"

"I would like that." He smiled lightly.

"Perfect. Are you ready, then?"

He nodded and stepped in close to me. Reaching his arms out, he slid them around my waist and pulled me near him. The familiar scent of bergamot and sandalwood relaxed me.

"You look really pretty," he whispered before we galed away.

We landed outside the town's wards, and I looked up at him and swallowed. He held me for longer than he needed to, but I didn't mind. He kept my eye contact but dropped his hands from my waist.

"Which way is the saloon?" I asked.

"It's this way." Cash nodded his head in the direction.

"What's this town called?" I picked up my dress and started walking.

"This is Hallowshade." He fell in step next to me.

"There are a lot of stores here."

"It's a great place to shop during daylight hours."

"Oh, really? What do they sell?"

"The Lycans sell a lot of things, but they have the best fur pelts in the lands."

"Does it get colder in Ashbern than in Mazuria?" I could hear music playing close by.

"Much colder. You will need a pelt and a cloak for winter. I also suggest wool gloves. You don't want your pretty... um, your hands getting cold."

"I will ask Ember to bring me here to get some things." I smiled because I knew he was about to call my hands pretty.

"We're here."

Looking up, I saw a big wooden building. Tiny little lanterns were hanging on each side of me as we strolled up the pathway. We entered the saloon doors, and the music got louder.

"Stay by me." Cash reached down and interlocked his fingers with mine. The familiarity of his manly hand soothed me. When you worked with weapons and chopped wood as much as he did, you were bound to have rough hands.

He led me through the saloon until we found some of our friends sitting at a table. I could hear them talking as we approached.

"There is no way, Asher! That's impossible."

"Do you want to bet on it, Zayn?"

Zayn scratched his chin as he thought of his answer.

"Challenge accepted." He put his hand out and shook Asher's.

"Hey guys!" Cali smiled at us. "We just ordered food."

"I'm not hungry." Everyone looked at Cash with wide eyes. "I'm going to get a beer." He dropped my hand and headed to the bar.

"I'll go with you, buddy. I need a whiskey." Val's eyes wandered to Ember as he stood up. "Do you want anything, love?"

"My usual, thanks." The two men wandered toward the bar and I took a seat.

"I could eat. I haven't eaten since I had lunch with Zayn."

"That was yesterday, Cinder." Zayn smiled.

"Oh, I forgot. I was so busy making pies today, I skipped lunch." I yawned lightly.

"Where did you have lunch yesterday?" Cali asked.

"A sandwich place on Tessalone." I smiled at the memory of that delicious sandwich.

"You ate at Milo's without me?" Ember's head shot toward Zayn.

"Sorry, but not really. It was delicious." Zayn gave her a mischievous smile before he took a swig of his drink.

"Did you get to see the booth?" Ember asked.

"Yes. Zayn said it needed paint, but other than that, it's perfect. I had a lot of fun, too."

"I'm glad you had fun," Ember said with a smile.

"There you guys are." Zila walked up with Natsu and a male Lycan next to her. I figured it was her brother.

"You must be Cinder," the male Lycan said.

"I am." I smiled kindly at him. He was extremely handsome with black hair and the same silver eyes as Zila. His dark skin tone made his eyes even brighter.

"Cinder, this is my brother Kage." Zila smiled proudly.

"It's nice to finally meet you, Cinder. Zila has told me so much about you. Welcome to the Howling Moon."

"It's nice to meet you, too. I love your place. Oh, and happy birthday." I blushed as he took my hand and kissed it.

"Thank you." Kage turned his attention toward Cali. "Would you like to dance, Calista?" He lowered his hand to her, and I watched as her cheeks turned pink.

Since when does Cali blush?

"Okay, but only one dance. I have food coming." She took his hand and stood up. I watched as they made their way to the dance floor.

"Nice to see you again, Cinder." Natsu gave me a slight bow of his head.

"You too, Natsu."

"Emilia said you came to see your booth," he said.

"I did. Thank you for all your help. She said you were the reason I got it."

"I didn't do much. Turns out that Henry, the previous owner, wanted to retire but has been having trouble walking lately. He was in too much pain to pack up his stuff. He was waiting until his son came to visit in the spring and have him do it. So, I took my crew to his stand and got it done."

"That was so kind of you, Natsu. I'm very grateful, and I'm sure Henry is too."

"You're welcome, Cinder. A friend of the King's Guard is a friend of mine."

Zila's eyes filled with love as she stared at Natsu.

"Okay, guys. We are going to go mingle." She strolled off, and he followed behind her.

"I have an odd question, Zayn," I said as I turned toward him.

"Okay," he said suspiciously.

"If that old owner of my booth had trouble walking, why couldn't he just get an Angel like Cali to heal him?"

"That's actually a great question. Blessed Angels can heal wounds and stuff, but they can't cure the elderly. Once the body breaks down, no one's magic can help."

"Oh." Sadness filled me as I thought about the old man not being able to be healed.

"It's a part of life, Cinder."

"I know, Zayn. I just feel bad that he can't work anymore."

"Oh, believe me. Henry hated working. He was damn good and ready to retire. He would have told you himself." Zayn took a swig of his drink and I laughed.

"Well, I'm glad he got what he wanted then."

"Speaking of healing. Cali said she had to heal your arm." Zayn asked.

"Yeah. You can't even tell anything was there." I looked down and ran my finger across it as I thought about Cash.

"I can't believe Cash flapped." Zayn laughed lightly, and I looked up at him.

"Flapped?" My face scrunched up at the unknown word. "What does that mean?"

"Zayn." Ember's eyes locked dead on his and she shook her head.

"Um. It means his wings popped open accidentally."

"Is that normal?" I curiously glanced at Zayn, who looked over at Ember.

"It's normal," he said.

"So, why do they pop out accidentally?"

"It just happens sometimes, Cin." Ember smiled at me. I felt like I was being left out on what the truth really was.

Zayn ran his hand through his hair. "Would either of you ladies like a drink?" he asked, changing the subject.

"I'm good. Val's getting me a whiskey sour," Ember said.

"Val *got* you a whiskey sour." Val set the glass down with a smile and slid into the chair next to Ember.

"Thank you." She smiled brightly at him and picked up her drink.

"Would you like a drink, Cinder?" Zayn asked.

"Sure. I will take whatever." I shrugged.

Zayn stood up and held out his hand. "Come on. You can come with me and look at the options."

I took his hand and stood up. Cash was sitting at the bar alone as we walked up.

"What would you like?" Zayn asked.

"I don't know." My eyes wandered over the variety of bottles behind the bar. I had no idea what any of them were.

"I'll take a brandy while she decides."

"Coming right up, Zayn," the bartender said.

"I will take the same thing you're having." I didn't know what brandy tasted like, but I figured trying it won't hurt. The name sounded pretty, so I assumed it tasted good.

"Make that, two brandies," Zayn said.

"You're not going to like that," Cash said and eyes drifted over to him.

"How do you know?" I asked.

"Because I know you." His blue eyes gazed into mine and a slow smile spread across my face.

The bartender set the drinks in front of Zayn, bringing my attention away from Cash.

"Thanks, Libby." Zayn picked up our drinks and handed me mine.

Grabbing it, I raised it to my mouth and took a small sip. My throat burned and it tasted bad.

"That's disgusting, Zayn." I handed the drink back to him and he laughed.

"I knew you wouldn't like it." Cash smiled at me, and my heart sped up. "Hey Libby can you get the lady an amaretto on the rocks with a splash of pineapple juice?"

"No problem, Cash." The bartender turned around and quickly made another drink while I moved closer to Cash. "Here you go."

She slid the drink to Cash and he handed it to me. I took a small sip worried it would burn again.

"Oh." I was pleasantly surprised.

"Better?"

"Much better." I smiled brightly at him and he smiled back.

"I'll be back. Ember needs me." Zayn walked away taking both brandies with him, leaving me with Cash.

Looking toward our table, Ember was in a full-on conversation with Val. That's odd. I wonder how he knew she needed him.

"Take a seat." My attention went back to Cash. He reached his hand out to me. I hesitated for a second before I took it. Using his hand as leverage, I stepped onto the bottom rung of the barstool and slid my butt onto it.

"Thanks for the drink," I said.

"You're welcome." He smiled before staring back at his drink.

Admiring his side profile, I loved what he had done to his hair. His long sandy blonde hair was half pulled up and on each side of his head were three tightly woven braids.

"I love your hairstyle." Reaching my hand out, I took one of his braids in between my fingers. He stiffened slightly, so I dropped it.

"Cali did it for me. She usually braids it before battle, too."

"Well, it looks lovely."

"Lovely?" Cash's eyes widened as he slung his head toward me.

"What's wrong with 'lovely?'" I asked, and then giggled.

"I'm a warrior, Cinnamon. I don't want to be lovely." The sound of my nickname made me smile. His eyes locked onto mine and he grinned.

"Well, handsome then. Very manly, might I say, dear sir." I tried using our playful regal banter, hoping he would, too.

His eyes saddened and then drifted down to my cleavage. Reaching out his hand, I held my breath with excitement as it headed toward my breast.

A shiver ran through me as his hand lightly grazed my skin. He picked up the angel necklace hanging from my neck—the one that he had given me before things got weird. Holding it between his fingers, he admired it with a sad smile.

His eyes wandered up to mine and held my gaze for a few seconds before he dropped the necklace.

"Sorry." He shifted in his seat, turning back toward the bartender. "Can I get another beer?"

Sadness rose in me as I glanced down at my drink. Picking it up, I downed it. My insides warmed as it went down my throat.

"Whoa. Easy there." Cash's eyes widened.

"I will take another, too, please. Actually, save yourself time and just give me two." I smiled big at her.

"Coming right up," Libby said.

Cash shook his head and smiled at me.

"What?" I asked.

"Nothing," he said, his huge smile still there as he stared at me.

The bartender broke our eye contact as she set two more drinks in front of us.

Cash grabbed his beer and I watched as he took a swig. He had foam in his beard, and I laughed.

"What?" he said as he looked over at me.

"You have foam in your beard, silly."

He took his hand and wiped it off.

"Yeah. That happens a lot."

"What does beer taste like?" I asked.

"Try it." Cash grinned widely as he handed me his beer.

I put the tall glass to my mouth and took a drink. Bitterness filled my mouth.

"Yuck. This is bad, Cash. I think it's spoiled or something."

I heard the bartender giggle. Cash laughed as I handed him his drink back.

He took a big swig and made a refreshing sound with his mouth after he swallowed.

"That's how it's supposed to taste, Cinnamon." He grinned from ear to ear.

"Gross." I smiled and laughed at him. Cash's eyes locked on mine as he continued grinning. Then they drifted over my shoulder and his smile dropped. He shifted in his seat and stared at his beer.

"Hey guys. The food is cold, but there is some left." I turned toward my sister.

"Okay. I will be there in a second, Ember," I said.

She nodded, and I watched as she headed back to our table. Then I turned my attention back to Cash.

"Are you coming?" I asked.

As I looked at his face, waiting for an answer, I could see the pain and the struggle in his eyes again.

Placing my hand on his thigh, he looked down at it. His chest rose and fell at my touch. My Cash was in there, and I was going to get him back.

"Thank you for the drink, dear sir. But I must retire to my table. Do you mind helping a lady down?" Removing my hand from his leg, I held it out to him.

His eyes met mine and I smiled big, not letting my mood be altered by his. In return, he grinned widely.

"A gentleman would never leave a lady in distress." Cash took my hand as I stepped off the bar stool.

I picked up one of my drinks and downed it. Cash's eyes widened at my actions.

"Have a good evening, sir." I picked up the edge of my dress and curtsied.

"You too, my lady." He bowed his head at me.

An enormous smile was on my face as I grabbed my other drink and sauntered away from the bar. I was feeling better. I wasn't sure if it was the small amount of his normal personality coming back through, or if it was the alcohol, but hope filled me as I headed to our table.

Making my way across the room, I saw Zayn sitting alone.

"Where is everyone?" I asked.

"Dancing, mingling." He shrugged.

Looking out toward the dance floor, I saw Val pull Ember in close to him and I smiled big as I watched them dance. You could feel the love radiating around them and it made me yearn for some of that type of closeness.

"Aww." I sighed.

"Would you like to dance, Cinder?" My eyes met Zayn's as he smiled.

A new song came on, a slightly faster one, and I decided that, since I came here to have fun, that's what I was going to do.

"What the hell. I would love to."

"How many drinks have you had?" Zayn laughed as he stood up.

"A couple!" I took a big swig of my drink and set it on the table. "Come on." I grabbed his hand and pulled him toward the dance floor.

Once we were out there, I put one hand in Zayn's and the other on his shoulder.

"So, have you decided on a name for your stand yet?" he asked.

"No, and you're not going to let up on that are you?"

"No, I'm not." He laughed.

"I keep thinking about it, but I can't come up with anything catchy."

"How about Zayn's My Favorite Angel?"

I laughed and shook my head.

"Who said you were my favorite?"

"Hey, I took you to the best sandwich shop in all the lands, so I must be at least at the top of the list."

"You definitely are." I laughed even though, deep down, Cash would always have my heart—no matter what happens with us. He would always stay number one on my list.

"How does tomorrow sound?"

"For what?" I asked.

"To go get paint."

"Oh, I will have to ask Val if I have any training."

"I already did. You have morning classes, but you're free in the afternoon. Unless you have any other obligations…?"

My mind instantly went to Cash and my chest felt tight because my calendar was completely empty now.

"I don't." I shook my head.

"Perfect." Zayn smiled brightly. "We will go early, and I can show you where the best ice cream shop is."

"Oh, yay!"

I thought about the last time I had ice cream—it had been years.

The song turned slow, and I looked up at my dance partner.

"Thank you for being so kind to me, Zayn."

"You're welcome. I just hope that you're less lonely now."

"I miss Cash." The confession fell out of my mouth before I could stop it—it must have been the alcohol.

"I know, Cin. I know." He put his hand on my back and rubbed it lightly. I laid my head on his chest because I needed closeness, or comfort, I wasn't sure. I could hear his heart beat steadily with the rhythm of the music as he soothed me, and I let out a long breath.

Once the song ended, Zayn led me back toward our table and I caught sight of something I wished I hadn't. Pain spread through me, and I sucked in a large breath. My body stopped itself from moving as my heart ripped into pieces.

Chapter 16

Cash

Downing the last of my beer, I decided to see what everyone else was up to before I went home.

"Thanks, Libby." Our drinks were free, but I knew Libby lived off tips, so I threw a pile of cash on the bar.

"No problem, Cash. Have a good night."

"You too, honey." I stood up from the bar stool and started toward my friend's table.

Seeing something that I didn't want to see, I stopped dead in my tracks. I watched as Cinder strolled onto the dance floor, hand-in-hand with Zayn.

"Fuck," I whispered to myself.

Zayn was an honorable man, more perfect for Cinder than I could ever be. He had only been with a few women—unlike the man whore I had been in the past.

Turning around, I took a seat back at the bar.

"Here." Libby set another beer in front of me. I looked up at her, confused. "I know that look all too well, Cash." She smiled kindly.

"Thanks, Libby."

"No problem."

Looking back at the dance floor, my heart sank. Cinder was laughing at something Zayn said. She looked happy, and that was all I ever wanted for her.

"They're cute together." Libby's voice brought me back from the mental anguish I was causing myself.

"Yeah. He's perfect for her."

"And you're not because...?" Libby tilted her head as she dried off some glasses she had washed.

"Because she deserves better than me. She deserves the entire world." I shook my head and took a swig of my beer.

"Cash, I don't know what's going on, but I know you very well. You are a *damn* good man, and any woman would be lucky to have you." She sighed.

"Thanks." I took another swig of my beer and then looked back at the dance floor.

The song had turned slow, and they were still dancing. She laid her head on Zayn's chest and my heart broke.

I let out a hard breath because I knew I had fucked up.

Libby looked over to the dance floor, then back to me. "Don't get me wrong, Zayn is a very good-looking man, but I saw the way she looked at you, Cash. The world faded away, and you were the only one she cared about."

"I fucked up, Libby. I pushed her away."

"Almost anything is repairable, especially relationships."

"I can't change my past, so there's that." I downed the rest of my beer as Libby came from behind the bar. She scooted onto the stool next to mine and sighed.

"I'm so tired," she said.

"What time do you get off?" I asked.

"Ten minutes ago." She smiled big.

"Why are you still here?"

"You needed a friend, Cash."

"I appreciate that."

"Well, I must get going. I hope you figure things out with the pretty redhead."

"Do you need an escort home?" I knew she lived on the other side of town, and it was a long walk this late at night.

"No, I have my buggy. I brought in the alcohol that came off the ships for Kage. He pays me extra for doing it."

"Did you ever get your wheel fixed?"

"No. I can't really afford to pay someone. It's still wobbly, but the horses manage to pull it. It will have to do for now."

"I can look at it." I would do anything to help Libby because she was a good woman. I knew she lived alone and struggled with things sometimes after her brother left town.

"That would be wonderful. I don't have the money now, but I could pay you in installments."

"Unnecessary. Is your carriage outback?" I asked.

"It is." She smiled. "But you don't have to—"

"Let's go look." I stood up and took her hand. She slid off the barstool and followed me through the bar.

Once we were outside, Libby grabbed a lantern on the walkway, and I wondered what she was doing.

"So we can see," she said.

"Good idea." We went around the back of the bar and walked up to her carriage. One of her horses neighed when it saw me.

"Hey, Benny Boy." I ran my hand down his soft mane. "I missed you too, buddy."

"I will never understand the bond you have with my horse."

"He's a powerful male like me. We tend to stick together," I said with a wink. She laughed and shook her head. "Which wheel is it?"

"The back one." She walked around the back of the carriage and held the lantern down by the broken wheel.

Crouching down, I ran my fingers down the inside and could feel the wood had a crack in it.

"I hate to say it, but you need a new wheel. This one is cracked and warped. It won't last much longer."

"Great. Well, I guess I will start saving up for it." She sighed. "Thank you, Cash."

"No problem."

I said my goodbyes to Benny, and we walked back to the front of the building. As we approached, I saw the back of Zayn and Cinder as they were leaving. Together.

"Shit…"

"I'm sorry, Cash." Libby hung the lantern back where it came from.

"It's okay. You should be careful going home, Libby."

"I will. Thanks again." She smiled kindly and walked back around the building.

Not wanting to bump into Zayn and Cinder, I wandered towards the other end of town because the walk was twenty minutes longer. I could gale back to the portal from there.

As I walked the dark streets with only my thoughts, images of Cinder's beautiful face kept popping into my head. Her light red hair and her freckles. Her smiling, her laughing, her just being happy.

My friend better take good care of her.

Chapter 17

Cinder

My chest felt like I was being squeezed to death as the pain radiated through it. Seeing the man that I want more than anything, walk out of the bar with another woman made my heart stop working.

This was a horrible feeling that I had only felt once before—the morning my sister told me our mother was gone. Heartbreak, that's what this was. I was heartbroken.

"Are you okay?" Zayn asked. I had stopped walking and was staring at a closed door and didn't even realize it.

"Can you take me home, please?" my voice cracked coming out.

"Of course. Let's go tell the others first." I nodded as we walked toward where our friends were.

"I'm going to take Cinder home," Zayn said as we approached the table.

"Already?" Cali's beautiful blue eyes looked sad.

"Are you okay, Cin?" Ember asked.

"I'm fine. I've just had a long day."

"Don't forget you have training in the morning." Val smiled big at me. "I'm going to teach you how to mind converse and Cash is going to give you axe training."

"Oh, that's outstanding. You're going to love that, Cin. It was one of my favorite things to learn." Ember smiled big.

"That would be wonderful. Thank you." I smiled at my sister and her mate, but on the inside, I was screaming. I didn't want Cash anywhere near me.

Ember stood up and hugged me. "Are you *really* okay?" she asked in a whisper.

"I'm fine." I pulled away with a big smile, pretending to be okay. "I'm just tired."

"Okay. I'll see you tomorrow."

Zayn said his goodbyes, and we left the saloon.

We walked outside the wards and didn't say much. He galed me back to the portal, and we stepped on it. With a swoosh, we landed back in Ashbern. I didn't speak as we entered the manor.

"I had fun tonight," Zayn said.

I nodded as we ascended the stairs.

Zayn fell in step next to me. "Are you okay?"

"Yes. No. I don't know."

"Do you want to talk about it?" I stopped walking and met the Angel's eyes as mine filled with tears.

I took a seat on the top stair and put my face in my hands. After a few seconds, I felt Zayn set next to me. He rubbed his hand down my back to comfort me. I looked up at him as tears fell from my eyes.

My hands started flailing about in the air as I spoke, "I'm just sad right now, Zayn. I don't know what to think. Cash used to be so attentive to me but has been avoiding me for days. I don't know what I did or what I said. Maybe I'm a terrible kisser. Do you think that's what it is? I hope not, because then how would I get experience in kissing if I'm not actually kissing? He has probably kissed plenty of women, and I didn't know what I was doing and then tonight he was super nice and called me Cinnamon a bunch of times and smiled at me and—"

"Hold on. Slow down." Zayn grabbed both of my arms and looked me in the face. "Take a breath."

Taking a deep breath, I blew it out slowly.

"Again." I did what he said, and I did it again.

"Okay. I'm good."

"My room is right here. Do you want to talk?"

I nodded. He took my hand and we stood up.

Zayn's room was right next to the stairs. He opened the door, and I followed him inside. Seeing a chair, I immediately plopped into it.

"Would you like some water?" he asked.

My eyes wandered over to the minibar—alcohol sounded better.

"Wine please."

Zayn walked over to the bar and poured me a glass of wine and handed it to me. I downed the whole thing and handed it back.

"More."

"Cinder, I don't think—"

"More please."

Zayn grabbed the bottle and poured more wine into my glass. He stood there patiently waiting for me to be ready to talk.

"I'm a fool, Zayn."

"You are not a fool."

"I am–for thinking that Cash would want someone like me."

"There is nothing wrong with you, Cin."

"Then why is he doing this?" I looked up as tears streamed down my face.

Zayn set the wine on the floor, kneeled beside me, and took my hand. "I'm sure there is a perfectly good explanation for it."

Blinking back tears, I downed my wine and held my glass out again.

"I have never seen you drink this much. I don't think that's wise." Shoving the glass further into his face, he took it with a sigh. He stood up and refilled it, then took the bottle back to the bar.

"Everything was perfect. I don't know what happened, Zayn."

"Have you tried talking to Cash? He's a good listener."

"I did. He said he couldn't tell me anything, so I don't know what to do."

Zayn swallowed and shook his head.

"Have you talked to Ember about it?"

"Not really." I downed my wine and stood up. My insides were warm. "Should I?"

Waiting for his answer, I made my way over to the bar and picked up the prettiest decanter. I didn't know what he filled it with, but I didn't care.

"I think you should. She may have better answers for you. Umm, that's brandy."

"I don't care." I filled my glass with the light brown liquid and drank it. It was warm going down. "Oh, this isn't that bad."

"Shit," Zayn muttered as I refilled my glass.

I turned around too fast and my head was slightly spinning, so I made my way over to Zayn's bed. Setting my glass down on his nightstand, I crawled on and then picked my glass up.

Zayn let out a sigh and ran his hand through his hair. He came and sat on the edge of the bed.

"I don't know what else to say, Cinder."

I took a sip of the drink.

"This is actually delicious, Zayn."

"It's because you're already buzzed."

"I think I could get used to this." I giggled uncontrollably for a minute and then started crying. Zayn rubbed his hand on my arm, and I downed the apple brandy. My insides were on fire as I swallowed it. I stuck my tongue out to blow the hotness away.

"Okay, that's enough." Zayn took my glass from me and set it on the nightstand.

"Can you get Noreen for me?" I asked.

"Of course." Zayn stood up and headed toward the door. "I'll be right back."

Zayn left the room, and I wiped the tears from my face. My head was spinning slightly, so I laid down and got comfortable. I nuzzled into his pillow and relaxed.

Zayn

Walking down to Noreen's room, I was pissed off at Ember. She caused this mess, and I was stuck in the middle. I had been doing everything I could to make Cinder happy after she told me she was lonely. I didn't mind, but Ember should have been here for this. If Cash was here, I would tell him to get his head out of his ass and get his woman out of my bed.

I knocked on Noreen's door. No answer. I thought about the schedule. It was her weekend off so I knew she went back home to the Elven land. "Shit!" I turned around and headed back.

Opening the door to my room, I saw Cinder had laid down. With a sigh, I headed over to her. She was sleeping soundly, so I pulled the blankets up over her and made my way to the minibar. Pouring myself some apple brandy, I took a sip and grabbed an extra blanket out of the closet.

Setting the glass on the table, I made a makeshift bed in the chair because there was no way I was sleeping next to Cinder. That would be awkward, especially since she's in love with one of my good friends. I was hoping she figured that out sooner rather than later.

It was late summer, and the nights get cold in Ashbern, so I threw a log on the fire before taking a seat in the chair. I ran my hand through my hair and sat back with a sigh. Grabbing my brandy, I took a swig as I watched the fire burn. I turned the oil lamp down, so I had just enough light to read. After picking up my book, I opened it to where I left off. I eventually fell asleep with it in my hands.

Chapter 18

Ember

Lying in bed with Val, I was snuggled up close to his side, my head in the crook of his arm. It was early morning, and I was dreading getting out of bed because I knew I had to tell Cinder what I said to Cash. I couldn't let it go unsaid any longer.

"I don't want to tell her, Val. She is going to be so mad at me."

"She will, but she will work through her emotions and will eventually forgive you." Lifting his hand, he pushed my hair out of my face.

"I know but—"

There was a knock on the door.

"It's Zayn. He said he wants to talk to you."

Stumbling from the bed, I sighed as I headed to the door and opened it.

"Hey, Softy."

His face was stone cold. He was upset and I immediately wondered what happened.

"Come get your sister out of my bed."

"What?" Confusion ran through me as ten different scenarios played in my head all at once.

Zayn stepped into our room, and I shut the door.

"Don't give me that face, Ember. I didn't touch her." He ran a hand through his shaggy hair and sighed.

"I know you wouldn't, but how did she end up in your room?"

"She was upset, and we got to talking and she just kept drinking and crying over Cash. She fell asleep in my bed, so I covered her up and slept in the chair."

"Thank you for taking care of her."

"Don't thank me. I did it for her, not you." His face was angry.

"Zayn, I—"

"Don't, I don't want to hear it. Just come get your sister out of my bed so I can get on with my damn day!"

I let out an enormous sigh as he opened the door. He looked back over his shoulder at me. "You tell her what you said to Cash—today—or I will." He slammed the door when he left.

"Shit!" I stomped my foot.

Looking over at Val, I was waiting for an 'I told you so' but he didn't say anything.

"I have to fix this." I shook my head as a million thoughts flew through it.

Val hopped off the bed and strolled over to me. Putting his hands around my waist, he pulled me close to him. I laid my head on his chest and he kissed the top of it.

"I'm going to go shower, love." He let go of me and headed into the bathroom. I was on my own now.

Taking a deep breath, I opened the door and headed to Zayn's room. I knocked softly and he opened the door.

"Come in." His face told me he was still mad but was grateful I was going to take care of things, finally.

Looking over, I saw Cinder peacefully sleeping. I walked over to her and pushed her light red hair out of her freckled face.

"Hey, Cin." She didn't move.

Walking around to the other side of the big bed, I crawled onto it. I reached my hand out and shook her arm slightly.

"It's time to get up, Cin."

Her eyes fluttered open, and she stretched.

"No, it's too early." She covered her head with the heavy comforter and then quickly flung it off her. "This isn't my quilt." She bolted upright in the bed and looked around. Her eyes stopped on Zayn, and they went wide.

"I will leave you two alone," Zayn said and then left the room.

"Oh Gods. I slept with Zayn!"

"No." I laughed. "You got drunk and fell asleep. He slept in the chair."

"Thank the Gods." She rubbed her eyes and then looked at me.

"We need to talk, Cin."

"Okay." She gave me a half smile and then yawned. "As long as you talk quietly, my head hurts."

"I need to tell you something and you have to promise me, no matter what I say, that you won't leave Castleva."

"Why would I leave?"

"Because what I need to say is going to make you mad."

"I already know, Em. I saw Cash leave with that bartender last night. That's why I got drunk."

"Oh. That's not—"

"It's okay. I will eventually get over it," she said with a sad face.

I took a deep breath and blew it out slowly.

"That's not what I was going to tell you."

"Oh. What is it then?"

Her emerald-green eyes bored into mine. I was about to break her heart and it broke mine thinking about it. I decided to rip the bandage off quickly.

"I said some things to Cash, and that's the reason he's been acting the way he has been."

"What did you say to him?"

I swallowed hard as I tried to come up with the words.

"Remember the day we fought about you going to Direbreak without me?"

"Yeah." Her face had gone blank.

"Well, after Val and I left your room, we ran into Cash in the hallway. He was on his way to your room." She stared at me, and I swallowed. "I told him you were a virgin and that he should take his time with you."

Her face softened and she let out a breath she had been holding. "It's okay. I already told him that." Her face paled as she blew out a breath slowly. "Can you get Cali to come heal me? My head is pounding, and my stomach is queasy."

"That's not all I said. I dishonored him, Cin." My heart raced as the words fell out of my mouth.

"What do you mean you dishonored? How?" she asked.

"I basically called him a man whore."

"What?" She jumped up off the bed. "What exact words did you say, Ember?" Her face was now angry.

"I told him I knew he was no saint and that I knew he had slept with plenty of women."

She glared at me, her eyes filling with tears.

"Why would you say that?"

"I was just trying to look out for you."

"I'm a grown-ass woman. I don't need you to look out for me."

"I'm sorry, Cin. Ever since mom died—"

"Get out, Ember."

"Cin, wait."

"Get out!"

I looked at her beautiful face as tears rolled down her cheeks. I had broken her heart.

Getting up, I made my way to the door and left. I saw Zayn leaning against the wall.

"How did it go?" he asked.

I wiped tears from my cheeks.

"Not good. Can you get Cali? Cinder has a class with Val in thirty minutes, and she's queasy."

"Of course."

"Thanks, Zayn." I started walking toward Cash's room. I had one more conversation to have.

"Hey, Demon Spawn," he said. I turned around to a smiling Zayn. "I love you and I'm proud of you." More tears filled my eyes.

"Thanks, Softy. I love you, too." I turned back around and continued my journey.

I made sure my face was free of all tears before I knocked on Cash's door.

"Do you ever wear a shirt?" I asked as he opened it.

"Good morning to you too, Ember." I stepped into the room and shut the door behind me.

"I need to apologize to you, Cash."

"You already did." He grabbed a shirt and slid it on.

"No, a genuine apology."

"I forgave you days ago, Ember. There truly is no need." He smiled.

"I told Cinder what I said to you," I blurted.

He plopped down on the bed and his eyes went wide. "Oh."

"Yeah. I made her angry enough that she kicked me out of Zayn's room. So, I figured I would come talk to you and tell you I'm sorry. I royally screwed things up."

His face looked like he was thinking about something for a minute. Then he nodded.

"Apology accepted." He looked down at the ground.

"You're a damn good man, Cash. I was just protecting my sister."

"I know. Val and Zayn said as much. That's why I forgave you days ago."

"Then why are you not grinning like a fool and eating? You've been very un-Cash like and none of us know how to deal with that."

He laughed and a small smile crept onto his face.

"Being a King's Guard is lonely, Ember. When I left my family, I had a hard time transitioning. I slept with a lot of women that first year, but if I knew I was going to meet Cinder, I wouldn't have."

"Everyone has a past. I wasn't a virgin when I met Val, and I know he wasn't either."

"He definitely wasn't." Cash grinned, the way he used to. "Shut up, Cash."

"You deserved that." He laughed.

"I did." I smiled and took a seat on the bed next to him. "I'm really sorry."

"It's okay. I'm okay. I just have some things to work through. Personal shit."

I was going to tell him to be kind to my sister, or start seeing her again, but my meddling had already caused enough drama, so I kept my mouth shut, for once.

"Take all the time that you need, but at least eat something while you're doing it." I smiled as I stood up.

"Thanks, Ember." Cash rose from the bed and pulled me in for a hug.

"You're welcome. I have to go shower. I'll see you later."

"Bye," he said as I shut the door and went back to my room.

Chapter 19

Cinder

"Get out!" I screamed.

Ember stared at me for a few seconds before she got up and left the room.

Tears poured down my face as I thought about my sister ruining my happiness. My heart raced and I couldn't breathe. As I gasped for air, my stomach felt uneasy. I ran to the bathroom and fell to my knees in front of the toilet and hurled.

After about ten minutes of puking up my soul, I laid down on the bathroom floor. Tears streamed out of my eyes as memories of Cash from the last few days came flooding back to me. Everything was her fault. Cash was avoiding me because of her.

Hard sobs came out of me while my body convulsed. I heard the door creak, and looking through blurry eyes, I saw two figures staring at me. One of them kneeled next to me.

"I'm going to heal you, so you won't be sick anymore, sweetie." Cali's voice was sweet and gentle. She laid her hands on my back, and warmth spread through my whole body as she cured my hangover.

More sobs came out of me as she took a seat on the floor. She pushed my hair out of my face and rubbed my back as I cried.

"Do you want me to heal your emotions?" Zayn asked. "You have a class with Val in twenty minutes. The effects will last for the whole day if I give you a good enough dose."

"Can you give me just enough to get off the floor? I don't want to be without emotions."

"Of course." Zayn kneeled beside me and placed his hand on my cheek. The warmth of his magic spread through my body and settled.

"Thank you," I whispered.

"I'm going to go take a shower in Cali's room. Take all the time you need, Cinder," Zayn said before he left the room.

Cali stroked my hair as I laid there for a while. My chest felt better. The sadness that broke my heart had eased, but it was still there, ready to deplete me at a moment's notice. My emotions felt off—not really numb, but masked—like they were there and waiting to come back and eat me alive.

"Do you want me to tell Val that you can't come to practice today?" she asked.

"No." I set up and wiped my face. "I'll go. Thank you for helping me."

"You're welcome. I'm here anytime you need me, sweetie." She smiled kindly before standing up. She offered me a hand and helped me off the floor. "You may want to change first," Cali said as we exited.

We said our goodbyes in the hallway, and I went down to my room. I threw on pajama pants and a top. I didn't bother brushing my hair or anything because I really didn't care what anyone thought. After a quick bathroom break, I headed downstairs. I made my way out of the manor and around the back.

It was a warm summer's day as I crossed the fields to the gym. I was jealous of the happiness I heard coming from the birds that were singing their morning praises. I wanted that kind of happiness again. If I knew it was going to be ripped away from me so bluntly, I would have savored every second.

Opening the door to the training center, I went inside and headed down to where I usually met Valarian.

"Good morning," he said as I staggered into the room. "If I knew it was pajama day, I would have worn mine."

"Sorry, Val."

"No need to be sorry. You look... comfy." He tilted his head and smiled.

I giggled. "Thanks."

"Are you ready to get started?" he asked, and I nodded. "Perfect. Take a seat on the floor."

I took a seat right where I was standing and crossed my legs. I put my elbows on my knees and leaned into my fists.

"So, we're going to work on you wielding your thoughts to me. Don't put your shield down while we do this. When you want to say something to me, think about me and then say it in your head. Think about saying it to me. Does that make sense?"

I nodded.

Can you hear me?

Yes. That's weird. Is this what you hear all day?

When people don't shield, yes. He laughed lightly.

That would suck.

It does sometimes, but most know how to shield. The worst is young children. Their mind goes a mile a minute, kind of like Ember's. Hearing her name, I looked up at him. *So, first, I want you to think of a color.*

Why did she do this? I asked, completely ignoring his request.

It wasn't intentional, Cinder.

She said you were with her.

I was. He took a seat on the floor and crossed his legs.

What happened? I asked.

Val sighed. *She was mad at me for wanting to train you. She saw Cash and took it upon herself to make sure you were protected.*

Why does she care what I do with my love life? I'm a grown woman.

Sometimes when you lose people you love, you hold on tight and try to protect the others in your life. Ember wasn't trying to hurt your relationship with Cash. In her own way, she was trying to help.

I just don't understand why she said anything to begin with. A hard breath of air escaped me.

She told me she wanted him to take his time with you. She was just trying to protect you. I'm not saying she wasn't in the wrong—she was.

I don't know if I can forgive her, Val.

To Ember, you not forgiving her would be a far worse punishment than death. She may be a powerful warrior on the outside, but on the inside, she's a hot mess. I know this because for weeks I heard her thoughts.

I laughed lightly. *I know she is.*

Her vulnerability is one of the many reasons I love her. He smiled sweetly.

I love her so much, Val.

I know you do, and she knows that, too.

Would she still be like this if our parents didn't die?

I think she would. That's just who she is as a person. She loves deeply.

I sighed. *Oh, blue.*

What?

You told me to think of a color. Blue is my favorite.

I really don't think you need the practice, Cinder. You're a natural.

Thanks. I smiled proudly. *Better than Ember?*

Yes, but don't tell her I said that. She'll kick my ass.

I laughed as he stood up and gave me his hand. I took it and he pulled me up from the floor.

"Do you want unsolicited advice?" he asked.

"Sure."

"You should talk to Cash. He was torn up over what she said. He wasn't mad that she said it, he was mad at himself since he believes it to be true."

"I appreciate you. I couldn't ask for a better brother." I reached out and gave him a hug.

"And I couldn't ask for a better sister. Unlike my blood sister, you can cook."

I giggled.

"Oh, that reminds me. What is your favorite flavor?"

He rubbed his hand across his chin while he thought about it. "Most definitely chocolate. Why?"

"It's a secret." I smiled big.

"Well, I hope I get something with chocolate in it."

"Maybe." I smiled mischievously as he opened the door to the outside.

"Good job today. I have to go check on my mate. Don't forget that you have axe throwing with Cash."

I let out a large sigh. "I don't want to see him right now."

"Why not? I figured you would want to work things out with him."

I just shrugged and bit my lip. I wasn't about to tell him I saw Cash leave with the bartender.

"I'm sorry, Cinder. I usually do the axe classes, but when the king set yours up, I gave Cash that assignment because you both were good then."

"It's okay."

"I can have it changed for next week if you decide. Just let me know."

"Thanks, Val." I smiled lightly, trying to hide my confused mind.

"Head toward the outdoor training center. He'll be there waiting for you."

Valarian took off toward the manor and I headed the opposite way. Hearing wings flapping, I looked up and saw Arna swoop in. She landed next to me and squawked.

"Hi, Arna." I reached my hand up and rubbed her soft feathers. "I know you can hear me, but I can't hear you. Can I vent for a minute, and you listen but not tell Ember?"

She squawked.

"I hope that's a yes."

She squawked.

"I'm really mad at her, Arna. She said some things that ruined my relationship with Cash." Arna tilted her head like she was listening attentively. "I don't know if I can forgive her, but a big part of me knows I couldn't live without her being in my life."

She squawked.

"I know she only did what she did because she loves me, but that doesn't make it right. I still must work through this on my own before I can speak to her. Do you think that's selfish of me?"

She squawked and ruffled her feathers. I felt like she was agreeing with me.

"See, I don't think it's selfish either. Thank you for listening, Arna." I petted her head and she vibrated. "I'll talk to you later."

She squawked, flapped her wings, and flew off. I continued walking toward the training area.

"Hey," Cash said as I shuffled up. He had a light smile on his face. "Are you wearing pajamas?"

"Yep."

"Should I have worn them, too?"

Visions of him leaving the bar with another woman flashed in my head.

"Nope." I narrowed my eyes at him. I was not amused.

"Okay. Well, are you ready to become a lethal weapon?"

He held out an axe to me.

More visions of the blonde-haired beauty went through my mind.

Maybe I should throw the axe at him. Checking my shields, they were super tight. I decided murder wasn't on my agenda for today since I wasn't strong enough to drag a body anywhere.

Especially Cash's big, sexy body. With a deep breath and a sigh, I took the axe.

"I'm ready."

"Great! I love throwing axes, so this will be fun."

Completely ignoring his excitement, I decided I wanted to clear the air before I started.

"Ember told me what happened." The light smile on his face dropped at my words.

"Yeah. She came to my room earlier and told me you knew."

"I'm sorry she made you feel the way she did, Cash."

"She didn't do anything but make me realize you deserved better."

"Why would you think that?"

"Because what she said was true, and you deserve better than that. I would never dishonor you, Cinder."

Usually, I was open about my feelings, maybe too open at times. I wanted to tell him I didn't care what he had done in his past. We all have pasts and sometimes we regret things we have done, and I would never use that against a person. I knew he was a good man, and I also knew he wouldn't do anything to intentionally hurt me, but all I kept picturing was him leaving the bar with that pretty Lycan bartender.

Deep down inside, I knew he only left with her because he was hurting inside, too. Even if he didn't want to dishonor me, it still hurt thinking about them together. Afraid that tears might roll out of my eyes if I spoke about it, I just nodded instead.

"So, are we good?" he asked.

Looking up at his beautiful blue eyes, how could I say no? For once, I would have to hide my feelings so I could get my training done.

"Yeah, we're good." I held up my axe to him. "How do I use this thing?"

"I thought you would never ask!" A real Cash smile came across his face and my heart just about leaped out of my chest.

Taking deep, slow breaths, I pushed my feelings for him aside and smiled. He held up his axe with one hand and pointed to the target.

"So, the goal is to throw your axe and hit that target in the middle. I'm going to show you how to hold it first, then—"

I lifted the axe above my head and flung it toward the target. It landed almost in the middle.

Looking over at Cash, his mouth fell wide open.

"Should I go again?" I asked.

"Holy shit! How did you do that?"

"I don't know, I just threw it." I shrugged my shoulders.

"I think axes may be your thing, Cinnamon." He smiled big as he retrieved my axe from the target.

"Thanks." I pretended that him using my nickname again didn't give me goosebumps.

"If Ember saw you do that, she would be super proud of you," he said as he handed me back my axe.

Part of me felt proud because my whole life, all I wanted, was Ember's approval. I wanted her to be proud of me. But the part of me that was still mad at her didn't want to acknowledge that right now. Cash must have seen the sour puss face I had because his smile dropped.

"Sorry."

"It's okay. I just don't want to talk about her right now."

"She didn't do anything wrong, Cinder. She was just looking out for you."

"I don't care."

"She just made me realize that—"

"I'm not speaking to her, so I don't want to talk about her." I threw my axe again, and it hit close to dead center.

Cash grabbed my axe off the target. "Wow. Good job!"

"Thanks." He handed me the axe again.

"I really think you should talk to her."

"It's not your concern, Cash." I threw the axe again and this time, hit the bullseye. I smiled big as pride filled me.

"Damn! Nice." He retrieved my axe again.

"Thanks." I took my axe from him.

"You really should talk to Ember."

"I'm done." I threw my axe into the dirt and turned away.

"Cinder, wait."

"No. I said I didn't want to talk about her, yet you insist on doing it."

"Only because I care about you, and I know how much you love her."

"We aren't together anymore, Cash. So, like I said, it's not your concern." I put my hands on my hips as I glared at him.

"Do you want me to have Val change your class so he can train you instead, since we aren't together anymore?"

"Actually, I think that would be best."

He looked hurt as his eyes wandered over my face.

"Your training is done for today." He turned and left. My heart cracked with every step he took.

Part of me wanted to stop him as I watched his sandy blonde hair sway lightly with each stomping step he took, but I think staying away from him until I healed was best. If I ever healed.

Chapter 20

Cinder

Thoughts swarmed through my head like killer bees buzzing while they looked for the threat to their hive. They were loud and dangerous, and I wasn't used to dealing with them. A part of me wanted to find Ember so I had someone to talk to about my feelings, but I definitely wasn't ready to patch things up with her yet. It had only been a couple of hours.

Trying to focus on my day with Zayn, I pushed my feelings aside as I stepped through the door of the manor. Glancing over into the study, I saw him sitting in a chair, reading.

"Oh, hey." Zayn smiled and then his eyes went wide as he saw my clothing.

"Hi." I held my head high like everything in the world was perfect as I strolled up to him. Even though I was wearing pajamas.

"Is your class over already?" Zayn asked, as he looked at the clock.

"Yep." I smiled, completely hiding the fact that it was only over because I got mad, and possibly hurt Cash's feelings.

"Are you ready to go then?" he asked as he shut his book.

"I'm ready when you are."

"Are you going to wear that?" He looked down at my pajamas.

"No, I have to change."

"Wear something light because it'll be hot," he said. "I'm going to change into something lighter, too. I'll come to your room in about thirty minutes."

"Okay."

Quickly going to my room, I took the fastest shower of my life. I threw on a light white sundress with thin straps and a pair of white strappy sandals.

Looking in the mirror, I was about to braid my hair when I caught sight of the necklace hanging from my neck. An overwhelming feeling filled my chest as I laid my hand on it. A single tear fell from my eye, and I wiped it away. Deciding that I shouldn't be wearing it anymore, I reached up and unclasped it. Heading out of the bathroom, I set it on my dresser and glared at it. I had no clue how long I stared at it before a knock on my door brought me back to reality.

"Come in," I said.

The door opened and Zayn strolled in. He was wearing a black t-shirt with brown slacks and had two swords strapped on his back.

"Your dress is cute." He smiled big. "Are you ready to... oh. What's wrong?" he asked.

"Nothing, I was just about to braid my hair." I spun my back to him, so he didn't see my face, and headed into the bathroom.

Grabbing the brush, I ran it through my wet hair as Zayn entered.

"Do you want me to help you?" he asked

"Do you know how to braid hair?"

"I do. Cali taught me."

"Did she teach you so you could braid her hair?"

"No. I lost a bet with Cash and had to learn."

"Do I even want to know what that was about?" I shook my head and giggled.

"You don't." Zayn smiled wickedly. "So, do you want me to?"

"It would save us time."

Zayn smiled as he took the brush from my hand. He ran it lightly over my head and it felt good. I closed my eyes as each stroke made my head tingle.

He set the brush down and divided my hair into three sections. Shivers ran down my spine as his fingers grazed the nape of my neck. I closed my eyes again as I thought about how Cash's hands would feel.

"What scent is your shampoo?" he asked, bringing me out of my visions.

"Umm, coconut and hibiscus. Ember got it at the market."

He leaned in and took a sniff of my hair and my breath caught.

"It smells delicious."

"Thanks." I swallowed hard as I blushed.

"I need a tie," he said as he held out his hand.

Picking up the tie off the bathroom sink, I handed it to him over my shoulder. I felt the slight tug as he tied off the end.

"All done." He put both hands on my shoulders as he looked at my reflection in the mirror.

Watching his smiling face, a small part of me wished it was Cash's face and I immediately felt like an asshole.

"Thank you, Zayn."

"Turn around and have a look."

Facing my back toward the mirror, I glanced over my shoulder and looked at the braid.

"Wow, you're better than I am at braiding."

"Thanks. Don't tell Ember. She busts my balls enough as it is."

"I won't be speaking to her anytime soon," I said.

"I really think you should talk to her."

I held up my hand, stopping him before he went on a rant.

"I appreciate your concern, but I will speak to her in my own time and only when I am ready."

"I respect that, Cinder. I agree with you, and I won't mention it again." He smiled big. "Are you ready to go?"

"I am." My body relaxed, knowing that Zayn wasn't going to bring it up again, and I gave him another fake smile.

"Come on, then." He nodded his head and left the bathroom.

Holding my fake smile in place, we made our way out of the manor and headed toward the portal. Zayn willed the portal to go, and we swooshed through the air as the rush hit me. Excitement filled my body, and I embraced it. Then we landed in the country of Cerulean.

There were two female guards at the portal and I smiled at them.

The sun was bright, and the air was hot as I stepped off the portal. My feet sunk in the sand as the smell of the sea hit me. Looking around at the beautiful, white, sandy beaches surrounding me, my mouth gaped open.

"This is amazing," I said. I took a deep breath, inhaling the salty sea air. It was very relaxing, and I immediately felt better. I was going to try hard to not think of Cash on this trip.

"Asher wants to go swimming before summer is over. We should go here."

"That would be amazing. Can we, Zayn?" I asked.

"I will talk to the group and set up a day."

"Thank you!" I clasped my hands together as more excitement filled me.

"Come on." He smiled big as we walked across the sand. "So, because of the amount of water that runs between all the aisles, we can't gale very far. We will have to walk most of the way, but it's not far."

"That's fine." I watched a crab cross right in front of me and I smiled. My eyes wandered up to the big, exotic trees it went under. "What trees are those?" I asked curiously.

"Those are called palm trees."

"They're weird, but beautiful. I have seen nothing quite like it. What are those green balls hanging from them?"

"Those are coconuts." Zayn laughed.

"Why are they green then? I have only seen brown coconuts at Mazuria Market."

"They aren't mature yet. Once they are mature, they turn brown."

"Oh, there's a mature one on the ground." I sauntered over to it and picked it up. "Look." I held it up for Zayn to see.

"Have you ever had coconut water?" he asked

"No, I don't know what that is," I said as I made my way back to him.

"Do you want to try it?"

"Absolutely!" I looked down at the brown coconut in my hands. "How do we open it?"

"You don't want the brown ones. You want one of the green ones that is just turning brown. They have the most water in them."

Looking around on the ground, there were only a couple, and none were green.

"These are all brown, Zayn."

"We need one from the tree."

I looked up at all the hanging coconuts, they were really far up.

"How will we get one?" I asked.

Zayn smiled brightly as a gust of wind from his wings hit me. They were solid black with blue and green highlights, just like Cash's. He flapped his wings and I watched with a gaping mouth as he ascended to the top of the tree and plucked a coconut from it. Slowly lowering himself back to the ground, he landed right in front of me.

"This one is perfect," he said as he held the coconut out to me.

"That was amazing, Zayn. I can't believe you just did that!" Adoration filled me as I stared at his face, which was gleaming with pride.

"Angels are the best species," he said with a wink.

"I agree. So, how are we going to open it? It took Ember an hour to open one that I bought at the market. She was mad at me." A mischievous smile played on my face.

"That's easy. Hold out both hands." I dropped my coconut and did as he said and held my hands out in front of me. He set his coconut in them and took a step back. My eyes widened as he pulled his sword from his back.

"Oh," I whimpered. "You're going to slice it?"

"Are you good with that, Cinder?"

"Yes," I whispered.

"Do you trust me?"

"Yes." This time I think I just mouthed the words.

"Then hold it far away from yourself and don't move."

Zayn locked eyes with me for a split second before he swiftly sliced the coconut, and I gasped as the top of it flew off.

"There you go," he said nonchalantly.

"What? How?"

"I told you, Angels are the best." He smiled proudly.

"Wow. You are amazing!"

"Drink it." Zayn smiled as he watched me. His sparkling blue eyes seemed to bore into my soul, like they knew I had secrets.

Quickly averting my eyes, I peeked down inside of the coconut and saw some liquid. Slowly lifting it up to my mouth, I took a sip.

"Oh." The juice had a weird taste, but in a good way. It was slightly sweet, which surprised me. I actually thought it was going to taste like water, and I felt a little dumb when it didn't. I wasn't going to confess that to Zayn, though.

"Do you like it?" he asked.

"It's good. I didn't expect it to be slightly sweet. Do you want a sip?" I asked.

He took the coconut and held it up to his lips, and I watched as he took a drink. A small part of me wondered if Zayn was a good kisser as he handed it back to me. My breathing got a little heavy at the thought as he wiped his wet lips with the back of his hand. Zayn was a very strong, and exceptionally sweet male—he also paid attention to me, and I liked it.

"Come on." He nodded his head in the direction we were going. "You can drink the rest on the way."

We continued walking on the beach for a few miles as I finished my drink. The warm sand felt squishy under my feet as I thought about how nice Zayn was for doing this. An intrusive thought came to my mind as I wondered if I was developing a little crush on him, but I quickly put the thought out of my head as I took the last sip of coconut water.

"I'm done with this, Zayn. What shall I do with it?"

"Just toss it on the ground. A coconut crab will probably eat it. That way, it doesn't go to waste."

I tossed the coconut to the side under some trees, hoping one would find it.

"So, when does the beach end?" I asked.

"It doesn't end. The sand covers the entire land mass here. It's a giant winding beach."

"What?" I stopped walking and looked around. "That is amazing. I would love to live somewhere like this."

"You would get tired of sand in your shoes, and other places," he said with a wink, and I giggled as I thought about getting sand in my underwear.

"I'm already tired of the sand in my sandals."

"You can take them off, Cinder."

"Can I?"

"Yes." He laughed. "Just use my arm as leverage."

I grabbed his arm and held it to keep myself steady. Noticing immediately how big his muscles were, I tried not to focus on it. I lifted my foot and took off one of my sandals, and then the other.

"Thanks, Zayn." I reached down and picked my sandals up.

He smiled and we continued our journey until we came upon a small town with little colorful canopy covered stands.

"Welcome to Anahita market!" A woman said as we entered. I smiled at her kindness.

"The place we are going is over here. It's crowded since it's the weekend so stay by me." I felt Zayn's hand brush against the inside of mine and then grip it.

Looking down, it confused me, but I liked it, so I tightened my hand into his. A smile was on my face as we walked.

Making our way through the crowd, I noticed everyone showed a lot of skin, which wasn't shocking because it was hot here.

"Here we are." He pulled me up to a stand and let go of my hand.

Looking around, there were tons of colored pictures that were beautiful. My eyes landed on one that was a starry night sky with a pair of white Angel wings in the middle, and I thought of Cash. Before I had a chance to scold myself, a sultry woman's voice brought my attention away.

"It's not every day that you see a sexy Angel standing in the middle of town."

Glancing over my shoulder, I watched as a very tan, and tall, exotic looking woman strolled up to us. Her hair was dark and up in a high ponytail, that was braided down her back.

She was wearing a pair of multicolored, baggy pants that hung super low on her hips—a kind I had never seen before—and a matching colorful top that stopped not far past her breast with a pair of gold shoes.

She was covered in gold jewelry—three necklaces, lots of bracelets, hoop earrings, a hoop in her nose, and even a hoop in her belly button. My eyes widened when I saw it. Looking back up, she was absolutely gorgeous, and she mesmerized me.

But the best thing I got to see was the Water Caster tattoo in the middle of her chest. It was an axe with waves of water—she was a King's Guard.

"Zarya, how are you, darling?" He kissed her on the cheek.

"I get a kiss from Zaynith fucking Storm. This day couldn't get any better." She smiled brightly, then her eyes wandered to me. "Oh, she is much prettier than your usual partner in crime. Where is Cash, by the way?"

"He was busy." Zayn ran a hand through his hair.

"Are you going to introduce me, Angel? Or should I do it myself?"

"Zarya Novak, this is Cinder Lavaris."

"Nice to meet you, Cinder. I wasn't lying when I said you're much prettier than Cash." She had a sweet smile on her face.

"Nice to meet you, too. I love your jewelry and your clothing. All of it is so beautiful. You're beautiful. Actually, you're gorgeous! I'm jealous, to be honest." I smiled big.

"Oh, wow. Thank you." Her smile widened. "We can get you some clothes like this before you leave, or we can get you a piercing." She winked.

"Oh. I have always wanted my ears pierced but my father said that it wasn't very ladylike, but come to find out, he wasn't even my real father anyway, he was a Changeling. So, I don't think that matters now. Oh, I bet Ember would be mad, which makes me happy because I'm mad at her right now, anyway." I clasped my hands together in excitement as Zarya's eyes widened. "Let's do it!"

"I don't know who Ember is, but I'm all about defiance." Another wink.

"Ember is my sister. We aren't speaking right now because she told Cash—"

"Cinder." My eyes met Zayn's, and he shook his head.

"Let her go, Zayn. I'm rather enjoying her rambling." Zarya tilted her head and looked at me like I was a small child doing something cute. I took a breath and slowed myself down.

Deciding that I was going to embrace my newfound freedom and make all my own decisions, I let my intentions be known.

"I would like to get a piercing today, Zayn. So, you can either come with me, or I will go by myself." I put my hands on my hips as I stood my ground.

Zayn smiled and shook his head.

"Whatever you want to do, Cinder. But you should pick out your paint colors first, so they can mix them while you get it."

"Of course." My heart raced with excitement.

Turning back toward the booth, I picked out a handful of colors. The lady behind the counter said they would be done in a bit, so I turned my attention back toward Zarya.

"Can we go now?" I asked.

"Sure." She smiled big. "Are you coming, Angel?"

Zayn sighed and ran his hand through his hair. "Yes, but I take no responsibility when Ember kills you."

Zarya smiled and walked away.

"I take full responsibility for anything I do, Zayn. Plus, we aren't speaking, so she can't kill me." I smiled big at the amount of defiance that filled me.

"Well, don't get anything too crazy or Ember will kill me. Plus, you're pretty the way you are." I blushed at Zayn's words.

A huge smile was on my face as we followed Zarya. She stopped in front of a small shop and talked to a blonde-haired woman there. Once they were done talking, she turned toward me.

"So, what are you wanting, Cinder?" Zarya asked.

"I just want earrings. Can I have small hoops?"

"Of course. Take a seat," the blonde woman said.

"Can you hold these?" I handed Zayn my sandals.

Taking a seat on the wooden stool, excitement filled me. Looking up at Zayn, he was smiling big.

"Why are you smiling?"

"I enjoy seeing you happy," he said.

"I enjoy being happy, for once." I took a deep breath as contentment filled me.

"I'm glad I could help with that." He ran his hand through his hair as I patiently waited for the woman to set up her supplies.

Ten minutes and a little archaic pain later, I had my earrings. The woman who pierced them handed me a small mirror, and I stood up from the stool.

"How do they look, Zayn? I want to know before I look."

His eyes looked back and forth between my ears.

"They're perfect, Cinder."

"Good." I held up the mirror and looked for myself. I had never felt more alive or more in control of myself than I did as I looked at the tiny gold hoops. "Oh, they are perfect!"

"I think you are ready for a tattoo now," Zarya said.

"Oh, can we, Zayn?" I looked at the Angel with pleading eyes and a pouty lip.

"Umm. One thing at a time, Cinder." Zayn chuckled. "Our paint is probably ready."

"Thank you for this, Zarya." Catching her off guard, I pulled her into a big hug.

"Oh. Well, you're welcome." She pulled back and smiled brightly at me.

"We have to go, Zarya, but I'm sure I will see you around." Zayn kissed her on the cheek, and she smiled.

"Take care of my new friend, Zayn. Bye, Cinder." Zarya winked at me before she strolled off.

Curiosity filled me and I couldn't help but ask what I had been thinking since I met Zarya.

"Are you in a relationship with her?" I asked.

"Zarya? No, it's not like that. We are just friends. Plus, I'm not her type."

"What do you mean?" I asked. A dreadful feeling came over me as I anticipated the answer. I was hoping Cash *wasn't* her type.

"She only likes women, and I think she likes you," Zayn said with a smile.

"Oh." A large breath escaped me at the relief that Cash wasn't mentioned. I also had a slight relief that Zayn wasn't seeing her, and I didn't know what that meant. But I wasn't going to analyze that right now, not while I had other questions that needed to be answered.

"Cali doesn't seem to have a gender preference. How does that work?" I asked.

"Well, some are born attracted to one or sometimes more than one. In Cali's case, she doesn't see gender. She likes people for who they are as a person, not what gender they identify as."

Zayn grabbed the paint from the woman at the stand as I thought about what I liked. The only thing I could think about was Cash with his shirt off, chopping wood. So, I was pretty sure I only liked men... or maybe just Cash. For some reason, Zayn was really growing on me. Confusion filled me as I thought about how nice and attentive he was.

On the way out of town, we stopped and got some ice cream at a little booth that was also run by a woman.

"A lot of women own shops here," I said before I licked my ice cream.

"They do." Zayn ran his tongue slowly over his ice-cream. My mouth gaped open as I stared at him. I immediately snapped it shut when I noticed what I was doing.

Still staring at him, I swallowed hard. "I'm kind of proud that I own one."

"You should be. It's an enormous accomplishment, Cinder." He smiled big. "I'm proud of you too, by the way."

Zayn took another lick, and I watched as his tongue slowly lapped up the side.

My eyes unfocused more and more with every lick that Zayn took. My imagination took over as I envisioned Cash's tongue licking ice cream. The vision took a turn when it included me covered in the ice cream and Cash licking the sticky, melted liquid off my skin. My breathing got heavy, and I had weird feelings down in my...

"Are you okay, Cinder?"

Blinking a few times, my eyes refocused on Zayn's face.

"Yes, I'm fine. Why?"

"Your cheeks are beet red."

"Oh, I think it's the heat." The actual heat was not the problem... The heat I felt for Cash was.

"As soon as we are finished, we will head home." He licked his cold treat, and I looked away before more thoughts of Cash intruded their way into my brain.

Once we were done, Zayn carried the paint as we made our way back to the portal. We were almost there when I noticed something.

"Zayn, look!" A crab was eating the chunk of coconut I threw under the tree.

"See, never a waste."

I smiled big as we passed.

We finally made it to the portal and stepped on. Zayn willed it to go, and I felt the exciting rush. Goosebumps covered my skin, and I closed my eyes as it reminded me of the goosebumps Cash gave me. When we landed back in Ashbern, it yanked me out of my happy thoughts.

"Now that you have paint, you have to decide on a name," he said as we stepped off the portal.

"Naming my booth has been hard. I just want it to be a good name."

"I'm sure whatever you choose will be great." He smiled as we walked up to the manor. I opened the door for him since his hands were full.

"Where are we putting those?" I asked.

"I figured we would stick them in the study for now." Zayn turned into the study and I followed.

He walked over to a table by the window. I dropped my sandals on the floor so I could grab some paints out of his hands.

"Thank you for today," I said.

"You're welcome. I hope you had fun."

"I did, Zayn. It was perfect." He smiled big as he set the last can of paint down.

Without even thinking, I pulled him in for a hug. His body was warm as it pressed against mine. I closed my eyes for a split second.

"Are you okay, Cinder?" I looked up at him, still in a full hug.

Locking eyes with him for a second, I blushed and looked away as I let go of the hug.

"I'm just tired and ready for dinner." I sighed.

"Okay. I'm going to go find Val. We've got guard business. I'll see you at dinner."

I nodded and smiled as he left the room.

Chapter 21

Ember

I was sitting in a field of flowers and the sun was shining down on me. I could hear birds chirping as I picked a flower from its stalk.

Thunder clouds formed above my head, so I started walking home before the rain came down. A flash of lightning hit hard, followed by a thunderous roar. Deciding I needed to get home quickly, I opened a portal in my mind to gale before the storm broke loose. It didn't work, and I couldn't understand why.

Everyone born in our world can instantaneously transport by using our minds. Mine wasn't working. I took off through the field of flowers at a light jog, trying to beat the storm. A wall of dark smoke suddenly met me.

'Oh no, not again,' I thought to myself.

Tall flowers with thorns on them shot up from the ground all around me.

A large flower opened in front of me, revealing a face inside of it. It was Erebus, the king of the Demons. He wanted me and wouldn't stop until I was his.

I reached down to grab my dagger and, as I pulled it from its sheath, it turned to ash. The Demon flower laughed in my face.

Vines started wrapping around my legs, holding me in place. I started yanking at them, trying to get them off. They were tearing into my hands and blood dripped all over the ground.

'Val, help!' I shouted to my mate, hoping he could save me.

I thrashed and screamed, trying to break free. A storm cloud came down from the sky and surrounded the area. Erebus let out a thunderous laugh as I screamed.

"Ember, wake up, my love." I woke up with my mate in my face.

Val was shaking my arms, trying to pull me out of my own personal hell. I had been having nightmares since I was killed and brought back to life by the God of Fire, Volcanis.

Erebus would never stop invading my dreams and my life until I was either his or dead.

"Val," I whispered. Leaning into him, I started crying.

"It's okay, my love. It's okay," he whispered as he ran his hands down my back.

"I'm sorry. I didn't mean to wake you again." I blinked tears out of my eyes.

"Don't ever be sorry for a nightmare, Ember. This isn't your fault." He kissed my forehead and pulled me in tight. "Do you want me to run you a hot bath?"

"Yes, that would be great." I was the luckiest woman to have such an amazing man. I leaned in and kissed him softly.

"I love you, my *hertis rote*." He laid his hand on my cheek.

"I love you, too, Val." I kissed him again, this time a little more passionately.

The kiss got steamy, and Val pulled away.

"You know we—"

Not caring what he had to say, I yanked his face back to mine. After a good make-out session and some heavy breathing, Val pulled away again.

"Don't stop, Val," I pleaded.

Locking eyes with me, he grinned widely and shoved me back onto the bed. I gasped and then giggled as I landed. Yanking my nightgown up around my waist, he pulled my panties off in one swift motion. He wasn't wasting time, and I was grateful for it.

Settling between my legs, he took his hands and spread my lips apart and then slowly lowered his mouth onto my core. I moaned at the feeling. His tongue was warm and wet as it consumed every little inch of me.

Letting go of my lips, he pulled away and I groaned in protest.

"Have we tried here?" he asked.

"No," I whispered. I knew what he was going to do, and excitement filled me. I moaned loudly as soon as I felt his strike.

His fangs pierced my lip right next to my clit and the feeling was amazing. As he sucked my blood, my back arched off the bed. A beautiful burning sensation ran through my veins, filling my body with pure bliss.

"Spread them open," he purred.

Reaching down, I spread my lips for him. He grabbed my thighs and yanked me close. He knew my body better than I did at this point, so his warm tongue was rolling around exactly the way I liked it.

The sensation of his bite was still flowing through me, lighting my body on fire in an exceptionally good way. It was the opposite of my nightmare—it was the most amazing feeling one could ever hope to have. It was completely washing away all the negative things from this past week.

His tongue rolled in circles as he gripped my thighs tightly. Reaching down, I twined my fingers into his hair, and pulled him into me, urging him to go faster.

Every cell in my body lit up as the overpowering feeling of my orgasm exploded through me. As I squirmed away, Val growled and tightened his grip on my thighs, making me feel all the sensations at their highest peak.

My orgasm ended and my muscles went loose, but he continued to lick me until I was twitching. He didn't pull away until I tried to crush him with my thighs.

Smiling big, he crawled on top of me. My wetness glistened on his lips. He slammed his mouth onto mine, entering me as we kissed.

Spreading my legs wider, I pulled my knees up as far as I could, letting him take all of me he wanted. I have already given him my heart, so what are a few more inches going to hurt?

He wrapped one of his hands around my thigh and pulled it up high as he growled. I could stay like this forever, with him inside of me. The bond we have is unbreakable.

His cock glided in and out of me while he rolled his tongue around mine. Breaking away from the kiss, he started kissing my neck, making his way to my shoulder.

The feeling was building, and I was about to come again, so I dug my nails into his back. He growled and struck out, biting me but never losing his stroke. It was rare that I got bitten twice in one day, but I had a feeling he knew I needed the extra blissfulness.

I immediately came when the venom flooded me. I felt his body tense as he sucked on my blood. He was about to come, too.

Tilting his head back, I could see a small amount of blood on his lips as he moaned and got his release. We laid there breathing heavily for a minute before we finally broke free.

"Come on." He picked me up and threw me over his shoulder. "We need to bathe." I laughed as he carried me off to the bathroom.

Val ran us a bath, and we both hopped in. He sat in the back of the bathtub, and I sat between his legs.

"What are your plans for the day, love?" he asked as he ran a washcloth over my back, cleansing me, like he always did.

"I'm going to get Cinder to talk to me."

"That sounds like a good plan to me. I hate that this has been going on for over a week."

"She needed time and I gave it to her. Her time is up. Either she is going to jump on this buggy, or I am going to run her over with it."

"That's not how the buggy metaphor works, love. You can't run people over with the buggy."

"Then I guess she will just have to hop on then."

Val laughed at my words as he pulled me close to his body. I relaxed in the hot, soapy water as it washed away the remnants of our lovemaking and my nightmare.

Chapter 22

Cinder

A week has passed since I got into an argument with Ember, and we still weren't speaking. Well, at least I wasn't speaking to her. She tried a couple times, but I completely ignored her, so she finally gave up. I have a feeling Val told her to give me some space.

All my classes were with Val now. I tried using a sword in a class with Zayn, but I wasn't good at it, so I figured I would stick with axes. Val told me I was "damn good at throwing axes" and I had never been prouder of myself. I made him promise not to tell Ember because I'll be damned if the moment that I finally get approval from her would be when wc weren't speaking.

Currently, I was carrying a basket and walking to the gardens with Zayn. I had finally come up with a name for my stand and he had suggested a picnic to celebrate.

He unfolded a blanket and spread it on the ground, then took the basket from me.

"Take a seat. Since this is your celebration, I will take care of everything," he said.

I smiled and took a seat.

This past week I had been hanging out with Zayn almost every day. We even baked together again, and I was enjoying his company. But no matter how hard I tried, Cash would never leave my mind.

My intrusive thoughts of him were like a thunderstorm that was making sure it was heard. There was no way I could avoid them, and I had given up on trying. Today, I had another plan, and I was hoping it worked, otherwise, I may look like a fool.

"I can't wait to hear the name you came up with," he said as he took a seat next to me. He crossed his legs and pulled the basket close to him then pulled random items out of it. Pouring a cup of iced tea first, he handed it to me.

"It's not that good, so don't get too excited," I said before I took a sip of tea.

"I'm sure it's perfect, Cinder."

He pulled out two plates and made us both a sandwich and a side of mixed fruit that he had cut up.

"Thanks. I wouldn't have been able to get through this last week without you," I admitted.

"No need to thank me. That's what friends do," he smiled brightly as he handed me a plate. My heart raced as I took it.

Avoiding his face, I grabbed a grape off my plate and popped it in my mouth.

"Are you okay?" he asked.

"Yes. Why?" I glanced up into his eyes.

"You just seem off today." He shrugged his shoulders as he uncrossed his legs and stretched them out in front of him. He leaned back onto one elbow and relaxed as he turned toward me. "So, what's going on?"

"What do you mean?" I asked, as I glanced away nervously.

"Cinder, look at me."

"What?" My eyes went back to his as I shoved more fruit in my mouth, afraid of what I was going to say.

"We have been hanging out every day, so I know you pretty well now."

I swallowed the bite I had taken and wiped a napkin across my face.

"I don't know what you're talking about, Zayn."

"I can tell you have something on your mind that you want to talk about, so stop being coy and just spill it."

My heart sped up as I tried to decide what I was going to do. I had been thinking about this moment for the last couple of days.

"Aren't you going to eat?" I asked, completely changing the subject.

A sly smile spread across his face, and he shook his head. "Stop avoiding it and spit it out."

Moving my plate to the side, I stretched my legs out in front of me and leaned back onto my elbow, mirroring Zayn's position. As I laid next to him, my heart raced with fear and excitement. I was about to do something that I wasn't sure he would like.

Raising my hand, I placed it on his neck, pulling his head toward mine. Leaning in close to him, I parted my lips slightly and placed a gentle kiss on him. He sat still as he let my lips move against his. After a few seconds, he pulled away.

"Oh, no." I shook my head as the feeling hit me.

"Umm, Cinder... I..." Zayn got quiet as he ran a hand through his hair.

"I'm sorry, but I had to do that to make sure and it was what I thought it was and now that I know, I don't know what I'm going to do."

"I don't know what's going on, Cinder, but you're rambling again. I think we need to talk."

Looking into his eyes, they were beautiful. He was a very handsome Angel, but he wasn't the Angel I wanted. Not the Angel I was in love with.

"I love Cash," I whispered as I looked down at the pattern on the blanket.

"What?" he asked.

"I love Cash." My eyes met his.

"Oh. Then why did you kiss me?"

"I had to see if there was anything between us."

"And?" he asked.

"And there isn't. Not on my end, anyway. I'm sorry, Zayn."

He sighed loudly and ran a hand through his hair.

"You have a way of shocking the hell out of me, Cinder. I adore you for it." He grabbed my hand, pulled it to his mouth, and kissed it.

"I'm sorry, Zayn. Please don't be mad at me."

"I'm not mad. I'm relieved."

"What?" Confusion settled on my face as I noticed how relieved he looked.

Am I that undesirable? I thought.

"Listen, I love you, but it's like the way I love Ember. You are my buddy's girl, even if you both are too stupid to see that. Respectfully, of course."

"I don't understand. I thought you liked me."

Shaking my head, I looked down at my hands. I was relieved that he didn't like me, but I was also slightly hurt. It made me feel like a broken toy that no one wanted to play with.

"Look at me," he said as he grabbed my chin, forcing my face toward his. "I know what you're thinking and there is nothing wrong with you, Cinder. You're a beautiful girl, but you're like a kid sister that amuses me. Not someone I want to bed."

"Then why are you nice?"

"Because you were sad. I was just trying to make you happy until everyone figured their shit out. We just ended up becoming friends during it."

What he was saying made perfect sense to me. Zayn was a good friend, and I loved him, but not the way I loved Cash.

"I cannot believe I just did that." I shook my head as I blushed.

"You caught me off-guard, Cinder. I went into shock and had no clue what I was going to say."

"Sorry." I giggled.

"Well, I'm glad that you finally figured out what you want. Maybe you can tell Cash now."

"Maybe." I bit my lip as I thought about Cash.

"Cinder, I think—"

"Zayn."

"Just hear me out, okay?"

"Okay." I nodded as I glanced into Zayn's eyes

"You should tell him how you feel, Cinder. You've already told me you love him. What's the harm in telling him?"

"And I told you what he said about not being good enough for me."

"That doesn't mean he doesn't want you. He absolutely does."

"I know he does, I can see him struggling with it, but he doesn't think he is good enough, so what am I supposed to do, Zayn?"

"How about not taking no for an answer? Let him know you think he is good enough."

"I can't do that." I looked down at my hands.

"You're a woman that goes for what she wants. You wanted a bakery stand, so you went for it and got it."

"This is different, Zayn."

"It's no different. You want something, go get it. You may not be a King's Guard, but I know damn well you are brave enough to be one."

"What if he rejects me again?"

"Then you will move on. But at least you can move on knowing you tried your hardest."

"Maybe." I plucked a dandelion from its stalk and rolled it through my fingers, remembering how Cash used to do that every day.

"Ember–," Zayn said, and my eyes shot to him.

"Nope. We still aren't talking about Ember."

Zayn nodded. I was grateful that he respected that I wasn't ready to give in.

"Okay. Well, you may want to rethink the whole talking to Ember thing because she is heading this way." Zayn glanced past me. Looking over my shoulder, I saw Ember making her way toward us.

"Oh shoot. I must leave."

"Nope." Zayn grabbed my arm and pulled me back down to the blanket. "At least hear what she has to say."

Looking at his pleading face, I figured it was time to at least hear her out.

"Hey, Ember," Zayn said.

"Hey guys. Can I sit?" she asked.

"Sure." Zayn smiled brightly at her as she took a seat on the blanket.

"Shit, Val just wielded that he needs me, I have to go." Zayn hopped up off the blanket and walked away. Ember furrowed her eyebrows at him because she knew, as did I, that he was lying. He just wanted to leave us alone so we could patch things up.

"Can we talk?" Ember asked.

I nodded and she continued.

"I'm sorry for ruining your life. You were so happy, and I just wanted it to stay that way." Looking into her beautiful emerald eyes, my heart ached. I could see the pain behind them, and I felt bad. "I ruined your only chance for happiness now and I can never get that back..." She threw her hands over her face as she cried hard.

Leaning over, I grabbed her and pulled her into a hug.

"Shh. It's okay, Em. We'll figure this out," I said as I sniffed back tears. I grazed my hand down her back.

"I'm sorry, Cinder," she whispered. "I promise I'll never get in your business again. I swear on my King's Guard honor." Her body shook against mine as the words came out.

We stayed in a hug for I don't know how long. Just leaning into each other. No more words were needed. We both knew that we had made bad decisions, but we had forgiven each other, and that was all that was important.

Once we were done crying, we ended up talking while we munched on fruit. I told her everything about this past week.

"You kissed Zayn!"

"Yeah." I blushed.

"Why?" she asked.

"I realized yesterday that I was in love with Cash, so I figured—"

"Wait. You're in love with Cash?"

"Yes." I looked shamefully at her.

"Whoa," was all she said as her eyes widened. I laughed and she did, too.

"Yeah. It's scary, but in an exciting way."

"I know the feeling all too well." She smiled big. "So, why did you kiss Zayn if you're in love with Cash?"

"We have been hanging out a lot and have gotten close. I was hoping it was more than friendship so I could get over Cash. But it's not, on either end."

"I can't imagine kissing Zayn. He's cute and all but, gross." Ember made a disgusting face and I laughed.

"It was like kissing my brother or something."

We both laughed hard.

"So, what are you going to do now, Cin?" she asked.

"I'm going to talk to Cash." Nervousness filled me as I took a deep breath and sighed.

"I think that's a good idea." She smiled at me. "He's gone right now. He went to Valmeyer."

"Oh." I sighed. "Well, I will talk to him later then."

"By the way, I love your earrings."

I smiled as I touched one of my little gold hoops. "Thanks."

"Hey," Zayn said as he and Val strolled up. They were both only wearing swimming shorts. "You ladies want to go swimming?"

"Yes!" I quickly hopped off the blanket. "I have been dying to go!" I clasped my hands together in front of me and smiled. Zayn and Val both laughed at my excitement.

"Come on, love," Val said as he reached a hand down and helped Ember up.

We made our way into the manor so we could change. My heart raced with every step I took as I thought about how I was going to tell Cash. The fear of him not wanting to be with me was strong, but my will to tell him was stronger. He needed to know that I was in love with him.

"Yes! I was hoping you would go. I put a suit on your bed, Cinder," Cali said as we walked into the manor.

"Bring a towel," Ember said. "Her suits are revealing."

Cali smiled big as my eyes widened.

Ember and I both headed upstairs and parted ways. I went to my room and saw a very tiny black bathing suit.

Picking it up, it noticed it was in two pieces. I sighed and threw it on.

Making my way back downstairs, I saw Ember, Cali, and Zayn waiting for me.

"Holy shit, Cin." Ember's eyes widened. "I told you to bring a towel."

"I'm fine," I said. She gave me a strained smile and nodded.

Looking over at Zayn, his eyes were wide.

"Cash just went upstairs to change into shorts, he said he will meet us there," Zayn said with a smile.

I nodded and stayed quiet as we left the manor.

"There's my love," Val said to Ember as we walked up to the rest of the group. "I love your new bikini." He kissed her, and I looked away wondering how long Cash would be.

"Cali, I have a question."

"Yes, Asher."

"What did you do with Cinder?"

"Shut up. She looks great." Cali clapped her hands together.

"Yes, she does. She looks very, um, very..."

"Pretty is the word I think you're looking for, buddy." Zayn patted Asher on the back and everyone laughed. I blushed at the attention.

The manor door opened, and Cash came running out.

"Sorry guys, I had to... oh." Cash stopped dead in his tracks as his eyes immediately went to my body. A gust of wind hit me when his wings popped open. He met my eyes and his face turned red.

I watched in wonder as a beautiful emerald-green mist fell from his wings. In the mist was sparkling magic dust that seemed to be alive as it danced its way toward me. Everyone around me gasped, except for Ember. Her face was just as confused and mesmerized as mine.

"What is that?" she asked.

Looking back at Cash, his face was mortified.

"I'm sorry, I forgot something." He took off into the air.

"Where did he forget it, in the sky?" Asher asked and Cali giggled.

"Asher," Zila warned.

Looking around at everyone, something was off. The men all looked stunned. Cali and Zila both had a look of pure joy and love. Ember looked confused.

"What is going on?" I asked.

No one said anything. My eyes stopped on Cali.

"I know you know, Cali. Tell me!"

"Sometimes our wings pop out when we have strong emotional responses. That's all."

"Okay. I'm not following." I shook my head. What Cali said just made me more confused.

What do emotions have to do with wings?

"You gave Cash a strong emotional response," Asher said with a smile. "Very strong one since he dusted, too."

"Dusted?" Ember asked.

"I don't understand. What do you mean by emotional response, and what is dusted?" I looked around at everyone. Zila blushed and looked at the ground. Asher cracked his knuckles. Cali giggled and looked away.

I met the eyes of Val and Ember.

"I don't even know what dusted means," Ember said with a shrug.

"But you know what flapped means. Tell me." She blushed and I looked at Val.

"What does flapped mean?" I asked.

"Nope." Val shook his head as he looked back at Ember. "I'm not telling her."

I was getting tired of my friends. My face shot to Zayn. "You're an Angel. Can you explain?"

"You gave him feelings, Cinder," Zayn said as he ran a hand through his hair.

"Someone, tell me exactly what that means!"

"Oh, for the love of the Gods. He saw you in a bathing suit and got excited," Ember said. "It means you turned him on, Cin."

"Oh, I... uh..." My face got hot with embarrassment. My memories of the night we went to Direbreak came back. He had flapped them then, too. Relief hit me and a small smile played on my face as I realized Cash still found me attractive.

"I have never seen Cash do that," Cali said. "I can't believe he dusted. I have read about it, but I have never seen that happen before in real life. It was amazing." Tears filled her eyes as she looked at me.

"I have never seen it either," Zayn added with a big smile on his face.

"What is dusted?" Ember asked.

Val must have been telling her secretly because she locked eyes with him for a few seconds. Her mouth gaped open as she looked back at me.

"Oh, Cinder." She put her hand over her mouth as her eyes filled with tears.

"What is it?" Worry filled me. "Is he injured?" I asked.

"Why don't you guys go, and I will meet you there," Ember said. "I need to talk to my sister alone."

"See you in a minute, love." Val said.

The group walked outside the wards, leaving me standing there with Ember.

"I can't believe he flapped, or whatever. I don't understand. I didn't think he liked me anymore."

"Men are weird sometimes, Cin."

"That is true." We both laughed.

"Are you okay?" she asked.

"Yes. Are you going to tell me what dusted means?"

"I'm not." She shook her head. "You should hear it from Cash, and no one else."

"Why?" I asked.

"You'll have to wait and see." She smiled big. "Don't worry about swimming right now. Go find Cash."

I nodded, still not understanding what was going on.

"Have fun," she said with a smile before she walked away.

Chapter 23

Cinder

Confusion and anticipation filled me. I was dying to know what dusted meant since everyone got weird. Nervousness also filled me as I opened the manor door. I was about to tell Cash I loved him, and it scared me.

Closing the door behind me, I saw him in the study, his wings now gone. He was sitting in a chair with his elbows on his knees and his face in his hands. From here, he looked upset.

"Hey," I said as I walked up.

Cash's eyes glanced up at me. A gust of wind went through the room as his wings popped open again, knocking over the lamp next to him.

I would be embarrassed if everyone knew anytime I was horny, so I put my hands over my mouth to keep from laughing.

"Shit!" He hopped up and picked up the lamp. I saw his wings in full glory from behind. The spread of them was around twelve feet wide. The blue and green hues of color shining off the stark blackness of each feather were beautiful.

"Are you okay?" I asked.

"Yes. I'm fine, Cinder."

He set the lamp back on the table, surprisingly it hadn't broken.

"They told me what flapped means." My heart raced as I glanced down at the bare chest in front of me. I averted my eyes and locked onto his gaze.

"Of course, they did." His bright blue eyes wandered over my face. "I'm sorry."

"You have no reason to be sorry, Cash." I took a few steps forward, closing the distance between us. The smell of bergamot and sandalwood relaxed me as I laid my hand on his arm. "I don't think it's a bad thing."

"Shit," he whispered as his eyes closed.

Green mist with magic dust left his wings and fluttered around me. I looked up with wonder as I watched it swirl.

"You're dusting again, Cash." My eyes wandered back to his face and his eyes popped wide open.

"Did they tell you what that means, too?" he asked with a panicked face.

"No. Ember said I should hear it from you. I'm dying to know what it is because it's beautiful."

The mist swirled around my face and sent shivers down me. Looking down, I watched as it swirled around my arm. It was like a presence in the room that you could feel. Compassion, kindness, lust, pride, happiness, honor, devotion, love... every possible feeling seemed to radiate through me as it grazed my skin like a gentle breeze. I never wanted it to end.

"I'm not sure you really want to know," Cash said, bringing my attention back to him.

"Tell me, Cash," I whispered.

He looked down and cleared his throat like he was nervous.

"Before I tell you what it means, I have to tell you something else first."

"Okay." The dust swirled on my face, and I giggled as it tickled me.

"I can't control what happened," he said with a sad smile.

I laid my hand on his cheek and his eyes met mine once more. "It's okay. You can tell me."

His face seemed to soften as the dust traveled up my arm and onto his cheek. He swallowed hard before he spoke again.

"When we dust, it means we are... um, in love."

The air in the room felt like it had disappeared completely, as the dust seemed to double with his confession. My heart sped up like it was going to run away and my hand fell from his face as shock hit me.

His head dropped in shame.

"I'm sorry. I didn't mean to fall in love with you. It just happened and—"

"I love you, too," I whispered. The dust swirled in a circle around us.

Cash's face looked back at mine as shock filled it. "What did you say?" he asked.

My heart raced, and I had a hard time finding my words. "I said um..." The dust swirled faster and my eyes kept darting between it and Cash's shocked face.

"Do you love me, Cinder?"

"Yes, I do." I swallowed hard. "I love you."

He smiled a genuine Cash smile, and I couldn't help but smile back. Yanking me close to him, his warm body pressed against mine.

"Oh." I let out a light yelp at his strength.

"I'm sorry. I didn't mean to hurt you," he whispered.

"A proper apology would be to kiss me."

"Is that what you want, Cinnamon?" I smiled at his nickname for me. I was excited to hear it again.

"I would love that more than I love baking."

"Then I shall aim to please you, my lady," he said playfully, and I smiled wide. My Cash was back.

"And I shall enjoy it, dear sir," I said with a giggle.

The sparkly dust encased us like it was hiding our love from the world. My eyes kept wandering toward its beauty. Cash lifted his hand and slid my hair behind my ear, and I turned my attention back to him. He ran his finger down my cheek and onto my chin, tilting my face up.

"If I kiss you, that means you're mine."

"There are no objections from me."

His face went serious as he leaned in.

"When I say mine, I mean forever, Cinnamon." My heart sped up with his words. "Which means being mated, eventually."

My mind raced as I thought about how life with Cash would be. Happy visions of smiling, laughter, love, and eventually children, were what I saw. Then a vision without Cash formed. Emptiness. That's all it was. A black hole with no way out. I knew then that I would never want to be without him. Spending the rest of my life with him sounded great.

I slid my hands around his neck.

"Forever sounds like a plan to me." Joy spread through me as he smiled.

"Good." Lifting his hand, his finger ran across my lips, and I closed my eyes. He dropped his hand, and I felt his lips press against mine.

His lips were warm and inviting, soft yet firm. I could feel his dusting grazing my skin as we kissed, and it was amazing. My lips parted slightly as I enjoyed every second. The entire world around us fell away, and I forgot where we were. Cash pulled back from the kiss and I opened my eyes.

"Wow," I whispered.

"Did you miss kissing me?" he asked with a wink.

My heart raced at a confession I had. There was no way I couldn't tell him about me kissing Zayn. I also needed to mention the situation with him and the bartender. It was best to have a clean, new beginning.

"We have a couple of things we need to talk about before our forever can start," I said.

"Okay. Let me try to get rid of these wings." His face concentrated hard. After a minute, the dust seemed to dissipate.

He pulled his wings in and took a seat in the chair. Wrapping his hand around mine, he pulled me down onto his lap.

"Go ahead." He smiled big as he wrapped his arms around me.

Anxiety filled me and my heart sped up once more. His smile had just come back, and I was afraid of taking it away again. But there was no way we could start our lives together on secrets.

I took a deep breath.

"You will probably get mad at me, and at Zayn, but you have to promise not to kill him."

"Why would I kill Zayn?" His eyebrows scrunched up in confusion, then a look of shock went across his face. "He didn't. I'll kill him."

Cash rose from the chair with me in his arms.

"Stop it, Cash. It's not like that." I tapped on his chest, trying to get his attention as he held me. "Sit down," I said. After a few seconds, he lowered himself back down onto the chair. There was a glare on his face, and I was glad that Zayn wasn't home.

"Let me explain. That's the least you owe me after you went home with the bartender, and I forgave you for that."

"Wait, what?" His face filled with confusion.

"I saw you leave the Howling Moon with her. I know we weren't technically together, but it hurt."

He started laughing.

"I don't find it funny at all, Cash. It actually hurt me."

"Cinnamon." He laid his hand on my cheek. "It's not what you think, either."

"Then what was it?" I asked.

"She needed me to look at her buggy. I went out back and told her she needed a new wheel. When I came back out front, I saw you leaving with Zayn. She went home, and so did I, but not with her. I came back here and went to bed."

"Oh." My face wandered to the floor as fear ran through me. He never went home with her—but I had kissed Zayn.

"So, tell me what you and Zayn did."

I looked back at his hardened face.

"Um. I kissed him."

"Even if I love him, I will kill him."

"You're not killing Zayn. Do you hear me?"

I gave him a stern look as I pointed at his face. He smiled like I was adorable. He then relaxed his body, which put me at ease, too.

"He didn't kiss me, Cash. I kissed him. If you're going to be mad at anyone, it should be me. He didn't even like it, he said."

"Why did you kiss him?" he asked with saddened eyes.

"Because I realized I was in love with you."

His eyes widened. "And that makes you want to kiss other men?"

"No, silly. But since I had been hanging out with Zayn a lot, I was hoping kissing him would make me forget you. It didn't work."

"I'm glad it didn't work." He pulled me in close to him. "But I'm still going to kill him."

"You are not. Now stop it!"

"I might."

I laid my hand on his chest.

"Promise me you won't hurt him, Cash. He was a victim of circumstances. Promise me." He looked up into my eyes and sighed.

"Only for you, Cinnamon."

"Kiss me," I said.

He tilted his head and smiled. Reaching out his hand, he slid it behind my neck and into my hair. Yanking my face toward his, his lips stopped only an inch from mine.

"I could never say no to you," he whispered before his soft lips pressed against mine.

Kissing Cash was like magic in my soul—absolute pure bliss. It was the same feeling as holding a newborn baby, or the sound of your mother's voice calling you for dinner—it was home, and I was glad that I'd brought my luggage.

Scooting forward on his lap as much as I could, I twined my hands into his hair. My lips parted further, so I slid my tongue into his mouth. A small moan escaped me as his tongue rolled around mine. Then he broke away, both of us breathless.

Mesmerized by how something so small can make you feel so much, I reached up and ran my finger across his lips. When I went to pull it away, he grabbed my hand, holding it in place. His lips parted and he slowly kissed my finger, all the way to the tip. Once he got there, his tongue rolled around it and my nipples tightened at the contact.

Staring into his eyes, my mouth fell open as my heart raced with excitement.

"Sorry," he said and let go of my hand.

Shifting on his lap, I put both knees on each side of him and his eyes widened. Looking down at his bare chest, his golden King's Guard tattoo caught my eye. Lifting my hand, I ran a finger across it, tracing the outline.

"I want a tattoo someday," I confessed.

"I can take you to get one," he said excitedly.

My hand left his tattoo and continued down his body. I went past the patch of hair on his chest and over to his nipple. His breath caught as I circled my finger around it, and it hardened at my touch.

There was a tingling, needy feeling between my legs. Every time I brushed slightly against his lap, the needing inside me seemed to grow.

Curiosity got the best of me, so I placed both hands flat on his chest and lowered my core onto his lap and was met by something hard. That was when I realized my neediness wasn't the only thing growing.

His body got knocked toward mine as his wings popped out again. His hands shot out quickly and grabbed me before I fell onto the floor. This time the lamp broke.

"Fuck," Cash said.

"Oh." I threw my hands over my mouth.

"You have to stop, Cinder. I'm dying here." He sat back in the chair as much as he could with wings behind him.

"I'm so sorry, Cash." I raised up on my knees, so I wasn't touching his lap, and hung my head down in embarrassment.

"Oh, no. It's okay, baby. Look at me." He laid a hand on my cheek, and I looked up. "I understand you're curious, you're just killing me in the process."

"I'm not trying to kill you. I just want to touch you."

"You touching me makes me want to touch you, and that's what's killing me."

"You can touch me," I said.

He swallowed and shook his head.

"If I touch you, we're going upstairs and you're not ready for that."

"I'm ready, Cash." He shook his head again, disagreeing with me. "Can I still touch you?" I asked.

He bit his lip as he thought about it. He looked over at the clock and sighed.

"Just don't go too far south."

I giggled as I raised my hand. This time, it headed straight for his stomach. He sucked in a breath as my finger traced the outside of one of his stomach muscles. Then over to the next one and then the one below it. I continued touching each hard muscle until I got to the last one. My finger wandered across a small patch of hair that went down into his swim shorts.

"Ah, nope." He grabbed my wrist. "That is south." His breathing was heavy from the small touches. It made me want to see how many more reactions I could get out of him.

Gripping his shoulders, I pulled on them as I pressed my body close to his. My nipples brushed against his chest, and it sent tingles through me.

"Kiss me again," I said. My mouth was only a breath away.

He tilted his head in contemplation, but before he had time to decide, I closed in the distance and pressed my lips against his. Within seconds, I parted my lips and slid my tongue into his mouth. It was needy and greedy, going after what it wanted.

His warm hands moved to my lower back and held me as I continued the passionate kissing. There was a pounding sensation in my core that I needed to stop. A moaning sound escaped us both when I lowered onto his hardness again.

I felt a wetness in my panties that I had never felt before.

"Oh," I whispered, as I gripped his shoulders tight.

"Excuse me, my lord." Hearing Noreen's voice was like a shock to my system. Apparently, I didn't close the study door. I buried my face into my hands in shame.

I felt a small breeze as Cash curled his wings around me, hiding me from the world. His plush feathers were soft against my bare back. It would have felt amazing if I wasn't so embarrassed.

"Yes, Noreen," Cash said. He sounded like he needed air.

"Would you like me to shut the door?" I knew Noreen well, and by the tone of her voice, I knew she was struggling to keep from laughing, but I refused to look.

"That would be great, Noreen. Thank you."

"You're welcome, my lord. Also, dinner is almost ready."

I heard the double doors shut and I uncovered my face. Cash and I both busted up laughing.

"That did not just happen. I'm so embarrassed, Cash."

"At least it was your friend, and not Helena."

Helena was an Angel who was about to retire, and she was extremely modest. She was the oldest servant here at five hundred years old. She would have gasped and clutched her pearls if she would have caught us.

"Thank the Gods it wasn't Helena."

His wings were still around me and I was dying to see what they feel like. Lifting my hand, I reached out and touched one.

"Your wings are so soft." He shivered as I ran my finger across them. "Can you feel that?" I asked.

"I can. They're super sensitive, with lots of nerves running through them.

"Does this tickle?" I ran my finger slowly down the black feathers.

"Yes," he whispered.

I heard the front door open and people talking.

"Shit. Get up," Cash said, and I jumped up.

"Put your wings away," I said, as I fixed my bathing suit.

"I'm trying. Get the lamp."

There was no time to fix the lamp, so I shoved the pieces of it behind the chair. Cash's wings finally sucked in and I crossed my arms over my extremely hard nipples and eased my face as the talking got closer.

"Who closed the study doors?" I heard Asher ask as he opened one. "Oh. Sorry, guys."

"It's okay, we were just chatting," I said.

"We are all going to change and eat. Are you guys coming?" Asher asked as he stepped into the room, swinging the other door open.

"Yep." Cash said.

Everyone else walked into the study, too.

"How was swimming?" I asked with a light smile, trying to seem normal.

"It was fun," Zila said. She sniffed the air and gave me a wide-eyed look. Knowing that she could smell lust, I blushed.

"We're going to try to go again before fall comes," Zayn said with a smile, then his smile faded. "Why are you looking at me like that, Cash?"

Glancing over at Cash, he had a scowl on his face. Oh no.

I told Cash I kissed Zayn, I quickly wielded to Val. I knew he was the only one big enough to stop Cash if he indeed tried to kill Zayn.

What? His eyes went wide in shock.

He's mad. As soon as I thought the words, Cash strode across the room toward Zayn.

Val must have told Ember, because her eyes went wide, and she moved to the side while Val stepped in close to Zayn.

"You kissed my woman," Cash said through gritted teeth.

"What?" Cali's eyes widened and darted to me.

"Actually, she kissed me," Zayn said with a shrug.

Asher's mouth dropped open, and I moved in close behind Cash.

Move back, Val said. I wondered if he had the capabilities to wield to us all at once, because Ember, Zila, Cali, and Asher all moved out of the way at the same time. I stayed where I was.

"Cash, stop it. You promised me." I laid my hand on his shoulder to soothe him.

"I'm not going to hurt him." My hand fell away as he stepped in close to Zayn, who didn't seem scared at all.

Raising his hand, he put a finger on Zayn's chest. "You. Are. Lucky. I. Love. You," Cash said, each word coming out with a poke.

"Ow." Zayn rubbed his chest. "I love you too, buddy," Zayn said with a laugh.

Cash yanked Zayn into a hug. He gave him two pounds on the back that echoed through the room.

"Let's eat!" Cash walked out of the study, leaving us all standing there breathless.

"I think he broke me," Zayn said. "I'm not sure if my back or chest hurts more."

"You'll be good." Asher smacked Zayn on the back as he left the room.

"Now I know why Cash calls you Ass," Zayn said over his shoulder, and I heard Asher laugh from the hallway.

"Hell yeah, Cinder!" Cali's face was full of adoration as she clapped her hands. "Making the men fight for you—I have never been prouder."

"Cali," Zila and Val said in unison.

She rolled her eyes at them.

"I'm just saying. It's best to make them beg, honey." Cali winked at me and sashayed out of the room.

Zila sighed and shook her head as she followed her out.

"Let's change and eat. Come on, love." Val took Ember's hand. She gave me a sympathetic smile before leaving me alone with Zayn.

"If I could get a warning next time, that would be great." He rubbed his chest as he smiled at me.

"I'm sorry, Zayn." I laughed nervously.

"It's okay. So, did you guys... work things out?"

"Yes." I blushed and looked at the ground as I thought about what we had been doing in the chair.

"Oh, I know that look."

"You don't know anything, Zayn. Be quiet."

"I know that you probably need to change out of those bottoms before dinner."

"Zaynith!" My mouth dropped open, and my cheeks flamed red hot.

He laughed as he walked away.

Making my way upstairs, I knew he was right. My swimsuit bottoms were wet, and I didn't even go swimming. I was going to have to casually ask one of the girls about that.

I smiled as I entered my room. There was no time to shower, so after using the bathroom, and cleaning up, I threw on the first dress I saw.

A knock came upon my door, and I strolled over to open it.

"Hello, my lady," Cash said with a bow.

"Hello, dear sir." I curtsied. "Come in."

Cash's eyes widened for a second before he stepped into my room. His eyes darted around, taking in the scenery.

"So, this is your room, huh?"

"Yes." I smiled brightly at him. He seemed uncomfortable.

"It's lovely, in a girly way," he said.

"You will have to show me your room someday."

He nodded.

"Someday. So, are you ready to head down?" he asked.

Heat poured through me as I stared at his beautiful blue eyes. My gaze traveled down to his soft lips and visions of what happened flooded my mind. I stepped up close to him and slid my hands around his neck. The smell of bergamot and sandalwood took over my senses.

"I would like to see your bedroom sooner, rather than later," I whispered.

His eyes widened.

"Um. I want you to see my bedroom, too, but you have never seen someone else's bedroom before, so I think we should wait to visit it."

"Cash, just because I'm a virgin, doesn't mean I don't have wants. I have been wanting you since I met you."

He smiled big.

"I will gladly fulfill your wants, just not right this second. Especially when we are late for dinner. Will a kiss do for now?"

His voice was like butter melting across my skin.

"Yes," I whispered.

Leaning his face down, his lips pressed against mine. The kiss was sweet and perfect. It was like having the best flavor of ice cream on a hot day, or finally icing a cake after it was cool. It was magic.

He pulled away and gazed into my eyes.

"Come on. We have plenty of years to do this, but the food only stays hot for so long."

I dropped my hands from him as I laughed.

He took my arm and escorted me downstairs to the dining room.

Chapter 24

Ember

Val and I were hand-in-hand as we walked in for dinner. He pulled out my chair and I took a seat. For once, we were the first ones here.

"I'm starving," Asher said as he strolled in. He stood to the side and didn't take a seat.

"Why aren't you sitting?" I asked.

"Well, I'm not sure where my seat is anymore. Cash booted me out of my normal seat, so I had to sit next to Cinder. I don't know if they are back together or not, so I'm just going to hang here until Cash comes and tells me what to do."

"So, you're going to let Cash dictate where you sit?" I asked.

"Yep. Oh, bread." Asher grabbed a piece of bread and leaned against the wall.

"Pussy." I shook my head and laughed.

"Cash is three times bigger than I am."

"Four," Val said as he poured me some wine and I couldn't help but laugh.

"Okay, four times bigger than I am, so I'm good with being a pussy." Asher smiled before he took another bite of bread.

"What's on the menu tonight," Zayn asked.

"Spaghetti," I said.

"Yum." He took a seat across from us. "Why are you standing against the wall, Asher?"

"He's scared of Cash," Val said.

"Fair enough." Zayn nodded as he poured some wine and I giggled.

Zila and Cali entered the room and Cali squealed.

"Spaghetti night! My favorite." Cali clapped her hands as they both took a seat.

"How is your chest, Zayn?" Zila asked.

"Sore. I never realized how strong Cash's finger is."

"Congratulations, Cinder!" Cali grinned and I tried hard to not let any mental images of Cash's fingers fill my brain.

"I'm being serious, it hurts." Zayn rubbed his chest and pouted his lip.

"Oh, stop whining. Give me your hand and I will heal you." Cali reached her hand out to Zayn.

"No. I don't need my sister to heal me. I'm a man." Zayn smacked his own chest, to show how strong he was. "Ow."

"Are you sure about that, Softy?" Cali asked.

"Hey, don't call me that." His eyebrows furrowed at Cali.

"Why not?" she asked. "Ember calls you that."

"Ember calls me Softy because... well, it's not your business."

"Ember calls him that because he is a softy," Cash said as he and Cinder entered the room, hand-in-hand.

Everyone's eyes landed on them, including mine. Cash was grinning ear to ear, and I was never happier to see him smile again.

"Here you go, my lady." He pulled out her chair and bowed. She pulled up her dress and took a seat.

"Thank you, dear sir." He scooted her seat in and sat next to her. The pure happiness on both their faces made me smile as I watched them.

"Why are you standing there, Ass?" Cash asked.

Asher sighed as he pulled out his chair and I giggled again.

"Can you pass the bread," Val asked.

"Here you go, Val." Zila handed the bread to him.

"What are we doing this weekend?" Cali asked.

"I don't know. We haven't made any plans," Zayn said.

"It's the third weekend of the month, so there is karaoke in Tessalone." Zila smiled brightly.

A memory just came to my mind, and I panicked.

"Oh, no."

"What is it, my love?" Val asked.

"I forgot we got invited to a burlesque show on Dazeth." I smiled nervously at everyone. I was worried they would be mad at my last minute invitation.

"Yes! I love burlesque." Cali clapped her hands. "When is it?"

"Tomorrow night," I said shamefully.

"Who invited us?" Zila asked.

"Oren. He said that we should all come." I looked over at Cali.

"We definitely should all go!" Cali clapped her hands again. I was relieved that she was excited to go, and curious to see if she would give Oren the time of day.

"Which includes me," Cinder said.

"Of course, that includes you, Cinnamon." Cash winked at her. She batted her lashes at him, and he grinned.

"Who is Oren?" Asher asked.

"He is this extremely sexy Elven," Cali said. She put her elbow on the table and rested her chin on her fist. "I saw him with his shirt off."

"Me too," Zila said, as she blushed.

"We all did," Cinder said. She had a big smile on her face, and Cash furrowed his eyebrows at her.

Shifting in my seat, I poured myself some more wine as the room got quiet. I grabbed another piece of bread and buttered it up and then got myself a little more spaghetti.

"Why were you talking to Elven with their shirt off?" Val asked as soon as I took a bite. My eyes wandered over to his as I swallowed my food.

"Um. I was checking on the progress of the barn." I held his stare because I had nothing to hide.

"And he was shirtless?"

"They were working, Val." I shook my head and smiled at his jealousy.

"Working out those hard muscles," Cali said with a wink.

A low growl came from Val, and everyone's eyes darted toward him.

"Really, Val?" I shook my head. "Stop that." I laid my hand on his thigh and rubbed it, making sure he knew he was the only man I wanted.

"I just don't want my mate hanging out with a shirtless Elven."

"Sexy, shirtless Elven," Cali said.

Another growl from Val.

"You are not helping, Cali," Zila said.

"Are you seriously jealous?" I asked as I removed my hand.

"I'm not jealous." Val shook his head and poured himself some more wine. "I'm sexy, too."

"Yeah, you are, buddy!" Cash nodded his head in approval, then looked at Cinder. "Cinnamon, you said that you saw this Elven. Was he sexy?"

"Yeah." She blushed. "Are you jealous?" she asked.

"Hell no. I know I'm sexier than him." Cash grinned and I think everyone at the table felt relieved to have him back to his true self. Well, at least I was.

"You are way sexier than him," Cinder said shamelessly.

"Gross." Asher sighed and scrubbed his hands over his face. "Is this what it's going to be like every night now?"

"Pretty much. There are mated couples here, and that's kind of what happens," Cali said.

"I am unmated," Cinder said.

"For now," Cash grinned, and my eyes widened. Cinder's eyes shot over to me.

I shrugged my shoulders and smiled.

"Where was I at when you saw him?" Val asked.

"For the love of the Gods, Val. Are you still on that?" I set my fork down. I was finally getting annoyed.

"I was just wondering, since we are always together."

"Jealousy isn't sexy, so stop it." I shook my head.

"This coming from the girl who would stab anyone who flirted with Val."

"I would not, Asher. Shut up."

"I agree with Asher," Zayn said.

"You would totally stab them," Cali added.

"Not before she kicked both their asses," Cash said.

Zila clasped her hand over her mouth to keep from laughing.

Something was off. Val could be jealous if it was a real threat, but he would never be jealous of a conversation. I watched as Val locked eyes with Zayn, and Zayn laughed. Looking around the table, everyone was trying to keep from laughing. Then the realization hit me.

"You asshole." I turned toward Val and smacked him with my napkin. "You're not even jealous. You've been messing with me."

"What's the time, Ass?" Cash asked.

"Three minutes," Asher said.

"Yes. I won!" Cali jumped up and clapped her hands.

"You were all in on it?" I asked.

"Sorry, love." Val winked at me.

"What did you guys bet?"

"How long it would take before you either got mad or caught on," Val said with a smile.

I shook my head.

"You did good, Ember. I said ten minutes." My eyes shot to Cinder.

"You were in on it, too? You're my sister!"

"Yeah, but I wanted to win." Cinder shrugged and continued eating.

"What was the win?" I asked.

"Winner's choice. In this case, I get to pick the one who gets to dance at burlesque. They always have an amateur hour." Cali smiled big.

"No way am I doing that," Asher shook his head.

"It's my choice, but I'm not picking you, anyway. I've seen you dance."

Asher's face looked appalled yet relieved.

"Who will my victim be?" Cali's eyes scanned the room and stopped on me.

"Um, I wasn't in this bet, so don't even think about it."

"You wouldn't show enough skin, anyway. Neither would Zila nor Cinder, so all the girls are out. Zayn is my brother, and I definitely don't want to see that. Val is..." her eyes met mine, "yeah, I don't want to get stabbed, so I pick Cash." Cali smiled big.

"That will be easy, he's a regular," Zayn said.

"You guys are too much." I shook my head. "A bunch of assholes."

Val pulled me in and kissed the side of my head.

As an apology, we can have sex under the tree tonight if you want. It's been a couple weeks, my love.

Excitement filled me as I heard Val's voice in my head. Unfortunately, I had no time to respond because a small swoosh sound went through the room as a messenger Imp appeared.

"Greetings," the Imp said. I immediately noticed that his face was gloomy, and his orange eyes weren't as excited as usual. My heart raced in fear as I wondered which land was attacked.

"Thanks," Zayn said as he took the letter from him.

"Salutations," the Imp said before disappearing.

"We have a mission." Zayn ran a hand through his hair as he looked at the letter.

"Who's on the order?" I asked.

Zayn's eyes widened before he looked up. His face had gone pale. "All of us."

"What?" Cash stood up in a panic.

"The king is requesting our presence now." Zayn stood up and pushed in his chair, as did Val.

"What about me?" my sister asked.

"King's Guard only, Cinder," Zayn said.

"It's probably just a meeting, Cin. No big deal" I smiled at her, hoping she found comfort in it and didn't freak out.

Zayn furrowed his eyebrows at my lie. I knew whatever happened was bad, but I stayed sitting, trying not to panic my sister.

"Okay. I'm going to help Noreen clean up then. I will see you guys when you get back." Standing up, she smiled as Cash kissed her cheek, then she headed out of the room.

My eyes glanced over at Zayn, and he was shaking his head.

"Not now, Zayn." I held my hand up.

"When then, Ember?"

I rolled my eyes at him.

"What are you two talking about?" Cash asked, his eyes darting back and forth between us.

"Nothing, Cash." I gave Zayn a look that said I would stab him if he said anything.

"We don't have time for arguments. What does the code on the letter say, Zayn?" Val asked.

"There were Demon attacks."

"Attacks. More than one?" Zila asked as she stood up.

"Yes. Cerulean, Tessalone, Mazuria, and Mayhem." Zayn's eyes were sympathetic as he met Val's. "It says death SPC."

"We need to get down to the armory," Val said, and left the room.

"What's SPC?" Asher asked. I was wondering the same thing as I stood up. I was now panicking.

"It's a special case. It's something we probably haven't seen before." As soon as Zayn said the words, I took off after Val. I knew he would be worried about his father and sister.

Sprinting to catch up with him, I grabbed his hand and held it while we went downstairs. I said nothing, because I knew he needed me to be quiet right now as he dealt with his emotions.

Entering the weapons room, Val immediately grabbed his short sword. I went over and took my bow off the wall.

The tension and fear in the air were thick and stagnant as the others entered. The room was silent, the only sound was the clinking of metal as everyone chose their weapons.

Asher stood in the corner looking at his staff, his face in full contemplation. He put it back on the wall and grabbed a spear instead. He spun it around with a slight smile.

"Nice choice, Asher," I said, breaking the silence.

His fear-filled eyes wandered toward me. "Thanks."

I gave him a sad smile and then grabbed some arrows and stuck them in my quiver. Fear was quickly building in me, and for a split second, I even thought about asking Zayn to heal my emotions.

"Are you ready, love?" Val asked as he slid his arms around me from behind.

"Yeah," I whispered. He kissed the side of my neck before letting go of me.

"Let's go, team." Val was nervous and it was bringing the commander out in him—the alpha male out in him. It really turned me on, but now wasn't the time to think about sex.

Val left the armory and I looked at Zayn and sighed. Zayn was usually the leader because Val hated the politics of having to deal with the royalty. That and he told me he hates the paperwork. Knowing that he was the rightful leader, Zayn let him take control and didn't say anything when he got in these kinds of moods.

"He'll be fine," Zayn said, and I nodded. He headed over toward me and put his arm around me. "Come on, Demon Spawn."

Leaving the armory, we headed upstairs, our crew following us. We met Val outside the manor, where he was pacing back and forth with his arms crossed.

"About time," he said.

About time? We were literally only a minute behind him. I refrained from rolling my eyes at him. Grabbing my hand the second I got close to him, he practically dragged me outside the wards. I glanced over my shoulder toward the portal, fearful that Erebus was going to step off it at any second.

Are you okay, love?

I'm fine. Don't worry about me, Val.

That will never happen. That's the same as telling me not to breathe. I will always worry about you.

I know.

Erebus won't touch you, love. I will kill him first.

"We can gale from here." Zayn said bringing my attention to him.

Val put his arms around me, and we landed outside the king's wards. Our friends all came in one by one.

"How bad do you think it is?" Asher asked as we started walking.

"I don't know, buddy?" Zayn said.

Val kissed the back of my hand as we started our journey. Fear was eating me from the inside out as we took the long trek toward the castle.

The sun had completely set by the time we made it there. The shadows of the trees looked like long pointy fingers dancing off the side of the castle as we entered. I nodded at the two guards posted at the door. They both gave us flat smiles.

Heading to the throne room, we turned into the hallway where all the statues were. I stopped in front of the one that was Tartarus. Anger took over as I stared at his face. I despised this God and everything he stood for. I stepped up as close as I could.

"I hope you're listening, Tartarus, because I have something to say. Just so you know, Erebus' plan won't work, and you won't be awakened. You cannot break us because we have something you don't. We have loyalty and a bond that you will never understand! Erebus will die. Me and my family will make sure of it."

"Damn right we will!" Cash's voice was like a shock back into reality.

Looking over my shoulder with tear-filled eyes, all my friends had stopped to watch me. Some of them looked fierce, some were smiling with pride, and a couple were teary-eyed. Deep down, I knew they all had the same thoughts I did. We were a family, and we were going to kill this asshole.

Val stepped in close and slid his arms around me. "You have no idea how much I fucking love you." He kissed the side of my head before he dropped his hands. I wiped away tears from my cheeks, as did some others, and we continued our journey in silence.

Once we got to the throne room, the doors opened immediately, and we stepped inside. Our group was quiet as we made our way down the red carpet.

Meyers stepped forward and clasped his hands in front of him.

"Welcome to Castle Elderfall, currently residing is Your Majesty, King Reign, the God of the Sun."

We all bowed our heads.

"Thank you, Meyers." The king's voice was strained. "As you all know, there were tragedies on multiple lands. Before I continue, I need to put some of you at ease. Your families are all safe. As a matter of fact, they're here, along with the rest of the dukes, and the new duchess."

Duchess?

"Since I am stressed, it is hard for me to block everyone's thoughts. If you could quiet your heads so I can think, I would appreciate it."

We all nodded as the king rubbed his hand across his forehead.

"Especially you, Valarian. Your thoughts are extremely loud."

"Of course, Your Majesty." Val cracked his neck and tried to relax his body.

"If everyone would follow me, we have some business to attend to."

The king rose from his throne and walked towards us. I would never get used to seeing how tall he was—over seven feet. Meyers walked next to him.

King Reign's long black hair swayed lightly as he passed us and headed out the doors. I gripped Val's hand tight as we followed him.

Chapter 25

Ember

We were like an anxious pack of wolves ready to defend our territory as we followed the king and Meyers through the corridor.

Reign walked up to a huge set of doors that opened with his arrival. We stepped through and I looked around. We were in a massive banquet hall.

There were beautiful candles lit on crystal chandeliers above our heads. One of them had a candle that was blown out. The ceilings in the king's castle were probably twenty or thirty feet tall, so I immediately wondered how a person would go about lighting them. They would have to have a tall ladder.

I noticed that the king slowed down and fell in step next to me.

"Like this," he said with a smile. He cast a small fireball that went straight to the chandelier and lit the candle that had blown out.

"And before you think it, I use wind magic to get new candles up there once those burn down." I smiled at his confession.

As we walked, my eyes wandered more. The room was filled with dozens of round tables covered in crimson tablecloths. Each table had a glass vase as a centerpiece that I assumed would be filled with flowers during an event. At the front of the room was a massive rectangular table that could seat at least twenty people. There were over a dozen sitting at it as we strolled up.

Glancing around, my heart eased immediately when I saw Val's dad and sister. His uncle, Lazul, was also sitting with them. I smiled at them.

Looking around at the table, I saw every eye color in the land except for red—the Demon's eye color.

There were a couple dukes I knew, including my uncle. There were also some that I had never met before. My eyes landed on a woman that I knew immediately. It was Katzia. She was sitting with another woman I didn't know.

"Thank you all for coming today. As most of you know, this is my acting Guard." The king pointed to us. "Considering recent events, it is understandable that emotions are high. As you express your concern today, I ask that you give my Guard as much respect as you give me." Reign pulled out his chair at the head of the table. "Guards, take a seat."

He pointed to the side of the table opposite where the people were already sitting. We all pulled out chairs and took a seat.

"As everyone knows, the Demons committed some horrendous acts today. Let's take a moment of silence for those we lost."

The air in the room seemed to thicken and I had trouble breathing. My mind immediately went to the dead bodies on Mazuria that I saw during the last battle. I closed my eyes tight, trying to make the visions disappear.

The king is going to have Zayn heal your emotions because he can't think, love. Is it okay if he does? As I heard Val's words in my head, I felt relieved.

Yes.

A few seconds later I felt Zayn lay his hand on my thigh under the table. Calming feelings overwhelmed me as I felt the surge of his magic. That was the biggest dose I had ever had. I laid my hand on top of Zayn's as a thank you to him before he removed it. I was never more grateful to have my feelings healed and wished I had done it earlier.

"We will be dropping formalities today. So, let's start with the Duke of Mayhem. Ryker, please tell everyone what happened on your land."

Val's father was a dark-haired man with violet eyes. He was handsome, sweet, and kind—just like Val. He stood up before he started his story.

"It was close to dinnertime when I was alerted to the casualty. I followed my guards out to see for myself because I couldn't believe that someone could do something so horrendous. Strung up on the edge of my land was a citizen. He was hanging from two large pieces of wood in the shape of an X. My flag usually hangs there. His throat was slit and carved into his chest was the number one. The Vampire they murdered was a local fisherman and had a small rowboat. I'm assuming that's how they caught him."

"Thank you, Ryker."

He took a seat, and the king turned his attention toward my uncle.

"Hendrick, Duke of Mazuria, please stand and tell your story."

My uncle ran his hand through his light red hair before he stood. His emerald-green eyes were sad when he spoke.

"My story is quite similar. I was in my study handling paperwork when I was alerted. Like Ryker, I had to see for myself. Unfortunately, some kids playing near the beach found the body and alerted the guards. When I got there, she was laid across a large rock. Her throat was also slit, and on her chest, they carved the number two. She was a local jewelry shop owner and was always on the beach looking for shells."

"Thank you." The king rubbed a hand across his forehead.

Hendrick quickly took a seat and gave me a sad look. I felt Val's hand lay upon mine under the table. He was on a mission with me when he met the jewelry store owner a while back. My heart hurt to know that she was gone.

The room was silent as the king continued rubbing his hand across his forehead. I knew he was probably struggling with everyone's thoughts as their emotions ran high.

"Who's next?" The king looked around at the table.

"The Duke of Tessalone, Your Majesty."

"Ah, yes. Thank you, Meyers. Next is Kavan."

The duke of the Fae lands stood up. He was a dark-haired, dark-skinned man with hazel eyes. I had met him before on a mission, and he was just as handsome as he was kind.

"Like the others, I have almost the same story. We started doing perimeter checks three times a day after my lands were attacked a few months ago. One of my guards was doing the evening check on the beach when she came across the body of a citizen. The man was a local tradesman and did a lot of traveling from land to land. He was tied around the trunk of a tree at the edge of the forest. His throat was also slit, and the number three was carved into his chest."

"Thank you, Kavan," the king said, and the duke took a seat.

"That brings us to the last land that was attacked, the water casters." The king sighed before he continued.

"As some of you know, the Duke of Cerulean is over two hundred years old. He was scheduled to retire next year, but the incident that has happened today has upset him dearly. He asked if he could step down early, so I granted his wish."

The king stood up and strolled around the table.

"For many, many years the reigning seat on each land has been passed down to the sons of the dukes. We ran into an issue when the Duke of Mazuria needed to be replaced, since he hadn't had children yet. I had to appoint a new duke from a different bloodline. A bloodline I trust."

The king stopped behind my uncle and patted his shoulder, then glanced over at me and smiled.

"Since that worked out well, I figured it was time for a change."

The king continued walking around the table, and my eyes followed his every step.

"I had already thought long and hard about who I was going to have take the position. I had been talking to this person for months and had them trained with the duke. They have already been making council decisions jointly, too. She is extremely good at it."

The king smiled as gasps went through the room when he said *she.*

"So, if you all would, please welcome Arien. The new Duchess of Cerulean."

We all clapped and *most* of the dukes congratulated her with smiles—all except one.

"Having a duchess rule without a duke is unheard of," a duke with emerald-green eyes said. Since there was only one other duke that was a Caster, I assumed he was the Duke of Windcrest.

"Yes, but Cerulean is a very independent land, run mostly by women. I think it is an excellent choice," Ryker said. I had to try hard to keep from smiling.

"I agree. Arien is also the daughter of the duke. With no rightful male heirs, I don't see what the problem is," Hendrick added.

"The problem is, we have never had a woman run an entire land before," the Windcrest Duke said.

"I'm sorry, Erjon, but is there something wrong with women ruling?" My eyes went to the Lycan man with silver eyes that spoke. He was the Duke of Direbreak.

"I wasn't saying there was, it is just unheard of," Erjon said. "There will be no duke in place to guide her since she is unmated. It could cause instability in the system."

"Why? Because she is a woman?" I asked, and all eyes shot to me.

Before I even realized what I was doing, I pushed out my chair and stood up.

"I'm a woman and a member of the King's Guard, as are these two." I pointed to Cali and Zila who both stood up in my defense, even though they had no idea where I was going with my argument. "We fight Demons to protect the lands, *your* lands..." I pointed at him, "so what is the difference?"

"You aren't making decisions that alter the lives of many."

Katzia smacked both her hands on the table and stood up.

"Oh, yes, she is! They all are!" The room quieted as all eyes went to her. The look on her face was heated. The new duchess laid her hand on top of Katzia's, and her face softened with the touch.

"My sister is right," Arien said, in an elegant voice. "She has told me a lot about Ember since she is her student, and I'm close with the Guards at the castle. Every split-second decision they must make can alter the lives of many. They put their lives on the line every single day to keep us all safe."

My eyes went between Kat and Arien. Now that I knew they were sisters, I could see the resemblance the brown-haired beauties shared. Arien must have been the water Caster sister Katzia mentioned when I first met her.

"Absolutely. The women in the King's Guard are fiercer than you will ever be, Erjon. If you don't think they make life-altering decisions every single day, then why don't you go fight the Demons in the next battle," my uncle said, and I couldn't help but smile as Erjon's face paled.

I glanced at Katzia, she and the duchess were both smiling, too.

"That is absurd, Hendrick," Erjon said.

"Why is it absurd?" The Lycan duke asked.

"I have never wielded a weapon in my life." Erjon shook his head. "I would die if I had to fight the Demons."

"Well, that's a pity for you." The Lycan duke said with a smile. "All of us other dukes, except for Hendrick, were King's Guards and went through training."

"I may not have the mark of a warrior, but since my best friend is the king, I went through the training many years ago. I had nieces I wanted to protect." Hendrick smiled at me. "Plus, Reign would be able to call upon me, when needed."

"Maybe that's a rule that should change, too." My eyes went to the blue-eyed Angel with blonde hair that was speaking. He was the Duke of Valmeyer. "There is no reason the dukes, excuse me, and duchess, shouldn't know how to defend themselves. I went through King's Guard training because I have the mark. I feel like everyone would benefit from it."

"I agree with Ezra," Ryker said. "I also have the mark, and I am trained. I trained my entire staff." Ryker leaned back in his chair and crossed his legs. "I even started training my kids when they were very young. That is why my son and daughter can wield any weapon in these lands." I smiled at my father—by mating—as respect went through me.

"I am also marked, so I am trained," the Lycan duke said with a smile. "As is my staff."

"I don't have the mark, but my father does. He trained me and Katzia, too." Erjon's eyes shot over to Arien. "My staff is also trained, by the way," she said as she smiled proudly.

"My son and I both have the mark," the brown-eyed Duke of the Elven land said. "I also made sure all my staff, including the servants, went through simple weapons and self-defense training. It's the least I can do to help them protect themselves if the Demons ever get to the castle. My son Oren currently leads the training for me."

My breath caught as I realized that Oren was the duke's son.

"So, it looks like the only one not trained is you, Erjon." The Lycan duke smiled big. I had a fondness for him.

"I wasn't born with the mark, so I didn't see a need to be trained."

"That's right." Hendrick leaned in on the table with a smugness on his face. "You only became duke because your brother—"

"Leave my brother out of this, Hendrick!" Erjon's face reddened. "We are not here to talk about training the dukes, or our children. We are here to figure out the Demon problem!" Erjon's voice rang through the room.

"What we should be talking about is training for citizens," Katzia said. "If we had more trained civilians, maybe the death count on Mazuria wouldn't have been as high."

"Yes, we should just give everyone a weapon! That's your solution?" Erjon's eyes were like daggers on Katzia as he stood up.

"That sounds like a plan to me," Hendrick said as he leaned back in his chair. His smile was smug.

"I agree," Ryker said.

"Agreed," The Elven duke said.

"You all are a bunch of imbeciles!" The veins on Erjon's neck looked like they were about to pop in frustration as he screamed.

King Reign slammed his giant fist on the wooden table, making me jump. I was surprised it didn't break as the loudness echoed through the room.

"Enough!" As the king's voice demanded attention, everyone standing took a seat—including me.

Reign leaned back in his seat and rubbed his forehead. There was no sound in the room and I was pretty sure everyone was holding their breath in the quiet. I know I was. He lowered his voice as he continued.

"Roslyn has noted your concerns and we will revisit them at another meeting." My eyes went to the other end of the table where the king's secretary was writing as fast as she could. "But today, we are here to talk about the Demon attack, and for me to appoint the new duchess. So, that is what we are going to do. Now, Arien, will you please tell the story of what was found on your land."

"My father was alerted that there were Demons on our lands. Fortunately for us, a couple of King's Guard stationed at the portal caught three Demons in the act. The victim was out checking her traps when she was caught.

They had already tied her to a tree and carved the number four in her chest and were about to slit her throat when the guards found them. A fight ensued and all three Demons were destroyed. Thankfully, no one else on my land was harmed."

"Thank you, Arien," the king said. He shifted in his seat and crossed his legs before he continued. "With everything going on with the Demons, I'm not sure having a ceremony would be ideal, but I know that is what the citizens will want. Especially with this new change. So, I will have Roslyn send notes to everyone with the date. I'm considering next weekend, or the one after."

"What will we do about the Demon attacks?" Erjon asked.

"For now, there is not much we can do. I have a few suggestions, but I'm not sure everyone is going to like them." The king uncrossed his legs and set up in his seat. "We all know that the King's Guard starts training at twenty-two. Some guards were born to dukes, like Valarian, and Cashmere."

Whoa!

My eyes shot to the Duke of Valmeyer.

Holy shit.

Cash was definitely a bigger version of his father. If Cash cut his hair, shrunk down, and aged some, they would be twins.

The king shifted in his chair. "I have been discussing this with a few of the dukes and we think that having the guards train at an earlier age might benefit everyone."

"How old were you thinking?" Arien asked.

"We were considering starting their training at eighteen," the king said.

"That is too young. Our kids will be slaughtered!" Erjon said.

"They wouldn't go on missions at eighteen, they would just start training." The king turned toward us. "I would like to hear the opinions of the actual people who have gone through this training. Valarian, since you are commander, what are your thoughts?"

"I think it's a great idea. It would give them a head start on what they must learn."

The king nodded in approval. "Zaynith?"

"I agree with Val. I think it's a wonderful idea."

"Ziliana. You are a smart girl, with a very good political view on the world. What are your thoughts?" The king asked, and I looked around wondering who the hell Ziliana was.

"If we incorporated it into the curriculums at each of the academies, then they wouldn't have to leave home," Zila said.

How the hell did I not know Zila's real name?

"And who will pay for that?" Erjon asked. "Are you going to?" He asked Zila.

"I would be willing to use any of my efforts to raise funds for the school in my homeland and devote my off time volunteering to help." Zila said elegantly.

"As would I," I said, and Erjon's eyes narrowed on me as his face filled with hatred. I had a feeling this duke didn't like women in charge, so I smiled at him.

"If you disagree then let it be known, Erjon," Val said calmly, and my eyes wandered to him. "But I highly suggest you not give my mate that look again." My eyes widened at Val's extremely polite words.

"I agree with my son. If you have something to say, then say it. But don't look at my daughter like that."

"I third that. She is my niece," Hendrick said with a wink.

Arien looked over at Hendrick and smiled big.

"I... I apologize." Erjon leaned back in his chair and got quiet.

Looking over at the king, he had a smirk on his face. "I think what Ziliana suggested is an amazing idea. I'm sure there are a lot of guards, or even citizens, who would be willing to help."

"I agree," the Duke of Direbreak said.

"Since we have all had a stressful evening and it's getting late, I think that will be all for this meeting. We will have another meeting in a few weeks after the elevation of the new duchess. Feel free to mingle with your loved ones before you go."

Erjon immediately stood and walked toward the exit. I turned toward Val.

"I can't believe you said that in front of the king, Val. What is wrong with you?"

"I said it politely, love." He shrugged and I shook my head at him.

"He deserved it, Ember. He's a pompous ass at every meeting." My eyes went up to my uncle as he and the king walked up.

"A very pompous ass," Reign said, then he and Hendrick laughed.

"Are we going to the Howling Moon?" Hendrick asked.

"We are, as soon as everyone clears out," the king said. "Would anyone like to join us at the Howling Moon?"

"I haven't been to Direbreak in years! Count me in," Ryker said, and my eyes went wide.

"Kage is going to flip his shit when the king and half of the dukes show up," the Direbreak duke said.

"Um, and duchess," Arien said as she walked up. "I'm ready for a big shot of tequila."

"I'll buy you a shot if you honor me with a dance," Hendrick said.

Her eyes narrowed at him, then she smiled. "Deal!"

"It is settled, we will all go," Reign said. "I'm going to change. I will meet everyone by the front door in twenty minutes." Reign turned toward us. "Thank you, Guards, for coming tonight. I think it was a successful meeting and I will see you soon. Have a good night." The king walked off. I guess that was his polite way of saying we weren't invited.

"Ember!" Wynter came running up. I stood up and she slammed a hug into me.

"Hey, Wynter. I missed you!"

"I missed you, too." She turned toward Val and hugged him.

"Valarian, would you mind escorting your sister home so I can go to Direbreak with King Reign?"

"Of course, father."

"I can do it!" Zayn smiled brightly and Wynter blushed.

"Thanks, Zayn. I appreciate it," Ryker said.

"I'll come with you," Val said, and Zayn's smile faded. "Okay, buddy."

"Do you want to come with us, love?" Val asked.

"No. I'm tired. I'm going to head back and read my book for a while. I will see you when you get back if I'm still up."

Val leaned in and kissed me before he left.

The rest of my friends and I said our goodbyes to everyone and headed out of the castle. I stayed in deep thought about the Demon attack as we walked.

"Hey, guys, I have a weird request."

"What is it?" Zila asked.

"I don't want anyone mentioning the attacks to my sister. I have been keeping them from her."

"Okay." Zila got quiet and looked a the ground as she walked.

Asher side eyed me and didn't say a word as he spun his spear.

"I know, Zayn told me." Cali gave me a slight smile and bit her lip.

"If she asks, I'm telling her," Cash said.

"Cash."

"I'm not going to lie to the woman I'm in love with. Sorry, Ember."

Cash walked ahead of us, and the group got quiet. I had a feeling no one wanted to lie for me. As we continued walking I couldn't help but wonder if I had made a mistake and if it was going to cause more issues.

Chapter 26

Cinder

Breakfast was over and I was headed out for my sparring class with Val. Making my way across the grounds, I saw a sexy Angel waiting for me outside the training center.

"Well, hello," I said with a smile.

"Are you ready to spar with me, my lady?" Cash winked at me, and my eyes widened.

"Are you my teacher today?"

"I am." A slow grin spread across his face. I felt hot all over, thinking about the positions we were about to be in as I smiled back.

"I am more than ready, dear sir."

"Perfect! Let's get going."

Cash took my hand and led me into the building. My heart raced with excitement and anticipation as we entered the sparring room.

"Val told me some things you have learned. So, we won't start with the basics. I want you to show me everything you know in a full-on match." My eyes widened.

"I can't defeat you, Cash."

"You don't always have to defeat your attacker, doll. Sometimes you just need to disable them enough to get away so they can't abduct you."

"What if I *want* you to abduct me?" I said as I stepped in close.

Cash's eyes were the ones now widening.

"Um, you'll just have to pretend like I'm a Demon today." He stepped to the side of the room and took off his shirt. I bit my lip as I watched him stroll back over. "Are you ready?" he asked. He was now in trainer mode. Unfortunately, I was in a *lay me down and make love to me* mode, so I wasn't sure how well this class was going to go.

"I'm ready," I said as I tried to calm my racing heart.

Cash took a stance, and I did the same. Trying to clear my mind from my lust-filled thoughts, I tried hard as I could to pretend that Cash was a Demon. It was going to be difficult since he was so beautiful.

We both stood there in a standstill for a few minutes, then Cash lunged for me. I tried to sidestep him, and he grabbed me from behind. I had to focus hard on not rubbing my butt on him.

"So, when you're in this position, you have a couple moves you can do," he said in a low voice that sent shivers down my spine.

Thinking about what Ember told me, I stomped his foot and he let go of me. Turning around as fast as I could, I ran my shoulder into him, trying to knock him down—it didn't work. He wrapped his arms around me once more, but this time I was facing him, and my breasts were pressed against his chest.

With my arms pinned under his hug, I had very minimal reach, so it was hard to defend myself. Since he was so tall, I couldn't even headbutt him. Needing to get out of his grip fast, I did the only thing that I knew would make Cash let go of me.

I reached my hand down and gripped the front of his pants, wrapping my fingers around his crotch.

His mouth went wide as he sucked in a large breath and let go of me. Like a bull going for his target, I slammed into him as hard as I could with my shoulder. He fell, as did I, landing right next to him. Getting onto my hands and knees, I crawled away from him as fast as I could. Grabbing my ankle, he yanked my body back toward his.

"Kick your feet. Never let them keep hold," he said.

I kicked my feet as hard as I could, and when he didn't let go, I took the loose foot and kicked toward his chest, but accidentally got him in the face. He immediately let go of me and I scrambled toward him in a panic.

"I'm so sorry, Cash. Are you okay?"

A huge grin fell upon his face. "You are supposed to be evading me, not comforting me." He grabbed me and pulled me close to him, crushing my body against his.

As he laid on his back, with me lying against him, I couldn't help but feel lustful. My eyes searched over his face for a second as I thought about my next move.

Before I had a chance to think, Cash's lips were upon mine. The smooth wetness of his hungry kiss consumed me and sent a chill down my body. After a very passionate minute, he pulled away.

"I'm... I'm sorry," he said breathlessly. "You're just too beautiful. I couldn't not kiss you."

He loosened his grip on me, but instead of getting up, I attacked him—but not in the way you think.

My hands slid around the back of his neck, and I yanked his face back towards mine and kissed him hard. After a brief second of shock, his arms went around me once more.

Sliding my knee over his body, I straddled him as the kiss deepened. Every cell in my body lit up as he slid his hands onto my butt and gripped it. He hardened beneath me, and I moaned into his mouth, making him squeeze tighter.

Breaking away from the kiss, his lips moved to my neck. I tilted my head as far as I could and moaned again.

The throbbing between my legs was back. Needing to satisfy it, I rubbed my core on him, and we both moaned at the amazing feeling.

Turning my head back toward him, my lips went instantly to his. My tongue darted into his mouth, and he sucked on it.

Moving my hips back and forth, the need kept building. I felt like I was at the finish line of a race, and I was getting breathless. It was about to happen...

Then Cash quickly pulled away.

"Get up," he said frantically as he pushed me off him and stood up.

"What's wrong?" I asked as he reached his hand down, helping me get off the floor. My breaths were fast and ragged as I stared at his panicked face.

"Val just wielded to me. He and Ember are coming down the hall." He tried to adjust the front of his pants and my eyes widened at how hard he was.

"Oh." I quickly ran my hands through my hair, trying to make myself look presentable.

"Take a stance," he said, and I did. I pulled my fists up as did he, right when the door flung open.

"Hey, guys," Ember said.

"Oh, hey," I said breathlessly. I dropped my fists and turned toward her with a smile.

"Wow, you are beet red, Cin. Is Cash working you hard?" she asked.

"Uh, huh." I smiled and nodded. He was working me hard alright...

"Cash, you have a mission with Cali. I will finish Cinder's class." Val said, and Cash nodded.

"I'll head out now." He turned toward me and kissed me on the lips—in front of my sister. Grabbing his shirt, he slung it over his shoulder. "I'll see you later, doll." He smiled then strolled out of the room. I looked at Ember in a panic and her eyes were wide.

"So, I guess you guys are doing good."

"We are." My smile was pained as I looked at her.

"Well, I'm really happy for you, Cin." She had a genuine smile on my face, and it eased me.

"Thanks."

"Well, I have to go meet Zayn. I'm taking him to the library in Pyreland."

"That sounds like fun." I continued my fake smile when, deep down, all I could think about was Cash's bare chest, and the wetness in my panties.

"Do you want to go?" she asked. "You can visit some of your friends."

"Thanks, but I have some baking to do."

"Okay. I'll see you later, Cin." Ember kissed Val and left.

"So, you had a good class, huh?" My eyes met Val and he tilted his head as he narrowed his eyes.

"Uh, huh." I bit my lip and immediately blushed.

"Considering what you two were doing, I'm assuming you have had enough training today." He smiled big and I could see his fangs. I giggled and covered my face in embarrassment.

"I'm so embarrassed. How did you know?" I asked.

"For the first time ever, Cash's shield was down. His thoughts were super loud when we entered the building."

"Oh. My. Gods." My cheeks turned red hot as the blood rushed to my face.

"It's natural, Cinder. When you're near someone you're attracted to, it's easy to get lost in the moment. Especially while sparring. The adrenaline kicks in and it can't be helped. Believe me, I know. That's why no one comes down here when Ember and I spar." He smiled big, and I giggled.

"Did Ember know?" I asked nervously.

"No, because she wielded her thoughts to me when we walked in."

"What did she say?"

"She said, 'Thank the Gods they're only sparring.'"

"Well, that makes me feel better."

"So, um... you're dismissed." Val busted out laughing, as did I.

"Thanks," I said as we made our way out of the training center.

We headed into the manor. Val took off to do Val things, and I headed to the kitchen. I immersed myself in baking until it was time to get ready for burlesque tonight.

After I made two desserts, I took a short nap, showered, and was getting dressed when there was a knock on my door. Opening the door, I saw Cali.

"Oh, hey. Come in." She sashayed into the room with clothes in her hands.

"I have an outfit for you to wear tonight."

"Okay..." My eyes wandered curiously over the clothes. "I draw the line at short skirts."

"Actually, it's pants. Here." She handed me the clothes and I scrunched up my face.

"I had a cute dress picked out to wear tonight, Cali."

"You don't want to wear a dress. It can get chilly on Dazeth. Wear those."

"Oh." I was saddened by not being able to wear the beautiful dress, but I didn't want to get cold. "Thank you."

"Go throw them on and let me see." I nodded and went into the bathroom.

Setting the clothes down, I held up each piece. The pants were high-waisted, black, and had tight ankles. They were nothing I was used to as I slid them on. The shirt was white with long sleeves that were baggy. It looked cute on me, but I was completely shocked that it was super low-cut.

"My boobs are showing, so how will that keep me warm?" I asked when I emerged from the bathroom.

"Us women must sacrifice sometimes to look beautiful. Which you do!" She gave me a mischievous Cali smile and clapped her hands.

"What are you up to, Cali?"

"Nothing. Come here." I gave her a suspicious look as I walked toward her. She pushed her brown hair behind her ears and picked up something off the table.

She wrapped a black belt thing around my waist. "What is that?" I asked as she laced up the front.

"It's a corset belt. It's like a corset, but shorter. They are very popular on the Elven land." She took a step back and looked at me. "Eek! You look perfect!" She clapped her hands together again as her face lit up in excitement.

"Thanks." I smiled politely. I needed to see a mirror before I decided if I looked good or not.

"Oh, I almost forgot." She stepped out in the hallway and came back in with a pair of boots in her hand. "Since we wear the same size shoes, you can wear these."

Taking the boots from her, I was shocked. They were knee-high boots with laces all the way up them. They had heels on them, too.

"I only wear small heels, Cali."

"Oh, you will be fine. Just humor me and try them on."

I nodded and put them on for her amusement. She made me walk around the room so she could look at me.

"Wow! You look sexy as hell, Cinder."

"I do?" I looked down at my outfit, wondering if Cash would think the same thing.

"Can I do your hair?" she asked.

"Um, like how?"

"I don't know. I can braid the back, or something."

"Can you braid the sides like you do Cash's?"

Her eyebrows raised and she squealed. "That would be perfect!"

An hour later, I was all dolled up and ready to go, but I was exhausted. Cali took off to go get dressed and I headed downstairs to wait for the others.

Stepping into the foyer, I saw Zayn sitting in the study. He was wearing all black like he usually did.

"Hey, Zayn." He looked up from the book he was reading. His eyes widened as he took in my outfit.

"Oh, wow!"

"Do I look okay?" I asked.

"You look amazing, Cinder. If you weren't with my buddy and I didn't know you, I would totally hit on you." He smiled big.

"Thanks." I laughed and shook my head.

"Hey guys." Zila walked into the room. "Oh wow, Cinder. You look great!"

"Thank you, Zila. So do you."

Zila was wearing a brown, white, and black plaid skirt with a black sweater. I immediately wondered if she knew it was going to be cold. I didn't have time to ask her because Asher walked in.

"Are we ready to go? Whoa!" Asher's eyes widened as he stared at me and Zila. "You ladies both look beautiful."

"Thank you, Asher," Zila said.

"Yes, thank you." I smiled proudly.

"Is everyone ready?" Ember asked as she and Val strolled into the study, hand-in-hand. She was wearing a pair of black pants and a light cream-colored sweater.

"We are waiting on Cash and Cali," Zayn said as he stood up.

"I'm here!" Cash said as he stepped in the foyer.

"Me too! Let's go." I heard Cali's voice but couldn't see her as I heard the front door open. Everyone went out the door, leaving me standing there with Cash.

"Wow, Cinnamon!" He stepped in close to me. "You look amazing. I love your hair." Raising his hand, he ran his fingers down one of my braids. Leaning in close, he pressed his warm lips against mine. He pulled away quicker than I wanted him to.

"Thank you. You look very handsome." Cash was dressed in all black just like the other men. His shirt had buttons all the way up the front and had the top few undone. It made my heat rise.

"Let's go." He took my hand and we left the manor.

Chapter 27

Cinder

Once we were outside, we headed to the portal. I immediately noticed that Cali had a skirt on and I was mad that I didn't wear a dress. After hopping on the portal with the others, we landed in Dazeth. It, indeed, was not cold.

"It's not cold here," I mumbled.

"Not yet, maybe in a month or two, doll."

My eyes narrowed at the back of Cali's head as I wondered what she was up to.

Stepping off the portal, we were surrounded by fir trees.

"There are a lot of trees, though."

"Since the Elven are builders, they go through a lot of wood." Cash smiled and took my hand as we walked.

After a few minutes of walking, I felt the small wave of magic hit me as we crossed the wards.

"We can gale from here," Val said. Wrapping his arms around Ember, they disappeared.

"Yep." Zayn galed away, too. Then, one by one, everyone disappeared.

"My lady." Cash held out his arms and I stepped into them. Wrapping them around me, they slid onto my back.

"Lower," I said.

Cash's eyebrows raised, then he slid his hands to my lower back.

"More." Cash grinned at my words and slid his hands onto my butt. He squeezed it hard, and I fell slightly forward into his chest.

"Better?" He asked.

"Yes," I whispered. He winked and we galed away.

We landed a short walk outside of a small town. Cash told me it was called Arnlean and it might have been small, but it was busy. The Elven really did know how to party—there was a saloon, or some sort of activity on every corner.

We stopped in front of a big building that had music pouring out of it. I looked up to see that the building was two floors high, and I could see people mingling on a balcony.

"Come on, Cinnamon. The show will be starting soon."

We stepped inside and it was gorgeous! The entire inside was covered in black wood—the bar, the stools, the stairs, the floor–everything. We walked to the front and sat at a table. When Cash pulled my chair out, it was lined in a beautiful blue velvet.

Taking my seat, I looked around. Each table had a beautiful white flower centerpiece—a glass vase in the middle with a lit candle in it.

Looking toward the front of the room, I saw a huge black stage with a blue velvet rug in the middle, and a matching curtain hanging in the back. There was a band set up in front of it playing music.

"What would you like to drink, ladies?" Zayn asked.

"I already know what Cinder wants." Cash winked at me.

"I will take a bottle of white wine," Cali said.

"My usual. Vodka cranberry," Zila said.

"Do you want a whiskey sour, love?"

"Yes, Val. Thank you." Val kissed Ember and stood up.

All four men took off, leaving us women to chat. Remembering I had questions, I immediately turned toward them.

"Ladies. I must ask something, but you cannot make fun of me for not knowing."

"Of course," Ember said.

"When I kiss Cash and... other things, something odd happens to my body sometimes."

"Your nipples harden?"

"Yes, Cali, but that has happened before."

"Your lady bits twitch?"

"Cali! Let her finish." Zila shook her head. "Go ahead, Cinder."

"I mean, that happened, too." I blushed and everyone giggled. "This is something that has happened a few times now." I swallowed hard as I thought of words to say.

"We can talk privately later if you want, Cin." Ember gave me a sympathetic look.

"Oh, no. I'm completely comfortable talking with the girls about it. I just don't know how to say it and be respectful."

"Oh, this is going to be juicy." Cali clapped her hands.

"Um, sometimes, my um... my panties get wet."

"Oh, that's normal," Ember said.

"Completely normal." Cali smiled.

"What does it mean?" I asked, and all the women looked at me.

"Did mom not talk with you?" Ember asked.

"She didn't." I shook my head. "I never asked, either."

"Oh. Well, when your puss—"

Ember held up her hand.

"Cali, I can handle this one. So, when, um... See what happens, um..." Ember uncomfortably scratched her neck.

"I thought you could handle it, Ember?" Cali asked sarcastically.

"You two are so immature. I will handle it." Zila set up straight in her chair. Cali leaned in close, like she was excited to hear this. I realized then that Zila was the mom of the group.

"When you get turned on, sometimes the vagina gets wet, but not always. Once you are turned on and wet enough, it makes the entrance of the penis easier. That way, it doesn't hurt," Zila said.

"Then sex is more enjoyable. Well, most of the time. It really depends on who it's with. Some men act like they're trying to hammer in a nail." Cali shook her head and rolled her eyes.

I stared at her and blinked. I heard a sigh come from Zila.

"It's true, Zila," Cali said. "Anyway, Cinder. It just means your, I'll say it nicely, *vagina,* was ready for some action. Which is a good thing."

"Oh. So, my body is saying that it's ready for Cash's penis?" I asked.

"Cock. But, yes," Cali said with a huge smile.

"What about the twitching... um, pulsating feeling down there?"

"Oh! That's a happy clit!"

Zila shook her head at Cali. "That's what happens when the blood flow to your genitalia increases due to sexual arousal. It can make the clitoris, or other parts, pulse."

"So, it's all normal?" I asked.

"Completely normal. You just got turned on." Zila smiled sweetly.

"You can get turned on from a lot of things," Ember said.

"Fighting turns me on," Cali said.

"Me, too!" Zila and Ember said in unison and then laughed.

"I'm the horniest after a good battle." Ember added with a smile.

"Yes, me too!" Cali clapped her hands. "The adrenaline rush from a good fight makes the sex so damn good." She made a moaning sound.

"Should I leave?" Val asked. "All I heard was adrenaline, sex... and moaning." He set Ember's drink down and took a seat.

"That's a disgusting sound coming out of my sister's mouth." Zayn handed Cali and Zila their drinks.

"You can stay, V. I was done." Cali smiled and poured herself some wine.

"Here you go, doll." Cash set my drink down and sat next to me. Asher sighed and took a seat next to Cali. He was super quiet tonight.

I lifted my glass and took a sip of my drink. "Oh, this is delicious, Cash."

"Zayn said you liked coconut water, so I figured you would like this. It's pineapple juice, coconut cream, and rum."

"I love it." I took another sip.

"Hey, everyone," Oren said as he walked up. "It's nice to see fellow King's Guards here." He smiled big.

"Oh, hey. Everyone, I would like you to meet Oren. He's the one who invited us," Ember said with a smile.

"It's nice to meet you." Val shook his hand, then put his arm around Ember. I had a feeling he *was* slightly jealous.

"Thank you for inviting us, Oren."

"The pleasure is all mine, Zila."

"Would you like to dance, Cali?" he asked. All eyes shot to her as she sipped her drink. "Um... maybe later, the show is about to start." She smiled slightly like she wasn't interested.

"Okay. Well, it was nice meeting everyone," Oren said before walking off.

"So, that is the notorious sexy Elven?" Val asked.

"Shut up, Val." He laughed and kissed Ember on the cheek.

"He is pretty sexy," Cash admitted, "but still not as sexy as me." He raised his arm and flexed it and we all laughed.

"Oren has taken a liking to Cali," Ember said.

Cali smiled brightly. "I mean, I am amazing."

"Conceited, but close," Cash said.

"This coming from a man who walks around shirtless." Cali rolled her eyes.

"Touché." Cash raised his drink and Cali clinked hers against it.

My attention was brought to the stage when the band stopped playing.

"Oh, the show is about to start." Cali clapped and made a woo-hoo sound when the announcer stepped onto the stage.

"Is everyone ready to see some beautiful people?" The crowd roared loudly. "As always, do not touch the dancers. Without further ado, please welcome the boylesque dancers!"

The crowd roared loudly as five male dancers, dressed in very provocative clothing, strolled onto the stage. They all had feathers on their outfits and were carrying big, feathered fans.

The show was sexy, funny, and amazing. I loved every second of it. The dancers even came into the crowd and gave people dances.

"How was that for entertainment?" The crowd cheered in response to the announcer. "Now, let's welcome the burlesque dancers!"

Five women, dressed similarly, sashayed onto the stage. Their performance was equally entertaining, and I also loved it.

There was about a twenty-minute pause between each show. Cash had taken off, and I didn't know where he went. Zayn and Val got us all our third round of drinks.

A man came up onto the stage and the music stopped.

"It's the time you have all been waiting for..." The crowd roared as I looked around, wondering what was going to happen now. "Amateur hour has now started. Our first dancer is no stranger to this stage. At this point, I'm not sure he is even an amateur!" The crowd laughed.

"Here we go again."

"Stop complaining, Asher. I rather enjoy his performance." Cali smiled at me. "I think Cinder will, too."

"He's very good at it," Zila said as she blushed.

I finally realized where Cash went...

"Please welcome back the Angel of Seduction!"

The crowd roared loudly. Women, and even some men, all around the room screamed, hollered, stood up, or clapped. I was a bit overwhelmed that they were that excited for a man that was just squeezing my ass a few hours ago.

Glancing back at the stage, my heart raced as I saw Cash stroll out. He was wearing the same button-up shirt and pants, but now had a red tie and a black hat on.

I glanced at my sister with wide eyes. She shrugged her shoulders. "This is my first time seeing it, too."

"Pay attention, Cinder." Cali nudged my arm. "Woo! Come on, Cash!" She clapped her hands in excitement.

My heart raced with anticipation as I watched Cash grab a chair and set it in the middle of the stage.

"Do we have any volunteers for this dance?" the announcer asked. Dozens of men and women raised their hands.

"You should do it, Cinder," Cali leaned over and whispered in my ear.

"We have a lot of volunteers tonight. The Angel will have a lot of options." The announcer's eyes scanned the crowd.

"If you have volunteered for this dance before, lower your hand."

Half the people lowered their hands. I was nervous to see Cash dance with another woman, so I grabbed my drink and downed it. I contemplated putting my hand up, but I didn't.

"Okay. You have fewer options, Angel. Now pick your victim!"

Cash hopped off the stage and strolled through the audience, slowly wandering around. He went from table to table as women batted their lashes at him and men gave him seductive smiles.

I waited with bated breath as he passed our table. He stopped right in front of me and looked down into my eyes. With a huge grin, he lowered his hand to me. Out of instinct, I took it and stood up.

"Her hand wasn't even up!" a woman at the table next to us said.

"Nobody asked you," Cali said. "Woo-hoo! Go, Cinder!" She clapped loudly.

Cash held my hand as he guided me through the crowd and onto the stage. He sat me in the chair and I laid my hands nervously on my lap. I had no idea what to expect, so my eyes wandered nervously.

Looking out at the crowd, I found our table. Locking eyes with Ember, she smiled at me and clapped with excitement. It made me relax knowing that she approved. The announcer left the stage as a sultry song came on, bringing my attention back to Cash.

Sliding down onto his knees in front of me, he bowed his head. Glancing up at me, he smiled, his blue eyes sparkling from under his hat.

"Are you ready for your dance, my lady?" My body trembled with the excitement of the unknown as I nodded.

Grabbing my knees, he slowly spread my legs apart. I was never more grateful to be wearing pants. Now I knew exactly why Cali had insisted I wear them.

Grabbing my ankle, he placed it over his shoulder, then ran both hands down my leg. Heat poured through my body as my legs shivered from his touch.

Stopping halfway up my mid-thigh, he slid his right hand back down to my ankle, leaving his left hand on my inner thigh. Lifting my leg off his shoulder, he ran his nose slowly up my leg. It traveled all the way to my core. He stopped just before he got to the apex of my legs, and I gasped. Avoiding that area, he dropped my leg and his nose traveled up my hip and onto my stomach. He stopped just right before my breast and looked up at me from under his hat.

"Are you okay?" he asked.

"Never better," I whispered. My breaths were ragged.

He smiled as he raised up from his knees.

"Woo!!" Cali was loud over the sound of the music and roaring crowd.

Cash slowly unbuttoned his shirt in front of me. As it gaped open, he put each hand on the side of my head and guided my face from his abs down to his groin, and back up again before he freed me. Laying his hand on my chest, he pushed my body back into the chair.

Sliding his shirt off slowly, my heat rose as I saw each huge muscle revealed. Reaching up, he untied his tie and slid it off. Throwing it around my neck, he yanked my head toward his groin again. It touched my face slightly as he grinded his hips and I blushed.

He slid the tie off, releasing me from the prison of his seduction. Turning away from me, I watched his sexy tattooed back as he slung his tie into the crowd. Two women started fighting over it and I laughed.

Turning his attention back to me, Cash unbuttoned his pants. He moved in close to me once more. My entire body was on fire as I stared at him. Leaning his face close to mine, he whispered in my ear.

"Pull my pants down with your teeth."

Air had completely escaped my body with his sensual words. Not wanting to disappoint the crowd, or myself, I did as I was told.

Sitting on the edge of my seat, I reached my neck out and clamped my teeth onto the top of his pants. My nose lightly brushed against the skin of his pelvic region as I pulled, and I thought I was going to lose it.

Sliding off the chair and onto my knees, I continued pulling his pants down with my teeth until my head was almost to the floor. Once I let go, he put his hands under my arms, picked me up, and sat me back on the chair. Leaning his head in close, he whispered again...

"I like you on your knees." He winked. I wasn't one hundred percent sure what he meant, but I had an idea, and my eyebrows rose at the thought. He grinned wide when he noticed that I figured it out.

Cash kicked his pants off the rest of the way, and they landed across the stage. My eyes widened when I saw him in only a pair of tiny black shorts. They were almost tiny enough to be underwear, and my heat rose further.

Cash planted his feet on each side of the chair and stepped up onto it. From this position, I was completely making eye contact with his... um, cock, which seemed to have hardened. Grabbing the back of my head, he entangled his fingers in my hair, sending shivers down my back. He swirled his hips to the rhythm of the music. His hard cock was close to my face, and I felt wetness in my panties again.

Stepping off the chair and lowering himself onto my lap, he sat on it. He took his hat off and placed it on my head. His face was now even with mine as the song ended. We were both completely breathless from the dance. His eyes wandered around my face, and I did the only thing my body wanted to do. I placed both hands on his neck and yanked him toward me. My lips parted, and I smashed a kiss on him.

"Hey, hey. No touching the dancers," the announcer said, and I pulled away from the kiss.

"Thank you for the dance," I said.

"Thank you for the kiss." Cash's face was red and sweaty as he smiled big.

He stood up and took my hand, pulling me up from my seat.

"What is your name, dear?" the announcer asked.

"Cinder."

"You can't touch the dancers, Cinder."

"She's my mate," Cash said as he pulled me close to him, and my breath caught.

"Oh, okay then." The announcer turned away from me and looked out at the crowd. "Let's give Cinder a round of applause." Cash raised my hand in the air and the crowd roared.

My heart raced, and I laughed uncontrollably as I looked out at the people. My eyes landed on our table and all our friends were cheering loudly, including my sister.

Cash grabbed his clothes and took my hand.

"Come on." He led me through the crowd and back to our table.

I was just seduced and called a mate by the man I'm in love with and a thousand thoughts were running through my head as we walked.

"Holy shit!" Cali clapped excitedly as we approached. "That was amazing! Your best performance yet."

"Good job, Cinder." Zila smiled. "You, too, Cash."

"That looked like fun!" Ember said.

"You can go next time." Cash winked at Ember and Valarian growled. "I'm kidding, buddy." Cash clasped him on the shoulder.

"I know, and if you weren't my friend, you wouldn't have arms." Valarian held up his glass with a wink, and Cash laughed.

"Believe me, I know." Cash picked up his drink. The two men smiled as they clicked their glasses together.

Cash set his drink down and slid on his pants, my eyes kept darting from him to my sister as she spoke.

"I'm proud of you, Cinder. You have more balls than I do. I would have never gone up in front of a crowd!" Ember smiled and, for once, I felt closer to being her equal.

"Thank you." I smiled back at her as pride filled me.

"I'm going to go mingle." Asher downed his drink. "Maybe I will find a woman to pay attention to." He stood up with a sigh.

"We will come with you, buddy." Cash nodded his head in Asher's direction. Zayn and Val stood up and followed Asher.

Cash slid his shirt on and leaned down into my face. "Thanks for the entertainment, doll." He kissed me and took off with an unbuttoned shirt.

"What is wrong with Asher?" I asked as I took the hat off and sat it in the table.

"His girlfriend ended things with him," Ember said.

"After two years." Zila's face saddened.

"Oh, no. That is horrible!" My heart hurt for Asher.

"It is." Cali sighed. "Especially since he was madly in love with her."

"Why did she end it?" I asked.

"She was unhappy. Being a King's Guard isn't easy on relationships," Cali said.

"Val and Ember are fine." I looked at my sister.

"It's different. We get to live together. It makes things easier when you see your mate every day."

"She could have come to Castleva," Cali said as she shook her head, "but she didn't want to."

"Yeah. Asher said she didn't want to leave her family, which is understandable. I didn't want to leave Cinder." Ember glanced over at me, and I smiled.

"Me getting abducted worked out well, I guess." Everyone laughed at me.

"It did. We are grateful to have you here." Cali scooted to the seat next to me and pulled me in for a side hug.

Feeling at home with these people was a great feeling. I hadn't felt that way since my mother died. I was now surrounded by people who loved me in their own way. But there was one Angel that I couldn't stop thinking about. That dance was like nothing I had ever experienced before. I really wanted to be in his arms right now, but I knew he needed to be there for Asher.

An hour and a few drinks later, I was getting tired.

"How are you ladies doing?" Zayn asked, as he and Asher walked up.

"Wonderful!" Cali smiled big. I think she was a little drunk. "I think I'm going to find a hottie to dance with. Where did Oren go?" Her eyes scanned the room.

"I'm going to head home." Asher cracked his knuckles and sighed.

"No, you're not." Cali stood up and grabbed Asher's hand. "Come on, Ash. You can be my hottie." She sashayed onto the dance floor, dragging him behind her.

Val strolled up and lowered his hand to Ember. "Do you want to dance, love?" She took it with a smile, and they made their way onto the dance floor.

"Would either of you ladies like to dance?" Zayn asked.

"I'm good right now, Zayn. Thank you." Zila smiled. "I'm going to go settle the bill before it gets too late."

Everyone had left, and it left me alone with Zayn. He took the seat next to me.

"So, how was your night?" he asked.

"It was fun."

"It definitely looked like fun." He smiled and took a sip of his drink.

Looking out into the crowd, I saw Cash leaning against a wall, talking to a dark-haired, beautiful Elven. I bit my lip while I watched. The music was loud, and she leaned in close and whispered something into his ear. He smiled at her. I shook my head and sighed.

"What's wrong, Cinder?" Zayn asked.

"Cash called me his mate."

"Oh. Did you not want him to?"

"No, that's not the problem, Zayn. He called me his mate, then took off to console Asher. And he hasn't come back for a while, so I have been sitting here thinking about it, and I look over and I see that." I pointed to Cash and the Elven woman.

"Oh, well, I think that you have two options, Cinder."

"And what are those?" I asked confusedly.

"You can sit here and watch that woman flirt with the man you're in love with, or you can stake your claim. If he wants a mate, go give him one. If that's what you want, of course." He smiled mischievously.

Looking back in Cash's direction, I took a deep breath. I wasn't sure if it was jealously or not, but considering the situation, I *definitely* wanted her to know he was taken, and she was wasting her time. I *was* his mate.

"Maybe I shall stake my claim, as you say." I stood up and headed toward them.

Stomping across the room, I didn't know what I was going to say, but I knew there was no way I was going to sit there and watch this and do nothing about it. I walked straight up to Cash.

"Excuse me, can I talk to you?"

"What's wrong, Cinder?" Cash looked over my face, worry filling his.

"Can we talk, please?"

"He is a little preoccupied at the moment, sweetheart." The woman reached up and ran her hand through his beard. Cash looked at her and pulled back slightly, his eyes landing back on me.

A part of me wanted to run off, but something inside of me decided that wasn't the route I was going to take. Pulling something from deep inside, I did what I thought my sister would do.

"I suggest that, if you want to keep those hands, you get them off him," I said.

"Excuse me?"

"You heard me. Remove your hands or I will remove them for you!"

The Elven's eyes went wide, and she looked at Cash.

"Cash?"

"You heard her." Cash grabbed her wrist and removed her hand.

"You're both rude." She gave me an evil face before she stalked off.

"You have something to say to me, Cinnamon?"

"Yes. I do." I put my hands on my hips.

"What is it?" Cash grinned.

"I just wanted to tell you that... that you're a fool."

His eyebrows rose. "Why am I a fool?"

"Because you called me your mate and then took off. So I have been over there wondering what that means, and then I find you talking to—"

Cash yanked me into his body and his lips quickly found mine. Sliding his hands down my back, they stopped at my butt and gripped it. I slid my arms around his neck, and my fingers entangled in his hair. After a few minutes of what may have been considered inappropriate behavior in public, Cash pulled away.

"I want to ask you something," he whispered as I gasped for air.

"Okay," I said, breathlessly. Making out really took some energy.

"Will you mate me in the eyes of the kingdom?" he asked, his beautiful blue eyes sparkling with anticipation.

When an important decision like this comes up, it's usually best to think about things. Maybe consult some friends or look into oneself and see what you *actually* want. Cash and I hadn't even had sex yet, but I knew with every ounce of my heart that I loved this Angel more than I would ever love anything in the world. So my mouth and body wouldn't let me even think about it.

"Yes!" I screamed and jumped into his arms.

He caught me and held me in the air. "I was hoping you would say that!"

Placing a sweet, gentle kiss on my lips, I melted into him. He turned in a circle, swirling my dangling legs in the air.

Sitting me back on the ground, he smiled big.

"Come on." Cash took my hand and led me to our table. "Let's tell our friends."

Wait, what? I barely had a chance to comprehend that we were betrothed, and he wanted to tell our friends—tell MY SISTER!

My thoughts didn't come quickly enough, and we were at our table before I knew it. I immediately noticed that Oren was sitting there talking to Cali.

"Guess what, guys." Cash pulled me into his side. "I asked Cinder for a public mating, she said yes!"

All our friend's mouths dropped open in shock, and my heart raced with fear. It took them a few seconds to get over the shock, but one by one, they came back to reality.

"That is outstanding!" Oren said.

"Yes! I think we need a round of drinks to celebrate!" Cali clapped her hands as she smiled big.

"Congratulations, that is wonderful!" Zila had teary eyes.

"I approve." Zayn nodded and held up his drink.

"Me too," Val said with a smile.

"Me three," Asher said. "Who's going to start it?"

Start what? I thought.

"Do you approve?" Cash looked at Ember while he raked his hand through his beard, and I could feel the tension as everyone stared at her.

She stood up from the table and stepped toward us. She slid to one knee in front of us and looked up with her beautiful emerald-green eyes.

"As a fellow King's Guard, I, Ember Lavaris Grey, will honor this mating by always protecting your mate when you are not around, Cashmere Voland. And your mate when you are not around, Cinder Lavaris." She pounded her fist onto her heart twice. "Until death." Then bowed her head and stayed there.

My eyes filled with tears as Valarian fell to one knee and repeated the words. Then Zayn, Cali, Zila, Asher, and Oren.

Our friends stood up and I smiled at them with a full and happy heart.

"Congratulations," Oren said, and shook our hands.

"Thank you," I said.

Cash turned toward Ember. "So, I guess you approve?" he asked with a grin.

A slow smile radiated across her face. "I approve more than anyone. As long as you make her happy."

Cash fell to one knee in front of Ember and bowed his head. "I swear on my honor as a member of the King's Guard that I will not only make her happy, but I will also protect her."

"I know you will. You're an honorable man, Cash." Tears filled her eyes.

He stood up and pulled me in close to him. Ember smiled at us as happiness flowed through me.

"Am I supposed to drop to my knees?' I asked.

"Not in front of everyone," Cash whispered, and I felt my cheeks flush.

"Who's going to get the drinks?" Cali asked. "We need to toast this occasion."

"I already ordered them." Asher nodded his head toward a server who was carrying a tray of drinks.

"Damn you're quick, buddy," Zayn said. "You didn't even leave the table."

The server set the tray down and we all grabbed a glass.

"As soon as I saw that Elven woman stomp off, I knew we were going to need drinks, I just didn't know what for." Asher smiled.

"Elven woman?" Ember said, confusedly.

"Some girl was flirting with Cash, but Cinder handled it." Zayn smiled big.

"She definitely did." Oren grinned.

"What did you say to her, Cinder?" Zila asked.

"Nothing." I smiled politely.

"She told her to remove her hand from my beard or she would remove it for her." Cash smiled proudly at me.

"That sounds like something Ember would say." Val looked over at Ember and she shrugged.

"Don't expect anything less from the Lavaris women," Cash said.

"We don't." Zayn held up his glass. "To Cash and Cinder. Many blessings."

"Many blessings!" Everyone repeated.

We ended the night talking and just being with friends. Oren spent an hour talking with us and trying to get Cali's attention. Once it was time to go, he bid us farewell and we made our way back to the portal. Once we landed at Castleva, Cash grabbed my hand.

"I will escort you back to your room, but would you like a midnight stroll through the gardens first? It's a full moon." He smiled.

"I would enjoy that."

"I will see you tomorrow, Cin." Ember walked off hand-in-hand with Val.

Cash and I took our time slowly strolling towards the garden. Once we were there, the familiar scent of the roses made me feel at home.

Cash stopped walking and leaned into the flowers, searching for a perfect one.

"Here you go, my lady." He slid the rose behind my ear.

"Thank you, dear sir."

We walked over to the water fountain and took a seat. Cash pulled me in close to him. His face was lit by the moon, and I couldn't help but admire his manly beauty.

"So, did you like the show?" he asked.

"Yes. Maybe a little *too* much."

"What do you mean, Cinnamon?"

"Well, if I tell you, you have to promise not to judge me."

"I would never judge you." He pulled my hand up to his mouth and kissed it.

"I enjoyed it so much that my panties got wet."

Cash's eyebrows rose as his eyes widened.

"Oh." He got quiet. I left him completely speechless.

"Are you judging me?"

"No, no. I just don't know how to respond after that. All I could think to say was 'You're welcome,' but I didn't want to be rude."

I laughed hard as I blushed. "Thanks are definitely warranted."

"Well, if it makes you feel better, I got hard." He grinned as his eyes sparkled at me.

"I know. I saw it and I liked it." I laid my hand on his thigh and slid it close to his cock.

His eyes widened once more. He placed his hand on top of mine, keeping it from getting any closer to him.

"So, I have a surprise for you tomorrow, but it requires us to go to bed early, and leave before the sun rises."

"Oh, okay." I swallowed as he removed my hand from his thigh.

"We better get inside," he said. "It's getting late." He stood up and held out his hand as he smiled.

"Okay." I took his hand and stood up.

"Oh, make sure you wear pants tomorrow."

"Why?" I asked.

"You'll have to wait and see." His smile widened.

As we walked hand-in-hand back to my room, I couldn't help but think that he was avoiding being intimate with me. Once we got to my room, he pulled me close.

"I will be down here before dawn with breakfast. We can eat in our pajamas."

"That sounds like fun. Where are we going?" I asked.

"It's a surprise." Leaning in, he quickly kissed me.

"Goodnight, Cinnamon."

"Goodnight."

He left me in the hallway standing next to my door, exhausted, horny, and slightly annoyed. I sighed as I entered my room and shut the door.

Chapter 28

Cinder

Waking up with a smile was the best way to wake up. The sun wasn't even up, and I was still in my pajamas when I opened my bedroom door to Cash. He had a tray with fruit and bagels on it, and a huge smile on his face.

"Come in," I said as I held the door for him.

He walked into the room, and I watched the angel wing tattoo on his back move with his muscles as set the tray on the table. Looking down, he had light gray lounge pants hanging low on his hips. For some reason he had a single axe stuck in them pulling one side of his pants lower than the other. Heat poured through me as he turned toward me.

"Your pajamas are cute." He smiled big as he pulled me in. My heart raced as I laid my hands on his bare chest. "And sexy," he added. He placed a kiss on my cheek.

"Thanks." I blushed as he pulled away. I was wearing a light pink tank with little white flowers. The bottoms were shorts that matched.

"Sit!"

"Yes, sir." I smiled big and took a seat.

"I made you some fresh squeezed orange juice," he said as he set the glass in front of me.

"You squeezed it yourself?"

"I did." He grinned proudly. "My axe is going to smell like oranges all day." He furrowed his eyebrows as he pulled his axe out of his waistband and looked at it.

"Why would your axe smell like oranges?"

"How else was I going to cut the oranges up, doll?"

"Cash, there are kitchen knives for that." I giggled.

"The axe is quicker." He smiled as he set it on the table and I shook my head at his silliness.

"So, what are we doing?"

"I told you, it's a surprise. Don't forget you have to wear pants."

"Why?" I grabbed a strawberry and sucked on it.

"I mean, you can wear a dress, but once you see what we're doing, you're going to wish you were wearing pants."

"Is what we're doing safe?" I asked.

"Safe is like taste, it's subjective."

"What?" My eyes widened and he laughed.

"You'll be fine. I'll protect you with my life. On my honor."

I smiled big and nodded. "I know you will."

We ate quietly for a while. Cash inhaled his food quickly, and I nibbled as I wondered what we were doing.

"Are you almost done, Cinnamon? We must go before the sun comes up."

"I'm done," I said with a mouth full of bagel.

He grinned at me while I swallowed and took a drink of my orange juice.

"You're so adorable."

His confession made me smile. His facial expression turned to one more serious, as he picked up my hand. He ran his thumb across it as he stared at it.

Bringing my hand up to his mouth, he kissed it. His eyes met mine when he said, "I love you."

My heart skipped a beat, or maybe four, as I looked into those gorgeous blue eyes. Tears threatened me, but I held them back as I whispered, "I love you, too."

"I'm sorry I pulled away, Cinnamon. I should have just talked to you."

"It's okay, Cash. It's in the past and we have both moved on. I think we are stronger for it."

He leaned over the table and kissed me before he hopped up.

"I have to shower. Meet me downstairs in thirty minutes."

"Shower with me," I said before I even realized the words came out of my mouth. I swallowed hard as his eyes widened.

"That, umm..." He ran his hand over his beard. I smiled at the fact that I made him completely speechless again.

"Please." My smile was seductive.

Cash took a deep breath and blew it out hard. "I appreciate the offer, and believe me, I want to... but if we don't go now, we won't make it in time."

"It would be just as quick," I added in hopes that he would agree.

"Umm. If we shower together, we aren't leaving this house." He grinned and I giggled. "And I really want to show you this." His eyes grew sad.

"Okay. Maybe another time."

"Oh, definitely another time!" He grinned as he grabbed his axe and walked backwards toward my bedroom door. "See you in thirty minutes," he said as he pointed his axe at me.

He left the room, and I quickly got in the shower... alone.

Once I was done, I threw on a pair of black leggings and short black boots. I paired it with a white, lightweight sweater that hung slightly off my shoulder. It was long and came to my mid-thigh. Grabbing the angel necklace off the dresser, I headed downstairs as fast as I could as excitement poured through me.

"Even in pants, you're magnificent," Cash said as I glided down the stairs.

"Thanks." I smiled proudly and held the necklace out to him.

"Oh." He smiled as he took it from my hands.

I turned away from him and moved my hair to one side. He slid it on my neck and latched it. I felt his breath bounce off me for a second before he kissed my neck. Shivers ran down my entire side as I wondered what kisses would feel like on different body parts.

"Okay, let's go," he said, pulling me out of my blissful thoughts.

He took my hand as we left the manor.

"Why can't you just tell me where we are going, Cash?"

"It's a surprise!" he said as he dragged me to the portal.

"A surprise that involves pants, and nighttime. I'm not sure I will like this surprise."

"You won't like it, Cinnamon, you will love it. I swear on my honor. The sun will be up soon, anyway." He grinned as we stepped onto the portal.

The rush hit me as the portal went. The amazing feeling shot through me, making my belly tingle. Goosebumps formed on my arms, and I felt a hug from behind me. The smell of bergamot and sandalwood caressed my senses, and then we landed.

"We're here," he said.

I looked around and the land we were in was beautiful, from what I could tell. The grass and the trees were the greenest I had ever seen next to the first bits of daylight. There were beautiful light pink flowers in a field next to us.

Cash took my hand as we stepped off the portal.

"Hey, Cash," a portal guard said.

"Hey, guys."

"My lady." The portal guards bowed to me, and I smiled in return.

As we walked through the field of pink flowers, my senses were on fire. It was the best smell I had ever had the pleasure of smelling in my life.

"This is amazing, Cash."

"I knew you would like it here."

"Where is *here*?" I asked.

"Valmeyer. Land of the Angels."

"Wait." I stopped walking as my eyes widened.

"We aren't here for you to meet my parents. We aren't even going into town. There're just so many beautiful things here that I was dying to show you. For now, we are going to gale. We are low on time, so we must hurry."

"Hurry for what?" I asked as he slid his arms around me.

"You'll see," he whispered before he galed us away.

He galed us to the bottom of a large mountain. My eyes wandered up as I took in its massiveness.

"This is Arcross Mountains. One of my favorite places."

"Cash, I am not rock climbing." I shook my head at the thought.

I met his eyes as he tied his blonde hair up into a bun. I couldn't help but drool as I saw the muscles in his arms flex.

"You won't even be getting your hands dirty, doll." He put one hand behind my back, and the other under my legs and scooped me up. "Hold on," he said, as his wings popped out.

My eyes widened when I realized we were going to fly up the mountain. I quickly slid my hands around his neck and held on for dear life. Before I had a chance to panic, he flapped his wings and off we flew.

The wind blew my hair back and, at that moment, I wished I would have had time to braid it. Cash's grin was irresistible as we flew through the sky. The rush was intense, but exciting. It was like riding the portal, but better.

"Woo-hoo!" I yelled, and Cash laughed.

"Are you enjoying this, Cinnamon?"

"Yes!" I looked down at the dark land. It was hard to see so far away. "This is amazing, Cash. I wish I had wings."

"I don't."

"Why?" I asked with a pouty lip.

"Because then I wouldn't have an excuse to fly you around."

I smiled big and laid my head on his chest.

After a while, Cash slowed down. I watched as we headed toward a small cliff. He landed on it and set me down.

"How was your ride, my lady?"

"It was perfection, dear sir. I will forever be grateful." He smiled as he took my hand.

"We can sit here," he said as he took a seat on a rock that was only big enough for one person to sit on.

"Where will I sit?" I asked.

He pulled me down onto his lap and I smiled as I wrapped my arms around his neck.

"You didn't have to bring me all the way here to get me to sit on your lap. I would've done it at home."

"Oh, I know," he said with a grin. He leaned back against the mountain. "But we wouldn't have had this view. Turn around and watch."

Turning away from him, I stared out into the horizon. He wrapped his arms around my waist as I leaned into him. His wings curled in and wrapped around us and laid across my lap. It was slightly chilly out, so I kept my arms underneath them, and ran my hand along the inside of his soft feathers.

The gentle glow of the sunrise soon showed itself. Orange, pink, and yellow hues kissed the sky as we both watched.

"It's almost as beautiful as you," he whispered in my ear. I snuggled in closer and laid my hands on top of his.

Love poured through me as he held me on that mountainside. I wanted to build a fort right there on the cliff and live there forever. No worries in the world—just me in Cash's arms.

After the sun was up enough that it hurt my eyes, I turned toward him.

"Thank you for this. I loved every second, Cash. It was beautiful."

"You're welcome, Cinnamon." He raised his hand and pushed my hair behind my ear. "I should have told you to braid your hair. I'm sorry."

"That's okay. It'll probably take me an hour to brush these tangles out, but it was worth it."

"Turn around," he said with a smile. He uncurled his wings and put them behind him.

I shifted in his lap and turned my back toward him once more. He pulled all my hair behind my back. Tingles ran across my scalp as he ran his fingers through my hair, removing the tangles.

With each stroke he did, the faster my breaths sped up. Once he was done, he moved all my hair aside and yanked me back toward him.

My heart raced as he pulled my baggy sweater down, showing my bare shoulder to the world.

"I've been wanting to do this since I saw your shoulder sticking out." Leaning his head down, I felt his lips touch my skin. He kissed all the way across my shoulder and close to my neck.

His fingers grazed my neck as he moved the fine hairs out of the way. I tilted my head out of instinct, and his lips slowly made their way up to my neck. A moan of pleasure fell from my lips.

Parting his lips more, I felt the wetness from his tongue as his kisses deepened. Reaching my hands down, I gripped the side of his thighs as another moan escaped me. The tingling feeling between my legs was back, and I was ready to find out what it wanted.

Raising my hair, he continued kissing across the back of my neck and shivers ran down my spine, lighting my soul on fire.

As his kisses made it to the opposite side of my body, I tilted my head in the other direction. He continued kissing across my shoulder as far as he could go, then made his way back over to my neck and up to my ear.

A small pleasurable gasp left me as his fingers wrapped around my throat and his other hand tightened on my stomach. He tilted my head back as he sucked on my earlobe.

The feeling inside me was building, and my clit twitched. Without thinking, I reached down and grabbed the hand that was around my waist and pulled it up to my breast and ran it across my hard nipple.

He seemed to slow for a minute, like he was thinking. I squeezed his hand, making him squeeze my breast, hoping he would realize what I wanted.

When his hand finally squeezed my breast on its own, he released my earlobe and went back to kissing my neck. Dropping my hands back to his legs, I dug my nails into his thighs as I moaned again.

The twitching at the apex of my legs got stronger, so I shifted my butt on his lap. Hardness pressed into my butt cheek, and I gasped with excitement. The hand on my breast, and the one on my throat, tightened slightly as I continued rubbing on him.

Not being able to take it anymore, I laid my hand on top of his. Pulling it away from my breast, I ran it slowly down to my lower stomach. I let go to see if he would leave it there, he did.

Once I realized he was doing what I wanted, I pressed my luck to go further. I moved his hand down between my legs and onto my inner thigh. He gripped it tight on his own, and I gasped from the closeness.

Getting even braver, I slid his hand in between my legs. His kisses seemed to stop for a minute, but I didn't care.

Pulling his hand as close as I could to my core, I rubbed his fingers on my achy spot. A large moan left me as I felt the highest pleasure I had ever felt at this point. My panties were soaked with wetness, and the need I had was overwhelming.

His hand started moving on its own, so I let go. He rubbed it on my clit, and it was the best feeling I had ever felt in my entire life.

I rolled my butt around on his cock as his fingers moved against me. The feeling was building, and I was about to orgasm for the first time. Then Cash stopped...

"Okay, okay," Cash said breathlessly as both his hands dropped from me.

"No, don't stop," I whispered as I picked his hands back up. I was about to put them back where they both were when he stopped me.

"I let it go too far, and for that I'm sorry. It's hard to not touch you, Cinnamon."

"Then touch me! Or make love to me, just don't stop." I was in a panicked need.

"Your first time isn't going to be on the side of a mountain."

"Why not? It sounds perfect." I reached for his hands again when he yanked them away.

"Look at me," he said. With a sigh, I turned around to face him.

"What?" I asked with a pouty lip.

"Oh, come on. Don't do that." He ran his thumb across my lip. "We have plenty of time to do all the fun things. There's no reason to rush."

"Yeah, except for there is. I want it, and I want it now!"

He laughed and shook his head.

"It will happen naturally when the time is right, and neither of us will stop it. You deserve nothing less than that. Nothing less than perfection," he said.

I nodded and bit my lip in disappointment.

"Are you ready to head back?" he asked.

"Yeah." I stood up from his lap filled with sexual frustration. My clit seemed angry at me and I tried my best to ignore it.

He reached one hand behind my back and one behind my legs and picked me up. I grabbed onto his neck as he grinned

"That was way too much fun, by the way," he said.

"I would have enjoyed another hour or two."

His eyes widened. "Two hours? I may not be man enough for you, Cinnamon." We both laughed.

"You're definitely man enough."

He leaned in and gave me a quick kiss.

"Do you want to feel something that is as almost as amazing as sex?" he asked.

"I would rather have sex, but if my second option is something close, I guess I'll take it." I said the words sweetly, but there was definitely a bitter tone to them.

"You better hold on real tight this time." He grinned big as he stepped close to the edge.

My breath caught as he dove headfirst off the cliff. We flew fast and hard, and my heart raced with excitement.

The feeling was magnificent. It was like being on a portal while eating your favorite cake, after making out with Cash for hours.

The ground seemed to come up fast and I held him tight as the fear of us not stopping hit me. Cash pulled up about ten feet from the ground and flew straight across.

"Holy shit, Cash! That was amazing!"

"I knew you would like it." He winked at me before he looked back toward the trees we were headed for.

"Where are we going?" I asked.

"For a ride." He pulled up and shot higher in the air. We sailed slightly over the treetops. I was in complete bliss as I looked down.

After a long ride, we eventually passed the forest and were above a clearing.

"Oh, you're going to want to see this, doll!"

He dove again and it gave me butterflies in my stomach. He flew close to the ground, and we passed a family of four large doe. They had two little fawns with them.

"To the Gods. Those were the cutest babies I have ever seen."

"Until you see ours," he said with a grin.

"Cashmere Voland, I love you and I want babies someday, but not anytime soon."

"It wasn't an offer, just more of a heads up. Our babies are going to be gorgeous!"

"Well, obviously." I shook my head because I knew they would be. "How many kids do you want?" I asked.

"I don't know. Do you think six is too many?" he asked, and my mouth gaped open.

"Yes! I was thinking.... two."

"Okay, we will meet in the middle. We'll have five."

"That's not the middle. Four is the middle."

"Four sounds good," he said as he flew up. He grinned and I had a feeling that I got played.

Did I just agree to have four kids with this Angel? Yeah, I did...

"Are you ready to head back to the portal? I'm hungry and I want to take a nap."

"I'm ready when you are," I said.

We flew for another twenty minutes or so before I saw the portal in the distance. Without an ounce of shame, Cash flew right up to the portal. The guards there smiled big at us as he sat me down.

"Did you have a good flight, my lady?" a guard asked.

"I did. Thank you." I smiled as Cash took my hand and we stepped on.

Cash wrapped his arms around me as he willed the portal to go. The rush hit me, but the amazing feeling was nothing compared to what I felt flying off the mountain—or on top of it.

We walked hand-in-hand into the house and went straight to the kitchen. Cash made us both a sandwich and handed me mine. He grabbed my hand and pulled me toward the stairs.

"We don't even have plates, Cash."

"I do it all the time. I'll have mine gone before we even get upstairs."

We ascended the stairs and turned toward my room. I noticed when Cash opened the door to my room, that his sandwich was long gone. I had only taken two bites.

"Nap time," he said as he shut the door. "Are you napping, too?"

"Yes. I'm tired." I stifled a yawn. "Are you napping with me?" I asked, and then took a bite of my sandwich.

"No. You're going to stay here and I'm going to go to my room."

"Oh." I took one more bite of my sandwich and laid it on the table.

"Are you going to eat that?" he asked.

"No. I'm full. You can have it if you want. I'm going to change."

He picked up the sandwich and started eating it as I grabbed my pajamas and went into the bathroom. I used the facilities, changed, and came back out.

"Have a nice nap, doll. I'll see you before the show." Cash stepped up and wrapped his arms around me. He placed a gentle kiss on my lips as I slid my arms around his neck.

"Stay with me, Cash. And before you say no, hear me out."

He nodded. "Go ahead. I'm dying to hear what you came up with to get me to stay." He grinned and I smiled.

"Well, I will promise to keep my clothes on, and so will you. Also, if you stay here, we will get to cuddle together while we take our naps. If you go to your room, you will be lonely without me." I poked my lip out as I pretended to be sad.

"Cinnamon..."

I let go of his neck and placed my hands on my hips.

"Listen, I'm not taking no for an answer. Now, you go get your pajamas on and come back here and nap with me."

"Yes, ma'am. Remind me to have you act like this once we eventually get naked." He grinned.

"Go, Cash!" I pointed to the door. He laughed as he headed out.

Running over to the window, I closed the curtains. I wanted it to be as dark in my room as possible. I hurried into the bathroom and quickly put on some perfume.

Making my way back to my bed, I fluffed up the pillows. I slid my pajama shorts off and kicked them under the bed, so Cash didn't see them. I crawled into bed and covered myself up, so he didn't know I was in my underwear.

Yeah... I kind of lied when I said I wouldn't get naked. I wasn't technically naked yet—but that was on my agenda.

After a few minutes, Cash came back into the room. He was wearing his gray lounge pants again, but this time he wasn't shirtless. He had a white tank on. He walked over and stood next to the bed with a blank face.

"I don't know if I can do this, Cinder."

"Cash, just get in—"

"Just kidding!" The entire bed moved as he jumped on it.

"Ah. You're going to break my bed." I giggled.

"You think that's funny, do you?"

"Maybe." I gave him an adorable smile.

"You're going to pay for that." He crawled across the bed and leaned in toward my face.

His lips were only an inch from mine when he started tickling me.

"Cash, stop. Ah." I tried to crawl away, but he picked me up like I weighed less than a pillow. I ended up on his lap as I laughed uncontrollably.

"I told you that you were going to pay."

"Okay, okay. I can't breathe. Stop. Stop."

He stopped tickling me and I rolled away from him. His eyes went wide when he saw that I was in my underwear, but he didn't say anything.

Fluffing out his pillow, he laid back and relaxed. He put his hands behind his head and crossed his ankles.

Crawling over to his side, I laid on my belly so he had a nice view of my butt. I propped my elbows on the bed and set my chin into my hands. I was only about halfway up the bed, making my head very close to his groin that I quickly side eyed. I had a plan of attack, and I waited for him to get nice, and comfortable first.

"Are you going to come up here and cuddle with me so we can nap? Or are you going to stay down there and look at me with lust filled eyes?"

"My eyes are not lust filled. You don't know what you're talking about, Cash."

"Lust filled."

"That's it!" I sprang my plan into action and tickled him.

"Ah, don't. I don't like that."

"Oh, it was fun when you were tickling me!" I crawled up to him as I tickled him more.

He hugged me tight and pulled me into him. My arms were locked between his and my body. I was defeated quickly.

"Shoot!"

"You really thought you were going to get far with that, Cinnamon? I knew what you were doing." He grinned as he tightened his grip.

"Okay. Let me go, and I will call a truce."

He gave me a suspicious look before he finally let go. He put his arms back behind his head and I laid next to him.

"Goodnight," I said.

"You mean goodnap?"

"That's not a word, Cash."

"Well, it should be. I love naps and they usually aren't at night."

I crawled up to his face and laid my hand on his cheek. "And I love you."

Not giving him a chance to respond, I closed the distance between our lips and kissed him.

The kiss started off light and pleasurable. A sweet kiss that said I love you. After a while, it turned into more. My hand slid from his cheek and down onto his chest, and then to his stomach. I let it stay there for a while, not wanting to rush this.

His hands came out from behind his head. One went around to my back, and the other, surprisingly, went to my butt. He squeezed it, and my heat rose.

Deciding to be brave, I slid my hand down to his cock, which was rock hard. His hand left my ass and grabbed my wrist stopping me.

"Shit. You promised this wouldn't happen, Cinder."

"No, I didn't. I promised our clothes would stay on. We can do a lot of things with our clothes on."

Cash let out a large sigh.

"Maybe I should go to my room." He shifted like he was going to get up.

"Cash, wait. I'll stop. I promise." My eyes saddened because I really would rather cuddle than not have him here at all.

He rolled over to his side and faced me. "Roll over, I can't trust you," he said. I laughed and rolled away from him.

He scooted up behind me as close as he could. He pulled the blanket up over us and wrapped his arm around me. I immediately felt safe. It felt like this was where I was supposed to be.

"Your ass touches my cock, and I'm leaving," he said. I laughed hard because I was actually about to rub my butt on him.

"Goodnap, Cinnamon," he said as he nuzzled his head in my neck.

"Goodnap, Cash." I smiled big as I closed my eyes.

Chapter 29

Ember

Today was a busy day for me, I was headed across the field to meet Katzia for some ignitus training when I heard a squawk. Looking up, I saw Arna come swooping in fast and she landed in front of me.

"Hey, Arna."

Hi! Have you heard anything since the meeting with the new duchess?

"Not yet. I have a mission this afternoon. We are taking all our weapons to Vulcan so he can spell them. I may find out more then."

So, we aren't taking our weekly ride today?

"Yes, we still are. I figured you could go with us, and we could ride after."

That would be wonderful!

"Well, I must get going. I'll see you this afternoon."

Okay. Bye, Ember.

Arna took off into the air and I continued my walk. Seeing Katzia standing there waiting for me, I wondered what we were going to do today.

"Hey, Kat."

"Hey, Ember. Would you like to walk through the gardens with me?"

My eyes rose at her questions. "Um, sure."

We took off on a leisurely stroll towards the gardens.

"So, you were pretty fierce at the meeting," she said.

"As were you." I smiled big. I wasn't quite friends with Katzia yet, but we were slowly headed toward friendship, or at least I hoped.

"I just hate men who think that women aren't smart or strong. I could have burned that man alive if I wanted to, and he couldn't have stopped me."

"That's the kind of power I need."

"That's the kind of power you have, Ember. You must connect to your ignitus first."

We passed the roses as we entered the huge garden.

"I have tried, I don't know what else to do." I sighed in frustration.

"I have been talking to scholars and we have an opinion that we seem to share." She stopped walking next to some lilies. "These are my favorite flowers."

I smiled as her eyes lit up from the beautiful flowers. She leaned down and pulled one toward her face as she sniffed.

"So, what's this opinion?"

Her hand fell away from the flower as she looked at me.

"You haven't accepted it."

"What do you mean? I *have* accepted the fact that I'm a freak."

"Those words don't sound like you have accepted it, Ember." I sighed as she gave me a sad face. "For the bond to be able to take hold, you have to come to terms with the fact that you are a Demi-God."

"I know I am."

"Then say it! Say that you're a Demi-God."

My eyes wandered over her face as anxiety filled me.

"Um, I'm a Demi-God."

"Well, that didn't sound very convincing." She laughed and it was beautiful. I saw a real smile on her face and realized that I never really saw her happy.

"It's really hard to comprehend, Kat. I know I am one, but I don't feel like one. How can someone like me be one?"

"What do you mean, 'like you?'"

"I am not normal, Kat. I'm a broken, emotional mess. How can I be a Demi-God when I can't even control my feelings?" I wiped a single tear from my eye.

Katzia's face softened, and she laid a hand on my arm.

"I see the same fire in you, and the same love in you, that I have. I'm also an emotional mess, but that doesn't mean I'm not a badass emotional mess."

I laughed and sniffed back tears. For the first time ever, Kat hugged me. Pulling back, she held onto both of my shoulders as she looked into my eyes.

"I'm going to tell you something that's private." She took a deep breath. "My mate was killed over fifty years ago. I miss him every single day of my life. Some mornings I don't even know how I get out of bed." She dropped my arms as tears fell from her face.

"I'm so sorry, Kat." I put a hand over my mouth as sadness filled me.

She shook her head. "It's okay. I only told you that so you know that no one is perfect, not even a Demi-God."

I nodded my head and pulled her in for another hug. She broke away from me and pulled a handkerchief out and wiped her face.

"Now, I do want to say something else. Your ignitus will still work even when you are under the magic of another species."

Confusion filled me. "What do you mean?"

"I mean, you have Angels at your disposal that have amazing powers that can help you. One of them is even your best friend. You just need to learn to ask for help."

"I don't want to ask Zayn to do that."

"When things get bad, Ember, I go see my Angel friend. There was a point when I had to get daily doses to survive. There's nothing wrong with that."

"Maybe I will have a talk with Zayn."

"Meditating helps as well."

"I don't know how to meditate," I admitted.

"Well, I know a secret. You have an amazing friend in there that runs through the woods on four legs and meditates while she's out there."

My eyes widened in shock at the secret I didn't know. "Zila?"

Kat smiled. "Yes. She is very bound to the earth. I have spoken with her about it, and she said that she would love for you to join her when you're ready."

"Wow, I didn't know that. I will talk to her, too."

"Perfect! I wanted to tell you one more thing in case you bond with your ignitus before I see you again. Once you are able to turn it on and off, you can pick what you use it on."

"What do you mean?"

"I mean, only the things you want to burn will burn. If you want to sit on the couch, with your ignitus on, you can. But just know, the longer it is on the more exhausting it gets. Only turn it on when needed and turn it off when it's not."

"So, I could technically touch my mate and I wouldn't hurt him unless I wanted to?"

"Exactly!" She smiled big.

"Okay." I nodded my head. I had a little more respect for my fire skin.

"So, our class is done for today."

"We didn't do anything." I laughed.

"I think we did." She smiled big. "I will see you next week, Ember." She picked a lily from its stalk and strolled out of the garden while she sniffed it, then galed away.

Heading back toward the manor, I was in deep thought. Maybe Katzia was right. Maybe I should have Zayn heal me more often and not be ashamed about it.

Entering the manor, I saw Zayn in the study reading.

"You've been in here a lot more than normal," I said as I walked up to him.

"Well, you've been busy, so I was spending a lot of time with Cinder. Now that she and Cash are back together, I have little to do but read." He shut his book and smiled.

"I'm sorry for everything, Zayn. I know we've had a rough patch, and I just want us back to normal."

"We are back to normal, Demon Spawn."

I laughed and shook my head.

"So, I have a weird request." I bit my lip as my anxiety rose.

"Okay." His face was suspicious.

"Katzia said that maybe I should get doses of magic... um, from you. But you don't have—"

"I thought you'd never ask!" He stood up and grabbed my arm. I felt the warmth of his magic hit me and my heart seemed to slow down as my tight chest loosened. "There is a light daily dose for you. Let me know how well that works and we will work on altering it until we get it right."

"Wow. You didn't hesitate." I laughed.

"I do what I can to help." He pulled me in for a hug.

"Thank you, Zayn."

"No thanks needed, friend."

"Get your hands off my woman, Angel!" Zayn let go of me and I turned around to a smiling Val.

"And what if I don't, Vampire?" Zayn asked with a smile.

I watched as they both threw fake punches.

"You guys are so immature." I shook my head at them.

"You want some, Red?" Zayn threw a fake punch at me, and I didn't even flinch.

"Weak," I said as I stared at him.

Val laughed and pulled me into him. "That's my girl!" He kissed the side of my head.

"Are we ready for this mission?" Zayn asked.

"Val and I are. Where is everyone else?"

"Val, can you wield to everyone to head to the armory?" Zayn asked.

"Yep."

We took off towards the basement and headed to the weapons room. After filling two quivers full of arrows, I slung them on my back. I left my bow because it wouldn't do any good to add sulfur magic to it, so I grabbed two small throwing axes instead.

Val grabbed the short sword I gave him at our mating, and his other favorite. Zayn put his holster over his chest and stuck his twin blades in it.

"It's show time!" Cash said with a grin as he entered the room. Asher was right behind him.

Cash grabbed four axes and Asher grabbed two spears. Zila and Cali entered. Cali grabbed her katana and an extra one.

"I wish he could put sulfur magic in my teeth," Zila said as she grabbed two sai. I giggled.

"Is everyone ready?" Zayn asked.

We all said yes.

We headed out of the manor and toward the portal. I wielded to Arna that we were leaving. We stood there for a few minutes until I saw her swoop in. She landed with a loud squawk.

I'm ready!

"Hey, Arna." Asher reached up and petted her. She vibrated, showing her love for him.

"Let's go," Zayn said.

"I'll stay back so I can bring Arna," I said.

"I got her! You guys go ahead." Asher smiled and it was the first time I had seen it in a week.

We all stepped onto the portal, and it was wielded to go. Val pulled me in close to him like he always did, and

I felt his warm lips touch mine. Portal rides have quickly become a favorite of mine.

We landed in Mazuria and stepped off.

"Hey guys. There are a lot of you today," the portal guard said.

"We have business," Zayn said.

"Where is Arna?" The other one asked. "Isn't it flying day?"

"She's—" The portal swooshed, and Asher and Arna appeared. "Right there," I finished.

They both stepped off the portal.

"Hey Arna!" Both guards reached up and petted her, she vibrated lightly.

Hi!

"She said hi," I said.

"We have to go. You guys have a great day. Come on team," Zayn said. He was in commander mode, so we all followed, including Arna. She walked next to us.

"She vibrates more when I pet her," Asher said with a smile.

That's because you are hotter than them, Asher.

Val laughed and I shook my head.

"What did she say, Ember?"

"She said because you are her favorite, Asher."

That is not what I said!

Val laughed again. Asher's face looked like he didn't believe me. I was not about to tell him he was hot, so I ignored Arna.

We were walking on the outer edge of town, and I looked over and saw my old house. For once, sadness didn't fill me. I was content with my new life and new family. It also might have had a bit to do with a little Angel magic.

Once we entered the woods, Zayn stopped.

"We can gale from here."

I'm going to fly around and scare some town people. Val and I laughed as Arna took off into the air.

Everyone started galing away one by one. Val wrapped his arms around me and we galed, too.

We made our way past the wards and into the castle. Once we were inside, we were met by my uncle and an amazing guest.

"The King's Guard have arrived." Hendrick smiled big. "You all know Arien." He gestured toward the new duchess.

"Nice to formally meet you all. Hendrick has told me so many wonderful things about every single one of you. I'm honored to meet you."

She shook everyone's hand as they said their name.

She shook mine last. "It's nice to officially meet you, Your Grace."

"You, too, Ember. But please, call me Arien. Hendrick says the most wonderful things about you and your mate." She grinned and I could see a sparkle in her eye. I believed she had a crush on my uncle.

"Well, I'm glad to know that the things he says are nice." She laughed at my joke.

"Are you escorting us to the prison, Your Grace?" Zayn asked, still in commander mode.

"We are. I told Arien she could watch if you guys didn't mind. There is no need for formalities here, Zayn."

"Appreciated," Zayn said with a smile. "Lead the way."

We all followed Hendrick down to the prison and went down the stairs. I immediately went up to Vulcan's cell and smiled.

"Hey, Vulcan. Thank you for agreeing to do this. We appreciate it."

"Nice to see you again, Ember. When I read the letter you sent to Hendrick, I was thrilled to be at your service."

After Vulcan spelled Val's sword, Zayn checked it and it was filled with magic, so we knew he was being honest.

"Everyone, this is Vulcan. Vulcan, these are the other members of the King's Guard."

"I see everyone bought plenty of weapons to spell. I will be exhausted after this. Can you possibly entertain me with another deer?"

"Um.... I didn't bring my bow." My face saddened and I thought about running back home and getting it.

"I can send a hunter out to get you one. I will also have the butcher clean and quarter it for you so it's less messy" Hendrick gave me an accusing look and I just shrugged my shoulders.

"I would prefer to eat the entrails and other organs, Your Grace," Vulcan said, and my mind wondered about the fact that he was using royal formalities.

"No problem," Hendrick said with a flat smile. I bet he had the same nauseating feeling I did.

"Let's get this show on the road. I want the women to stay out here. Val, Cash, and I will go in with each person's weapon," Zayn said. His eyes wandered to Hendrick. "Can you unlock the door?"

Hendrick held out his hands and one of his guards dropped the keys into it. He unlocked the cell door. I immediately went inside and walked up to Vulcan. Val was right on my tail.

Ember!

"I really appreciate this," I said, ignoring Val.

"I told you, Ember. Anything you need." Vulcan smiled at me.

"Do you mind if I sit with you while you do this?"

Are you crazy, Ember?

"Be my guest." Vulcan waved his hand toward the bench, and I took a seat next to him.

Zayn is pissed, and so am I. I ignored Val again. He stood in front of me and crossed his arms. If looks could kill, I would be dead.... again.

Zayn stepped into the cell and took position on one the other side of Vulcan. "Cash, go first." His face was stone cold as his eyes locked on me. I swallowed hard under his stare, then looked away.

Cash stepped into the cell and pulled out one of his axes and handed it to Vulcan. "That's my baby, so be careful with her."

"Of course." Vulcan took the axe between his hands. It started glowing green, then got brighter, and faded away. He handed it back to Cash.

Cash inspected the axe with a confused face. I saw his facial expression change as he used his Angel magic and it glowed green. Satisfied that it worked, he slid it into his belt. He yanked out his other axe and handed it to Vulcan, who repeated the same magic.

Cash and Val brought Cali and Zila's weapons into the cell. None of the men would let them go near the Demon. Now that all my friends had their weapons spelled, that left only me.

"Did you bring a weapon, Ember?" Vulcan smiled at me.

"My dagger is already Demon.... um, sulfur spelled, but I was wondering if you could do arrows?"

"I absolutely could." He smiled proudly as I handed him a quiver filled with arrows. I was grateful that he was able to do the whole quiver full and not have to do each one individually.

"There you go." After doing the second one, he handed it back to me, and I slung it on my back. I handed him the two throwing axes I brought, and he spelled those, too.

"Thank you, Vulcan. I appreciate it." I laid my hand on his arm and smiled. He looked at my hand as his eyebrows furrowed in confusion. Looking back at me, his eyes filled with happiness and he smiled kindly.

"It was my pleasure." He crossed his legs with a look of peaceful content on his face.

Val reached down his hand and grabbed mine and pulled me up from the bench. I knew I was in trouble.

"I just got word that the hunter has brought the deer to the butcher. It will be here as soon as he is done," Hendrick said.

"Thank you, Your Grace." Vulcan bowed his head.

"You're welcome. Thank you for your service." Hendrick gave a nod of his head and we all left the prison.

We said our goodbyes to my uncle and headed outside.

"Are you crazy?" Val said as soon as we stepped outside the castle.

"Seriously, Val?"

"He didn't hurt her," Cali said in my defense.

"That's not the point, Cali!" Val said. She scrunched up her face and said nothing.

Then Zayn turned to me.

"Val is right. When we are on a mission, you are my soldier, my responsibility. Don't pull any crap like that again, Red, or your ass will be staying home for a month!"

Val nodded at Zayn's words as he looked at me.

"Zayn."

"No. I don't want to hear it. Do you understand me, Ember?"

"Yeah. I get it, Zayn. Sorry."

Zayn took a deep breath and sighed. "Alright, let's report back to the king."

He took off, walking ahead of us. Zila rubbed her hand down my arm, consoling me before she followed him.

Since I pissed Zayn off, I figured I wouldn't mention I was going to go for a ride with Arna, so I followed him, too. Val fell into step next to me.

Are you okay, love?

Yes. I'm fine, Val. Are you mad at me?

Of course not. I just want you to be safe, Ember. Are you mad at me?

No. I know you guys are right. I just have this feeling. I'm really sorry. I didn't mean to upset anyone.

We love you and don't want you to get hurt. That's why we both got so mad.

I know.

Why are you taking this so well? He asked, as he tilted his head at me.

Katzia said I should utilize Zayn's magic powers. She said that she must do it sometimes because of her anxiety. I figured I would try it, so he gave me a dose before we left.

Is it helping?

I think it is. I'm going to have him do it again tomorrow.

Good. Val put his arm around me and kissed the side of my head.

"We can gale from here." Zayn still looked pissed as he galed away. Everyone followed him.

"Come on, love." Val put his arms around me and we galed back to the outside wards of Pyreland.

After a ten-minute walk through the forest, Zayn stopped and turned toward me. "I'm not sorry for reprimanding you, you deserved it." He smirked. "But I'm sorry I yelled."

"It's okay. I know I shouldn't be trusting Demons."

"Yeah. He did seem awfully helpful, though. It was odd." Zayn's face looked like it was in deep thought.

"Erebus killed his parents. It was just easy for me to connect with him," I said.

Zayn gave me a sad smile. "Well, next time, wield to Val what you're going to do before you do it, so we can talk it out first."

"I will." I smiled so he would relax.

Zayn smiled back before he continued walking. We all followed.

Once we were at the portal, I wielded to Arna and she came swooping in within minutes.

It's about time. I'm hungry!

I don't know if I can go, Arna.

Why can't you go? she asked.

"Are you and Arna taking your weekly ride?" Val asked. I knew he had heard our conversation and was trying to break the ice between Zayn and I.

I shrugged and looked at Zayn.

"Go ahead, Red. We will see you back at the manor." He smiled and I nodded.

Val leaned over and kissed me goodbye. Grabbing her reins, I hoisted myself up on top of her. She flapped her wings and we ascended into the air.

The wind blew my hair back as the sweet rush of flying hit me.

Chapter 30

Cinder

Everyone was gone and I was in the dining room making a mess—also known as creating art. Since I had the day pretty much to myself, I decided it was time to make the signs for my stand. I had just spilled paint everywhere and I had a feeling Noreen was going to kill me.

"I'm so sorry, Noreen."

"It's okay, Cinder." Her smile was pained as she scrubbed the paint from the floor. I told her I would do it, but she refused to let me help.

"What are you ladies doing?" Cash asked as he walked into the dining room with a smile.

"Making a sign for my stand. I spilled some paint."

Cash looked down at the floor.

"Oh. Do you need help, Noreen?"

"No, my lord. I have it almost cleaned up." He nodded and headed over to me.

"Can I see what you're making, Cinnamon?"

"Sure." I stepped aside and he peeked down at my banner and his eyes widened.

"Primordial Pleasures?"

"Yep. That's the name of my bakery stand." I smiled proudly.

"Oh. Is that the only name you could come up with?"

"What? Do you not like it?" I asked.

"I mean, I like the name. I just don't know if it's right."

"Well, I named it Primordial after the Gods. I found an ancient cookbook with each of their favorite desserts in it. I have been making them and they have been delicious. So, I figured I could highlight a different God every week. Pleasures because dessert is very pleasurable." I smiled brightly, hoping he understood the name better now that he knew the meaning behind it.

"I understand that, but..." He tilted his head as he looked at my sign.

"But what, Cash?"

"Primordial Pleasures sounds like a whorehouse."

I gasped.

"Oh. Oh, no." My body sunk in defeat. I worked forever on the sign, and now I had to come up with a new name.

Cash laughed as I pouted. "You could still use the name."

"What name?" Zayn asked as he entered. I stood there, mortified. I couldn't speak.

"Her bakery name," Cash said with a huge grin.

Zayn made his way over to me.

"I'm so sorry, Cinder. I totally forgot to..." Zayn's eyes widened at my sign. "Primordial Pleasures?"

I nodded. "Do you like it?" I asked.

"It's kind of.... um. It sounds like a.... um."

"A whorehouse," Cash said.

"Yeah," Zayn agreed with a laugh.

I threw my paint brush down and took a seat.

"I guess I will start over."

"Have fun with that." Zayn strolled out of the room as he laughed.

"Do you want me to help?" Cash asked.

"I'm going to clean up so Noreen can set the table for dinner."

"I'll help with that, then."

Cash helped me clean everything up and put it away. He escorted me upstairs and left to go change for dinner. The meal was quiet and not much happened. Afterward, I went back to my room. It was after midnight, but I couldn't sleep. I kept thinking about what I should name my stand.

Deciding a little baking may help, I headed down to the kitchen. I grabbed the ingredients I needed and mixed up enough dough for two pie crusts.

Looking at the counter, I could only roll out one pie at a time because it was small, so I grabbed everything I needed and headed into the dining room.

Spreading the flour across the table, I pulled my dough out of the bowl and started kneading it on the table.

"What are you doing, doll?"

I jumped at Cash's voice in the quietness of the dining room.

"Oh, Cash. You scared me." He smiled as he walked up to me. "I'm making two pies."

"Yum. Can I have some when they're done."

"Yes. What are you doing down here?" I asked.

"I couldn't sleep, so I came down to get a snack."

"I couldn't sleep either. I can't stop thinking about a name for my stand. It's already past the date I wanted to have it open, and now I'm freaking out because I wanted to sell enough pies to have money to donate to the school thing that Zila was telling me about and—" Cash yanked me into him.

"Slow down. You have all the time in the world, doll. Your stand isn't going anywhere. You will get it done."

"I know." I sighed and relaxed in his arms.

Cash let go of me and pulled out a chair.

"Sit." I smiled and took a seat. "Let's just relax for a minute and then I'll help you finish these pies."

He took a seat across from me.

"Can I ask you something?"

"Of course, Cinnamon."

"Do you want to have sex with me?"

"Of course I do. Why wouldn't I?"

"I don't know. I just feel like sometimes you want to, then sometimes you don't."

Cash shook his head and bit his lip.

"I'm sorry if I'm confusing you. I really, and I mean *really*, want to have sex with you, but you're a virgin. You don't get to have a first time again. It's a lot of pressure to make it perfect for you. I just want to wait until it's perfect."

"I appreciate that, Cash. I really do." Cash took my hand in his and he ran it slowly over his lips—then kissed it. "But what if I don't want to wait?" I asked.

He dropped my hand and met my eyes.

"I think that's a decision you shouldn't make lightly." He raised his hand to my face and ran his thumb over my cheek.

"It's not lightly. I want you," I whispered.

He started to pull his hand away, so I grabbed his wrist, holding it in place. Closing my eyes, I pulled his hand close to my mouth. I could smell the hint of pine on his skin from some wood he must have been chopping as I ran my nose across it. Parting my lips, I kissed the top of his hand. Continuing the kissing, I made my way up to the tip of one of his fingers. Sliding my tongue out, I rolled it around the tip of his finger.

Opening my eyes, I met his as I eased his finger into my mouth and sucked on it. His wings popped out and knocked the wooden bowl I had my dough in off the kitchen table. I dropped his hand and threw my hands over my mouth to keep from laughing.

"I'm sorry," I said with a stifled giggle.

"You can make me flap any time you want, doll." He reached his arms around me, and I heard the chair scraping the wooden floor as he scooted me closer to him. "You're sexy and I want you, too, but I think you should get everything you want. So, if you want to wait until you're mated, I think you should."

"I never said we should wait until we are mated."

"I know, but you deserve better than that, better than me."

"I don't want anything else. I don't want anyone else. I want you, Cashmere Voland."

"My mom is the only one that calls me that."

"What made her name you that?" I asked.

"She said when I was born that my wings were as soft as cashmere."

I reached up and ran my fingers along the beautiful black feathers of his wings. "She's not wrong," I whispered.

"What are you doing to me?"

"What do you mean?" I asked.

"You're turning me inside out. Everything about you is perfect. I can't take that perfection from you." He shook his head with a frown on his face.

He wouldn't take it from me, but I was willing to take it from myself. I laid my hand on his knee and ran it up his leg.

"Cinder, don't," he grabbed my wrist.

"Do you want me to stop?" I asked.

He let go of my wrist, so my hand continued its journey until I reached a very hard part of him. He let out a moan when my hand grazed his cock.

"Do you like that?" I asked as I rubbed.

His response was quick. He pulled me in for a kiss. I scooted as close to the edge of my seat as I could as his tongue darted into my mouth.

He slid me off my chair and onto his lap. I wrapped my legs around him as his hard cock pressed into me and I let out a moan into his mouth.

Sliding his hands into my hair, he yanked my head back, and the roughness of his actions made me quiver. He kissed the front of my throat and then made his way up my neck. When he got to my ear, I shivered and moaned before his lips found mine once again.

I moved my core forward, and then back again. Another moan. The more I moved, the better it felt. The sensation was building and I knew if I continued that I was going to have my first orgasm. He let me rub on him until we were both breathless.

Needing to take a breath, I broke away from the kiss and tilted my head back as a large moan escaped me.

"Do you like that?" he asked with a smile.

"Yes," I said into his ear as I laid my head on his shoulder.

"Me too," he tilted his head and kissed my neck, "but we have to stop now."

"No, Cash!" I stopped moving.

"What's wrong?" he asked.

"It's just..."

"What, Cinnamon?"

"I don't want to stop. It feels so good, and I'm aching for more."

He laughed at my words and grabbed my hips and pulled me closer to him.

"I know, but we aren't having sex in the dining room."

"I've never had an orgasm before," I blurted. "But I feel like I may be close to one or something. I don't know."

"What? Not even alone?" he asked.

"No," I whispered into his ear as I started to rub on him again. He tightened his grip on my hips, stopping me.

"Are you serious?"

I met his eyes and nodded. "I have never, and I want it. I need it," I said breathlessly, as I started rubbing once more. I tilted my head back and moaned.

He stopped me from the blissful moment I was having when he lifted me off his lap and set me on the table.

"Your first orgasm will not be you coming on my cock through clothes. Lie back," he commanded.

I giggled with excitement at his words and did what I was told and scooted my butt down to the edge and laid down. I heard his chair scrape the floor as he turned it toward me. He slid my dress up, exposing my legs to the chilly air.

"Are you okay?" he asked.

"Yes, I trust you." I saw that huge grin of his on his face and it made my heart happy.

Lifting my foot, he kissed the top of it. Making his way past my inner ankle, he started kissing my leg. He kissed all the way to my upper thigh and across my panties and I gasped.

"Are you okay?"

"Yes!"

Sliding my panties to the side, he slid my lips open and ran his finger between them, I let out a loud moan. Pulling my panties back over, he stood up.

"What are you doing?" I asked. He grabbed my hands and set me up on the table. Grabbing my legs, he wrapped them around him and took off out of the dining room.

"We are going to my room," he said.

"Oh." I held on tight as he jogged up the stairs. I prayed to all the Gods that no one, especially Ember, came down the hall.

Cash opened the door to his room and stepped in. He set me down on the floor and quickly shut the door behind us. It was dark, the only light coming from the low burning fireplace.

"Turn around," he said. I turned away from him and was now facing his big bed.

I felt his hands as he unbuttoned all the buttons down the back of my dress. Both sides of it fell open and I could feel the cold night air on my back.

Brushing my hair to the side, Cash kissed my shoulder. His lips were warm and inviting. Taking their time and slowly moving away, heading down my spine. He kissed every inch of skin until he got to my lower back.

"Raise your hands," he said.

Putting my hands in the air, he slid my dress off. No one had ever seen me naked before, and I was nervous. I felt Cash drop to his knees behind me. He started kissing the back of my legs, and up to my butt.

His hands slid up my thighs and stopped on the side of my panties. Gripping them, he slowly slid them down to the floor.

"Step up."

I lifted my right foot, then my left as I stepped out of my panties. I was completely naked now.

Cash started kissing on my butt cheeks and I gasped. I felt his hand run up my inner thigh and stop right at my core. It slowly slid over my wetness as my head fell back with a moan.

Standing up, he pulled me in close to him. He kissed my neck, and I tilted my head. He stopped and whispered in my ear.

"Turn around so I can see your beauty."

Taking a deep breath, I turned around slowly and faced him. His eyes went from my face down to my breasts.

"Your breasts are perfect, doll," he said with a grin. I swallowed hard. I could barely breathe.

Lifting his arms, he pulled his shirt off and I stared at his beautiful chest. He undid his pants and dropped them. He was wearing nothing but a pair of shorts as my breaths came faster.

He pressed his warm body into mine and kissed me. My hands slid around his neck and his went straight to my butt and squeezed it. I moaned into his mouth as he lifted me up and carried me to his bed. Sitting me on the floor in front of it, he brushed my hair out of my face.

"Are you okay?"

"Yes," I said breathlessly. He smiled as he laid his hand on my cheek. Moving from my face, his hand traveled down my neck and across my chest.

A shiver ran through me when it went across my nipple. He stopped and squeezed my breast as his other hand went to my neck and yanked me into him.

My lips parted in a hungry manner as he kissed me. Our tongues rolled around each other as moans escaped into the night air. Lifting me from my feet in mid-kiss, he sat me on the bed.

"Lay back," he said. I scooted across the silkiness of his sheets and laid back.

Crawling on to the bed, he laid on top of me. I spread my legs, letting him in between them. I felt his hard cock press against me, and I really wished he had taken his shorts off.

His hand found my breast again as he leaned his head down toward it. I gasped when his wet mouth sucked in my nipple.

His other hand slid past my stomach and stopped at the apex of my legs. Finding my wetness, he spread it up to my throbbing clit and I moaned loudly at the sensation.

He continued sucking my breast as his fingers moved in a circle. My hands gripped the blanket tight at the marvelous feeling.

Releasing my breasts from his mouth, he slid down my body and I wondered where he was going. The bed shifted as he moved between my legs.

Running his hand up my thighs, he spread them wide open. A look of pure hunger radiated across his face as he stared at the place that only I have ever laid eyes on. His lips touched the inside of my thigh, making me jump with every kiss he placed. He made his way up to my center and spread my legs further. Running his finger over my clit, I shivered. He ran it down to my opening and back up again.

"Oh, fuck," I whispered.

"Since when do you cuss?" He laughed.

"Shut up, Cash."

My breath caught as I felt him kiss all over the outside of my most sensitive area. Spreading my lips open, he lowered his mouth onto me. His tongue rolled around my clit, and I moaned loudly. My hands gripped the blanket tighter as his tongue explored every part of me.

Heat was building, and I didn't know what was going to happen, but I was ready for it. A tingling sensation ran through every cell in my body. My muscles tightened and

I felt like everything was going to float away—I was going to float away.

My hands flung out and tried to grab the edge of the bed because I felt like my body would leave this world, and then everything exploded. Pure bliss ran through me as every nerve I had in my body lit up like stars in the sky. My hand reached down and grabbed Cash's head as the blissful feeling went through me.

My body went limp, and exhaustion hit me. Cash pulled away and crawled up next to me as I tried to slow my racing heart.

"Feel better?" he asked.

I couldn't talk, I just whimpered. If this was anything close to sex, I was ready for that, too. Running his hand up and down my arm, my eyes got heavy....

Chapter 31

Cinder

The sun was shining, and the birds were chirping as my eyes slid open. I felt a warm body snuggled up to the back of mine. Glancing over my shoulder, I saw Cash peacefully sleeping. Looking down, I could see his red blanket in the sunlight. I rolled over toward him and smiled at how beautiful he looked. His blonde hair was laying half across his face, and I pushed it out of the way.

"Oh, hey. Good morning," he whispered.

"Good morning, Cash. I'm sorry that I fell asleep." I felt terrible especially considering I knew what sexual frustration felt like and what the relief of it was. I also felt bad when I realized we left the dining room a mess. Noreen was probably going to kill me.

"Don't worry about it, doll. Last night was all about you." He grinned proudly.

"I can make it up to you right now," I said as I ran my hand across his chest.

"That sounds amazing, but I have plans for us today. We're going to go meet my parents. I want to tell them that we're betrothed, so we need to hop in the shower and get ready."

Panic hit me. I wanted to meet his parents, but I was nervous.

"What if they don't like me, Cash?"

"They won't like you, doll. They will *love* you." He kissed my forehead and slid out of bed.

I watched him with lust-filled eyes as he picked up our clothes and threw them in the chair.

"Are you coming?" he said as he entered the bathroom.

I slung the cover off me. My body was still naked from last night's events, and I smiled at the thought.

Gingerly making my way to the bathroom, I was excited. I had never seen a male's cock before, and I was ready. Hearing the shower turn on as I entered, Cash turned around and looked at me.

"You're so gorgeous, even with bed head."

I giggled as I stood there naked in front of him.

"Come on." He nodded his head toward the shower, so I walked over to him.

Looking down at his shorts, I bit my lip. I was overly excited for this moment.

"Cinnamon." I looked up at his face. "My eyes are up here." He pointed to his face and grinned. I laughed.

"Sorry, but since you have seen me naked, I think it's only fair that I see you naked, too."

"Good point." In true Cash fashion, he shamelessly slid his shorts off and stood there with a look of pride on his face. "Take a look."

My heart raced and I swallowed. My eyes traveled down his body and stopped at his hard, and might I say, *huge,* cock—or at least I thought so. It was the first I had ever seen, but it was glorious. Fear ran through me as I thought about where it was eventually going to go.

"Well?"

"It's beautiful," I whispered.

"Beautiful?" His eyebrows furrowed together.

"Oh, I'm sorry, dear sir. I meant glorious, very manly. It's the biggest and best looking one I have ever seen," I said, sarcasm lining my voice.

"It's the only one you have ever seen." He laughed and yanked me into him. I felt his hardness press against my belly since he was much taller than me. He laid a sweet, quick kiss upon my lips, then broke away.

"Ladies first." He took my hand and I stepped into the shower.

The warm water hit my face, and I immediately turned toward him as he stepped in. He smiled at me.

"Are you happy to finally get to shower with me?"

"Yes." I blushed as I glanced back down at his cock.

"We are here to get clean, not get dirty. So, keep your eyes up here, missy." I giggled as he grabbed the soap. "I'll wash you."

Grabbing the washcloth, he lathered it up. His hand raised up touching my nose with the cloth and left soap on it, then he laughed.

"Turn around," he commanded.

I did what he said and turned away from him.

He moved my hair out of the way and slowly ran the washcloth across my back. I sucked in a breath when it went across my butt cheeks. He continued until my entire backside was clean.

"Turn around."

"You are bossy," I said. I smiled at how authoritative he was and turned toward him.

He grinned as he soaped up the cloth again. Raising the washcloth, he ran it across both my breasts. I closed my eyes and enjoyed every second of it. He cleaned my entire front before he rinsed the cloth and worked on himself.

Tilting my head back, I lathered up my hair and washed and conditioned it. We switched spots and he did the same.

Once we were done, he pulled me in close to him and kissed me. My nipples hardened as they grazed his body. Stepping out of the shower, he handed me a towel, and grabbed one for himself.

We both dried off and wrapped our towels around our bodies before we left the bathroom.

"I have to go to my room and get clean clothes," I said.

"Make sure you braid your hair." He grinned again. "I will meet you by the front door in twenty minutes."

I held the towel tight as I opened the door. Stepping in the hall, I quickly walked to my room, hoping I didn't see anyone. Unfortunately, that didn't happen....

Asher's door opened and he stepped into the hall right when I was about to pass his room.

His eyebrows raised as he stared at me. "Um..."

"Hi, Asher." I smiled like everything was normal, tightening my grip on the towel.

"I'm going to pretend like I didn't see this." He smiled and walked past me.

"Thanks," I called over my shoulder as I continued my journey.

Slinging my door open, I practically fell in my room and slammed the door shut. I giggled from the excitement of getting caught.

Hurrying over to the closet, I peeked at every dress I had, trying to find a perfect one to impress Cash's parents. I grabbed a red dress that had tiny white polka dots on it, I threw it on and headed into the bathroom.

Looking in the mirror, my hair was a wet mess. Grabbing the brush, I quickly removed my tangles and braided it. Sliding on my shoes and then grabbing a white shawl, I headed down to meet Cash.

"You look beautiful," he said as I glided down the stairs. He was wearing a black t-shirt and black pants. It was very informal, so I was glad I went with the dress choice I had.

"Thank you." He took my hand and helped me off the bottom stair.

"Hey, Zila," Cash said as we strolled into the foyer. "Can you tell Zayn that we're going to Valmeyer to meet my parents since it's our day off?"

"And Ember, too. So she doesn't worry," I added.

"Of course. Have fun." Zila smiled as she walked past.

We walked quietly hand-in-hand as we headed toward the portal and stepped on.

He wielded the portal to go, and my stomach tingled in a good way as the rush hit me. We landed in the county of Valmeyer.

"Hey, Cash," a portal guard said.

"My lady," another said with a bow of the head.

"Hey, guys." I smiled as Cash took my hand and we stepped off the portal.

"This is even more beautiful in daylight," I said.

"Not as beautiful as you, doll." Cash winked and we continued walking for a bit.

The field of pink flowers was gorgeous with the rays of the sun shining on them.

"We can gale from here." He slid his arms around me with a smile and we galed away.

We landed just outside some woods. He took my hand as we strolled toward the direction that I assumed the town was in.

After a few minutes, a castle came into view and confusion hit me.

"Cash?"

"Yes, Cinnamon."

"Why are we going to the duke's castle?"

"Because my father is the Duke of Valmeyer."

"What?" I stopped walking, bringing him to a halt with me. "Why didn't you tell me?"

"It never came up." He shrugged his shoulders.

"I cannot meet a duke and duchess wearing this!"

"The duke and duchess are my parents. They wouldn't care if we came in pajamas."

"*I* care, Cash." I dropped his hand as my face scrunched up. "It was bad enough I met the king for the first time wearing dirty clothes and fresh out of a prison cell."

"You're gorgeous, doll. You have no reason to be worried. My parents are super easy-going and loving. Where do you think I get it from?" He grinned big.

I nodded my head as he took my hand once again.

As we continued walking toward the castle, I couldn't help but admire the beauty of it, even with anxiety flowing through me. Looking up, it was huge. It was entirely white brick with close to a dozen large, pointy, gray steeples, and one large gray spire. All the windows were arched, and some had etchings on them.

We walked across a huge drawbridge and a portcullis opened for us. A dark-haired man was standing there with a smile on his face.

"My lord, it is good to see you again."

"It is good to see you, Lucian. I hope you are faring well?" Cash's extremely royal tone was a shock to me. It was like his playful one, but it was real. Now I understood why he was the way he was. His parents were royalty.

"I am, my lord. Thank you for asking." The man's eyes wandered to me, and he smiled.

"Lucian, this is Cinder Lavaris. She is my guest."

"It is an honor to meet you, my lady. Welcome to Castle Angelcrest." He bowed to me.

"It is nice to meet you, Lucian." I started to pull my hand out of Cash's so I could curtsey, and he shook his head no.

"Where are my parents? I would like to see them."

"It is early morning, so they will be in the garden, my lord."

"Of course. Thank you, Lucian."

We stepped into the inner wall of the castle and entered the courtyard. My eyes widened and my mouth fell open in shock at the beauty. In the middle of the courtyard was a huge water fountain and in the center of it was a beautiful female Angel statue. Her wingspan was huge, and she was made with pure white marble.

I barely had time to admire it as Cash pulled me onto a cobblestone passageway. My eyes kept wandering around at the beauty of everything. Everyone that passed us bowed their heads and addressed Cash.

Once we took a corner, I could smell the roses before I saw them. We went under a large trellis covered in red roses and entered the biggest garden I had ever seen. My mouth gaped open as my eyes roamed over hundreds of red rose bushes.

We walked down a pathway that had roses lining each side. It took at least three minutes of walking to get to the middle.

In the center was a large white trellis gazebo covered in roses, and we walked right inside it. My anxiety rose when I saw a blonde man and a light brown-haired woman sitting on a white wooden bench. They were snuggled up next to each other, talking.

They both peered up at us as we approached, and the woman's eyes widened.

"Cashmere!" She hopped off the bench and hurried up to us. Cash dropped my hand as the woman hugged him.

"Hi, mother."

"I missed you dearly, son." She kissed his cheek.

She was wearing a gorgeous silver dress with beading and jewels. I immediately felt underdressed.

She turned to me and put her hands over her mouth. Her eyes filled with tears, and she shook her head. I held my breath as I worried what she would think of me.

"You must be Cinder," she choked. "Cash said you were beautiful, but my darling, you are completely gorgeous." She pulled me in for a hug and my eyes watered slightly as I thought about the last time that I hugged my mother.

"Hey, Pops." Cash's father hugged him and turned towards me.

"Are you going to let me see the girl, Aelia?" his father said.

"Oh, hush, Ezra. Let me be." She let go of me and took my hands. "Let me get a good look at you, dear. Oh, you are something else with your auburn hair and freckles. Wow. I love your red dress, too, it is my favorite color." She smiled widely as her beautiful blue eyes wandered over me.

"Can I at least shake the girl's hand?" Cash's father asked. His mother sighed and dropped my hands. "It is nice to finally meet you, Cinder."

"It is nice to meet you, Your Grace."

"You can call me Ezra," the duke said.

"Or Pops," Cash said with a smile.

"You can call me Aelia. Or perhaps you could call me mother." She gave Cash a side look like she was asking him a question.

"We came here to tell you both something..." Cash's mother's eyes widened as she stared at him. "I have asked Cinder to formally mate—"

"This is wonderful!" His mother threw her hands on her cheeks. "You will make a perfect duchess."

"What?" I tried hard not to have a look of shock on my face, but it was too late.

"Mother." Cash cleared his throat.

"Oh. My apologies. I got a little ahead of myself." She dropped her hands and raised her chin high.

"It seems discussions are in order. Maybe we should go inside and have some tea," Ezra said.

"That is a wonderful idea. Will you join us?" Aelia asked.

"Of course, mother," Cash said.

"Perfect! Come with me, dear." She took my arm and entwined it with hers and we strolled slowly through the garden with the men trailing behind us.

My heart raced at the mention of me being a duchess, and I wasn't sure I was ready for that conversation.

"Cashmere has told us so much about you. I hope this is not too forward, but I have never had a daughter of my own. I am delighted to finally get the opportunity to have female bonding time."

"I would love that as well," I said with a smile.

"Oh, you are so sweet. I just want to shower you in love and beautiful dresses." She laughed, as did I.

We made our way into a large sitting room that was completely open with a view of the garden. There was a round table in the middle of the room with a bright red tablecloth that matched the roses.

Ezra pulled Aelia's chair out and Cash pulled out mine next to hers before he took a seat on the other side of me.

"Would you like tea, Your Grace?" a servant asked.

"Yes, please. Thank you." The servant left the room and Ezra turned to me. "I am excited to hear that you two are betrothed, but I do have questions."

I nodded and swallowed hard.

"Relax, Cinder. He will not interrogate you. He knows better." Aelia smiled, and the duke chuckled.

"So, your uncle is the Duke of Mazuria?" he asked.

"That is correct."

"And your sister is a King's Guard."

"Yes. Her name is Ember."

Ezra turned toward Cash.

"Was she the redheaded one at the meeting?"

"She was." Cash's smile dropped and I immediately wondered what meeting they were referring to.

"She definitely speaks her mind freely," Ezra said and I stiffened as I worried about what Ember could have possibly done.

"That she does," Cash agreed with a smile.

"I liked her. She seemed fierce."

"She is." I smiled proudly at him and relaxed knowing that my sister didn't do anything stupid at whatever meeting they were at.

"I see that you speak eloquently. Have you had formal training?"

"I have. When I was younger, my father insisted that my sister and I both received formal training. He hired a pedagogue to come to the house and train us. I enjoyed it, but Ember hated it." I almost said that it was probably because our fake father planned on mating us off to the former Duke of Mazuria and the Demon King, but I decided to leave that story for a different time.

He laughed and smiled big.

"I bet. She does not seem like the type of woman who willingly bends to society's standards."

"No, Your Grace, she is not." Oops, that was out of habit.

"There is no need to use formalities with family." He smiled big.

A servant came in with a tea tray and set it down. Cash poured me a cup. Another servant dropped off a tray of small finger foods. Cash immediately made a plate and I was surprised when he passed it to me before making another for himself.

"Thank you," I said and he smiled.

"Now, Cinder. Has my son talked to you about the future?" he asked.

"Nothing other than mating and children."

"Oh, I would love grandchildren. How many?" the duchess asked.

"We decided on four." I smiled nervously.

"That is wonderful!" She clasped her hands together. "Have you talked about names?"

"We have not."

"Aelia, they are not even mated yet. We have other business we need to discuss first." Ezra said. "May I finish speaking to the girl?"

She rolled her eyes and sighed. "Be my guest, Ezra." She started making a plate of food and he laughed before turning his attention back to me.

"Since Cash did not discuss things further with you, I will just come right out and say it. He is the future Duke of Valmeyer, which would make you the future duchess. Are you up for that kind of task?"

Nerves filled me and I felt Cash's hand lay on my leg, easing me. I said the most honest answer I could think of at the time. "I am not quite sure what a duchess does, but I am willing to learn. With Aelia by my side, I am sure it would be a breeze."

Aelia smiled proudly at my answer, as did Cash.

"Well, I think you are right. So, I would like to put it on record that I approve this mating. Once the king has approved, then you can set the date."

"Thanks, Pops." Cash grinned widely.

"Can I get to know my new daughter now?" Aelia asked the duke, and he smiled.

"Yes, you—"

A loud horn brought our attention away. It sounded similar to the ones that I heard the night I was locked in the cell and the Demons massacred a bunch of Mazuria's citizens.

Cash stood up and yanked his axes from his belt. His father stood up as well.

"You stay with my mother and do not leave this castle, no matter what happens! I will send a guard in." Cash kissed my cheek and took off. His father walked over to a cabinet and opened it. He pulled out a sword and followed Cash out.

A minute later, a guard came into the room.

"We must get you both to shelter, Your Grace."

"Come on, dear." Aelia took my hand, and we followed the guard down the hall.

We entered a large chamber. Looking around the room I saw a table, couch, fireplace, and toward the back was a bed.

"I will be posted outside the door if you need anything, Your Grace." The guard shut the door and Aelia turned toward it.

She picked up a large block of wood. I immediately grabbed the other end and helped her slide it into some metal brackets on the door.

"This will keep us safe, but if I know my mate and my son, nothing will get in here." She gave me a sad smile.

She went to the table and lit a match and held it to a lantern. I was wondering what she was doing since it was daylight. Then she strolled over to the window and looked out.

"I'm worried about my people." She sighed and shut the wooden shutters and the room became dark.

"Would you like some wine?" she asked.

"Maybe one glass." With the Demons attacking and Cash and the duke out there fighting, I hoped the alcohol would take some of my nervousness away.

Grabbing a bottle from the bar and two glasses, she made her way over to the table and took a seat. I took one across from her.

"I have a question."

"Hopefully, I have an answer. What is on your mind, Cinder?"

"What meeting was the duke referring to?"

"Oh, the meeting with all the dukes after the Demon attack. That was a night for the history books. We now have our first duchess ruling without a duke by her side." She smiled proudly. "It was unfortunate that death came with it." Her smile dropped.

"When was the Demon attack?" I asked.

"It was a little over a week ago." Her face scrunched up. "Did you not know about it?"

I shook my head as I got quiet.

I had been lied to—again.

"Well, I will ask my son when he gets back why you were not informed." She shook her head.

Frustration and anger filled me as I wondered why Cash didn't tell me. Then, as I thought about it, I realized that it was probably not *his* idea to keep it a secret. But I knew whose idea it was.

Ember's...

Chapter 32

Ember

V al and I were sitting outside on the ground with Zila, trying to learn how to meditate when his voice brought me out of a state of zen.

"Zayn needs us, there is a Demon attack."

My eyes popped open, and I jumped off the ground. We all took off toward the basement. Since it was my day off, I was wearing leggings and a tank top and I immediately regretted the decision. If I had to fight Demons in that outfit, I would get torn up.

After grabbing our weapons, we headed toward the portal. Zayn was standing next to it, along with Cali and Asher.

"Let's go," Zayn said as he stepped on the portal.

"Where is the attack?" Val said as we stepped on.

"On Valmeyer," Zayn said, and my breath caught.

Of course, the day my sister is there is when the Demons would attack. My anxiety spiked. Val's arms immediately went around me as the portal was wielded to go. He kissed the top of my head.

She will be okay, love.

I stayed quiet.

Once we landed, I saw Cash, the duke, and two portal guards standing to the side. I drew my dagger from my thigh and immediately ran up to them as did the others. I didn't see my sister anywhere.

"What is the trouble, Your Grace?" Zayn asked. Cash's face was somber, and my breathing got heavy.

The duke sighed. "There is a body of a female Angel tied to an angel statue. The number seven was carved in her chest."

"Are there any other casualties, Your Grace?"

"No, Zaynith. We were lucky."

Zayn nodded.

I stared at Cash and I wasn't going to stop until he made eye contact. He knew exactly what I wanted when his eyes finally met mine.

"She is fine. She is with my mother."

I nodded.

"Would you like to see the body of the girl?" The duke asked.

"Yes. Then we will report to the king," Zayn said.

Everyone started walking, I stopped when I felt a hand lay on my shoulder. I looked up and met Zayn's eyes. The warmth of his magic soared through me.

"Daily dose." He smiled kindly and walked away.

"Come on, love." Val fell into step next to me.

As we got to the statue where the girl was, my stomach got uneasy. She was tied at the feet, her arms out to the side and tied to the wings of the statue. Blood dripped down her throat and her chest was carved up. I quickly looked away as did some others. Val, Zayn, Cash, and the duke all talked while they investigated and threw out ideas about the numbers. The rest of us had our backs turned.

Once they were done, they walked over to us.

"There isn't much left to do here. The duke's guards are going to handle the body. We need to report back to the king," Zayn said.

"May I check on my sister?" I asked Zayn.

Zayn turned toward the duke.

"May she, Your Grace?"

"She may. We will escort her up."

"Val, go with her," Zayn said.

"Thank you, Zayn."

He gave me a sad smile, then led the rest of our crew back toward the portal.

"It is nice to formally meet you, Ember. My name is Ezra."

"Likewise, Your Grace."

"Valarian." He shook hands with Val.

"Nice to see you again, Your Grace."

"If you will, please follow us."

We followed Cash and the duke into the big, beautiful castle. We were escorted into a sitting room.

"If you wait here, we will retrieve Cinder."

"Thank you, Your Grace."

Cash and his father left the room and I waited impatiently to see my sister.

Chapter 33

Cinder

It had been over an hour and neither Cash nor the duke had returned yet. I was in deep thought about how mad I was at Ember when there was a knock at the door.

Aelia walked over to it. "Yes?" She called out in a small voice.

"It's me, darling."

She lifted the wood off the door, opened it, and immediately ran into the duke's arms.

"Is everything okay?" she asked. She let go of the hug and grabbed Cash and hugged him.

"Everything is fine. We will talk about that in a minute." The duke turned toward me. "Cinder, you have visitors."

"Who?" I asked.

"Val and Ember are here," Cash said.

"I do not want to see my sister right now." I gave Cash a look that said don't push me.

The dukes' eyes went from me to Cash and back again.

"We will leave you two alone to talk. Come on, darling." The duke escorted the duchess out of the room and shut the door.

Cash strolled over to me with a flat smile.

"You know, don't you." He sighed.

"I don't know what all you are hiding from me, so why don't you tell me everything that I don't know."

He sighed and took a seat next to me.

"Ember has been having us keep all information about Demons and attacks secret from you."

"Why?"

"She said she didn't want you living in fear."

"And why have you been keeping it from me?" My eyes filled with tears as I looked at him. "And don't say because she told you to."

"The last time you two got in a fight, you didn't talk for a week. I didn't want you to be mad at her again. I did tell her that, if you asked, I wasn't going to keep it from you, but you never did."

"So, this is my fault for not asking?"

"No, Cinnamon. It's my fault. I should have immediately told you, or made Ember tell you. I messed up." He picked my hand up and kissed it. "And for that, I'm sorry."

"Well, I'm not that mad at you, but I am pissed at my sister. So, you can go tell her that."

"Cinder."

"No, Cash. I'm not going home, either. I'll go stay with my uncle for a while if I have to."

He nodded. "Well, you can't stay in my parents' bedroom all day, so at least let me take you out to a sitting room."

"To the Gods, I thought this was a guest bedroom." I jumped up and Cash laughed. He lanes in and kissed me.

"I'm really sorry. I love you, Cinnamon."

"I know. I love you too, Cash."

He took my hand and headed toward the door. Once we were in the hall, I saw his parents standing there.

"Are you ready to see them, Cinder?" Ezra asked.

"I have an odd question." I looked at Aelia.

"Go ahead, honey," she said as she smiled kindly.

"Can I stay here, just for the day? I do not want to go back to Castleva right now. I will send an Imp to my uncle to see if I can spend the night there."

"Of course, you can stay as long as you want. There is no need to leave—you can stay the night." Aelia pulled me in for a hug.

"Thank you." I realized that I did need to talk to Ember because I had something to say. "I just need a moment alone with my sister first."

"I will take you down there." Cash held out his hand and I put mine in it.

"Good luck," his mother said before we walked off.

Cash led me down to where Ember was waiting, and we entered the room. She jumped up, ran to me, and pulled me in for a hug. Val stood there with his arms crossed.

"I was worried to death about you," she said.

She pulled back and looked at my face.

"You lied to me. Again!"

"Cinder, I—"

"No! You don't get to talk. You get to listen."

She nodded.

"You have lied to me repeatedly. You have completely ripped away any ounce of trust I had in you. I know you say you're doing it for me, but it's for you, Ember. You are the one that is *so* worried about me that you are controlling my life and I am done with it!"

"I'm sorry, Cinder."

"Me too. I am sorry it has come to this." I shook my head. "I won't be home today. I don't know when I will be. I need time to think without you around. The duchess said I could stay here. I may go live with our uncle. I don't know. Whatever I choose will be *my* decision, and mine only."

She nodded as her eyes filled with tears. "I understand."

My eyes wandered to Val. *I know she is going to be distraught, so please take care of her, Val.*

I will, Cinder. You worry about taking care of yourself right now. I nodded at Val's words, and he smiled lightly.

"I love you, Ember," I whispered with tear-filled eyes.

"I love you, Cin." She closed her eyes tight as tears streamed down her face.

Unable to watch, I turned away as my own tears fell. Cash took my hand as we made our way back to his parents. He stayed quiet during the walk, as did I.

"Did everything go okay?" Ezra asked.

"Yeah, Pops. All is good."

"Perfect. Well, I will have a servant set up a guest room for you, Cinder."

I nodded and smiled. "Thank you."

"Are you staying, Cashmere?" Aelia gave her son a pleading look.

"Yes, but I'm only off today and tomorrow, so, unless I ask the king for leave, I can't stay too long."

She smiled big.

"Well, if you are staying, Cinder can just stay with you." She looked over at me with a knowing smile. "If you would like, that is."

Not wanting to look bad in front of either of them, I made a respectful decision.

"We are not mated yet, so I would prefer a guest bedroom."

"I will have one readied for you," Ezra said. "Now, I have some paperwork to do, so I will see everyone at dinner." He kissed Aelia and left.

"Cashmere, you should show Cinder some of the castle." Aelia smiled big.

"Yes, mother."

"I will go get some clothes for you, Cinder. They will be in your room when it is ready."

"Thank you."

"You are very welcome. I will see you both at dinner." She picked up the bottom of her beautiful dress and strolled off down the corridor.

"What happened today?" I asked as soon as she was out of earshot.

"We should sit, and I will tell you everything."

"Okay. Should we head back to the sitting room?"

"I have a better place."

He took my hand and pulled me through the corridor. We rounded a corner and stepped up to a door. He opened it and pulled me inside.

"This is my bedroom." Cash smiled as I entered the room. It was massive.

It was like the other bedroom I was in, but everything in here was black. Blankets, curtains, tablecloth, everything.

The first question that came to mind was probably the dumbest one I could have asked.

"Why is this entire bedroom black, but your blankets at home are red?"

He laughed. "Because it's my mother's favorite color, that way she is always with me." My heart grew at his confession.

"You're an amazing man, Cash." I stepped in close to him.

"An amazing man doesn't exist without an amazing woman beside him." He wrapped his arms around me as his sweet lips pressed against mine. He pulled away more quickly than I wanted.

"Now, let's talk. What do you want to know?" he asked.

"Everything. Start at the first thing she kept from me."

"Well, I didn't know she was keeping things from you at first. I just assumed you knew." He sighed. "The first Demon attack since you have been to Castleva was on Mazuria."

"Was anyone killed?" I asked.

"No, not that time."

"When was this, Cash?"

"It was the night that we were playing pool. When Val came in and you left."

"That was the night that Ember stayed with the king and my uncle to visit."

"Well, she wasn't visiting, she was reporting back what they found. We had a meeting with Val, and he told us about the attack and informed us about the thirteen guards and sulfur weapons."

"Thirteen guards? Sulfur weapons?" Confusion flew through me.

He sighed again. "She really has kept a lot from you."

"Apparently." I closed my eyes to fight back tears. I shook my head and took a deep breath.

Cash told me about every attack, a Demon prisoner named Vulcan, the sulfur weapons, the thirteen Demon Guards, and the numbers carved into the chest of some victims. By the time he was done, I was overwhelmed with concern. A part of me wished I didn't know now, and thought Ember was right, but I think that was because I had a lot of information thrown at me in less than an hour. If it would have been over the last month, like it was for them, it probably wouldn't feel like the end of the realm as we know it.

"Wow." I shook my head.

"Do you want me to heal your emotions?" He asked.

"No, I'll be fine. It's just going to take me a minute for my brain to catch up."

There was a knock at the door.

"Come in," Cash said as he shifted in his chair.

A female servant gingerly opened the door and peeked her head in.

"I am sorry to interrupt, Your Grace"

"Hey, Hadley. Come on in." The black-haired Angel stepped into the room.

"The room for your guest is ready, Your Grace." She stood there with hands crossed in front of her.

"Which suite is it?" he asked.

"The duchess had me give her thirty-three, Your Grace."

"Thank you, Hadley." The servant turned and left the room. Cash turned to me with a huge smile on his face. "Do you want to see your room?" He asked.

"I might as well." I stood up, as did he.

"Now, it's a long walk, but if you get lonely at night, you can come see me." He grinned as he opened the door.

"I probably wouldn't be able to find your room with these winding corridors," I said.

His grin was still huge as we stepped into the hall.

"Come on." He took about twenty steps down the hall and stopped in front of the door next to his room. "Here you go, my lady." He opened the door with a sly grin.

My heart sped up and a slow smile spread across my face. "Oh, maybe I will find your room," I said.

He laughed as he entered.

Looking around, it was the same size as Cash's. "This is too much, Cash."

"I don't know why you didn't just tell them you would stay with me. You slept in my room last night." He smiled big.

"I didn't want to seem like *that* kind of girl."

"You aren't *that* kind of girl."

"I'm not sure your mom understands that if she gave me a room this close to yours."

"I have a feeling that she is dying for some grandbabies."

My eyes widened.

"I hope she isn't holding her breath." He laughed at my words. "I can't get pregnant until I have my emergence, anyway. Thank the Gods."

"Do you want to see some of the castle before dinner?" He asked.

"Sure."

He smiled and took my hand. "Come on."

We left his room and headed through the winding corridors once more. He led me outside into the bright daylight where we walked down some cobblestone streets and toward a small section of town.

"There are residents inside the walls?" I asked.

"There are. There is also a market."

"That is amazing, Cash."

We walked through the streets and people waved or bowed their heads. After a while, we made it to the market.

"There is a spice stand," Cash said as he pulled me over to it.

"Oh, I am so sorry, my lord," a woman said. The very pregnant brown-haired Angel was sprawled out on a blanket in a comfortable position. She tried to get up as fast as she could. "My mate stepped away to get the children a snack." Cash stepped behind the counter and took her hand and helped her up.

"No worries, Lucy. Not much longer now, I see." To my shock, Cash reached his hand out and rubbed her belly and my mouth gaped open.

"You are frightening your lady friend, my lord." They both looked at me and laughed.

"Lucinda, this is Cinder. We are betrothed."

Her eyes widened and then she smiled big. "It is nice to meet you, my lady."

"Likewise." My face was still in shock as Cash held her stomach.

"I know you're in there. Where are you, buddy?" Cash asked her stomach. "There he is! My boy is getting stronger."

"That was a big kick, my lord. He always kicks the biggest when you are around."

"I told you before, Lucy. He is going to be a King's Guard." Cash smiled and released her stomach.

"Don't worry, my lady. He insists on feeling him kick anytime he is around." Lucy said.

"I can't help it. I love babies." Cash grinned as he walked over to me.

"Are you in the market for some spices?" she asked as she waddled over. I looked down at her belly with curious eyes. "Do you want to touch it, my lady?"

"Oh, no. It is very inappropriate." I shook my head and met her eyes.

"It is not inappropriate if you have my permission. Go ahead, my lady."

She stepped out from behind the booth and I saw her huge stomach in all its glory.

"May I have your hand?" She held out her hand and I placed mine in it. She laid it flat across her stomach. "If you talk to him, he usually kicks."

"Hello little one. My name is Cinder." I felt a thump against my hand and my eyes widened.

I looked up at Lucy.

"He likes you, my lady." I smiled as I removed my hand.

"That was amazing." She smiled kindly at my words.

"Would you like to look at the spices now, my lady?"

"Yes, please. Thank you, Lucy."

I skimmed over the spices and got two that I didn't have yet. She refused to take our money, but Cash slid some in her bag when she wasn't looking.

We were about to leave when a male walked up, and I assumed he was Lucy's mate. He had two little brown-haired, beautiful girls with him.

"Hello, my lord," the man said. He shook Cash's hand.

One of the little girls grabbed my hand and smiled, and I smiled back.

"My name is Parisa." Her rosy-red cheeks were slightly chunky.

I bent down next to her. "Nice to meet you, Parisa. My name is Cinder."

The other little girl hid behind her father's leg. She kept peeking out and smiling at me. My heart hurt for the amount of love I could have for two little girls I just met.

"Father, I have to pee." The little girl dropped my hand and ran to her father.

"Never a dull moment with children," he said. "Let's go." He took her hand and they strolled off.

"Are you ready?" Cash asked.

I nodded.

"It was nice meeting you, my lady. I hope we meet again soon," Lucy said.

"We definitely will. I want to see the baby as soon as he is born." I smiled big and took Cash's hand as we finished our stroll through town.

Once we were done, he headed back inside. He took me straight to the dining room since it was almost dinnertime.

The dining room was enormous, the table in the middle alone could fit twenty people. It was covered in a red tablecloth and had four golden candlestick holders with lit candles.

Cash pulled out the dark wooden chair and I took a seat.

"Did you two have a good day?" Aelia asked.

"We did," I said with a happy smile.

"Cinder got to feel Lucy's baby." My eyes widened as I looked at Cash in shock. I was embarrassed that he told his parents.

"Oh, that is wonderful. She is due in a month."

I smiled politely as Cash's father passed me a plate of potatoes. I put some on my plate.

"Are you two going to try for a baby when your emergence comes, Cinder?"

"We have not talked about that yet, mother," Cash said.

"They are not even mated yet. Give the kids a break, Aelia."

"I was just wondering, Ezra. I am not getting any younger."

"You are only a little over a hundred years old!"

"Do not tell people my age." Her face looked appalled.

"Angels can live a thousand years, so you have plenty of time for grandchildren, darling."

My mouth dropped open. A thousand years? Caster lifespan was only three hundred years. Someday Cash will have to watch me die of old age. Tears formed in my eyes from the thought.

"Would you like some more wine?" Cash leaned over and asked.

"Yes, please," I said as I met his eyes. He tilted his head and furrowed his eyebrows in concern. I smiled lightly, trying to hide my moment of sadness.

The rest of dinner was small talk. After we ate, we strolled slowly down the hall, hand-in-hand. My mind wouldn't stop thinking about me dying years before Cash. Then I wondered about the betrayal of my sister. Then I wondered about babies, mating, and my stand that I have been neglecting. Everything.

"Are you okay, doll?" he asked when we got to our rooms.

"I am. I was just thinking about Ember." He gave me a sad smile and I felt bad for lying. Well, I wasn't completely lying, I was thinking about her, amongst twenty other things.

"I know how upsetting it is." He slid his arms behind my lower back and pulled me into him. "Have I told you how gorgeous you are today?"

"Maybe once or twice." I giggled and smiled.

"You're gorgeous, Cinnamon." He leaned in and kissed me quickly. "Goodnight. I will see you in the morning." He grinned as he backed away towards his room. Once he opened his door, I opened mine and we entered at the same time.

Chapter 34

Cinder

The day had been long and tiresome so I ran a bath and hopped in. The warm water soothed my body and my mind. I was washing my body when my hand grazed my nipple and it hardened instantly.

Unlike Ember, I don't curse that often, but I couldn't help but to say — "What the fuck am I doing?" I immediately sat up in the tub.

Cash was next door, and I was in here. There was no reason not to be in the room with him—in the bed with him. We only had three hundred years together, and I wasn't going to waste one day!

I finished washing myself and dried off. I dug through the clothes that Aelia left for me and threw on the cutest, and smallest pajamas I found and opened my door.

Peeking my head into the hall, I didn't see anyone, so I slid out my door and walked over to his. Raising my hand, I knocked lightly.

Within seconds, the door flung open. Cash was standing there shirtless with a huge grin.

"It took you long enough, doll!"

One of his hands went into my hair as the other went to my lower back and he yanked me into his room. His warm lips instantly pressed against mine. He kicked the door shut as his hungry kiss took over my body. My hands dug into his back as I smashed his body against mine.

I started walking backwards to the bed, pulling him with me. Once I felt my legs touch the side of the bed, I fell on top of it, bringing him down with me. He put his hand on each side of my body, keeping his weight from crushing me as we kissed wildly.

After a few minutes, he pulled away and stood up. He was breathless as was I. His eyes stayed locked with mine as he lowered his pajama pants to the floor and slowly pulled them off.

"Scoot up."

I did as he said and scooted to the middle of the bed. Reaching up his hands, he pulled my shorts off. His eyes went wide and then he grinned when he saw I wasn't wearing underwear. He crawled onto the bed and kneeled next to my side. The cool night air hit my breast as he removed my shirt.

A gust of wind went through the room as his wings popped open. He looked over at one of his beautiful black wings, and I watched as he plucked a feather from it before they disappeared.

"Close your eyes," he whispered.

I did as he said and closed my eyes.

Laying there completely naked with my eyes closed, I was giving Cash all the power in the world. He had full control over me—over my body—and I was ready to be his puppet.

Cash shifted on the bed, and I felt the feather run across my forehead. It traveled across my eyelid, down my cheek, and over my ear. I giggled slightly as it tickled.

The feather left my ear and made its way down my neck and slowly across my chest. He circled it around my already-hardened nipple, and I gasped. Leaving one breast, it traveled to my other and did the same.

My skin puckered as he ran the feather across my rib cage and down onto my stomach, sending chills through me. It slowly made its way across my skin and traveled over to my side, and I jumped at the tickle it gave me.

Anticipation filled me as he ran the feather over my hip bone close to my core. It continued its journey onto my thigh, and down my leg.

He ran the feather across my ankle and onto the top of my foot before he moved to the other one. Now it traveled back up the opposite leg, sending shivers through me once it ran across my thigh.

The feather gently grazed across my pelvic region, and I gasped. Cash continued circling it over my core until I became breathless.

My eyes were still closed tightly when the bed shifted again. I could smell bergamot and sandalwood as his lips pressed against mine in the darkness. My hand slid up to his neck and he grabbed it and pinned it to the bed. I never would have thought that would have excited me, but as he gripped my wrist, my clit twitched, telling me otherwise.

His tongue slid in my mouth and rolled around mine as his other hand reached down and squeezed my breast.

After a while, he broke away from the kiss and let go of me. The bed shifted once more and I felt his hair graze my stomach right before his chest laid across it. His manly hands spread my legs open while pulling them up. I felt his beard tickle me as his tongue went instantly to my clit. I let out a huge moan at the touch of the warm, wet mouth that was now on me.

One of my hands gripped the sheets tight, and the other grabbed onto Cash's thigh that was by my head. Gripping it, I dug my nails into it as he swirled his tongue around, sending chills through my body. I felt the edge of his shorts hit the back of my hand, so I slid my hand into them. My hand found his hard cock and I wrapped my fingers around the silky skin.

For every lick he did, I gently stroked him. I wasn't sure what I was doing, but he moaned, so I hoped he liked it.

He reached around my legs and put them under his arms, holding them up. I was spread wide open, and the feeling was beyond amazing. His tongue rolled around from my clit to my entrance, and I could feel the orgasm building inside of me.

The feeling built and built until I exploded. I dropped my hand from his cock and gripped his thigh tight once more as every cell in my body lit up and the earth stood still. Cash licked until I was breathless, and my body went limp.

He dropped my legs, and I felt the bed shift again. He didn't lie next to me like he did last night, he slid on top of me.

"Are you okay?" he whispered.

"I am amazing," I said breathlessly.

"Do you want—"

"Yes, please." I dug my nails into his back so his warm body wouldn't leave mine. "Make love to me, Cash."

He sat up slightly and I felt him reach down and slide his shorts off. When he laid back on top of me, his cock was pressing against my core. I gasped at how warm it was.

"Open your eyes." I opened my eyes, and he was smiling lovingly at me. His face was half lit in the moonlight. He was the most gorgeous Angel in the world.

"Hi," I said with a giggle.

"Hi," he said back with a smile. "You do know this will hurt?" His face turned somber.

"I do. That's okay. Cali said it only hurts the first time or so."

"Do you want me to heal your emotions so you can relax?" he asked.

"No. I want to feel everything," I whispered.

He nodded and his lips gently pressed onto mine. I moaned as his cock laid against me. It felt amazing. I spread my legs further and it slid up between my lips and through my wetness.

He pulled back some and I felt the tip of it at my entrance. It was knocking on my door, begging to be let in. He stayed there like that, kissing me for a while before a tiny bit of it slid inside of me, then back out.

More kissing and it slid in a little bit further this time, and back out. One more time, this time he went in another inch, and I felt a slight pain, he pulled back.

I was ready to get it over with, so I dug my hand into his back and inched him in a little further.

A sharp pain radiated through me, and he pulled back. He went in again at the same depth and it seemed less painful.

He broke away from the kiss and looked into my eyes. His hand reached down in between us, and it circled on my clit. I closed my eyes as he slid inside of me again. The pain was unnoticeable, so I moaned.

He slid in further, only about half in now. His finger kept circling and I moaned again. His lips found my neck and sucked on it as he slid in almost all the way. My orgasm was building once more, so I moaned loud and dug my nails further into his back. I felt him ease into me slowly all the way, and he let out a soft moan.

"Oh God, don't stop, Cash."

He started thrusting slowly into me as his fingers continued their circling. My knees spread apart as far as they could at the amazing feeling. His thrust got a little harder with each moan that fell from my lips in the darkness. Sparks flew through my body once more, and I almost screamed as I dug my nails into his back. My orgasm took over and I gripped him tight. My insides clenched and a warm wetness filled me as he moaned along with me.

My hands fell from his body as my muscles went limp from exhaustion.

"Look at me," he whispered. I opened my eyes and looked at him. "I love you."

I choked down my emotions as I stared into those beautiful blue eyes of his.

"I love you, too, Cash."
He smiled big and kissed me.

Chapter 35

Cinder

The sound of bells woke me from my sleep. My eyes cracked open, and Cash was staring at me smiling. The sun was bright today and the birds were singing their morning praises along with the bells.

"Good morning, doll."

"Good morning. What are those bells?"

I rolled over toward him so the sun wouldn't be in my eyes.

"That's the morning prayer bells."

"Oh. It's too early for prayer," I said with a yawn.

"What do you want to do today?" he asked.

"I want to get a tattoo."

"What?" His eyebrows rose.

"I saw a tattoo stand at the market, and I want one."

"Okay." He grinned proudly.

"What?" I was now the one in shock as I threw the blanket off and set up.

"You want a tattoo, so let's go get you one."

I did not have to be told twice. I jumped off the bed and took off running into the bathroom.

"Where are you going," Cash asked.

"To shower!" I slammed the bathroom door shut and turned the water on. Before the water was even warm, Cash entered the bathroom.

I smiled at him as I slid into the shower.

"You're washing my back this time," he said as he hopped in behind me.

An hour later, I had him by the hand and I was dragging him through the streets of town. Cash stopped and stared at some weapons at a stand, bringing me to a halt with him.

"Look at that axe, Cinnamon."

"Come on, Cash." I pulled on his arm and started walking again.

"You're really strong when you want something," he said with a laugh.

"I'm just excited, so quit stopping!"

I pulled him up to a stand.

"Hi, I want a tattoo," I said to the man sitting there looking bored.

"What would you like?" he asked.

"Oh, I don't know." I knew I wanted one, but I hadn't even thought about what I was going to get.

"Well, I cannot help you choose. You pick it, we stick it. That is our motto." He pointed to a sign on the stand and that was *literally* what it said.

I nodded and looked over at Cash.

"It's your choice, Cinnamon."

I thought hard about what made me truly happy. "I know what I want."

"Perfect. Go behind the curtain and take a seat, my lady." I went behind the curtain and Cash followed.

"You cannot be in here, my lord. I do not know when she will be done, but you can check back later."

"I will go entertain my mother for a while, then. I will see you later, doll." He turned toward the tattoo artist. "Make sure your hands don't go anywhere they aren't supposed to."

The man's eyes widened, as did mine.

"Of course not, my lord."

Three hours, and a lot of archaic pain later, I was done. I emerged from the curtain with a big smile on my face. Cash was leaning against the wall next to the stand, waiting patiently for me.

"Let me see what you got!" He strolled up to me and I held out my wrist.

"Do you like it?" I asked. His eyes widened and nervousness filled me because there was no going back. It was permanent.

"You got a cupcake on your wrist?"

"Do you not like it?"

"I don't like it, Cinnamon, I *love* it." His eyes met mine and he grinned.

Cash turned to the artists and handed him a pile of money. The man counted it and his eyes widened. "This is three times as much as it costs, my lord."

"Did your hand go anywhere other than her wrist?"

"Of course not, my lord."

"Then keep it." Cash smiled big and took my hand.

"Stop saying stuff like that, Cash. You are going to scare people."

"Nah, he'll be fine. So, what do you want to do now, doll?"

"I hate to say it, but I want to go home."

Cash stopped walking and turned towards me. "Are you sure?"

"Yes. I need to talk to my sister."

He smiled big. "Let's go tell my parents goodbye."

Once we were inside the castle, we found his parents and said our goodbyes. We made our way out of town and hopped on the portal. We landed in Castleva, and my heart raced with anxiety as we walked inside.

It was everyone's day off and we heard laughter coming from the dining room. We walked in there and they were all playing cards. Everyone's eyes shot up to us as we strolled in.

"Oh, hey, guys. Welcome back," Zayn said.

"We just started a new hand. Do you want to play?" Zila asked.

I shook my head and walked up to my sister who was staying quiet.

She looked up at me with sorrow filled eyes. They were pink and puffy and I could tell she probably cried all night.

"I want to talk to you," I said.

"Okay. We can go somewhere private."

"No. We will talk here because these people are our friends, actually they are our family, and we don't keep secrets from family." She nodded and the room got quiet, as I continued my rant.

"I may not be a King's Guard, but I have the right to know what goes on, Ember. I also have the right to make my own decisions. You won't make any more choices for me. If you even attempt to, I will move out and you won't know where I am. I couldn't even enjoy a day and a half away from you because I had so many wonderful things that had happened to me and I wanted to tell you. I got to feel a pregnant woman's baby kick my hand, I had sex, and I got a tattoo!" Ember's eyes went wide and then shot over to Cash. Glancing back at him, he had a pained smile on his face. I looked back at her.

"And do you want to know who I wanted to tell first? You! I wanted to tell you, but you weren't around because you pissed me off. So, from now on, can you please try to refrain from doing that and just be my sister again?" I was breathless by the time I was done ranting... Or should I say over sharing. "Because I miss you, Em."

She smiled and almost laughed before she stood up and hugged me. "I'm so sorry. I missed you, too."

We hugged for a minute before Asher broke the silence. "Cinder coming home with a bang!"

I giggled and let go of the hug.

"Welcome home," Ember said. "Let me see your tattoo." She smiled big.

I held up my wrist and showed it to her.

"Oh, that is cute, Cinder. It fits you perfectly."

"Thank you."

"Let me see!" Cali jumped up and looked. "Cute!" She clapped her hands and I felt like I was home at the sound. "So, did you orgasm?" she asked.

"Cali!" Zila reprimanded.

"Don't say 'orgasm', Cali." Zayn made a puking face. "Gross."

A huge smile was on my face while I blushed.

"Oh, that's a yes. Good job, Cash!" Cali clapped again.

I'm pretty sure both me and my sister died inside as we stared at each other. I looked back at Cash, and he was grinning arrogantly. He walked up and put his hands around my waist and laid his head on my shoulder.

"Did anything happen while we were gone?" Cash asked.

"I got stung by a bee," Zayn said.

"I taught Val and Ember how to meditate," Zila added, and my eyes widened.

"Cali didn't come home until the sun came up," Asher said, and everyone's eyes shot to her.

"Snitch!" Cali scrunched up her nose at him.

Everyone laughed. I was grateful to be home.

Chapter 36

Ember

Three weeks had gone by since the last Demon attack and things were eerily quiet. The only mission we had recently was a food run.

It was late October, and the fall air was chilly as I stepped outside. This would be one of the last few rides I got to take with Arna before winter came. I had on a pair of pants and a long sleeve t-shirt, with my black corset over it.

I wielded to Arna, and she came swooping down.

"Hey!" I said with an excited smile.

Hi! Where is Cinder?

"She is coming. She had to grab a shawl."

Cinder and Cash emerged from the manor hand-in-hand. She was giggling at something he said.

"You ladies have fun," Cash said. He kissed her goodbye before he strolled to the side of the manor.

"He is so sexy when his hair is in a bun," Cinder said as she watched Cash walk away.

That is very true! Arna said.

We watched as Cash picked up an axe and started oiling it down. My attention was brought away when my own mate emerged from the manor.

"What are you ladies doing today?" Val asked as he strolled up.

"I'm going to meet an old friend for lunch." Cinder smiled happily.

"Arna and I are taking our weekly ride while they do that. Then Cinder wants to hit the market before we come home."

"Will you be home for dinner?" Val asked.

"We should be."

"Cinder, you will have to keep these two out of trouble," Val said.

I beg your pardon. Arna said, and Val and I both laughed.

"Oh, don't act like you're innocent, Arna. I know how you both are." Val shook his head. "We have to get a bunch of wood ready for winter, so I have to go. Goodbye, love." Val kissed me goodbye and headed over to Cash.

We strolled over to the portal. Arna went on first, then Cinder and I squeezed in next to her. I willed it to go, and I felt the rush of it before we landed.

We hopped off the portal on Mazuria, and I nodded to the two guards there.

"Hey, guys," I said.

"Hello, ladies," one guard said.

"Hello," Cinder said with a smile.

Tell the dark-haired one that every time I see him, I get feelings down in my —

Arna! I wielded and shook my head. "Arna said hi," I said to the guards instead.

Both guards smiled as they patted her on the neck before we walked off. We strolled about twenty feet away, and Arna crouched down so I could climb up.

"You're ridiculous!"

I'm just me. She said proudly.

I laughed as I pulled myself upon her. "We will see you in about an hour, Cin."

"Okay."

"Are we meeting here?" I asked.

"No, I will come to Wistar," she said before strolling toward town.

It killed me inside to let her go to town alone, but when we lived here, she had done it every day. I was trying hard to be less overbearing. I sighed once she passed into the wards.

Mountains first, then? Arna asked.

"Let's just do Wistar today." I slid the harness over my body and fastened it. "I want to get some reading done."

Perfect because I'm hungry. I can catch some fish while you read.

Arna flapped her wings, and we slowly left the ground. She ascended into the air but stayed about fifty feet above the water. Since we weren't going to the mountains, there was no reason to fly high today.

The wind blew my hair back as the scent of the ocean calmed me. Soon I would sit under the trees of my favorite place with a book in my hand, and I needed the relaxation.

A few minutes later, we rounded the corner of the mountains, and I saw a ship.

Whose ship is that?

"I'm not sure, it may—" A loud whizzing sound rang in my ear as an arrow shot past my face.

Shit. Hold on. Arna banked right as another arrow shot past us.

"Arna, go up!"

Going up is too slow. Hold on!

She shot down fast toward the water as another arrow flew past us. We were stuck between the mountains and the ship and only twenty feet above the water.

We took the tight corner around the mountain, and I believed we were far enough away that they wouldn't be able to shoot us anymore. I saw Wistar Aisle on my left and the Arna mountains still on my right.

"Who the hell was that, and why are they shooting at us?"

I don't know, but we are going home.

Looking around, I saw a Demon standing on the sand with a bow in his hands.

"Arna, watch out!" I screamed but, before I could get the words out, an arrow hit Arna in the side, and she screeched.

It hurts, Ember.

"I know. Get us on the ground so that I can defend us."

A few seconds later, Arna started descending rapidly toward the water.

"Arna, pull up!"

I can't feel my body.

I put my head down on her body and held on tight as we slammed into the ocean.

The water was chilly this time of year, and it took the bit of breath I had away from me. I struggled to get out of my harness, and Arna was dragging me down. We were both going to drown if I didn't do something quickly. I grabbed my dagger and sliced the leather straps of my harness. Once I was out, I immediately swam to the top and took a deep breath.

"Arna!" I screamed.

Looking down, I couldn't see her anymore. I couldn't hear her either.

Trying to reel in my feelings as tears ran down my face, I knew I had to get out of this water. I was a sitting duck. I looked around, trying to figure out what direction to go in, but it was too late. Something stung me in my shoulder, and my body went numb within seconds. The ocean sucked me under, but before I could go too far, I was pulled out of the water and dragged onto the sand.

Looking up, I saw the red eyes of two Demons. They left me on the sand and walked away. I couldn't see what was going on because I was facing the sky, but it sounded like they struggled to do something.

Another Demon picked me up, threw me over his shoulder, and carried me onto the small boat I had seen. While on his shoulder, I glimpsed over a dozen Demons pulling Arna out of the water with a net before he threw me down.

"You're lucky I'm immobile," I said to the Demon that dropped me.

His response was a kick in the side. The kick hurt, and it surprised me to feel it with a paralytic in me.

"I'm going to kill you!" I screamed as the pain sent shivers through me.

A sting to my arm made me gasp just seconds before my eyes closed.

Chapter 37

Cinder

After having a late lunch with my friend, I headed out of town. I walked into the tree line until I was well out of the wards. It was a beautiful fall day, and I was glad I had a shawl over my gorgeous tan dress.

Once I was outside the wards, I galed to Wistar Aisle and immediately regretted it. I gasped as I stood in front of two Demons. My heart started racing, and I tried to gale away, but it didn't work because my emotions took over.

Turning around, I grabbed the bottom of my dress and took off running. Within seconds, a Demon grabbed me.

"Stop it! Let me go!"

Thinking hard about what everyone taught me, I lifted my elbow and slammed it onto his face, and he dropped me to the ground. That hurt way more than I ever thought it would. As I crawled up from the sand, the Demon grabbed my ankle. Lifting my foot, I started kicking it toward him. It wasn't hurting him, but it was enough for him to lose his grip, so I took off running.

Only getting a few feet away, I felt a pain in my lower back. I fell to my knees and tried to grab what was sticking out of me, but my body went limp. I fell face forward into the sand as a Demon walked up to me. Not being able to move, I realized I got shot with a paralyzing dart, and I was, once again, a prisoner.

The Demon picked me up, threw me over his shoulder, and carried me toward the beach's edge. A boat pulled up and they handed me off to the Demons onboard. Looking around the ship while I was being set down, I could see Ember, who appeared to be asleep.

"What did you do to my sister?" I asked.

"She is just napping."

Hearing a squawk, it brought my attention to Arna. They stabbed her with a needle, and she went quiet before they removed the net from her.

"Where are we going?" I asked the Demon that set me down.

"To Mistlaven. Erebus needs you."

"Why?"

"You ask too many questions," the Demon said before I felt a needle stick in my arm.

Chapter 38

Ember

My eyes slid open slightly as the day's events returned to me. My instincts kicked in, and I immediately closed them. Needing to check out my surroundings, without notifying them that I was awake, I did what Katzia had taught me—I let my body tell me what was going on.

My muscles felt loose, but I twitched my finger to see if I was able to move again. I was. Exploring my senses, I started with touch. I could feel a cold marble floor beneath me, so I knew I was probably inside a castle.

Listening to sounds, I could hear two people talking, so I knew I wasn't alone. I could also hear a fireplace crackling and smell the wood burning. I was definitely in a castle.

Opening my left eye, the one closest to the ground, hoping no one could see me, I could see the feet of two Demons. I could also see Arna. She was lying down, and I wasn't sure if she was alive or dead. My heart instantly hurt, and I closed my eyes tight as a tear rolled out.

Arna? Can you hear me?

I got no response.

Arna, please don't be dead.

They say you can feel a broken bond and that the pain is excruciating. Opening my senses once more, I tried to see if I could feel anything different. I didn't, so I hoped she was still alive. I was praying to the Gods that she was.

As the conversation continued, I slowly opened one eye again. The Demons had their backs to me, so I reached my hand down to my dagger. It was gone. I also noticed that my shoes and leather corset were gone.

Shit. Opening both eyes, I lifted my head slightly to see if there were any weapons around.

Pain shot through my side as someone kicked me. I coughed out a breath as the air escaped my body.

"The mean one is awake," I heard a voice say. So, there were at least three Demons.

"I will go alert the Master," another said. Okay four.

Hearing the door close, I knew one of them left the room. I rolled over on my back and saw the Demon in my face.

"Get up," he commanded. "Now."

I slowly stood up, and he grabbed my arm.

"Where are we going?"

"To see King Erebus."

Ember, I heard Arna say.

Thank the Gods. You're alive. I yanked my arm out of the Demon's grip and elbowed him in the face. She didn't look good as I ran up to her.

Ember, run. Fight your way out. I heard them say that Erebus will mate you after you watch me and Val die.

"Do they have Val?"

Not that I know of. But he will come for you. You must go!

"No, I won't leave you!"

As I pulled frantically on the chains trying to free her, a Demon yanked me away by my hair and threw me to the floor.

"You don't do anything without my permission. Do you understand?" the Demon asked.

Anger filled my body, and I jumped up and immediately punched him in the face. His head flew back, and when it righted itself, I grabbed his neck and pulled his face into my knee. I ran over to Arna and tried to yank the chains off her again until I noticed there was a lock on it.

"Where is the key?" I squatted down next to her.

Ember! I looked up as both Demons were running toward me.

Jumping to my feet, I held my position. I tried hard to light my ignitus. It didn't work. A Demon lunged for me, and I stepped to the side as he stumbled past me.

The other Demon wouldn't fall for the same move, so I lunged for him first. I grabbed his shoulders and threw my knee into his groin. He fell to the floor, and I kicked him in the face.

Taking a few seconds to focus again, I tried to light my ignitus. I have never failed at anything in my life, but this, I was failing at.

Watch out! Arna screamed as I felt claws scrape my back.

I whirled my arm out and slammed the side of my fist into the first Demon's head. As I whipped my body around, I was met by the second Demon's fist. He punched me in the face, and it knocked me down. As soon as I landed, I kicked the Demon's leg out from underneath him.

He fell to the floor next to me, so I crawled on top of him, holding his arms down with my knees, and started punching him in the face. I stopped beating him, grabbed his head, and jabbed my thumbs into his eyes.

Good luck hitting a moving target without sight, asshole.

The Demon screamed and wailed as I felt his eyeballs squish below my fingers. He threw me off him, and I landed a few feet away. Jumping to my feet, I wielded a huge fireball. I was ready to throw it when I felt a sting on my shoulder. My fireball extinguished, and I reached back and pulled the dart out of my skin.

"Shit," I said when I realized it was another paralyzing dart.

My legs went numb, and I fell to the floor. The Demons who still had his sight, walked up to me and kicked me hard in the stomach. I tried to move my arms to grab it, but they no longer worked. They defeated me. I was going to die—along with Arna.

"Kick my mate again, and I will rip your head off, myself!" I glanced up and met Erebus's eyes as he strolled up.

Claws clicked across the floor, as I saw something possibly worse than Erebus following him in like a pet. The very large Chimera came close to my face and sniffed. It let out a growl as it stared me down. Erebus snapped his fingers, and I heard its claws clicking again as it walked away.

Erebus then kneeled beside me as his face looked over mine. Raising his hand toward me, he ran a claw lightly over my cheek.

"I'm sorry they hurt you, mate."

He is lucky my arms didn't work, or I would have punched him for touching me. So, my response was to spit in his face instead.

"Well, that wasn't very nice, now was it," he said as he ran a hand over his face, wiping my spit off.

"Fuck you, Erebus!"

"Oh, you will get to soon, dear." Ice ran through my veins at the thought of him touching me. He smiled wickedly like he knew what I was thinking. "Take her to my cell."

Two Demons grabbed me by my arms and carried me down a hall while my legs dragged across the floor, lifelessly. We entered a large, extravagant bedroom. There was a cell toward the back of the room and they threw me to the floor of it. They shut the door and locked it.

The paralyzer they gave me was strong. I couldn't even lift my head to look around as I lay on my side. Fear shot through me. This is where I am going to die, but not before Erebus had his way with me.

I love you, Val. With all my heart and soul. I'm sorry that you're going to die because of me, I thought, knowing he couldn't hear me from this far away. I knew he could feel me, I just hoped that was enough. I prayed to the Gods that it was enough.

I laid there, completely immobile for I don't know how long, before a Demon came into my cell. This one was different. It was the first female Demon I had ever seen.

The Demon squatted down next to me, and I met her eyes right before I felt a sting in my arm.

"Erebus wants you to get some sleep before the ceremony." That was the last thing I heard before my eyes closed hard.

Chapter 39

Valarian

It was getting dark, and Ember wasn't back yet. She had never been gone this long. I was standing in the study with Zayn, Asher, and Zila. Zayn had just sent a messenger Imp to the portal guards asking if they had seen them. I was pacing the room while we waited for a response.

"This isn't like her, Zayn. Something is wrong."

"Let's just wait for the Imp to return before deciding what to do."

"She will be fine, Valarian. She is strong." Zila patted my arm and gave me a sweet smile, trying to soothe me.

"I know she is."

"Do you want me to—"

"No, don't alter my feelings, Zayn."

"Okay, buddy."

The door flung open as Cash and Cali entered.

"What's going on?" Cash asked.

"Ember, Cinder, and Arna are missing." A low growl left me.

"We have to go—"

"Hold on, Cash. We are waiting for the Imp to return." Zayn ran a hand through his hair.

"Weren't they just going to Mazuria, like they do every week?" Cali asked.

"Yeah. That's what Ember said before they left." I cracked my neck in frustration. "But that was over eight hours ago."

The Imp appeared in the middle of the room, and I yanked the letter from his hand before he spoke.

"What does it say?" Cash asked.

"They haven't seen them since this morning. I'm going there."

"We all will. Weapons room," Zayn said and I took off out of the study.

I made my way down the stairs to the armory as fast as I could while everyone followed me. I slid my harness on and grabbed a short sword. Running, I took off up the stairs. Cash was right on my ass.

"Val, Cash, wait," Zayn hollered. I didn't stop. Neither did Cash.

Ember was my life. The blood that ran through my veins, my *hertis rote*. I wasn't stopping for anyone. I ran out the manor's front door and up on the portal.

"Stop!" Zayn screamed.

"Fuck." I waited on the portal as my team ran up.

"We have to tell the king first," Zayn said breathlessly.

"You can. I'm leaving now."

"Me too." Cash yanked his axe from his belt.

"Val, we have—"

"I love you, Zayn, but no one is stopping me. So, either get on the portal or let me go.... please." I wasn't a begging man, but I was begging.

He looked at me and sighed. "Everyone goes with Val. I'll tell the king. Be careful."

Everyone but Zayn stepped on the portal, and I wielded it to go. A few seconds later, we landed in Mazuria. I ran up to the portal guards on duty.

"Have you seen them?"

"Not since they got off earlier."

Galing as close as I could to their old house, I ran up on the porch. I turned the handle, but the door was locked, so I kicked it open, and Cash and I walked in. Looking around the house, it was empty, and sheets covered everything, just how Cinder and Cali left it.

The rest of our team was standing on the porch when we came outside.

"They aren't here," I said to them.

"Where the hell could they be?" Cash asked.

An overwhelming feeling hit me hard. I felt Ember's fear as it shot through me.

"The Demons have her."

"How do you know?" Asher asked.

"I just felt her fear run through me."

"What are we going to do?" Cali asked in a panic.

"Go get them the fuck back." Cash's face was stone cold.

"Can you tell if Cinder and Arna are with them?" Zila asked.

"No, I just know that Ember is scared and now pissed off. Which means she is probably trying to fight her way out."

"Well, what are we doing?" Asher asked while he spun his spear.

"You guys wait by the portal. I will be right back. I have a Demon friend I need to talk to."

I galed away and landed outside the wards of the duke's castle. Once it came into view, I saw a guard outside and ran up to him.

"Get the duke!" I yelled.

He went inside and I followed him. He went straight and I went right.

"Hey, where are you going?" He asked.

"Tell him to meet me in the prison, and hurry," I called over my shoulder. I took off running until I made it to the prison. Jogging down the stairs as fast as I could, I almost fell.

There was a guard at the door, and he said nothing as I flew past. Vulcan was sitting on a bench, staring off into a corner when I approached. His eyes shot to mine.

"Erebus took her!"

He jumped to his feet in a panic.

"He will turn her!"

"I know," I said breathlessly.

"We have to go get her back, Valarian."

"Do you know where they would do the ritual?"

"I do. Take me with you, my lord."

"You expect me to trust you enough to take you on a rescue mission to save my mate?"

"My friend!"

"Excuse me?"

"Ember is my friend! She is the only friend I have ever had. I would never do anything to hurt her." His red eyes saddened.

I stared him down as I thought about what Ember would do. She trusted Vulcan. She had even sat next to him and he never once even gave her a dirty look.

"Don't make me regret this." I turned toward the guard. "Keys." I held out my hand and his face looked shocked.

"I cannot give you the keys."

"Give me the fucking keys!" I growled and the guard jumped in fear. I knew the blood had rushed to my face in anger, causing veins to pop out. I tried hard to breathe and relax my body so they would disappear.

The duke came rushing in with a panicked face.

"What is going on, Valarian?"

"I need the keys so I can let Vulcan out."

My jaw tightened as he glared at me in shock.

"For what?" he asked.

"Erebus has Ember. I need Vulcan to show us where they are."

Hendrick's face looked like he was struggling with a decision, then he turned toward the guard.

"Keys." The guard dropped them in his hand, and he unlocked the cell. "Do not do anything stupid," Hendrick said as he opened the cell.

"Let's go, Vulcan." I nodded my head toward the exit and Vulcan emerged from the cell.

"I'm coming with you," Hendrick said.

"Do you think that is a good idea?" I asked.

"What good is my King's Guard training if I don't get to use it."

I shook my head.

"I appreciate the offer, but I feel like it would be best if you updated the king on what's going on. We left so quickly that we didn't have time to fill him in." I completely lied. I didn't need to worry about getting a duke killed on my watch.

"I will report to King Reign and see what he wants to do. Be careful and bring my niece back."

I nodded. "I'll do my best." I left the prison and Vulcan followed me out.

"I haven't been outside in over a month," Vulcan said.

I nodded and kept quiet.

Once we were outside the wards, I uncomfortably slid my hands around Vulcan and galed us to the forest.

"Come on," I said. He followed me as we jogged up to my friends. The look on their faces was priceless when they saw a Demon next to me.

"Are we breaking out prisoners now?" Cali asked.

"Hendrick knows. Come on," I said.

"Shouldn't we wait for Zayn?" Asher asked.

"Nope," Cash and I said in unison as we walked off toward the portal, and everyone followed.

"But isn't he in charge?"

I stopped walking and turned toward him.

"No, Asher, he isn't! I'm in charge since I'm the first in command. Zayn only does it because I don't fucking want to! So, shut up and do as I say or go back to Castleva!"

Turning back around, the portal guard's eyes were wide as I stepped on. I wasn't sure if it was from my yelling, or the fact that we had a Demon with us. Cash and Vulcan stepped onto the portal without hesitation.

"If anyone doesn't want to go, you can stay here and wait for Zayn."

"My woman is there. You know I'm not staying." Cash tied his hair up, ready for action.

"Me either," Zila said.

Cali had a sad smile as she came and stood next to me. "Obviously, I'm in."

I met Asher's eyes.

"In or out, buddy?" As I looked at his sad face, I felt bad for letting my temper get the best of me. I always worked hard to keep it under control.

"In," Asher said as he stepped onto the portal.

"I didn't mean to yell, Ash."

"It's okay. Let's go save them," he said as he patted my shoulder.

I wielded the portal to go, and a few seconds later, we were in my homeland.

"Where are we?" Asher asked.

"Mayhem," I said.

"Vampire land?"

"Yep," Cali said.

"I'm going to go talk to my father. You guys go to the docks and prepare a ship. Cash is in charge until I get there. Someone will have to take Asher since he doesn't know the way. Um..." I looked at Vulcan and he shook his head, "and Vulcan."

"I got Asher," Cali said, as she wrapped her arms around him.

My eyes landed on Cash.

Can you take him, please? I wielded.

"I got him." Cash put his arms around the Demon and galed away.

I galed and landed as close as I could outside the castle wards. An enormous surge of emotions came from Ember. It was love.

I love you, too. I'm coming for you, my love. I knew she couldn't hear me, but I didn't care.

Running hard and fast, I wielded to my father. *Father, I need you! I'm outside.*

Before I got to the castle, he was coming out the door.

"What is wrong, son?" he asked.

"The Demons have Ember. I believe they have her sister and Arna, too." My breaths were fast and ragged.

"What do you need me to do?"

"I need a ship, and I need it now."

"Don't waste time. Go! I will send a message to the docks immediately."

"Thank you, father." I pulled him in for a hug.

"Be safe, my son," he whispered.

"Always." I took off running back outside the wards.

As soon as I was far enough away, I galed to the docks. I landed and immediately ran up to the ship, and a guard stopped me.

"Like I was telling your friends, we haven't gotten word from your father, so you cannot take this ship."

"Get the fuck out of my way, or I will rip your head off." A low rumbling growl left me.

"V," I heard Cali say.

"I'm sorry, Valarian, but until your father—" Grabbing the guard by the throat, I threw him to the side and walked onto the ship.

When I heard footsteps behind me, I turned around to see my friends coming aboard.

"Come on, Vulcan," I said and he stepped onto the ship and six guards followed him.

"You cannot take this ship!" a guard shouted.

A large growl escaped me as a guard grabbed Zila's shoulder. She immediately elbowed him in the stomach, and he let her go. I grabbed him by the throat and threw him to the side.

Cash was pounding on any guard that moved. Asher started fighting a guard with the blunt end of his spear. Cali jumped on the front of one and head-butted him in his face. Another guard ran up to me, and I punched him and knocked him out. I was trying to immobilize them, not kill them. Three more guards came onto the ship. Vulcan stepped back, not engaging in the fight.

"Stop!" one of them yelled.

We all stopped and stared at him while we caught our breaths.

"We got the letter. You can go."

"Thank you," I said breathlessly.

His eyes wandered to Vulcan and back to me. "Good luck on your mission." He reached down to help the guard I knocked out, and they all left the ship.

"Now what?" Zila asked.

"Does anyone know how to sail this thing?" I asked.

"I do," Natsu said as he boarded the ship. He stopped hard and stared at Vulcan with wide eyes.

"How the hell did you know we were here?"

"I brought him." Zayn strolled on. "I figured we would need a sailor if the Demons had her. I see you broke out a prisoner."

I shrugged my shoulders.

"So, you guys just figured you would take out a bunch of guards and steal a ship?" Natsu asked.

"Absolutely." Cash said arrogantly. "We will do anything to save them."

"I got permission from my father. The letter just didn't come quick enough."

"What's with the Demon?" Natsu asked.

"Natsu, this is Vulcan." He eyed the Demon up and down. "He is Ember's, um... our friend. He spelled all our weapons with sulfur magic."

"Nice to meet you, Vulcan." His head bowed slightly, but his wide eyes never left the Demon.

"The pleasure is all mine. Would you like me to spell your weapon?" Vulcan asked. Natsu's eyes met mine and I nodded. He pulled his sword from his back and hesitantly handed it to Vulcan.

Vulcan took the sword between his hands, and it glowed green. The magic light got brighter before it faded away.

"Here you go." Vulcan handed the weapon back to Natsu.

"Thanks." Natsu looked it over with furrowed eyebrows and Vulcan smiled arrogantly.

"Can you sail this thing?" Asher asked Natsu. "It's bigger than yours."

"She is no Miss Conduct, but she will do." Natsu immediately started preparing the ship. Cash and Zayn started untying ropes as I watched.

Cali came up and hugged me.

"She will be okay, V, I just know she will. She's a fighter."

"Thanks." I let go of the hug, and she went and took a seat next to Zila.

Natsu took the helm and we left the dock.

"This is going to be a long ride," Natsu said. "The wind is against us."

"Of course it is." I looked over at Asher.

"I can use my wind, but I will be exhausted using that much magic. So, I probably wouldn't be much help during a fight."

I shook my head. We needed all the help we could get.

With a sigh, I crossed my arms and stared in the direction of the Demon lands for the next nine hours.

Chapter 40

Cinder

S omeone shaking me, startled me from my sleep.
"Wake up, Cinder," I heard Ember whisper.

"What?" I asked.

"Get up. We must devise a plan."

Looking around, I began to panic as I seen we were locked up.

"Where are we?"

"We are in a cell, in Erebus's bedroom. I don't know when they brought you in. They shot me up with a paralyzer and then a tranquilizer."

"Me too." I rubbed my eyes as I tried to wake up from the grogginess.

"How did they get you?" she asked.

"I went to Wistar Isle, and they were there when I got there."

"They must have been watching me for weeks to know my schedule with Arna."

"Where is Arna?" I asked.

"She is chained up in the main area."

"Main area of what? Where exactly are we?" I set up and pulled my knees up to my chest and hugged them.

"I believe we are in Nebulous. It's a town on Mistlaven, but I'm not sure. My guess is this is Erebus's castle, since he is here."

"How will we get out?"

"I'm not sure yet, but when the Demons come, you need to pretend to still be out of it. We need them to think that we are still drugged up."

"Then what?" I asked.

"I don't know, Cinder. Fight for our lives, I guess. I tried hard to use my ignitus, but it isn't working, and I don't have any weapons."

"Then how will we fight?"

"Use your fire as much as you can and use the skills you learned in sparring. If you get a chance to run, do it."

"Where to?"

"If I remember correctly from the map in the library, the castle isn't located that far from the prison. If you can manage to get out, go behind the castle and go into the forest and keep going until you reach the sand. Once you are on the beach, wait. If I know our friends, they will come up there."

"Okay."

"Fight back, do whatever you can. Don't let them—shit, lie down."

Ember hit the floor, so I did the same. As I lay on my side, I closed my eyes. I heard the lock on the cell click and the iron door open.

"Get up," a Demon said.

"Why?" I asked, but didn't move.

He yanked on my arm and pulled. "I said get up."

I slowly rose from the floor on shaky legs. I wasn't pretending, they were actually shaky.

"Where are we?" I asked.

"This one asks a lot of questions," one Demon said to another.

"She does. Get the mean one up." The Demon nodded his head toward Ember.

"Come on, get up." He yanked on her arm and lifted her to her feet.

They escorted us by our arms down a few hallways and out to a large central area of the castle. When we entered the large room, I saw Arna chained up. Her chest rose and fell, so she must have been sleeping.

They threw us both to the floor.

"Stay there and don't move."

We watched as over a dozen Demons ran around the room, getting things ready. They brought a bunch of wood into the center of the room—enough for an enormous bonfire. One Demon brought in a long table and set it next to the pile of wood. Another one set a large golden bowl in the table's middle, and laid three swords next to it.

"What are they doing?" I asked in a whisper.

"A ritual."

"For?"

"To raise Tartarus." My breath caught at her words.

The Demons set up another table along the front wall and covered it with suspicious food. A handful of Demons brought in a large marble altar and placed it on the right side of the room by the wood. A Demon wearing a long white cloak entered the room and placed two goblets and a knife on the altar.

"When I make a move, you run. I'm going to try to light my ignitus," Ember whispered.

I nodded.

Ember's eyes narrowed, and I could tell she was concentrating hard, but nothing was happening.

My eyes shot toward the white cloaked Demon as he made his way over to us.

"Are you the virgin?" he asked me as he approached.

"What?"

"I *said,* are you the virgin?"

"She knows what you said, asshole." Ember narrowed her eyes at him.

Another Demon punched her in the face, making her fall to the floor. I gasped and threw my hands over my mouth.

"I asked you a question," the cloaked Demon said. I looked over at Ember. She ran her hand over her mouth and wiped the blood off. She nodded her head slightly. I hoped I understood what she was saying.

"Yes, I am the virgin."

"Good. My name is Tellus. I will be handling the ceremony. What is your name?"

"Um, it's Cinder."

"It's now time to prepare you for your sacrament."

A Demon reached down and grabbed my arm.

"Don't touch her!" Ember screamed as she threw a fireball at Tellus, and he barely dodged it.

The Demon that had punched her, kicked her in her back and she fell over, he then proceeded to kick her in the stomach, and she grabbed it with a look of pain.

"If you know what's good for you, you will be quiet. Good luck fighting now," the Demon said as he tied her hands behind her back.

The other Demon grabbed my arm again and brought me to my feet. I could feel his claws scraping my skin as he escorted me to the other side of the room. He reached his hands up and started untying my dress, and I gasped.

"What are you doing? Stop that," I said as I swatted at the Demon. A fist came at my face, and I fell to my knees.

It was the worst pain I have ever felt. I didn't know how Ember took it so well. At that moment, I realized that she actually did hold back when we sparred.

"Don't fucking touch her!!" Ember's screams echoed loud through the castle.

The Demon yanked me up.

"Don't move this time," he said as he continued undressing me. I stayed still as he slid my dress off me, exposing my breasts to the room.

"I'm going to kill you all! Just wait and see!"

As I looked at Ember, I had a feeling she could have taken out all these Demons with just a butter knife, if given the chance.

"I said, shut up!" The Demon kicked her in the face, and I winced. This time she stayed down, and her eyes remained closed. Fear and sadness ran through me as tears streamed down my cheeks.

The Demon undressing me bent down and slid my panties down to my ankles.

"Step out," he said.

I lifted each foot as he removed them. Embarrassment filled me and I cringed as I looked around and saw every Demon staring at my naked body.

"The cleanser," Tellus said.

A Demon handed Tellus a bucket. He walked up to me and poured it over my head. I closed my eyes and shivered as the cold liquid ran down my body. I wiped the wetness off my face and opened my eyes.

Two Demons with scrub brushes in their hands started scrubbing my skin, and it hurt.

"Why are you doing this?" I asked as I sniffed back tears.

"This is just a cleansing, child. Nothing more. You are safe right now."

Tellus's words didn't make me feel safe. They scared me to death, and I just wished Cash was here to comfort me—to save me.

The Demons dried me off and started dusting me with powder.

"What is that?" I asked.

"It's a sacramental powder," Tellus said.

"What is it for?"

"To keep your skin safe once it catches on fire."

"What?!" Fear shot through me, and I backed up a few feet. I looked around, trying to see if there was anywhere to run. The Demons grabbed my arms and put me back where I was supposed to be standing.

"Calm down. The fire won't hurt. Once the God Tartarus accepts you, the flames will disappear."

"What happens after he accepts me?"

"He will mate you and bed you immediately to seal the mating, but not until after your sacrifice."

"What sacrifice?"

"You must sacrifice your soul so he can turn you into one of us."

I knew I wouldn't be accepted because I wasn't the virgin they needed for the ritual, so I wasn't concerned about my soul. I was, however, concerned about my life.

"What if he doesn't accept me?" I asked.

"Then you will be dead."

I gasped as my breathing got labored.

"Will the fire kill me?"

"No, Erebus will." Tellus shook his head and sighed. "But since you are a virgin, you have nothing to fear."

Turning away from me, he walked over to the altar and grabbed a knife and a goblet before returning to me. The two Demons grabbed my arms again and held them to my side.

"This will hurt, but it is necessary." He lifted the knife to my chest and my eyes widened with fear. He slid the knife across my skin, right underneath my nipple.

"Ow," I whimpered as the sharp pain of the slice ran through me. More tears fell from my face as I looked down at the dripping blood.

Tellus held the goblet up to my breast and let my blood run into it. Once it was about half-filled, he removed it and set it on the altar.

Demons started filling the room one by one until it was almost full. My breath caught when I realized there were probably close to fifty Demons. The last one to walk in was holding a torch. He walked up to the pile of wood and lit it on fire. I feared the smoke would kill us, but as I watched the smoke rise, my eyes followed it. I could see the bright full moon through a large opening in the ceiling.

Some cheering Demons brought my eyes back to the room. My heart stopped, and fear ran through me when I saw Erebus enter. He walked over to my sister and touched her face.

"Who did this?" He asked with an angry look.

"I did, your majesty, she was—"

Without even a second thought, Erebus yanked out a dagger and stabbed the Demon in the chest. He fell to the floor, and Erebus jumped on top of him. He then carved a hole in the Demon's chest and pulled his heart out.

Standing up, Erebus held the heart above his head as dark green blood dripped down his arm. He paraded around the room with it as I watched wide-eyed.

"If anyone else lays a hand on her, this will be you!" He threw the heart in the blazing fire before he strode over to Ember as fear ran through me. At least I knew she would be safe.

"My poor mate." My fear turned to pure hatred and disgust when he leaned down and kissed her.

Chapter 41

Ember

Waking up from one of my nightmares, I felt a kiss on my lips. But this dream had been *too* real because I still felt the pain from the hits I had taken.

Ember, wake up now! I heard Arna say.

Hearing her scared voice was like a shock to my system. Realizing my hands were tied, and the lips upon mine weren't the soft lips of my mate, I opened my eyes and saw that Erebus was the one kissing me. Not having any weapons or even hands to use, I immediately sprang into action with the only weapon I had—my teeth.

I bit down on his lip as hard as I could.

"Ahh!" he screamed and pulled away from me. His lip was still between my teeth, and I took a chunk with me.

Sitting up, I spit the lip onto the floor. It tasted bitter and rotten. I looked up at him as his blood ran down my face.

"Oh, I love your fierceness. You are going to be an amazing mate. I cannot wait to bed you." He grabbed his cock and squeezed. Disgust poured through me as he stared at me.

"You go near me with that thing, and I will bite it off, too," I said with an evil grin. A huge part deep down inside of me really wished he would try because I sure as hell wasn't lying.

"Even though I love your fierceness, Ember. I don't like the way you disregard my feelings."

"And that's my problem, how?"

"It seems you need to be brought down off your high horse." He turned around. "Sword," he said, and a Demon handed him one.

Looking over at Cinder, she was naked and crying. Two Demons held her still, and fear combined with anger ran through me when I saw her breast covered in blood. I knew it was her blood because it was red.

"Don't touch my sister!"

"Of course not. We need her for the ceremony, but do you know who isn't needed?" He glanced over at Arna, and my heart threatened to beat out of my chest.

"No! Don't!"

"Oh, that got a reaction," he said with a sly smile. Kneeling next to me, he lifted his hand and ran his sharp claw along my cheek. "Everything I do is out of my love for you, dear."

"You have no clue what love is," I spat.

"I know to get you to love me. I will have to eliminate the ones you love, so you have no one left but me."

"Forced love won't work. You're wasting your time, Erebus."

"We have thousands of years together to work on it. Don't worry, my love."

"Don't fucking call me that!" That was Val's name for me, not his. He had no right to use it, and it angered me.

"High horse. Tsk tsk." He snapped his tongue and shook his head at me. "As you wish then." He stood up and strolled over to Arna.

"Erebus, don't!"

"Will you give me what I want?" he asked as he turned back toward me. His red eyes bored into me. He knew he had the upper hand, and since my hands were literally tied, I had nothing to offer. Except for myself....

I hesitated to answer and focused on my ignitus. Once again, it failed me. It wasn't even lighting out of anger, and I had a feeling the sedative they stuck me with had something to do with it.

I realized that, if I wanted to save Arna or my sister, I would have to give in. Willing to give up my soul, or even my life for them, was worth it. So, I did....

"Yes, you can have me. Just don't hurt her," I breathed.

"This bird makes you weak. Your love for her makes you weak!" He turned toward Arna and held up his sword.

Ember, I love you. Arna's voice was sad as she closed her eyes tightly in fear.

"Erebus, please!" I cried out.

I thrashed against the restraints on my wrists, hoping they would break

"We can't have you weak!" He struck out with his sword and stabbed Arna in her chest.

"NO!!!!"

Ember. Tears ran down my face as Arna whimpered and collapsed to the floor.

"I'm sorry," I cried. "I love you. I'm so sorry!"

He raised his sword one more time and stabbed her again. All air had left my lungs as I watched him slowly pull the sword from her chest. Gasping for air a few times, her body convulsed before she finally stilled.

Severe pain rushed through me, and my face smacked the floor as I fell over. For a split second, I thought someone hit me. But then I realized, this pain was worse than any physical pain one could have.

This was pain from a broken bond.

The emotional pain was like poison running through my veins that threatened to eat me from the inside out. I had no thoughts of escaping now because I had no desire to fight back anymore. At that moment, I just wanted to die as my heart shattered and I lost a piece of myself. I was no longer a person. I was no longer whole. I was an empty vessel. The pain consumed me, and there was no way I could escape it—no way I could live with it, either.

I could barely feel the cold marble floor touching my cheek as my face laid upon it. Tears streamed silently from my eyes as I gave up on life.

Erebus handed the sword off, strolled over to me, and laid his hand on my cheek. "I'm sorry, but this will make you the strong mate I need, and a powerful queen."

I had no clever retorts.

I had no words at all.

Just pain.

He wiped the tears from my face with the back of his hand.

"Stop crying. That's a sign of weakness." He stood up. "Now, let's get this ceremony going."

I watched through tear-filled eyes as Erebus made his way over to the altar and grabbed a knife. He took it and sliced his hand open. He held it over a goblet and let the blood drip into it. Picking up both goblets, he strolled over to my sister.

"Let her go," he said to the Demons holding her. He handed her a goblet, and she took it. "Raise your glass."

She raised her goblet in the air, and he did the same.

"Tellus," he said as he looked at the white-cloaked Demon.

"We are here today to offer this virgin to the God Tartarus," Tellus said. Shouts of joy came from the Demon-filled room.

"The virgin must drink the blood of a Demon."

She glanced over at me, but I didn't move. I couldn't. The pain was too much to control.

"That means you, dear," Erebus said, bringing her attention away from me.

Cinder looked into her cup and squinched up her nose.

"Drink!" She jumped at the sound of Erebus' loud voice.

She raised the goblet to her lips and drank. She made gagging noises as she lowered it.

"Now, the Demon must drink the blood of a virgin." Tellus looked at Erebus.

Erebus raised his goblet and downed the blood. A Demon took their glasses and set them both back on the altar.

"Torch," Erebus commanded.

A Demon grabbed a torch, lit it off the raging bonfire, and handed it to Erebus.

"This won't hurt much." Erebus smiled as he walked up to my sister.

"No," I whispered. The emotional pain was still too intense. I couldn't move. I couldn't scream.

He held the torch to Cinder's body, and I watched the flames engulf her. Tears escaped my eyes as I let out a small, painful cry. The broken bond wasn't allowing me to move.

"Why are you crying again?" he asked me.

The pain was too strong—I couldn't answer. Whimpering sounds were all that left my mouth.

"For fuck's sake, stop being weak! This won't kill her," Erebus pointed at my sister.

I looked up, and she was still standing. She looked scared, but it didn't look like she was in pain. Relief filled me.

"See, now stop crying! We were not born to be weak!"

Thoughts of my fake father's words flew into me. Every terrible memory I had of him raced through my mind. Realization hit me and anger took over.

It was Erebus.

He was the one who did all of this.

He captured my mother and my father.

He sent the Changeling.

It was his words that the Changeling had said to me, daily. The words I was raised on—words that I now hated.

Something stronger pushed aside my pain, something more primal. Deep-seated anger threatened to consume me, and I would let it.

The floor started shaking below my body, and the Demons danced in celebration. Taking a deep breath, I used my shoulder to nudge my body up. Once I was sitting, I looked around. No one was paying attention to me now and that's what I needed. Because one way or another, I was a fucking Demi-God, and I was going to light my ignitus!

"Rise, Tartarus, rise!" Erebus screamed, and the floor shook harder.

A crack split in the marble, and I watched fire spit from the hole. The Demons danced and cheered while waiting for their God to emerge as the rumbling continued.

I may be a Demi-God, but a Demi-God without her powers was worthless. Thinking hard about everything I learned from Katzia, I took a breath. Never wanting my ignitus to begin with, I had always rejected it. Realizing that it's a part of me, a part I should own with pride, I reached deep down in myself and did the only thing I hadn't done before.

I accepted it.

Once I made that decision, I felt the connection. I felt the bond take hold. Every cell in my body sparked the moment my ignitus and I entwined as one. A low rolling fire covered my skin. This time, the flames felt different. I felt the control I had over them. They looked different, too—these flames were violet.

Seeing if I could, I stopped my ignitus. To my astonishment, it flickered, then subsided. I was now in control.

The floor stopped shaking, bringing my attention back. Glancing over at Cinder, the flames surrounding her disappeared. Then the hole sucked itself closed faster than it opened.

"What happened?" Erebus asked, his face filled with shock.

"He didn't accept her," Tellus said with a fearful look.

"Why not?" Erebus asked as his face filled with rage.

"I don't know. She said she was a virgin." Tellus shook his head frantically.

While they were talking, Katzia's words came back to me.

Only the things you want to burn will burn.

I immediately thought of the ropes that bound my hands, and I felt them break as they burned away.

Erebus stomped over to my sister and grabbed her chin. "Are you a virgin? Don't lie to me!"

"No, I am not." Cinder's eyes filled with fear.

"Hold her." Two Demons grabbed her arms as Erebus walked over to the table and grabbed a sword.

I jumped up and ran toward him.

"You won't be getting past me, Erebus."

He whipped around with the sword in his hand and a grin on his face.

"Is that so?"

"Yeah. It is." I smiled big as I lit my ignitus. His mouth dropped open as my flames shot high. I took off running and lunged for him. He dodged me with very little effort.

Three Demons surrounded me, and I immediately grabbed one of them. He caught on fire as I squeezed his arms. He fell to the floor screaming with me on top of him. He disintegrated and turned to ash beneath me, so I immediately hopped to my feet and the other ones backed away in a panic.

"How about you get rid of your fire skin, and we have an honorable sword fight?" I could hear the fear in Erebus's voice as he spoke.

"What are the terms?" I asked.

"If I catch you, I win. If I win, you mate me without running that pretty mouth of yours."

"Is that all?"

"And you respect me in front of my subordinates," he added.

"And what if I win?"

"I will let the Vampire live."

"Or you will be dead when I fucking kill you!"

"You might be good, Ember, but you aren't that good," he laughed. All the Demons started laughing with him, and he smiled with pride.

I quickly devised a plan and hoped it worked.

"Deal," I said as I turned my ignitus off.

Without hesitating, Erebus threw me a sword, and I caught it. I just hoped what I learned from Zayn was enough as I held the sword in my hand. The Demons formed a circle around the edge of the room. Erebus made his way to the center of the room, next to the bonfire, as did I. I could feel the heat coming off of it.

"No one interferes." He pointed his sword at the Demons watching. "Or I will kill you all!"

"You're going to regret those words," I said with a smile.

His response was quick. He swung his sword at me, and I jumped back. It barely missed me. I swung out at him, and he stopped my sword with his as the sound of clashing metal echoed through the room.

Slamming into him with my shoulder, he stumbled back, but didn't fall. Erebus was over a foot and a half taller than me. This battle would be to the death, even if it were mine.

"Do you need a break yet?" he asked.

I ignored him and swung my sword out, and he countered again with his. This went on until I was exhausted.

Standing there, panting and trying to catch my breath, I let my arms drop and rest for a second.

"Are you giving up?" he asked.

"Never," I said as I raised my sword and swung at him again.

We danced around in the middle of the room, swords clashing together as the Demons watched and cheered.

Erebus swung out at me, and instead of raising my sword, I dodged the blow. As he was in mid-swing, I swung out at his leg and hit my mark. I would have to thank Zayn later for showing me that move. If I lived.

Erebus fell to one knee, so I swung at his head. Reaching up, he caught my sword in the air, and I saw green blood ooze from his hand. He yanked my sword toward him, taking me with it. I fell to the ground in front of him, and he pulled me to his side in a chokehold.

"I win," he whispered into my ear. His nose ran up the side of my head and sniffed my hair.

Now was my chance to complete the only plan I had. I grabbed Erebus's arms as violet flames shot from my skin, consuming him. He instantly let me go and screamed. I immediately turned toward him and started punching him with flaming fists.

My moment of glory was ripped away from me as a net was thrown over me, yanking me away from Erebus. I saw Cinder wield some fireballs at the Demons dragging me away and was proud of her for trying. Grabbing the net with my hands, I willed it to burn, and it caught on fire. As soon as it fell from around me, I jumped to my feet, and a loud strike of lightning stopped me from moving.

"What was that?" Erebus asked.

A slow smile spread across my face because I knew what it was. My friends were here to rescue us.

Ember! Valarian wielded to me.

Cinder and I are okay, Val!

Thank the Gods. His voice sounded relieved. *We're coming in!*

Hearing a loud growl a few seconds later, the door flung open, and all the Demons turned toward it. The sound of my angry mate had never sounded more beautiful. I couldn't see my friends, but I could hear them as they engaged in a brawl.

Erebus had also turned his back to me—a dangerous move on his part. I ran hard as my bare feet slammed against the cold marble floor. I saw a Demon in my way and was about to plow him when one of Cinder's fireballs hit him and he fell to the floor in flames.

Jumping as high as I could, I lunged for Erebus and grabbed onto his back. I willed my ignitus to be as hot as possible as I held onto him. He yelled, fought, and slung his arms around, trying to get me off him, but I held on tight as the stench of burning flesh filled the air.

"Ahh," he screamed as he fell to his knees. I continued holding on while he squirmed underneath me.

Chapter 42

Cash

The shoreline wasn't that far away. My instincts were to take off flying to save the woman I love, but I had to wait for orders. I watched impatiently as Natsu lowered the anchor.

"All right, troops. Like Vulcan said, this will be a slaughter. This is the biggest ritual they have tried, so a lot of the Demons on the land will be here to watch. So, kill as many as those fuckers that you can, and try not to get killed in the process."

"Can we go now, Zayn?" I needed to get off this ship. It had been nine hours since we set sail and I was antsy.

"Yeah, Cash. You grab Val. Natsu, you can take Zila, and I will take Asher." Zayn's eyes landed on Vulcan.

"I can take myself, my lord." His batlike wings popped open with a smile. I bit my lip as I stared at him. This better not be an evil scheme because, even though he had been nice, I would have no problem killing him.

I took a deep breath and walked up to Val. His face was pained, and I grinned arrogantly at him, making sure to make him more uncomfortable.

"Don't touch my ass this time," he said.

"No problem, buddy." I picked his heavy ass up and released my wings.

Zayn took off into the air with a very uncomfortable Asher.

I jumped and flapped my wings and ascended into the sky. Val was a big man, almost as big as I was. He weighed a lot and I struggled to carry him, but I would never let him know that.

"Can't you flap those things any faster?" he asked, and I laughed.

"Only a few more minutes, buddy."

On the outside, I was still myself. I was trying to stay strong and keep my head in the game, but on the inside, I was dying. The woman I loved was in that Demon castle, and if anyone harmed even one hair on her head, I was going to lose my shit and kill them all.

After a few minutes, Nebulous Forest came into sight. I had never been so happy to see a bunch of half-dead trees before.

I stopped flapping and kept my wings back as I glided down toward it. We were coming in fast, but I was damn good at flying, so I wasn't worried about it.

The ground was getting closer, so I pushed back on my wings, slowing us down. Straightening my body out, we landed with nothing more than light thud. Val immediately jumped from my arms, and I pulled my wings back in.

"Thanks," he said. His smile was flat. I knew deep down he had the same feelings I did. He would gladly run into that castle and kill anything and everything in his path to get to the woman he loves, but we had to wait for orders.

Zayn ran a hand nervously through his hair and Asher was spinning his spear while we waited for the others to come in.

Cali landed next, with a sad smile on her face. You could tell she was worried. Natsu came in next, holding Zila. They landed next to us and he set her down. She blushed slightly before smoothing her curly hair back.

"All right," Zayn said. "We are—"

A painful sounding growl came from Val. He grabbed his chest and looked at Zayn.

"They are hurting her or something, Zayn. I can feel it."

"Let's get there as fast as we can."

"No," Val whispered. He closed his eyes tight. "This is the same pain I felt the night Ember died. The bond is breaking."

"What!" Zayn screamed.

"Did they kill her?" Zila asked frantically.

"No. Her bond broke." He shook his head and swallowed hard. "They killed Arna."

"What?" Asher's hands flew up and grabbed his head as he tried to catch his breath.

"No." Cali started crying and threw her hands over her mouth, and Zila did the same.

"We have to go *now*!" Val said, as his eyes met Vulcan.

"Let's go!" Zayn yelled.

"It's this way." Vulcan took off through the woods, and Val and I followed him, our friends right behind us.

We ran as fast as we could while tripping over the brush and fallen limbs of the forest. The entire Demon land seemed to be filled with wards, and it made things much more difficult than they should have been.

"I'm going ahead and doing a perimeter run, Zayn," Zila said.

"Okay. Be safe!" Zayn said.

Zila transformed into a massive black wolf and took off ahead of us. My heart raced as I ran as fast as I could.

About halfway through the never-ending forest, Val spoke. "Ember is pissed off."

I felt relieved to know she was mad. That meant that both her and Cinder were probably safe, and she was probably trying to kick someone's ass.

After what seemed like forever, Vulcan stopped at the edge of the forest.

"The castle is close to the tree line. It is usually heavily guarded," he said.

"Should we split up, Zayn?" I asked.

"No, we stay together."

"Where is Zila?" Cali asked.

"I'm sure she didn't go far," Zayn said as he emerged from the tree line slowly.

We crept across the dead lands, and I saw the castle in the distance. As we got closer, I realized we were at the back of it.

"Are we going through the back door?" I asked as I yanked one of my axes from my belt.

"I think it is best to go in the front," Vulcan said. "They won't be expecting that, my lord."

I had a couple front door, back door jokes, but considering the situation, I kept them to myself.

Zayn nodded. "Agreed."

We headed around the side of the castle.

"Shit. Zila needs us!" Val took off running around the front and we all followed. Once we rounded the corner, I heard growling coming from two different mouths.

My eyes widened as I saw Zila in a defensive manner, being stared down by a large Chimera.

The monster looked like a large lion equipped with a full mane but had big horns on its head. Its tail was long and snake-like and it was covered in scales with razor sharp spikes at the tip.

We all stopped dead in our tracks as the Chimera glared at us. Over a dozen Demons ran up and surrounded us, so I yanked out my other axe. Cali pulled out her katana, and Zayn and Natsu both grabbed swords from their backs. We were at a standstill. Val's fist tightened and he let out a low growl.

The Chimera snarled at him and then lunged for Zila, grabbing her by the throat as she yipped.

With his vampire reflexes, Val was the fastest, so he jumped on its back and started punching it. The Demons engaged us in a fight. I saw Asher quickly stab one with his spear. I slammed my axe into another's shoulder, and it immediately fell. It started convulsing as green blood oozed from it before it stilled. My mouth dropped open in shock at how easy it was to kill them now that we had sulfur magic weapons. I would have to thank Vulcan if we all get out of this alive.

Whirling around, I slammed my axe into the neck of a Demon that I saw out of the corner of my eye. I pulled my axe from him, and he fell.

Glancing up, I watched as Cali jumped up and spun her katana around and took a Demon's head off with one slice. I nodded with pride and then felt a scratch on my back. Whipping around, I came face to face with a Demon. Before I had a chance to react, Vulcan reached out and grabbed it by its throat.

Vulcan was a large Demon. I was six foot five and he had a couple of inches on me. He locked eyes with me and held out his hand. I threw him an axe and he caught it, slamming it into the Demon's head. Vulcan let go of the axe and the Demon fell to the ground with it still in its skull.

"Thanks," I said as I put my foot on the dead Demon's shoulder for leverage, pulling my axe free.

Zila let out a yip as she was thrown from the Chimera's mouth. Cali immediately ran to her, and I saw her bright light come from her hands. Knowing Zila was safe, I jumped in front of the beast that Val was still riding like a bull.

Zayn squatted down and sliced one of the Chimera's legs. He let out a massive roar and fell forward onto the ground. I ducked down and did the same, slicing its back leg.

Val yanked his sword from his belt and cut into its head. The beast fell completely flat on the ground and stilled. He was dead.

Val jumped off and we all immediately ran to Zila. Cali was helping her off the ground.

"Are you okay?" Zayn asked.

"Yeah. He got me good in the neck, but Cali healed me." She grabbed her neck out of instinct, but there wasn't a scratch on her now that she was healed. Natsu pulled her in for a side hug, a look of concern on his face.

We turned toward the door and took off in a run and were met by a dozen Demons.

"I got this. Stay back," Natsu said.

I pulled Vulcan back as he tried to run towards the Demons right when Natsu's lightning hit hard. They all fell to the ground, lifeless.

"Now *that* is impressive," Vulcan said, before turning to me. "Thank you, my lord."

I nodded.

"I wielded to Ember, they're both okay."

"Then let's go in," Zayn said.

Val kicked the door open. My eyes went wide with the number of Demons that were staring at us. He stepped inside with a loud growl and started ripping them apart. With an axe in both hands, I stepped inside and started slicing everything in my path to get to Cinder.

Chapter 43

Cinder

They threw a net over Ember, pulling her away from Erebus. I threw a couple of fireballs at the Demons near her, and they backed away. She grabbed the net with her hands, and it caught on fire.

A large strike of lightning sounded, and I jumped.

"What was that?" Erebus asked.

A slow smile spread across Ember's face, and I had a feeling we were getting rescued. The front door flung open, and I saw Valarian enter. He let out a primal roar that echoed through the room, sending chills down my naked body.

Everyone started fighting as I backed against the wall next to Tellus. Having no weapons and little skill, I figured I was better off staying out of the way.

Looking back at my sister, I watched as she took off running toward Erebus. There was a Demon in her way, so I chucked a fireball at him, allowing Ember to continue her journey. She flew and jumped on Erebus's back. He flailed his arms, trying to get her off him as her violet flames went high, but she wasn't letting go.

"Ahh!" Erebus's scream echoed loudly through the room.

A Demon grabbed Ember and yanked her off him. His hands caught on fire, and he let go of her. It gave Erebus just enough time to get to his feet. She lunged for him again, and he dodged it. Watching her determination to kill him, I realized I had to help her.

I looked around, wondering what I could do. There was a sword on the table, so I took off running. I grabbed it—it was heavier than I expected. It was also bigger than the one I used at practice, and it made my arms burn.

Running toward Erebus, I used all my strength and stabbed him in his back. He whirled around with a punch to my face and I fell to the floor. He reached down and squeezed my throat, and his long claws pierced my skin. I held onto his arm, trying to remove it as the life was being squeezed out of me. I kicked my foot out toward his groin, just like Ember taught me, and got him in the leg. All it did was anger him more.

He lifted my head and slammed it onto the floor, and pain radiated through my skull. I lied when I said the punch hurt more than anything. My head being slammed into the marble floor hurt more.

Seeing flames from behind him, Ember jumped on his back again and he let go of me. I quickly got to my feet and picked up the sword. I stabbed him in the stomach, and he stumbled back with the blade still in him. He fell to the floor with Ember below him. Her flames shot higher as he screamed.

Val, I need you!
Cinder, where are you?
Say it aloud so that I can find you.

"Cinder!" I heard Valarian scream. I ran toward the sound of his voice, squeezing my way through Demons and stepping over bodies before I finally saw him.

"Help, Val!" I screamed as I ran up to him.

He looked at my naked body, and his face angered. "Are you okay?" he asked.

"Help Ember! Now!" I pointed in their direction. I was really out of breath. "She's fighting Erebus!"

"Find a place to hide," Val said before taking off toward the fight.

A Demon grabbed my arm. I screamed and punched him in the face. I tried to run, but another Demon caught me around my waist, so I flung my head back into his face. In return, he hit me in the head, and it made me dizzy. Picking me up off my feet, he carried me off.

"Put me down!" I said as I punched and kicked as much as I could.

We had gotten about ten feet away when I finally got one good punch in on his face and he stopped walking. Then I was dropped suddenly. I looked up into a pair of beautiful blue eyes. Cash pulled his axe out of the Demon's neck, and he fell to the floor.

"Cinnamon," he whispered. He dropped to his knees next to me, laid down his axe, and grabbed my face in his hands. "Are you okay?"

"I'm fine."

Glancing at the scratches on my neck, his mouth gaped open. His eyes wandered down to the cut on my breast, and I could see pain fill his eyes.

"Who did this to you?" he asked. He rubbed his thumbs on my cheeks as he held my face.

"Erebus and Tellus."

"Did they... did they..." He closed his eyes and hung his head low, not being able to finish his words.

"No. They didn't touch me like that." I wiped tears from my face. "They thought I was a virgin and needed me to stay that way."

"I will kill them all!" He picked up his axe as he stood up.

Lowering his hand to me, he helped me off the floor. Grabbing the back of my head, he pulled me in and planted a short, sweet kiss on my lips.

"Take this." He handed me the other axe off his belt, which I was much better at using than the sword. "Stay close to me."

We started making our way through the room and were met by Demons. Cash quickly started fighting one as another attacked me. I didn't hesitate. I swung the axe right into his cheek, and he let out a gurgling cry. He fell to the floor, and I swung again, hitting him in the head, and he went still.

"That's my girl," Cash said. I met his eyes with a prideful smile, but he wasn't smiling.

He was staring at my body with furrowed eyebrows. I looked down, and green blood now covered the front of my body.

"Come on. We need to find you some clothes." He held his hand out and I took it.

We made our way through the room and killed a few more Demons before I saw Tellus.

"There is Tellus, the one that cut me!" I pointed to the cloaked Demon still hiding by the wall.

Cash pulled me over toward Tellus and dropped my hand.

"You. Take your cloak off," Cash said as he pointed his axe at him.

Tellus didn't hesitate. He removed his cloak and handed it to Cash who slid it over my body.

"There you go, doll." He kissed my cheek.

"Thank you," I said.

Cash turned his attention back to the Demon. "Did you hurt my woman?"

Tellus backed up against the wall and put his hands up. "I was just doing what Erebus told me, and—"

"Wrong answer."

Cash raised his axe and chopped straight into Tellus's neck, and I cringed as he let out a gurgling sound before he fell dead.

Cash pulled me in close to him and kissed the top of my head. "As long as I'm around, no one will ever hurt you again," he whispered, and I believed his words.

We made our way around the room, killing Demons along the way. I killed two more, and Cash killed a dozen or more. The Demons were all almost gone or had retreated when I noticed I hadn't seen Erebus. I also didn't see Ember or Val anywhere.

"They were right here before you found me," I told Cash as we stood in the center of the room.

Cash let out a loud whistle that rang through the room, and slowly, the rest of the King's Guard strolled up to us, stepping over bodies on the way. Everyone was covered in Demon blood and looked tired.

"I see you found, Cinder," Asher said.

"I see you found a bow," Cash said.

"Cinder!" Cali ran up and hugged me with tears in her eyes. "Arna is dead," she cried.

"I know." I patted her back and held her tight while we cried.

Zila came trotting up in her wolf form, she nudged my hand with her nose and whimpered. Out of instinct, I petted the top of her head. I hoped that was okay.

"I'm glad you're okay." Zayn hugged me.

"Me too," Asher said, "but I have to ask, what's with the cloak?"

"Long story," I said. "I'll tell you later."

"Where are Ember and Val?" Zayn asked.

"We don't know," Cash said. "Where are Natsu and Vulcan?"

"Vulcan?" I asked.

"I lost track of everyone once we all started fighting." Zayn ran a hand through his hair.

"I am right here, my lord," a large Demon said as he strolled up. I slid behind Cash's back and gripped his shirt tight as I peeked out.

"It's okay, Cinder. This is Vulcan. He is the Demon I was telling you about that spelled our weapons."

"It is nice to meet you, my lady." He bowed and I nodded.

All our attention was pulled away when a fearful Demon ran past us, trying to escape.

"I got it." Asher lifted his bow and shot it in the back of the head.

"You're an excellent shot," Vulcan said.

"Almost as good as Ember," he said with a smile that dropped quickly. "Where could they be?"

"I don't know, Asher." I shook my head.

"I killed at least ten Demons. Am I a King's Guard yet?" Natsu asked as he walked up, covered in Demon blood.

"You did great, my friend." Zayn patted him on the shoulder. "We can't wait until you come to Castleva."

Zila trotted over to Natsu, and he petted her.

"Where are Val and Ember?" Natsu asked.

"We don't know," Cali said. She looked distraught.

"Alright, let's find them. First, we will do a perimeter check. Natsu, Zila, Cash, and Cinder take the left side of the castle. Cali, Asher, Vulcan, and I will take the right side. We will meet up here in no less than—"

"Zayn, look," Natsu said. I followed his eyes and saw Val carrying Ember out of the hallway that led to Erebus's bedroom. I immediately ran toward them.

"Ember!" Zayn yelled.

She was covered in bruises and cuts. She had taken a beating today. I was glad that she was physically strong because I don't think I could have taken what she took today. She was a warrior.

Chapter 44

Ember

A Demon grabbed me and yanked off Erebus. His hands caught on fire so he let me go. But it had given Erebus just enough time to get to his feet. I lunged for him again, and he dodged it.

Letting out a loud yell, Erebus turned around and I saw Cinder holding a sword. Two Demons came at me, and I grabbed one by the throat, causing him to catch on fire. The other stared at me with wide eyes before he took off running.

Bringing my attention back to Erebus, I saw that he was choking Cinder. He grabbed her head and slammed it into the floor. Anger filled me, and I jumped on his back and wrapped my arms around his neck in a chokehold.

Hanging on with every ounce of strength I had left, I saw Cinder jump up and come at Erebus with a sword. She stabbed him in the stomach, and we fell backward. I was now stuck between him and the floor.

It was hard to breathe with his weight on top of me, but I wouldn't let go or give up. My flames were eating his flesh, but he refused to die. He yanked the sword out of his stomach as he fought to get out of my hold. I heard a loud growl and saw Val seconds before he landed on top of Erebus.

He started punching him in the face, but their weight threatened to kill me.

I can't breathe, Val! I wielded to my mate.

Val jumped up and yanked Erebus off me, throwing him about ten feet away. Reaching down, he picked me up without even thinking of getting burned by my fire. Thankfully, my fire didn't hurt him.

We both looked at Erebus. Once our eyes locked with him, the look of fear settled on his face. He took off running like a coward.

"We cannot let him live, Val!" I extinguished my flames.

"Let's finish this," he said.

We took off after him. As we were chasing him through the main area and down the hallway, I saw the last glimpse of him as he shut his bedroom door.

"I got it," Val said as we ran up.

One swift kick and the door flew open. Val ran into the room first. I saw Erebus holding a crossbow a mere moment before an arrow hit Val in the shoulder. I only had a few seconds before he loaded another arrow, and I had a hard decision to make—stop and check on my mate that I knew would heal or kill Erebus.

Knowing Erebus expected me to stop, I did what my gut told me to. I slid past Val and went straight for him. His eyes met mine, and his mouth gaped open in shock as I plowed into him, knocking him down and knocking the crossbow from his hands. Willing my ignitus, I started punching him in the face with flaming fists.

"Stop, and I will tell you where your parents are!" he screamed.

The shock of his words made me falter. He threw me off him, and I slid across the floor. I jumped to my feet, and he held up his hand.

"Stop. I know where they are," he said breathlessly.

"Lies!" I screamed.

"I swear." He was on his knees with his hands in the air. "I am not lying. May I walk over there so I can show you?" he pointed to the dresser. I couldn't help but be curious and hopeful that my parents were alive, so I nodded. I extinguished my ignitus as he slowly rose from the ground.

Val, please tell me you're okay. I wielded to him, not wanting to take my eyes off Erebus.

I'm okay, love. I'm almost healed. Don't trust him, Ember.

"Your answer is in here," Erebus said as he grabbed a wooden box off the dresser and slowly made his way over to me. "I was going to give them to you after we mated."

Reluctantly, I took the box from him. He opened the lid. I hesitated to take my eyes off him. Glancing into the box, I sucked in a breath. First my eyes landed on my dagger, and I was grateful it wasn't lost at the bottom of the ocean. Then I saw that the box contained two perfect golden rings that I would recognize anywhere. They were my parent's wedding rings.

Catching me off guard, Erebus grabbed me by the throat, and I heard the wooden box crash against the ground when I dropped it.

"I killed them, just like I'm going to kill you!" he said as he squeezed.

Dead—my parents were murdered. He had killed them. This whole time, the hope I had been carrying was destroyed. Sadness flooded back into me, and I struggled to fight back.

With a growl, Val was on him in an instant. Grabbing Erebus's by the throat, he squeezed. Erebus squeezed mine harder in return. Finally, coming to my senses, I willed my ignitus. The flames shot high, and Erebus dropped me. I fell to my knees in front of him.

Still holding onto Erebus' throat, Val punched his other hand into his chest. He let out a strangled cry and stilled.

"Do you feel that?" Val asked him. "That's your heart speeding up in fear of death. I know because I can feel it beating against my fingers as I squeeze it."

Erebus said nothing as green blood dripped from his mouth. The look of fear and shock was plastered on his face.

"Ember?" Val asked. I knew what he wanted. He wanted permission to kill him because, in his eyes, I deserved the kill. But seeing my mate kill him would be just as glorious.

"Do it!" I screamed.

Val yanked Erebus's heart out, and I watched as his body fell next to mine. He was dead. Erebus was dead.

Years of memories came back to me. Flashes of my parents, of our battles, the deaths, the crying, the fear... It was a glorious moment to celebrate as I looked at his dead body, but I wasn't going to celebrate because I had lost too much.

Val turned to me with the heart in his hand. I shook my head no. He squeezed the heart and threw it against the wall.

"Are you okay, my love?" he asked as he fell to his knees next to me.

It was over, but no, I was not okay. Erebus was dead, but at what cost? My parents were dead, and he killed Arna. I felt like it was all for nothing.

Frantically, I looked around the floor and saw a shimmer of gold. Crawling over to my father's ring, I picked it up. I looked around some more and saw my mother's. Crawling over to it, I grabbed it, and set it in my hand next to my father's.

As I held both rings, I started crying. Val got off his knees and walked towards me. He took a seat on the ground and wrapped his arms around me.

"He killed them."

"I'm sorry, my love," he said, then kissed the top of my head.

"He killed Arna!" My body convulsed with each painful cry.

"I know, baby." Val held me tight and rubbed his hand up and down my back.

He let me cry for as long as I needed. Once I was done, I pulled back and looked into his eyes.

"Are you ready to go?" he asked. I nodded, and he helped me off the floor. He leaned over and handed me my dagger. Reaching down, I slid it into my holster.

"I'm exhausted and everything hurts." My vision was blurry and I was dizzy.

Val didn't hesitate. He scooped me up in his arms and carried me out of Erebus's room. I gripped the rings hard as I snuggled into his arms. Every cell in my body hurt from the broken bond. As he walked us down the hall, I wondered if I was going to survive this pain, because even in Val's arms, I was okay with dying.

We made it out to the main room, and I heard my friend's voices as they approached.

"Ember!" I heard Zayn yell frantically.

"Is she okay?" Cinder asked.

"She's fine. She's exhausted," Val said.

"And Erebus?" Zayn asked.

"He's dead," Val said. "We need to get out of here."

"Let's go, team. *Now*!" Zayn said.

"No!" I yelled. I opened my eyes, and everyone was staring at me, including Vulcan, and I stumbled over my words for a second as confusion went through me. "We… We can't leave Arna." Meeting Zayn's eyes, he nodded in agreement.

"If we can carry her down to the water's edge behind the castle, I can pull the boat around," Natsu said.

"I'll go with him," Cali said with tears in her eyes. "I need to get out of here." She put her hands over her face and Asher rubbed her back.

Zila turned back into her normal form right in front of us. "Can we even carry her?" she asked.

"She's too heavy. We can't carry her."

"Val is right. Even with all of us, I don't think we would be able to," Cash said.

"Then I need to tell her bye." The pain was still there, and it was killing me. I felt like I was slowly dying.

"Do you want me to heal you first, Ember?"

"Not yet, Cali." The physical pain that my body felt right now was the only thing keeping my mind from the emotional pain that was slowly consuming me. "I need to see her first."

Val carried me over to Arna as my friends followed. He set me on the floor and I pressed my hand into his.

Hold these. I don't have the strength to tell Cinder right now. Val kissed my cheek and secretly took the rings.

I stumbled up to Arna and slid down onto the floor next to her. Reaching my hand out, I lightly petted her head.

"I'm so sorry." Tears strolled down my face as I looked at her dead body.

The pain broke free and devoured me as I threw myself against her. Her plush feathers touched my cheeks and all I could think of was that this was the last time I would feel their softness. Stinging sadness ran through my veins, and I started bawling.

"Ember?" Zayn said.

I ignored him as I cried hard. I had only had a minute with her, and I needed more time.

"Ember," Val said. "Your ignitus is on!"

Opening my eyes, I saw a low rolling violet fire flickering on my skin, and I watched as Arna's feathers caught on fire.

"No. No!!" I yelled as I tried to put the fire out with my hands, but the more I smacked, the more the flames engulfed her. Turning my ignitus off, I scrambled up off the ground, took a few steps back, and watched as the fire spread quickly.

"I didn't mean to." I put my hands over my face. I didn't understand why she caught on fire. My ignitus was only supposed to burn the things I wanted to burn.

As my friends watched her body fully engulfed in flames, I heard cries and sniffs.

"I'm sorry, Arna. I swear, I'm so sorry."

"We don't have to stay, love," Val said.

"I can't leave yet. I can't leave her like this."

Everyone backed up away from her as the flames shot high and burned her body away. I didn't move. I couldn't.

It wasn't a proper burial, but I was glad that the Demons couldn't do anything with her body now—like eat her.

"What the fuck?" I heard Asher say. I glanced over at him. "Her wing moved."

"What?" I asked.

"There it goes again," Cash said.

Looking back at Arna, I didn't see anything.

"It's the flames playing with your eyes," Zila said.

"No, I saw—" a large crackling sound cut off Asher's words as Arna's body rose into the sky.

A sharp stinging pain ran through my body, and I grabbed Val's arm to hold myself steady. My heart sped up, as the painful feeling burned through me. I fell to my knees and screamed as loud as I could.

Val crouched next to me.

"What's wrong, love?" He was grabbing me frantically, trying to look me over.

The red-hot pain shot fast through my body, and it hurt to open my eyes. I felt like I was dying, as every cell in my body felt like it was on fire.

Then the pain turned to bliss. Warmth spread through my veins, and I felt loyalty.

Kindness.

Friendship.

Family.

Then I felt a surge of love when the bond connected once more.

Peeling my eyes open, I looked up at Arna. My mouth dropped open as I watched her wings spread out. Violet flames flickered off her as she lifted her head and flapped her wings before she let out a loud screech.

"She's a phoenix," I heard Zila whisper.

"Yes. Only a phoenix can rise from the ashes," Natsu said.

Chills ran down my body as I looked up at the flaming bird. She slowly lowered herself to the grown next to me. She landed, and her flames subsided. She was now solid black with a purple head, and purple tips on her feathers.

"Oh, my Gods!" I slammed into her and hugged her. "I'm so sorry, Arna."

Don't be sorry. Nothing was your fault.

"What the hell?" Asher said.

"That's weird," Cash added.

"What are you talking about?" I asked.

"I can hear Arna," Asher said.

"I can hear her, too!" Cali added.

Can everyone hear me?

"Yes," everyone said, one by one.

"Your lips aren't moving, but I can hear you like I can hear Val," Cinder said.

I'm so happy I can be involved with the conversation now! Ember told no one what I was really saying. She wouldn't tell Asher that I thought he was hot. Everyone giggled, and Asher blushed. He looked relieved, and his eyes were filled with tears. *Did you see my feathers?*

I looked up at her and nodded as happy tears ran down my own face. "I did. They're beautiful."

She flicked her feathers, and violet flames shot off them all. She flicked again, and they disappeared.

Wow! she said. *Why are they violet?*

"Mine are too!" I willed my ignitus on and heard gasps coming from some friends.

Oh, wow! You bonded to your ignitus. Congratulations, Ember.

"Thanks." I extinguished it and smiled.

"Welcome back, Arna," Asher said. He wiped a tear from his eye and walked up to pet her.

Thanks, Arna said.

"I know this is a time to celebrate, but we need to get off this island. There were a lot of Demons that escaped," Val said.

"Who knows what they're planning," Natsu added.

"Or who they'll put in charge now," Asher reminded us.

We all looked at him, even Arna. Leave it up to Asher to say the things that everyone else was afraid to even think. The thought of another Demon like Erebus being in charge sent chills down my body.

"There will be another Demon in charge before the sun comes up, my lord," Vulcan said as he looked at Zayn.

Zayn nodded and moved next to me and kissed the side of my head. "I love you, Red," he said.

"I love you, too."

"Okay, let's get out of here, troops."

Zayn headed toward the exit, and we all made our way out of the castle. We didn't see one Demon on our way back to the ship.

Once we were at the edge of the water, Natsu took off with Zila, Cash had Cinder, and Zayn had Asher.

"I can carry you, but not Val," Cali said.

"Are you up to giving us a ride, Arna?"

Of course. Hop on.

"Okay. See you on the ship." Cali took off flying.

My eyes met Vulcan's.

"I am glad you are okay, my lady. My friend." He gave me a sad smile. I knew it might be a bad decision, especially if Zayn was around, but my gut instincts took over before I even knew what I was doing. I pulled Vulcan in for a hug. He seemed shocked for a second before he eased into it.

"Thank you," I whispered, and let go.

"I will see you on the ship," he said with a smile.

"Why would you go back to prison? You're free right now."

"Because I am a man of my word." He smiled that arrogant smile of his and his bat wings popped open. He took off into the sky and I turned toward Val.

"Please don't yell at me," I said.

"I'm not, love. Surprisingly, the Demon isn't half bad."

I laughed lightly as I turned toward Arna. Looking up at her, I vaguely remember cutting her reins off. I made a mental note to have her some new ones made.

"I got you." Val picked me up and set me on top of her. He then hoisted himself up behind me and wrapped his arms around my waist.

"Are we too heavy?" I asked.

You two together are still lighter than the king, Arna said, and I laughed.

The sun was just slightly peeking through the horizon as she rose into the sky and headed for the ship. I felt a huge wave of relief hit me when the wind blew my hair back. Having my familiar back and my mate killing my enemy was all anyone could ask for. Tears of happiness rolled down my face.

I love you, Ember.

"I love you, too, Arna." I patted her neck.

"I love you, too," Val whispered in my ear. He then kissed my neck and I let out a soft moan.

Oh no, I draw the line at any mating on me.

"Arna!"

She let out a laughing squawk as she lowered us onto the ship.

"Are you sailing with us, Arna?" Asher asked as I slid off the top of her and into Val's arms.

I am. I'm too tired to fly.

"Good. I'm sitting over here if you want to sit with me."

Sure! Arna followed Asher over to the other side of the ship.

"They're too cute," Cinder said.

"Yeah, he really loves her. How are you doing, Cin?"

"I'm good. Are you okay, Ember?"

"I'm doing the best I can right now." I shrugged.

"Yes. Me too. It's been rough." She had a sad smile.

"Can I heal you both now?" Cali asked as she walked up to us.

"Yes, please!" Cinder said.

"Absolutely." I sighed. My entire body hurt from the ass-whopping I had taken over the last two days.

Cali laid her hands on us both at the same time. I watched as beautiful light radiated off her and onto us. The blissful magic feeling was wonderful as my soreness eased.

"Thank you, Cali," Cinder said. She peeked down inside of her cloak. "Oh, thank the Gods."

"Were you worried that your breast would scar?" I asked.

"Yes. I have beautiful breasts." She smiled proudly and I laughed.

"I need to tell you a few things, Cin."

"Okay." The smile dropped from her face.

"I just want to tell you I am proud of you.

"Whatever for?"

"You're stronger than you think you are, and I underestimated you. For that, I am sorry."

"Thank you. That means a lot to me, Ember."

"We need to talk about the other thing when we get back."

"We can talk now."

"This should wait until we—"

"No, Ember. You promised me that there would be no more secrets. I want to know, so tell me."

I sighed deeply.

"Cash," I called out. Cinder looked over her shoulder as he walked up.

"What's up?" he asked.

"I have to tell Cinder something, and you need to be here for it." I looked into his eyes, and he nodded.

"What's wrong, Ember?" she asked.

"Val." I held out my hand and Val placed the rings into it, and I gripped them tightly. "This isn't easy to say."

"It's okay, Ember. I'm strong, remember?" She gave me a sad smile as tears filled her eyes. I think deep down, she knew what I was going to say.

"While we were..." I looked down at my tightly closed hand. I felt Val's arms slide around me from behind and I eased into him.

You got this, love, he wielded to me.

Taking a deep breath, I blew it out slowly. I was about to crush my sister's heart, and it didn't feel good.

Chapter 45

Cinder

Ember's eyes filled with tears and at that moment, I knew what she was going to say. Erebus wouldn't have let our parents live. He was a sadistic man, and I knew he would have either killed them, or turned them into Demons.

"While we were fighting Erebus in his bedroom, he gave me something." She sniffed back tears as she held out her hand and opened it.

Looking down at what she had, my chest got heavy when I realized what it was—my mother's and father's mating rings. Even though it hurt to see them, I had already come to terms with their death, unlike Ember. She had been holding onto hope, so I knew this crushed her—I also knew this was finally the closure she needed to move on.

"Are they dead?" I asked.

"Yes." Tears rolled down her face as she looked at me for strength.

"Did Erebus kill them?" I whispered as tears fell down my own cheeks.

"Yes. He said he did."

"How did Erebus die?" I asked.

"I ripped his heart out—literally," Val said

Wiping tears from my cheeks, I nodded my head. "Good. Thank you, Val." I hugged him.

"It was my pleasure," he said as he rubbed his hand down my back, soothing me. Then he turned the hug toward Ember, and I went from his arms to hers.

"I'm sorry you found out without me there. I wished I was with you." I sniffed back tears.

"I'm sorry that our family is gone," she whispered into my neck.

"We still have family, Em." It was the truest thing that I could have said as we hugged. "They are surrounding us now."

She pulled away from me and looked around. She smiled and nodded her head.

"You're right. We have more brothers and sisters than we know what to do with." We both laughed as we wiped away tears.

"Can we have a ceremony for our parents when we get back? Once we are all rested and stuff."

"Of course," Ember said. "I think that would be a great honor to them."

Cash slid his arms around me from behind and rested his chin on my shoulder.

"What are we going to do with the rings?" I asked.

"Well, I figured, since you and Cash are getting mated, maybe you guys could have them."

"No, I don't want to take them from you. You are the oldest, and they were supposed to bequeath them to you."

I shook my head, not being able to fathom taking what was always promised to her.

"I have the honor of wearing Val's mother's ring, Cin."

"And I don't wear rings, I wear a sword instead." Val smiled as he held up his sword that Ember gave him.

"So, you should wear our mother's ring. It would truly honor her." She placed the rings into my hand. "And I can't think of a better man to honor my father than you, Cash."

Cash stepped out from behind me and dropped to one knee as he bowed his head to Ember. "It would honor me to wear your father's ring."

"Thank you," Ember said with a sad smile. Cash rose from his feet and yanked her into a bear hug. "To the Gods, Cash. You're going to squeeze me to death."

I looked at Val and we both laughed at Ember's discomfort.

"I'm so grateful to have a sister, since I don't have one of my own," Cash said as he let her go.

"She is evil, Cash. You'll want to give her back," Zayn said as he walked up. He stood between Val and Ember and stretched one arm around each of their shoulders.

"I missed you too, Softy," Ember said and Zayn kissed the side of her head.

"Everyone did an amazing job today, and I couldn't possibly be any prouder of you all than I am right now." Zayn smiled big. "I know everyone is having a moment over here, but Natsu recommended we break open a barrel of Val's father's wine that Cali found. Of course, my sister has already poured glasses for everyone, but not before she downed one herself," Zayn said.

I glanced at Cali and smiled as she strolled over with a tray filled with glasses.

"Grab a glass, everyone," Zila said. She was carrying a second tray.

"We have so many things to be grateful for. What are we toasting to?" Asher asked as he grabbed a glass.

To being alive!

"That's a good reason, Arna." Asher nodded.

"And to the parents of these two beautiful women," Cash said.

"To our parents!" I raised my glass.

"And to being alive!" Asher said. Everyone held their glasses up and cheered.

Can I have some wine in a bowl or something? I'm parched.

"Can birds have wine?" Asher asked.

Excuse me, sir, but I'm not a bird. I'm a phoenix now.

Everyone laughed as Asher set a bowl in front of Arna. She took a drink.

Damn you, Asher. This is water!

"I think I read somewhere that phoenix's drink water," Asher said.

"I think I heard that, too," Ember agreed.

If I had fists, I would punch you both.

We all laughed at Arna and drank our wine. We mingled, hugged, cried happy and sad tears for the next few hours. Eventually, most of us got tired and found comfortable spots to sit. I was standing on the side of the ship with my arms crossed, staring out at the ocean when Cash called my name.

"Cinnamon! Get over here and keep me warm."

I smiled and made my way over to the perfect Angel.

"And why would I want to do that?" I teased.

"Because I'm yours?"

"Oh, I like the sound of that."

He grabbed my hand and pulled me down onto his lap.

"I'm sorry about your parents," he said as he pulled me close to him.

"Thank you. I'm sad, but I feel relieved. I'm just glad to know what happened to them, finally."

"Ember is going to take it harder than you."

"Yes." I nodded. "Yes, she will."

"It's because she is the physically strong one."

"Then what does that make me?" I asked.

"You're the emotionally strong one, my Cinnamon roll."

"Oh." Surprise filled me as he continued.

"That's why you two complement each other so well. You are both like puzzle pieces that fit together. What she lacks, you have, and vice versa. Since she isn't in control of her emotions, she makes up for that lack of control by making sure she's in charge of her body. That's why she does extra training. Then there is you. You understand people's feelings and how life works. You honor the life of someone that has died and cherish those memories instead of living in the past and regretting what you don't have now. It's very simple, really."

"I have never noticed that before."

Cash sounded so wise for his age. He was an extremely observant man and what he said made perfect sense. I'd always felt slightly inadequate since my sister was so physically strong—but emotionally, she was not. I was completely the opposite. Understanding emotions at a young age, I learned how to deal with them, but I wasn't physically strong.

"We should sneak off somewhere so I can get into that cloak of yours," he whispered, and just like that, the Cash that I loved was back. I laughed at his silliness.

"You can wait until I have showered and changed out of this ugly Demon cloak."

"It's cute on you. I was hoping you would wear it for me later."

"You're too much, sometimes, Cashmere."

"I'm even better with a little Cinnamon sprinkled on top."

"Have I mentioned you're cheesy, too?"

Very cheesy, Arna said, and I blushed.

"How did she hear us?" I whispered.

I have impeccable hearing.

"You better be quiet, doll. That bird might hear your dirty thoughts."

I'm a phoenix!

"You stop it right now, Cash, or I will kick your butt."

"You promise?"

"Anytime you want me to," I said.

He leaned in and kissed me. "I love you, Cinnamon."

"I love you, too, Cash."

Pulling me in close, I snuggled up in his arms. I felt safe enough to fall asleep on the ship ride home.

Chapter 46

Cinder

We had made it safely back to Castleva but were all completely exhausted from the trip. The sun was shining brightly and none of us spoke as we walked off the portal.

Zayn, Ember, Val, and Vulcan were all ahead of us, deep in discussion.

Zayn stopped walking and I saw him grab Ember's arm. He must have been easing her emotions. I gave Vulcan a slight smile as we passed, and he bowed.

Cash was holding my hand as we walked up the stairs and down to my room. He stopped at the door and gave me a look.

"You're either staying with me, or I'm staying with you. You decide," I said with a look that said I wasn't backing down.

"I'm too tired to walk to my room. Let's just stay here." Cash smiled big.

Hearing footsteps, my eyes looked down the hall and I watched as Ember slowly strolled up to us.

"Are you okay?" she asked.

"I am. Are you?"

"Yeah. Zayn just gave me an extra dose of magic so I could get some sleep. He and Val went to go update the king."

"That's good. You need the rest. What's going to happen to Vulcan?"

"Zayn is going to talk to the king, but I'm assuming he will go back to prison for now." She gave me a sad smile.

"Oh. Okay." I nodded, a small part of me was sad, because I got to talk to him on the ship. He was very nice for a Demon.

"I love you, Cin." She reached out and hugged me.

"I love you, too," I whispered. She pulled away and looked at Cash.

"I love you, asshole," she said with a smirk.

"Aw, that is the nicest thing you have ever said to me, Ember." He squeezed her in a bear hug and her feet left the floor. "I love you, too."

"You're killing me," she moaned. Cash set her on the floor with a smile. "Goodnight, guys."

She walked off and I opened the door to my room. Cash immediately plopped in the chair and took his boots off.

"I'm showering." I pulled the dirty, bloody Demon cloak off and headed for the bathroom.

I turned on the water and hopped in.

A few minutes later, a very naked Cash slid in with me.

"It's been a long day," he said as he stuck his head under the water and washed his hair.

"It has." I lathered up the washcloth and ran it along my body. "Can you get my back?"

Cash took the washcloth from me and lathered it up again.

"Be a good girl and turn around," he said with a smirk.

My eyes widened. "Yes, sir."

I smiled as I turned around and pulled my hair to the side. He ran the washcloth over my back, scrubbing away the dirt from the long two days I'd had. I felt his back press against me as he leaned toward my ear.

"Face me," he whispered.

I did what I was told and faced him. I watched as he rinsed the washcloth off and lathered it again. Lifting his hand, he ran the soapy cloth over my breast.

"I already washed my front," I said with a moan as my nipples hardened.

"I wanted to make sure you were extra clean so I can get you dirty again." He grinned.

The cloth left my breast and traveled down to my stomach before he dropped it.

Cash lowered to his knees in front of me and pushed me against the shower wall. His hands went up and spread my lips open and his tongue was immediately on me.

My head fell back at the feeling as I moaned. My fingers curled into his hair and held on as he rolled his tongue around my clit. One of his hands left my lips and grabbed my right leg, putting it over his shoulder. Then his other hand grabbed my left leg and did the same.

His hands slid under my thighs, and I gasped as he stood up with me still on his face. My back was against the shower wall, and I was holding on to his hair for dear life as I rode his face. His hands slid from my thighs to my butt and squeezed tight.

As his tongue continued to do a damn good job, one of his hands slid from my butt cheeks to the entrance of my core. I felt a finger go in me and I moaned. He pulled it out and slid it back toward my rear entrance and rubbed it around. I gasped at the unknown, but good feeling.

His finger slid inside my rear entrance slightly, as his thumb pressed against my core. Then they both slid inside of me at the same time.

"Oh, fuck," I whispered, as I had two fingers inside of me and a warm mouth on my clit.

I had nowhere to go as I was held in the air. My orgasm was building, and it was building fast. I gripped his hair even tighter as I exploded onto his face.

Every muscle in my body tensed as the glorious feeling ran through me. My body convulsed as he sucked my clit into his mouth.

Once I was done, he pulled away and took a deep breath. His hands slid up onto my waist. Sliding my legs off his shoulders, he lowered my body back down to the floor.

"What... what was that?"

"A different type of orgasm. Eventually, I will introduce you to them all."

I let out a breathy laugh as he smiled proudly.

"I want to try something," I said and then slid onto my knees in front of him.

His hard cock was right in my face, and I was a lot braver when I was standing. Gingerly lifting my hand, I wrapped my fingers around it and stroked my hand up and down.

I looked up at his facial expressions, trying to figure out what he liked.

Once he was moaning and breathing hard, I opened my mouth and stuck the tip of his cock in. My hand continued stroking him as my tongue rolled around his tip, then I sucked it in.

After a while, he stopped me.

"Fuck, okay. I'm going to come if you don't stop."

Pulling his cock out of my mouth, I looked up at him. "Come?"

"It's another word for orgasm, doll," he said as he took my hand and pulled me up from the shower floor.

"Oh. I didn't know that."

Grabbing both of my butt cheeks, he lifted me off the ground. I instinctively grabbed his shoulders and wrapped my legs around him to keep from falling. His hand slid down between us and rubbed on my clit as he kissed me. Once I was soaking wet again, his hand wrapped around his own cock, and I felt the tip of it at my entrance. Slowly, he put it in a couple inches and let go. His hands gripped both of my butt cheeks as he slid a little deeper inside of me.

"Are you okay?" He asked.

"Yes. Don't stop."

He slid a little further in and I moaned. Gripping his shoulders tight, I pulled him into me and slid my tongue into his mouth. His cock finally went in all the way and I moaned into his mouth.

He started thrusting slowly into me while his hands tightened on my ass. My orgasm was building once more as his cock slid in and out of me, hitting just the right spots.

Every muscle in my body clenched as my clit pulsed against him and then I exploded. Squeezing his shoulders tight, I was in ecstasy once more as we came together. My breathing slowed and I tipped my head back against the shower wall. I was exhausted.

Cash lowered me to the ground again. He lathered up the washcloth and we both cleansed. He hopped out first and left the bathroom. I washed and conditioned my hair before I hopped out.

After drying off, I wrapped the towel around me and went into the bedroom. Looking over at Cash, he was sprawled out in the bed, buck naked, on his back with his hands behind his head.

Dropping my towel with a giggle, I crawled into bed next to him. "You know it's past lunchtime."

"It's nap time." He said as he pulled me close to his side. He pulled the blanket over us and I snuggled in next to him.

"I love you," he whispered.

"I love you, too."

"Goodnap, doll."

"Goodnap, Cash."

Chapter 47

Cinder

Two weeks have gone by since Ember and I were abducted. Arna was now a phoenix and King Reign said something about her bond with Ember and how that made her come back in her true form. I know little about phoenixes, so I had no idea what they were talking about. Vulcan went back to his cell... for now, anyway. Everyone else was doing great. Cash and I had moved into a bigger bedroom, and we were having sex almost every morning, but today we woke up to a messenger Imp from his parents, so there was no time for breakfast, let alone morning sex.

"Come on, Cinnamon!"

Cash was dragging me across the bridge to his parents' castle.

"My legs are shorter than yours, Cash. I can't run that fast."

He hugged me and picked me up. I held onto his neck and wrapped my legs around him.

The portcullis opened and he ran under it.

"Good morning, my lord, my lady." Lucian's eyes were wide.

"Good morning, Lucian," I called out as Cash sprinted past him with me in his arms. "You do know this is highly inappropriate behavior for a future duke and duchess."

"The townsfolk will have to get used to it," he said, as he sprinted around a corner.

He stopped in front of a door and set me down.

"Are you ready?" he asked. His face was filled with excitement.

"Let me fix myself," I said as I smoothed out my dress.

"Like the baby is going to care about your dress." I ignored his remarks.

Cash knocked on the door and Lucy's mate answered. "Come in," he said. "They are in here."

We stepped into the house and followed him into a bedroom. Lucy was laying in the bed with a baby wrapped tightly in a blanket. My heart sped up with excitement as Cash and I slowly walked up to her.

"It's a boy, my lord." Lucy smiled as tears filled her eyes.

"Finally," her mate said with a prideful smile.

"I knew it," Cash whispered.

She pulled the blanket back from his face and I looked at him. He was absolutely gorgeous. He was pink, and tiny and I *really* wanted to hold him, but was also scared I would break him.

She raised him up to Cash and he took him from her. Cash slid the blanket off his head, and he had a bunch of brown hair.

"Look, my lord."

Lucy's mate pulled the blanket back slightly, and on the baby's chest was a tiny black King's Guard tattoo. Cash's mouth gaped open.

"I knew that, too," he whispered.

"You did," Lucy said with a laugh.

"What did you name him," I asked.

"His name is Gabriel the second. After his father," Lucy said. I smiled and looked back at the baby.

"You should hold him, my lady," Gabriel said.

I swallowed hard as Cash's eyes met mine and shook my head. He smiled and very gingerly held the baby out to me and slid it into my arms.

The baby fussed a little, so I started swaying out of instinct.

"You're a natural," Gabriel said.

"She is," Lucy agreed.

The baby stretched and a tiny foot popped out of the blanket. I let out an aww sound from my mouth as I saw it.

"His feet are so little." I reached my hand out and held his tiny foot. I pulled him close to my chest as I continued to sway with him until he went back to sleep.

I don't know how long I stayed like that before I heard a knock on the door. Gabriel took off to open it and I was shocked when I saw who walked into the room with a huge smile on his face.

"Your Majesty." Lucy started to get up from the bed before the king stopped her.

"Do not get out of that bed. You just gave birth, Lucy. You need to rest."

"Thank you, Your Majesty."

The king smiled and turned toward me.

"I believe it's my turn, Cinder." I smiled and nodded. The king took Gabriel from me and the look of awe on his face was priceless.

"I can't wait to have you join my team in twenty-two years," the king said to the baby, and I giggled.

Reign pulled the blanket back and a tiny pair of white wings were under it. I gasped.

"A healer." The king nodded with a prideful smile. "That is perfect. There has not been a male healer born in a few years."

"We were extremely excited when we saw, Your Majesty."

"I bet you were, Gabriel. You finally got that boy you wanted. You two should get some rest." The king smiled big as he handed the baby off to Lucy. "Let's go." The king nodded his head, and Cash and I followed him out of the house.

Once we emerged, there was the King's Royal Guard standing there. "I will see you two later." The king winked and strolled down the cobble streets with a Royal Guard on each side of him.

The crowd stopped and watched in wonder and excitement as he passed.

"So, are we having a baby soon?" Cash asked.

"Maybe." I shrugged, trying not to give away the fact that I wanted a baby as much as he did.

His eyes lit up and he grinned. "I will take a 'maybe' for now."

I giggled.

"We better get back. I have a lot of desserts to make for tomorrow."

"Yes. Tomorrow is going to be another exciting day." Cash took my hand and we headed home.

Chapter 48

Cinder

Today was the grand opening of my bakery stand. It was a little late in the fall to be opening it, but there was no way I was waiting until the spring.

Everyone was here helping me get started. Cash and Zayn were standing on stools and had just hung up my beautiful multi-colored banner. I stared at it proudly with tear-filled eyes.

"Primordial Sweets?"

"Yes. Is there something wrong with it, Ember?" I asked.

"No. I like it. It's cute." She smiled as she looked up at it.

"Tell her what you were going to name it," Zayn said as he jumped off the stool.

"Shut up, Zayn." My eyes shot daggers at him, and he laughed.

Cash jumped off his stool. "Primordial Pleasures," he said with a grin.

"Oh." Ember's eyes widened. "That sounds like a whorehouse." Everyone laughed and I shook my head.

"I hate you all," I said with a smile.

"We hate you, too." Asher said with a wink.

"I'm glad you used all the paint colors we bought. It looks great!" Zayn said.

"Cali, Zila and, Asher helped me." I smiled proudly at my sign until Cali's voice brought me out of the bliss.

"Sweet treats that are fit for a king. Today's special is lemon cake–King Reign's favorite. You should try some." Cali batted her lashes at a male Fae as she slid her hair behind her ear.

"Okay." He smiled and stepped up to the stand. He was my first customer.

She flirted with him and got him to buy enough dessert for three families before he left.

"Cali, you can't flirt with every customer," Zayn said. "Right, Cinder?"

"I disagree. Keep going, Cali." I smiled big and Cali winked at me. Zayn shook his head with a smile.

"What's in the boxes marked King's Guard Cupcakes?" Zila asked.

"Oh, they are filled with seven different cupcake flavors, one for each of the seven King's Guards." I grinned at the secret I had been keeping from everyone as Zila opened the box with wide eyes.

"Let me see!" Asher said as he peeked in.

"I made everyone's favorite. Banana nut for Asher, strawberry for Ember, Cherry for Zayn, Chocolate for Val, carrot cake for Zila, red velvet for Cali, and apple cinnamon for my mate."

Cash grinned widely at me using the word *mate* and I winked at him.

"That's an amazing idea, Cinder!" Cali clapped her hands in excitement.

"Thanks."

"Can we keep a box for the house?" Zayn asked.

"I brought an extra box with us for you guys to eat." As soon as I said the words, Val about knocked everyone down to get to the chocolate cupcake and I laughed.

He pulled back the wrapper and took a bite. "I've been waiting forever for this," he said with a mouth full. I laughed and shook my head.

After a few minutes, I got another customer, and then a third. I was excited. Then the crowd got loud, and I heard gasps.

"What's going on," I asked.

"I don't know." Cash pulled his axe from his belt and stepped out from behind the counter.

The crowd started to part, and the King's Royal Guard came through, with the king right in the middle. The crowd stood around watching with a look of wonder plastered on their faces.

"Your Majesty," we all said one by one and bowed.

The king looked up at the banner and then stepped up to my counter with a smile. "Primordial Sweets? Does the name have meaning?"

"Yes, Your Majesty. I found an ancient cookbook by Cora Nance at the manor, and it helped with my decision on the name."

"Oh. Corky. She was an amazing cook. So, what does that have to do with the name?"

"Since there is every Primordial God's favorite dessert recipe in the book, I figured I would make and serve them. So, Primordial Sweets just seemed fitting." I smiled nervously, hoping I hadn't made a bad decision.

"That is wonderful! Corky and her mate Jake were wonderful people. They may be long gone, but it is nice to know that her recipes live on."

"Thank you, Your Majesty."

"Since I came to buy some desserts, what is the best one?

"I would assume this one." I pointed to one of the cakes and watched as the king read the tiny sign in front of it.

"King Reign's Lemon Cake. I love it! I will take two."

"Coming right up." As I got a piece of cake ready, I noticed the king's face looked displeased.

"Is something wrong, Your Majesty?"

"I meant two *whole* cakes, Cinder."

"Oh! Coming right up, Your Majesty."

Since I brought two lemon cakes, I bagged them both—minus the piece my first customer bought—and set them on the counter. The king picked them up with wide eyes and handed them to a guard. Another guard stepped forward and threw down *way* more cash than the cakes cost.

"That is too much money," I said.

"I see the sign says all proceeds go to the schools, so keep it for the children."

"Thank you, Your Majesty."

"I am very proud of you, Cinder." His eyes were filled with pride, so I believed his words.

Without even thinking, I stepped out from behind the counter and slammed into him with a hug.

"Thank you. I wouldn't have been able to do it without you, Your Majesty."

"Oh, there, there, Cinder. It was the least I could do for a child of mine." He let go of the hug and I looked up at him.

"I am a child of the Tartarus." My face must have looked confused because he laughed.

"You live in my manor, so just like my King's Guard, you are my child. My daughter," he said proudly. He wiped a small tear from his eye. "Well, I have cake to eat. Good day Guards, Cinder." He turned and strolled away. I wiped a tear from my cheek and stepped back behind the counter.

We all worked the stand and sold every dessert I'd brought. After a hard day's work, we went back home, and all sagged into the dining room chairs. I was grateful it was dinner time because I was starving.

"It feels so good to be home," Cash said as he took a seat next to me.

"It is," I agreed. I got to thinking about the meaning of the word home.

Home is where family is. Home is where you feel loved, wanted, secure. Castleva was my home.

I looked around the table at my friends. Asher and Cali were play-fighting over the wooden spoon because they both wanted potatoes and the other wasn't giving in. I laughed at them.

This was indeed my home, and these people were our family.

Glancing around at everyone, I realized that I was in love with all these people and a tear escaped my eye. Every little quirk they had made me love them more. I wiped the tear away as I looked at Asher as visions came to me.

Asher spinning his staff, cracking his knuckles, or making jokes, all day every day. Constantly saying things out loud that some of us are just thinking, even if they are scary.

Zila with her sweet smile, blushing at the little things. She was extremely book smart, conservative and soft-spoken, but fierce as can be. She stepped up to be a mom to us when it mattered. She had no problem reprimanding us, but it was usually aimed at Cali.

I giggled as my eyes wandered to Cali.

Cali clapping her hands every time she got excited. She was what everyone called a free spirit, doing what she wants and not caring what anyone thinks of her as she cascades into a room, owning it. Societal norms were not in her vocabulary. Her beauty and confidence were mesmerizing.

She handed a bottle of wine to Zayn and my eyes wandered over to him.

Zayn running his hand through his shaggy hair. He was a natural leader, yet he was the kindest person I knew, even when barking orders at everyone. He would drop anything he was doing to help someone. He liked to seem sophisticated while he sat in the study reading a book, sipping on apple brandy, but we all knew he was just as immature as the rest of us.

I smiled big as he ran a hand through his hair while he was talking to Val. The amazing brother I didn't even know I wanted but I definitely needed.

Val, tilting his head with a fanged smile when he thought you were doing something cute. Crossing his arms in what Ember calls "That lazy stance of his." Comforting her no matter how much she was overreacting to her feelings. Growling when he was mad. He would rip someone's throat out to protect any of us, and we all knew it.

My eyes wandered to my beautiful sister.

Ember being Ember. Fierce, funny, and loving with every ounce of her soul. She wore her heart on her sleeve and we all loved her for it. She was an emotional mess, and neurotic at times, but we loved her for that, too. She spoke her mind, and she didn't care who disagreed with her. She would die for me, and a tear rolled down my cheek at the thought.

And that left Cash. I looked over at the grinning fool that I was madly in love with.

Cash was one who was always smiling. He liked to joke and have fun. He was always hungry, and he savored every meal like it was his last. I believed that Cash enjoyed life more than anyone else I had ever met. To me, he was a free spirit, too. His enthusiasm for life was one of the many reasons I fell in love with him.

"What are you thinking about, Cinnamon?" he asked, as I stared at him with worshiping eyes.

"Nothing," I said as I wiped another tear away.

"I know that face, doll. Tell me."
"I'm just glad to be home, Cash."
He grinned big and pulled me close to him.
"Me too, Cinnamon. Me too."

Continue reading for a sneak peek of

Silver Storms: Primordial Gods Book 3

Silver Storms

Zila

The Demons have been lying low, so there weren't many missions for us, which made the winter long and boring. I missed the warm days of summer, and I was glad that spring was approaching soon. Every time I thought of winter, there was one man in particular that I missed.

Natsu Amata.

I met Natsu one winter when I was eight years old. He was only two years younger than me when his mother had brought him to my mother's pelt stand on Direbreak. Our mothers talked for hours while we played in the snow. When Natsu's mother came back the next week to pick up her custom order, they talked for hours again. Our mothers quickly became friends after that. They took turns visiting each other once a week for many, many years. While they visited, Natsu and I would run through the woods together. He loved it when I turned into a wolf, and I loved it when he would spread his dragonfly like wings and fly after me.

We had our first kiss when I was ten. I had made him a bracelet out of twine, and he thanked me with a kiss. I mean, technically it wasn't a real kiss, but a kiss on the cheek to a ten-year-old was *real* and it was *magical*.

Natsu had come up with nicknames for us both by the time I was fourteen. He said it was a way of saying *I love you*, or *I missed you* without saying it in front of everyone. His nickname for me was Okami—it meant *little wolf*. He didn't use it very often and it warmed my heart when he did. He told me to call him Tonbo because it meant *dragonfly*, and that's what his wings looked like.

Since we were raised like brother and sister, we were super close growing up. Over the years, we have been there for each other, like friends are supposed to be, but somewhere along the line, in my late teens, my feelings for him changed. They were no longer just feelings of friendship—I fell *madly* in love with him. Natsu was everything you could want in a mate—kind, loyal, and protective—but, unfortunately, I never had the guts to tell him.

Since we had a friendship that most people in their lives wouldn't be blessed with, that friendship came with fear.

Fear that he saw me as only a sister.

Fear that me telling him would ruin our friendship.

Fear that he wouldn't love me the way I loved him.

That fear has kept me from forming any real relationships with other men. I have had sexual partners, but I have never had a relationship in my twenty-four years. Only one man in the world would ever have my heart, and he was standing in my kitchen.

"Hey, Okami!" He bowed his head and when he righted his body, he smiled big.

"Hey, Tonbo." He held out his arms and I slid mine around him. His hugs were warm and inviting. I didn't get those often either, but when I did, I cherished them.

"How have you been?" he asked as he let go.

"I have been faring well."

"That is good to hear." He smiled big and I felt my cheeks get warm.

"Happy belated birthday. I'm sorry I didn't get to see you."

"It's okay, Zila. I didn't expect you to sail across treacherous waters to wish me a happy birthday." I laughed and snorted. I was nervous because I knew why he was here.

He was twenty-two years old now, which means he was getting sworn in as a King's Guard and would now live with us—live with *me*. The thought excited me and scared me at the same time.

"How was the crab season?" I asked.

"It was great. Even though I love sailing, I'm glad to be off my ship. Hanging out with a bunch of sweaty crabbers for months gets to you after a while."

Knowing I should finally break the ice, I decided to mention his stay. "So, are you getting sworn in today?"

"I am." He smiled big. "Zayn already gave me my room, it's right next door to yours."

I wasn't much of a curser, but *Fuck* was the only word that formed in my head.

Recipe

Union Station Chocolate Chip Cookies

It has been said that this recipe that my grandmother, Cora Nance, acquired was a top secret recipe used in the Union Station Mall in St. Louis many years ago. I can say that I have had them on multiple occasions and they are delicious!

1 cup butter

1 cup sugar

1 cup brown sugar

Cream the above ingredients together in a bowl and set aside.

2 cups flour

2 1/2 cups of oats (powdered in a blender)

1 teaspoon baking soda

1 teaspoon baking powder

1 1/2 teaspoon salt

1 tablespoon vanilla

2 eggs

Mix together, then add to the first bowl.

Once combined stir in:

4oz. melted Hershey bar

1 1/2 cups chopped nuts (baker's choice)

12oz. chocolate chips

Roll batter into small golf-ball size balls.

Bake on an ungreased cookie sheet at 375° for 8 minutes.

Cookies will not appear done when removed.... do not over-bake!

ENJOY!

Also By P.S. Nail

Primordial Gods Series
Violet Flames: Book 1
Emerald Skies: Book 2
Silver Storms: Book 3

Argentium Vampire Hunters Trilogy
Raised by Venom: Book 1

Endless Reels of Thoughts: Snippets of Poetry from an Unsettled Mind

Acknowledgments

First and foremost, I would like to thank my husband and kids for putting up with my shit while writing another book! You four are amazing!

Thank you to the readers for supporting me along my journey. Without you all, I wouldn't continue writing. You have been more than supportive and I appreciate every single one of you.

This thank you is for you Ms. Heather "Peach" Shields! Thank you for all the hard work you did making my manuscript better! *happy tears* And thank you for helping talk me off the ledge every time I get imposter syndrome. You are so amazing, and I can't wait to come visit you. I will get the beef sticks ready, you get the playlist going!

April D. Berry, you're a light in my life that I didn't know I needed. You are the flame to my candlewick, the gas in my car, the scrunchie in my hair—you get the gist. You keep me going some days without even knowing it. I can't thank you enough for being so sweet and understanding and showing me that *most* authors go through the same emotions. If I could move closer to you, I would already be in the car! You're the best! *wink*

Having people who truly understand me and are there for me no matter how neurotic I'm being, is almost impossible to find—but I did! I struck gold when I found the beautiful women in my Romance Riot Discord. They are caring, honest, understanding, and make me laugh my ass off! You couldn't ask much more from a bunch of women than what I get from this group. *chef's kiss*

I would also like to thank Kelly from KDL Editing for getting me in at the last minute. You rock!

A huge thank you to my beta and ARC readers for being as amazing as always! I love you guys!

Thank you Diletta De Santis for yet another amazing, gorgeous cover. I cried when I saw it. It was more than I even thought I wanted.

And as *always*, a huge thank you to my amazing Aunt Vicky (she forced me to add this) who keeps me sane. I'm not sure how I feel about sharing you with all my author friends on TikTok. Lol. But truly, I love you with all my heart and your faith in me is the only reason I became a published author.

www.ingramcontent.com/pod-product-compliance
Lightning Source LLC
Chambersburg PA
CBHW031231310726
48971CB00004B/956